tiny titans

SEE?! NOW WE CAN ALL GO TO THE PET CLUB MEETING!
AWESOME! LET'S GO!

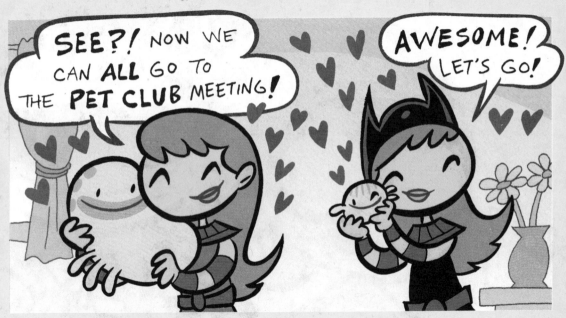

THE FIRST RULE OF PET CLUB...

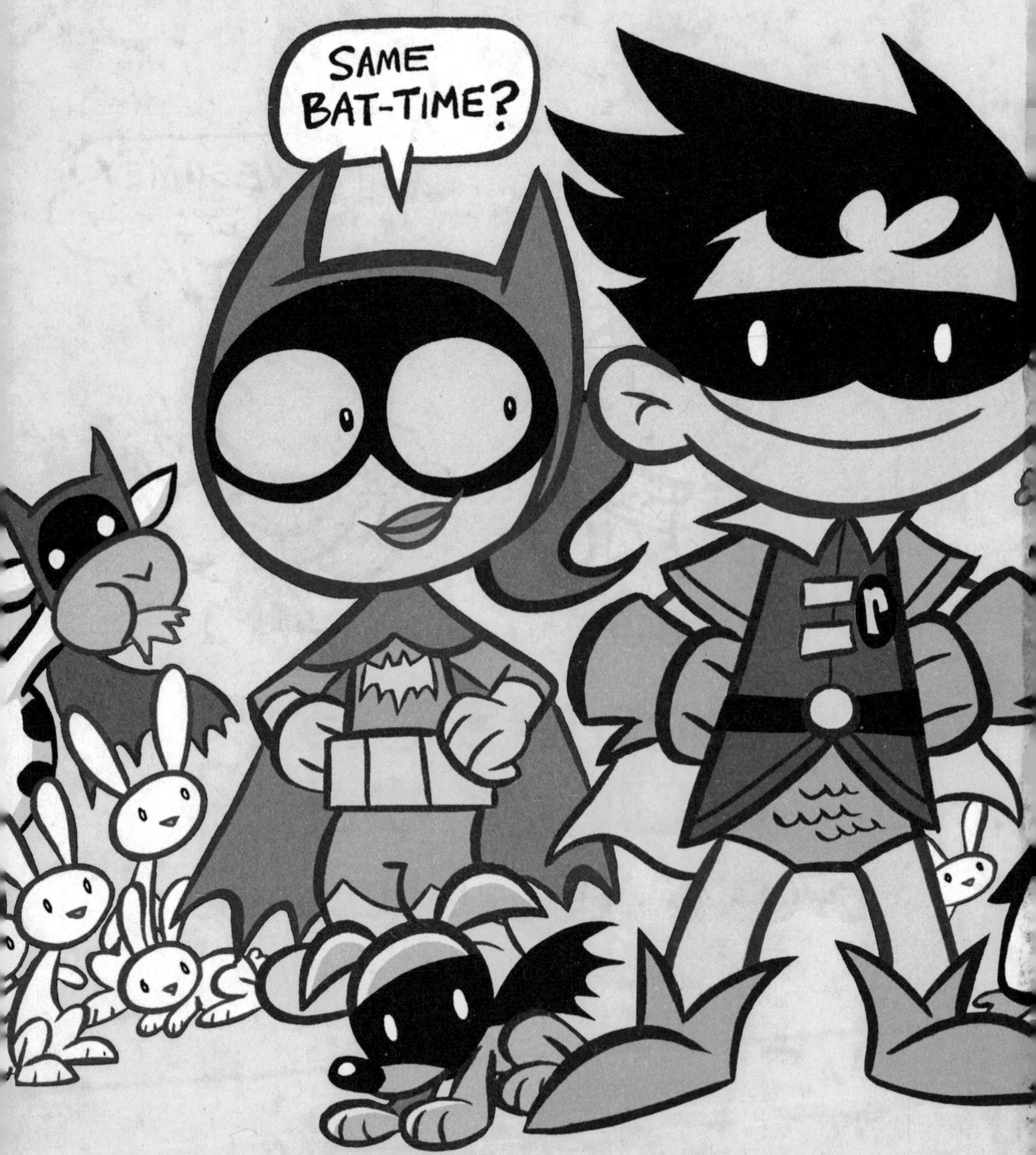
SAME BAT-TIME?

tiny titans

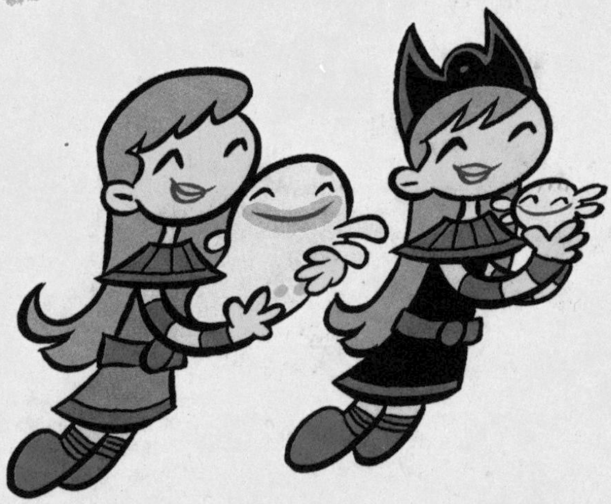

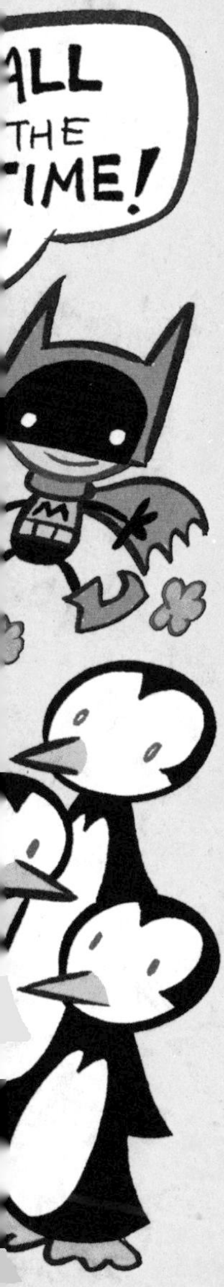
ALL
THE
IME!

THE FIRST RULE OF PET CLUB...

Art Baltazar & Franco
Writers

Geoff Johns
Special Guest Co-Writer on #25!

Art Baltazar
Artist & Letterer

Art Baltazar
Cover Art

Elisabeth V. Gehrlein Editor – original series
Simona Martore Assistant Editor – original series
Jeb Woodard Group Editor – Collected Editions
Anton Kawasaki Editor – collected edition
Steve Cook Design Director-Books

Bob Harras Senior VP – Editor-in-Chief, DC Comics

Diane Nelson President
Dan DiDio Publisher
Jim Lee Publisher
Geoff Johns President and Chief Creative Officer
Amit Desai Executive VP – Business & Marketing Strategy, Direct to Consumer & Global Franchise Management
Sam Ades Senior VP – Direct to Consumer
Bobbie Chase VP – Talent Development
Mark Chiarello Senior VP – Art, Design & Collected Editions
John Cunningham Senior VP – Sales & Trade Marketing
Anne DePies Senior VP – Business Strategy, Finance & Administration
Don Falletti VP – Manufacturing Operations
Lawrence Ganem VP – Editorial Administration & Talent Relations
Alison Gill Senior VP – Manufacturing & Operations
Hank Kanalz Senior VP – Editorial Strategy & Administration
Jay Kogan VP – Legal Affairs
Thomas Loftus VP – Business Affairs
Jack Mahan VP – Business Affairs
Nick J. Napolitano VP – Manufacturing Administration
Eddie Scannell VP – Consumer Marketing
Courtney Simmons Senior VP – Publicity & Communications
Jim (Ski) Sokolowski VP – Comic Book Specialty & Trade Marketing
Nancy Spears VP – Mass, Book, Digital Sales & Trade Marketing

TINY TITANS: THE FIRST RULE OF PET CLUB...
Published by DC Comics. Cover and compilation Copyright © 2010 DC Comics. All Rights Reserved.

Originally published in single magazine form in TINY TITANS 19-25. Copyright © 2009, 2010 DC Comics. All Rights Reserved.
All characters, their distinctive likenesses and related elements featured in this publication are trademarks of DC Comics.
The stories, characters and incidents featured in this publication are entirely fictional. DC Comics does not read or
accept unsolicited submissions of ideas, stories or artwork.

DC Comics, 2900 W. Alameda Avenue, Burbank, CA 91505
Printed by Transcontinental Interglobe, Beauceville, QC, Canada. 1/6/17.
Fifth Printing. ISBN: 978-1-4012-2892-7

Library of Congress Cataloging-in-Publication Data

Baltazar, Art.
The first rule of pet club/ Art Baltazar ; Franco.
pages cm.—
ISBN 978-1-4012-2892-7 (pbk.)
1. Graphic novels. I. Aureliani, Franco, illustrator. II. Title.
PZ7.B21386 Th 2010
741.5'973—dc23

2011290113

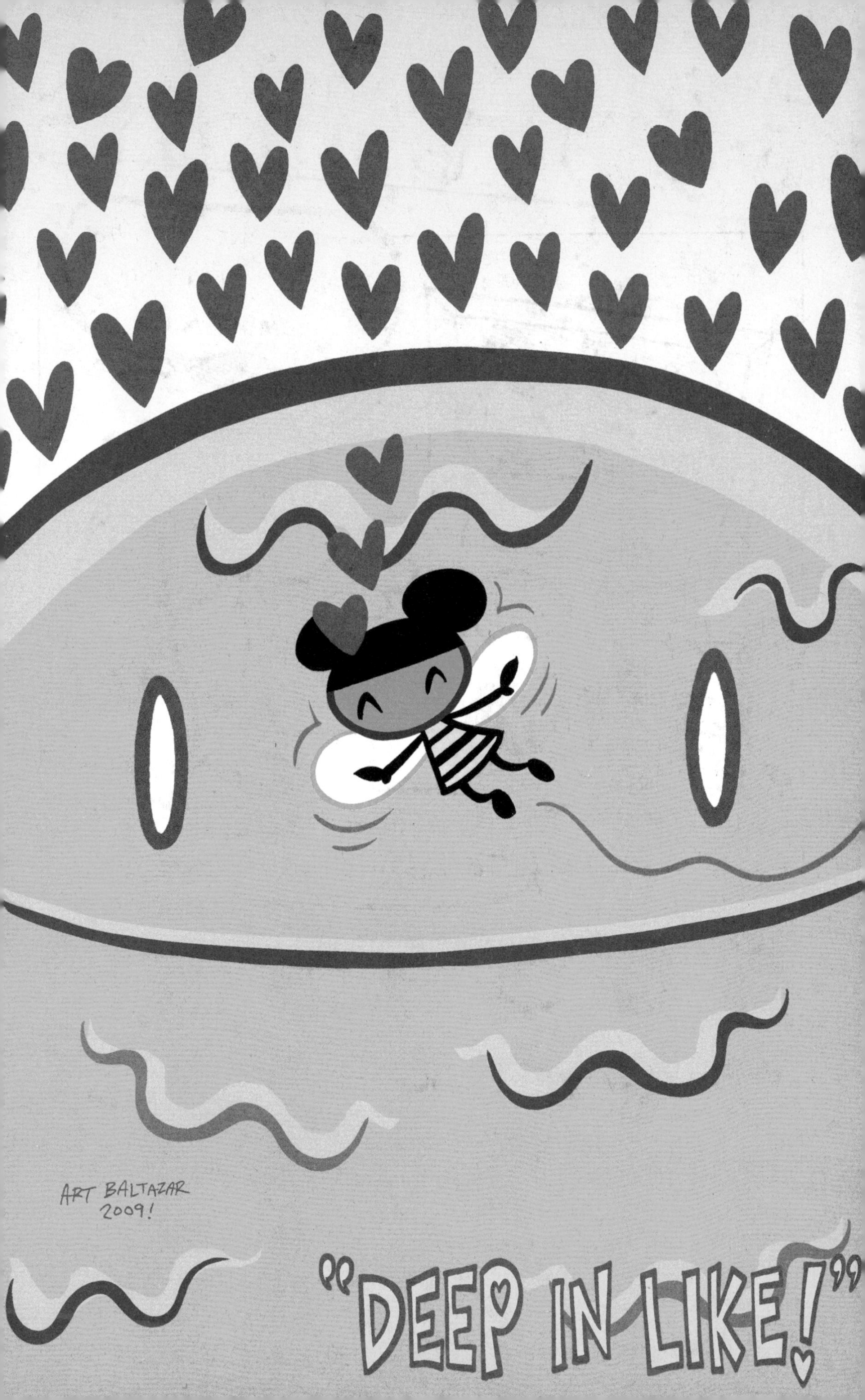
ART BALTAZAR
2009!
"DEEP IN LIKE!"

tiny titans

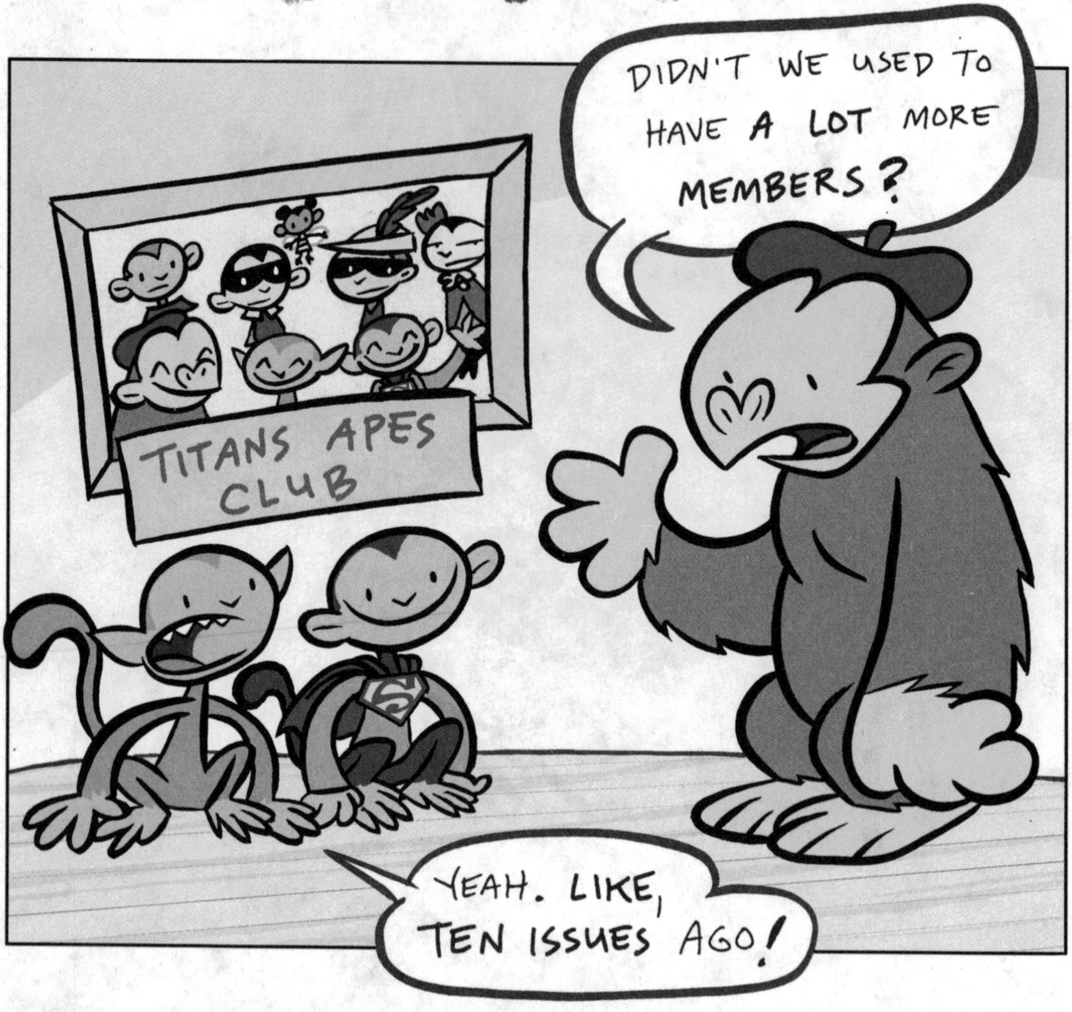
TITANS APES CLUB
DIDN'T WE USED TO HAVE A LOT MORE MEMBERS?
YEAH. LIKE, TEN ISSUES AGO!

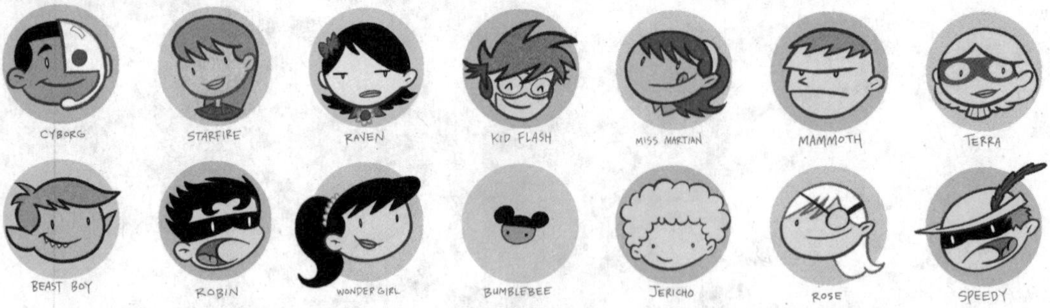
CYBORG
STARFIRE
RAVEN
KID FLASH
MISS MARTIAN
MAMMOTH
TERRA
BEAST BOY
ROBIN
WONDER GIRL
BUMBLEBEE
JERICHO
ROSE
SPEEDY

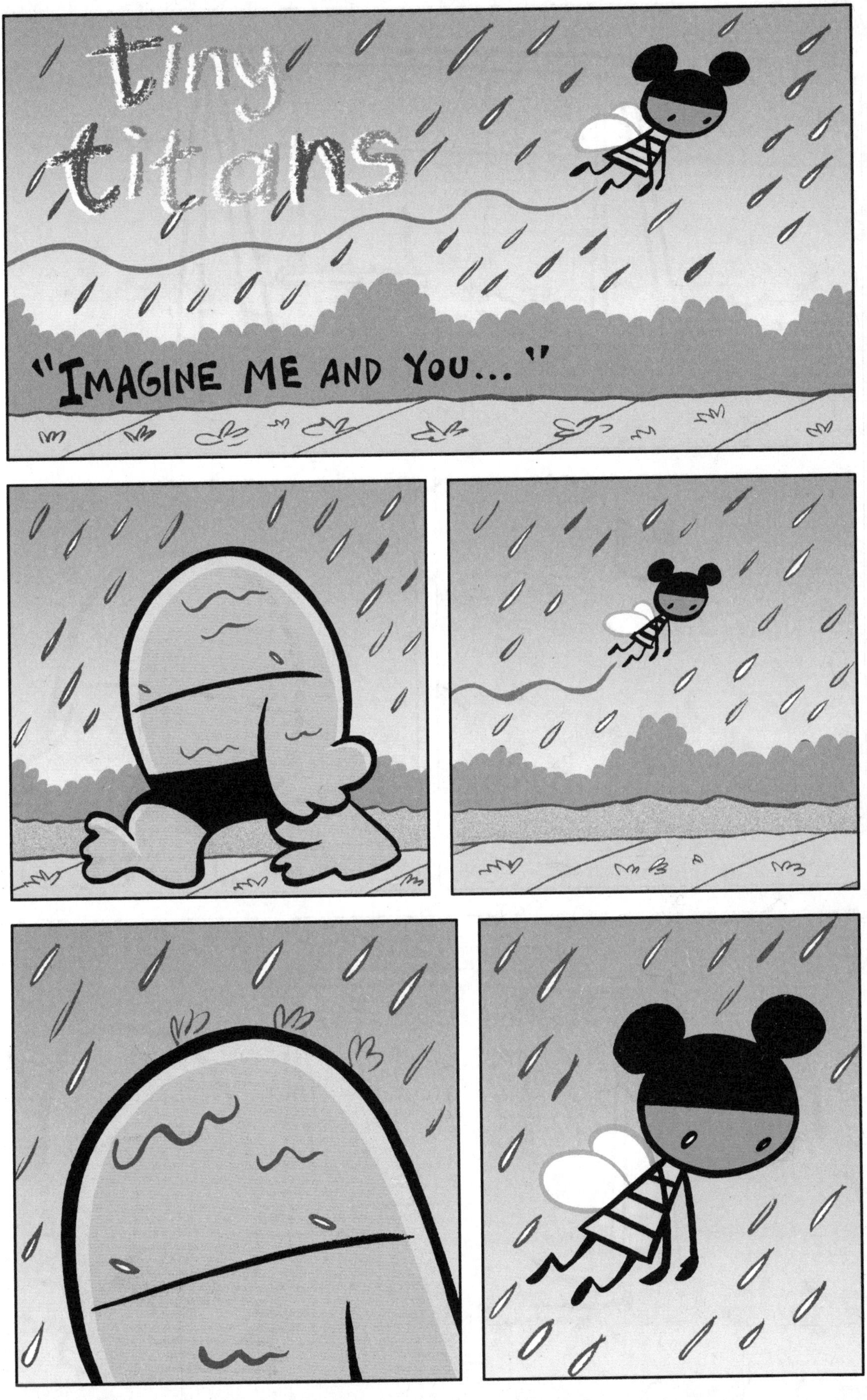
tiny titans
"IMAGINE ME AND YOU..."

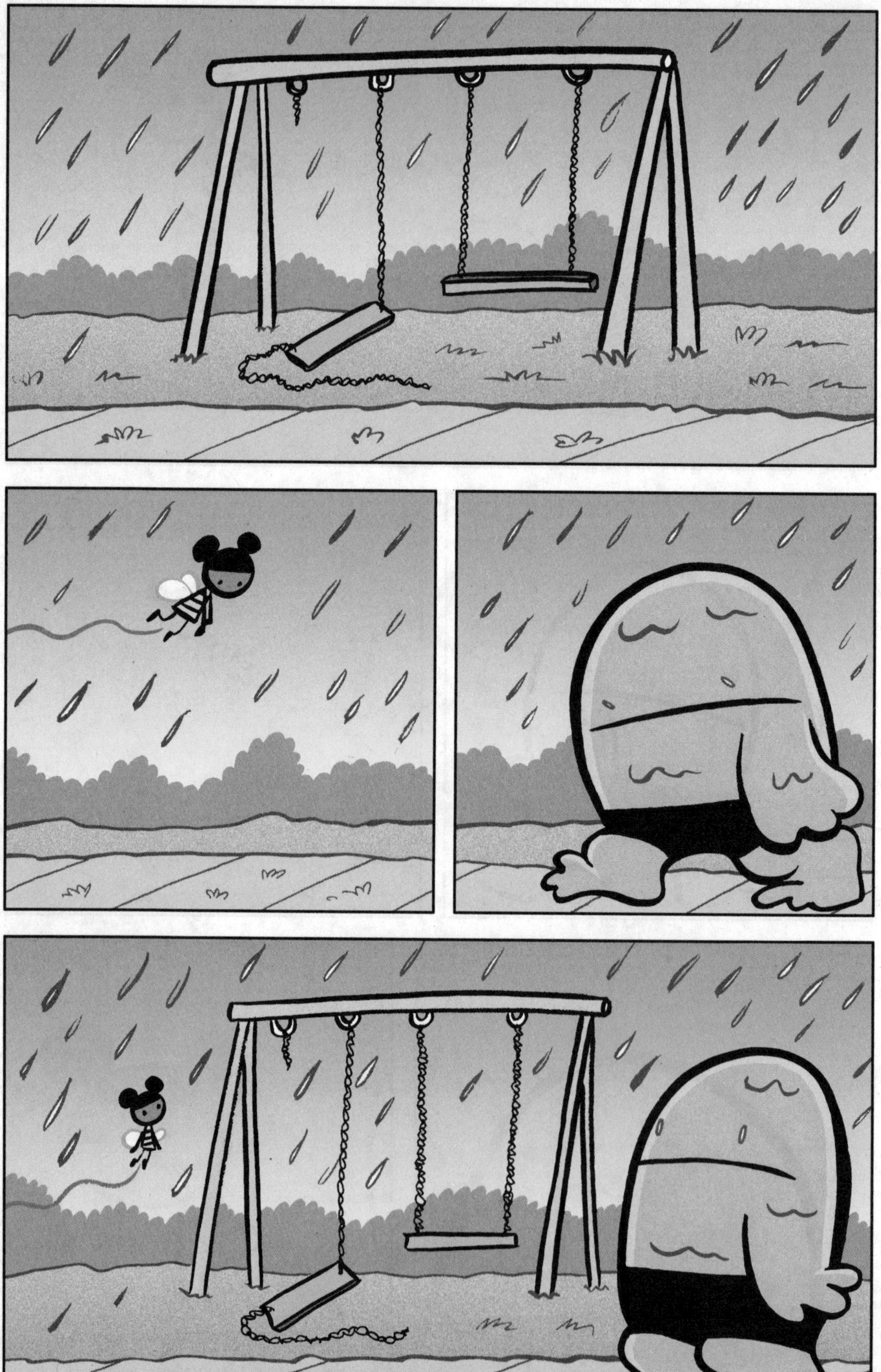

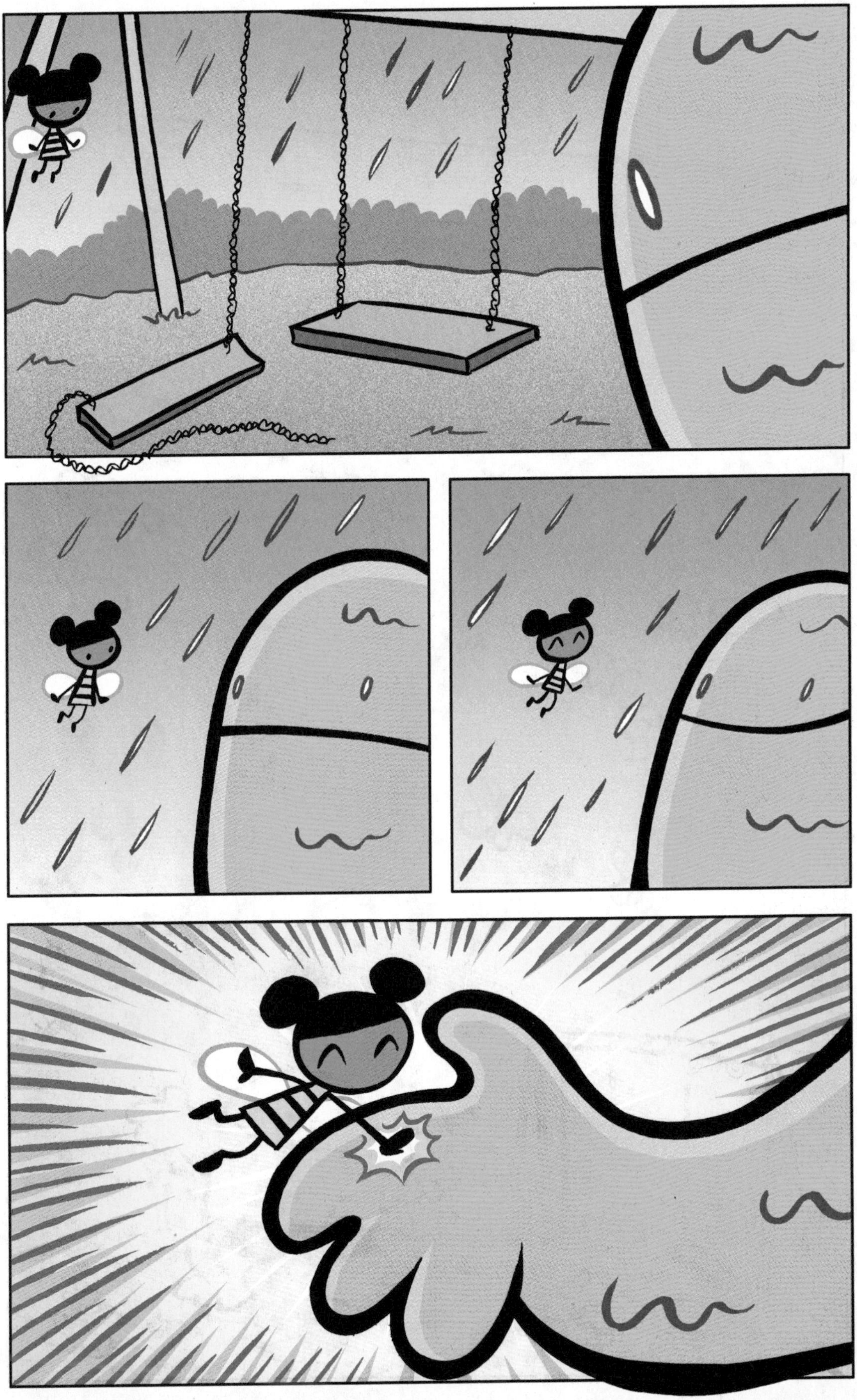

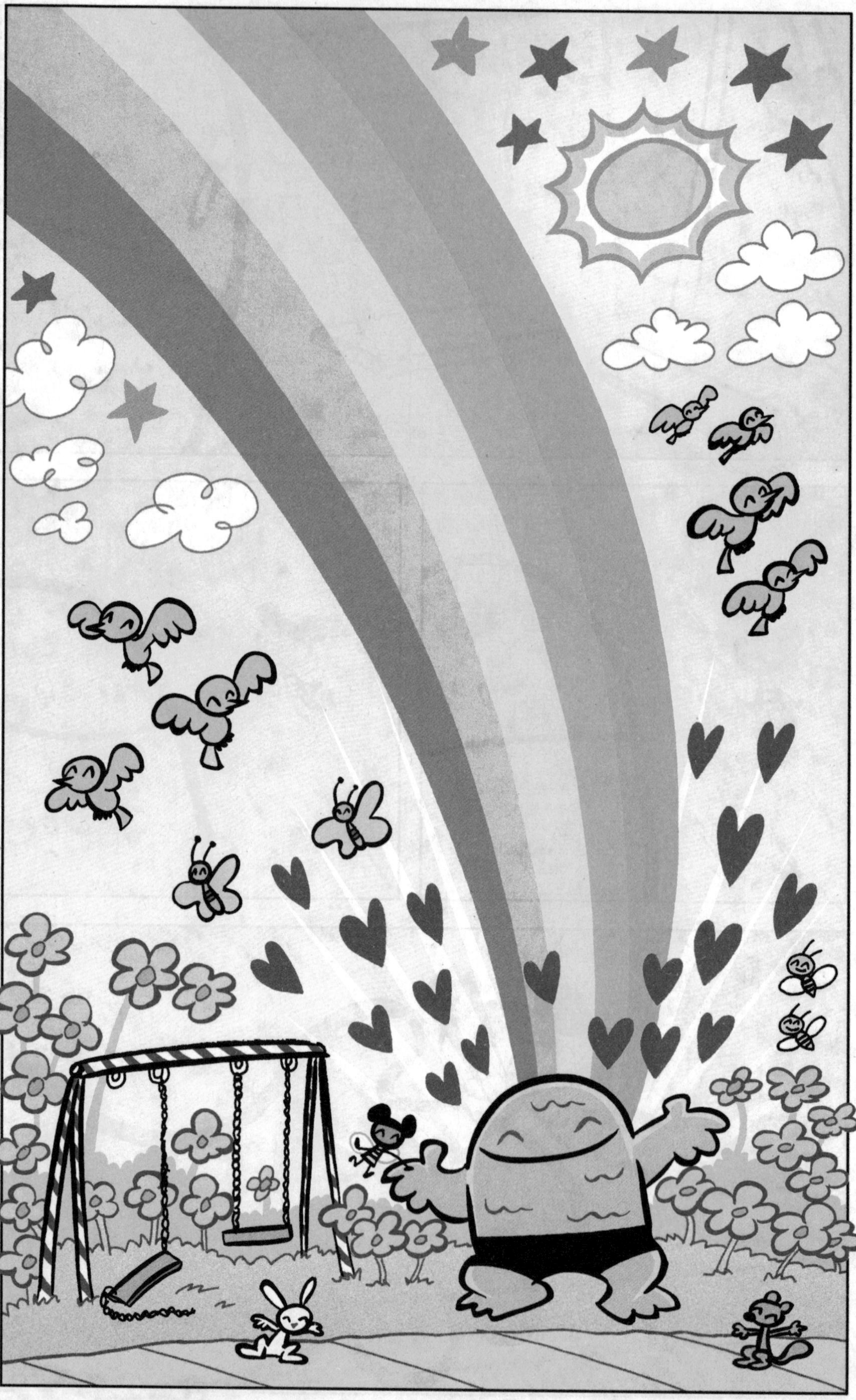

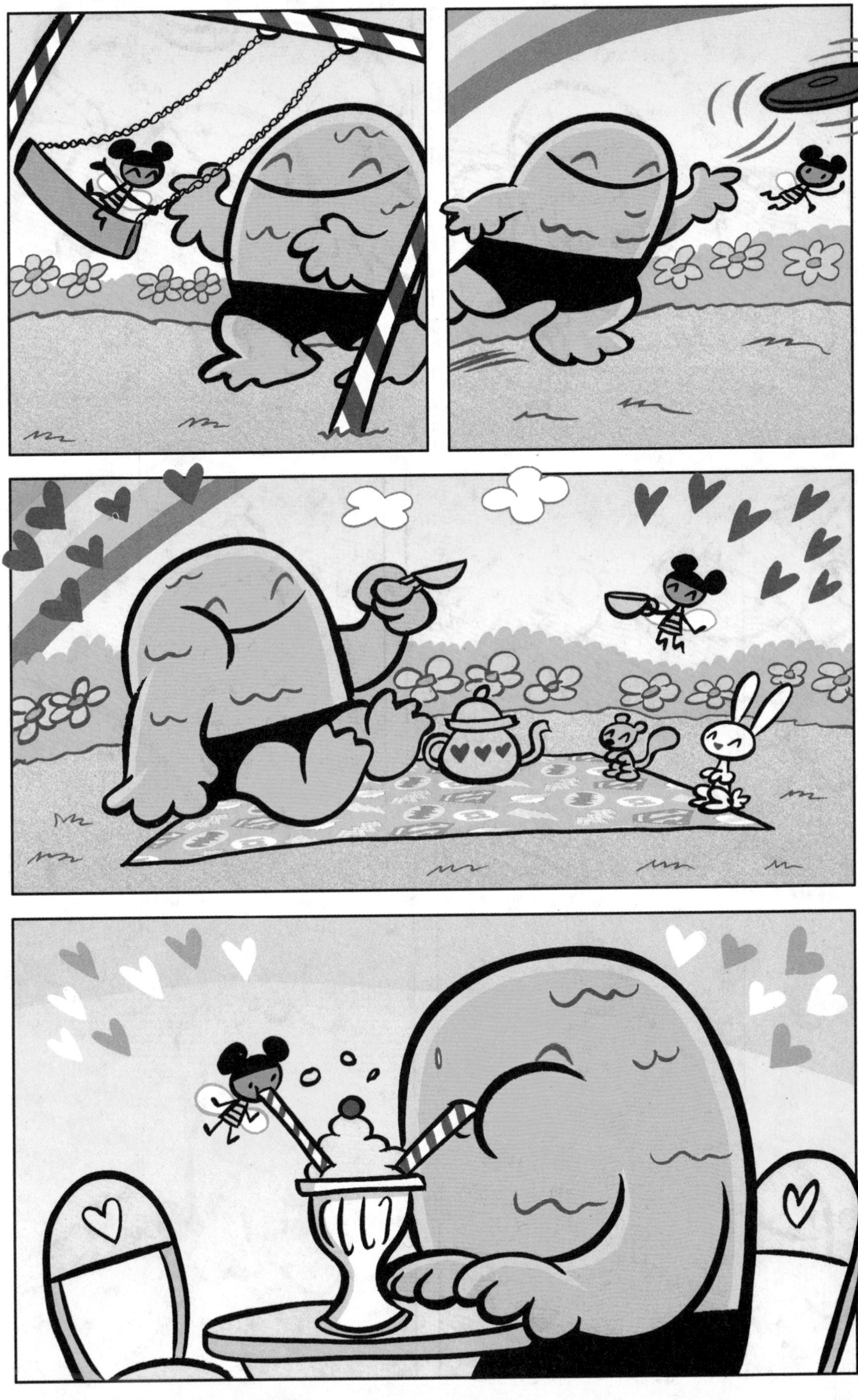

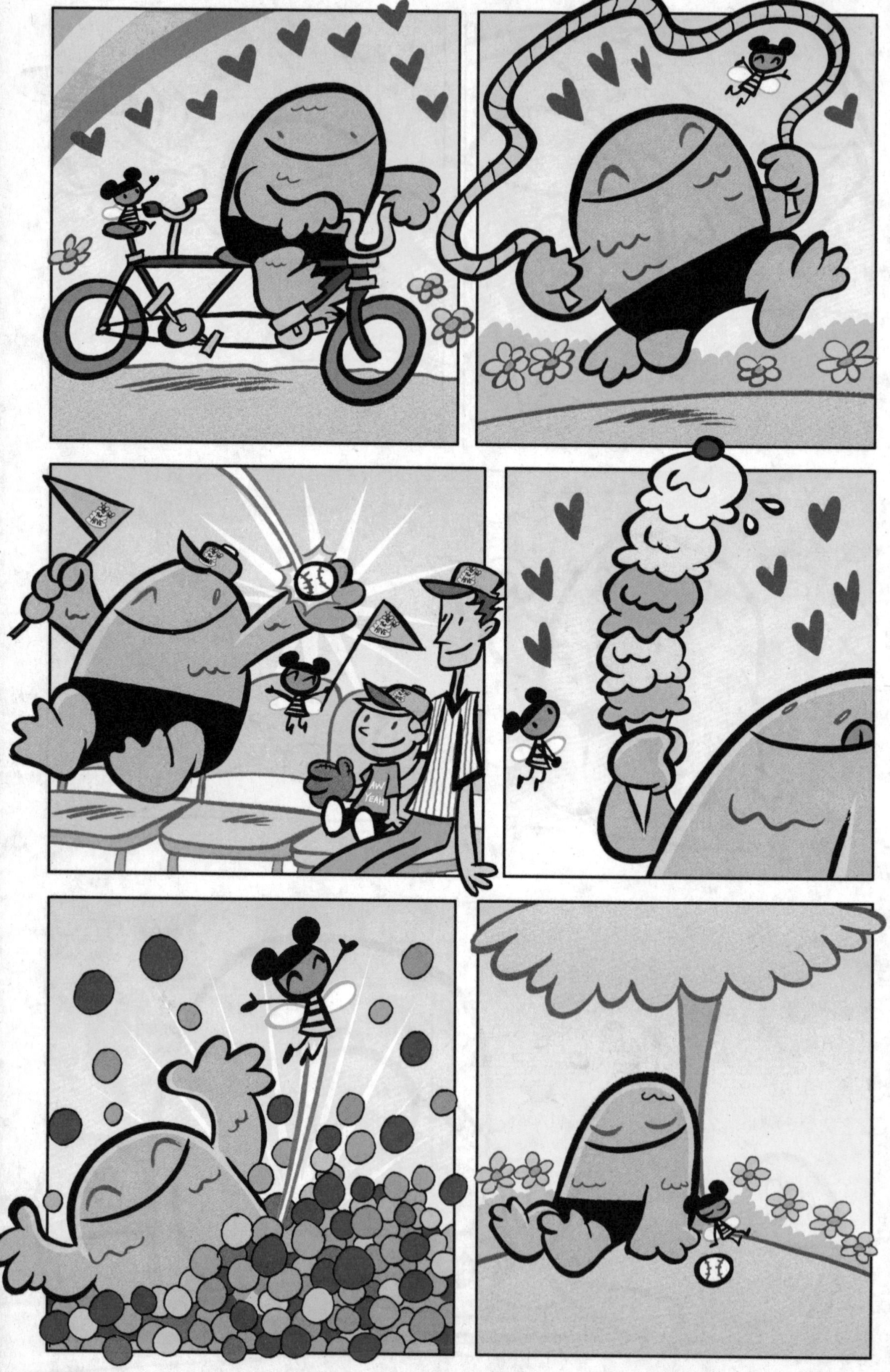
AW YEAH

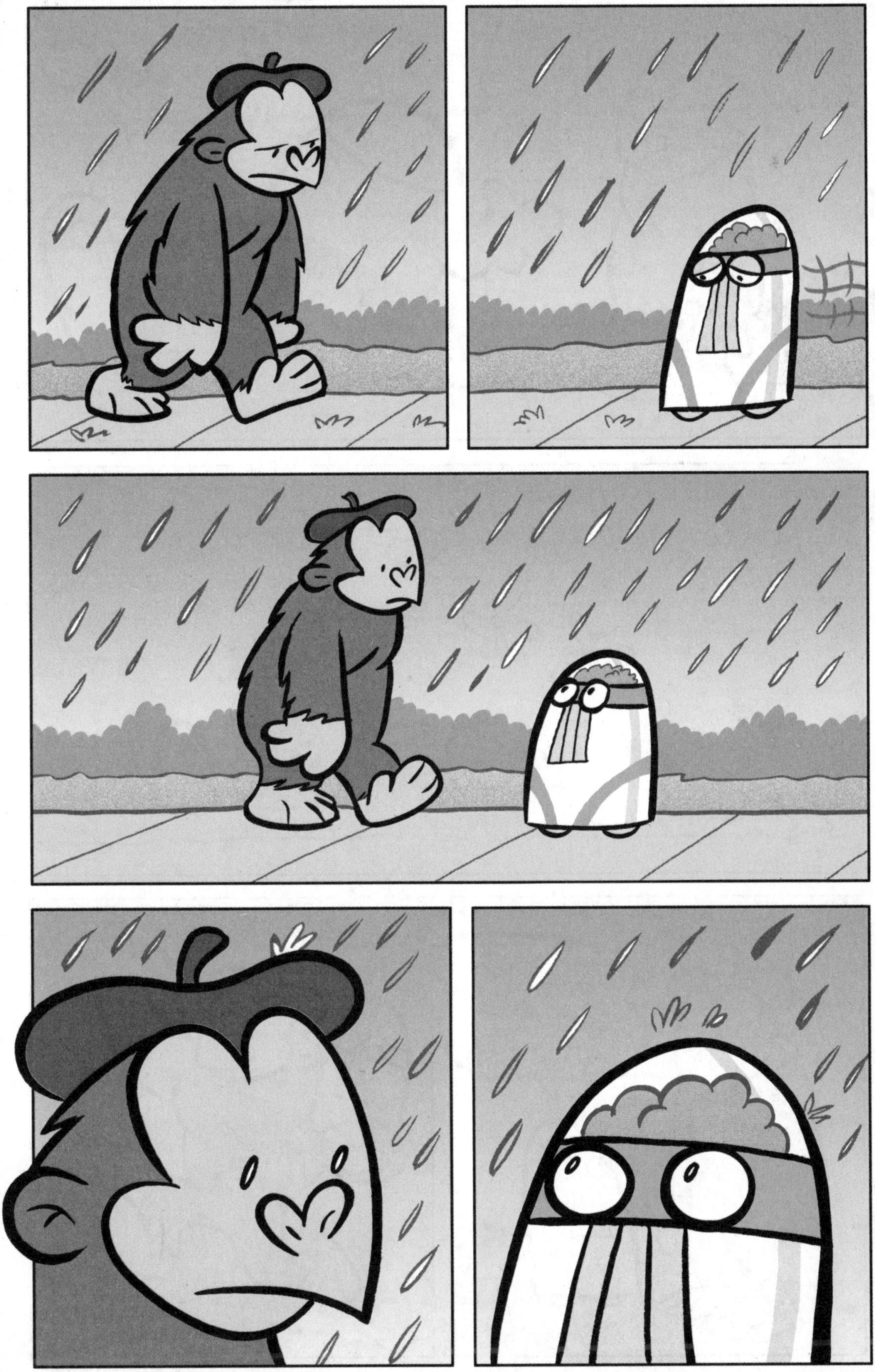

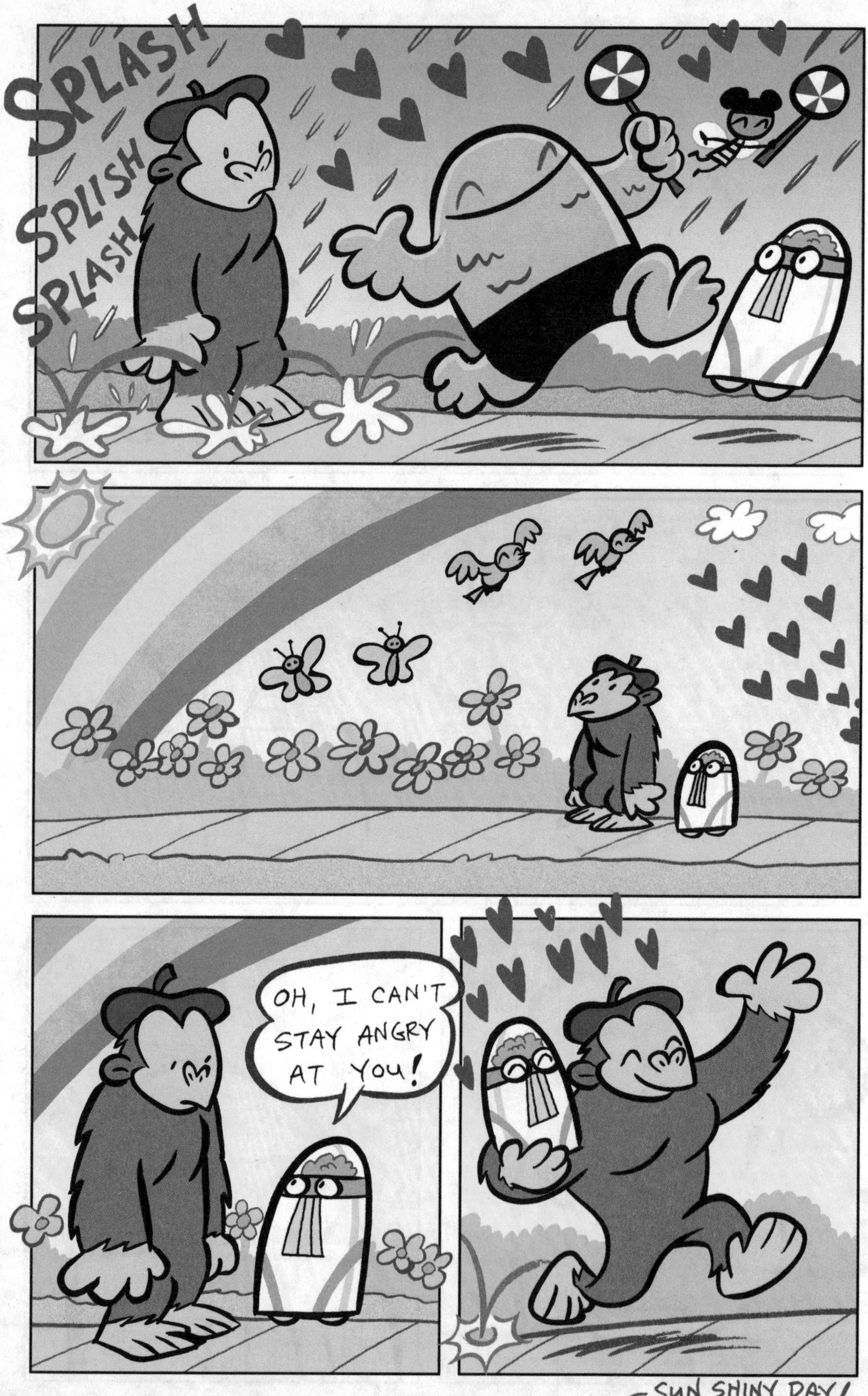
SPLASH
SPLISH
SPLASH
OH, I CAN'T STAY ANGRY AT YOU!

—SUN SHINY DAY!

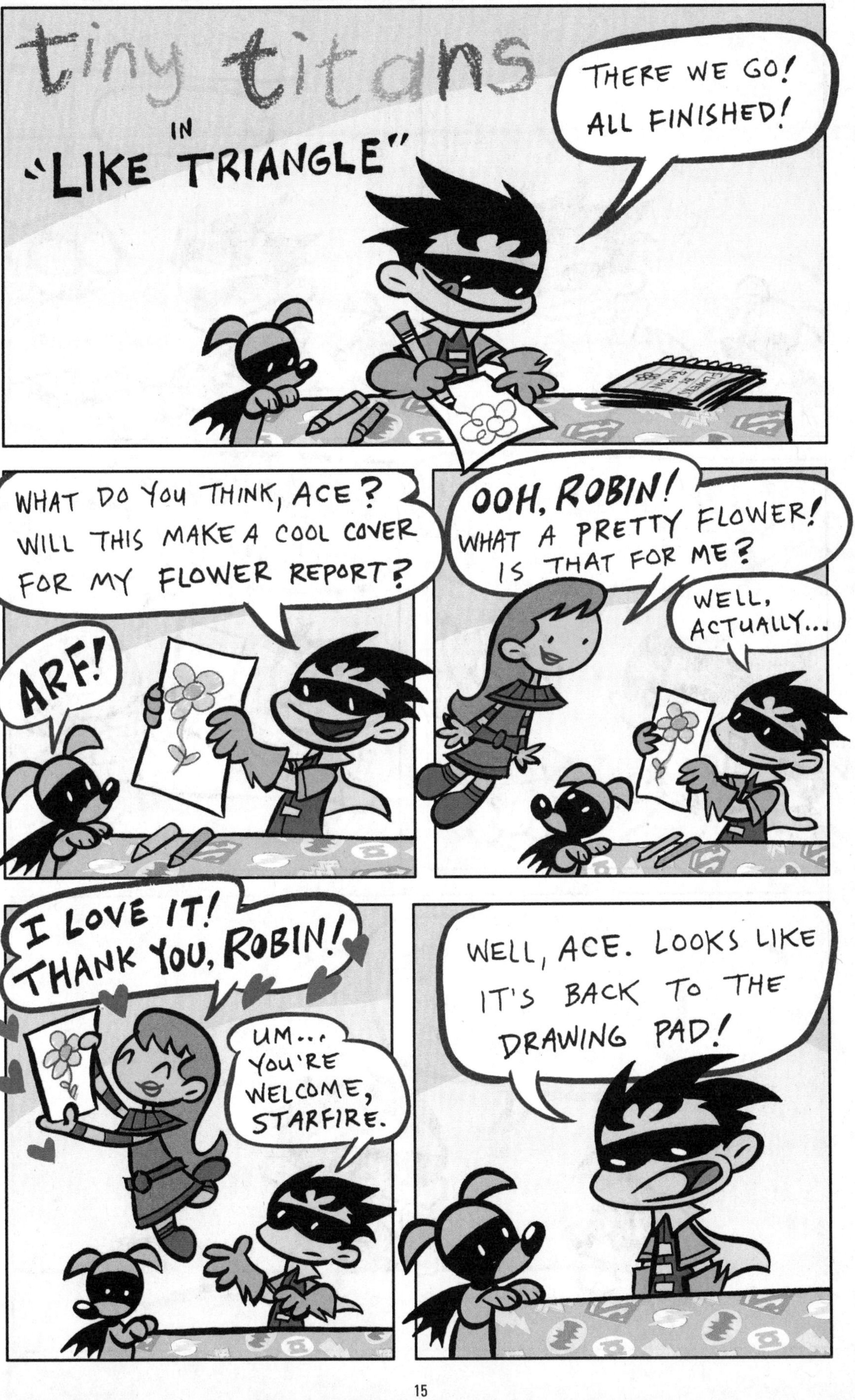
tiny titans
IN "LIKE TRIANGLE"
THERE WE GO! ALL FINISHED!
WHAT DO YOU THINK, ACE? WILL THIS MAKE A COOL COVER FOR MY FLOWER REPORT?
ARF!
OOH, ROBIN! WHAT A PRETTY FLOWER! IS THAT FOR ME?
WELL, ACTUALLY...
I LOVE IT! THANK YOU, ROBIN!
UM... YOU'RE WELCOME, STARFIRE.
WELL, ACE. LOOKS LIKE IT'S BACK TO THE DRAWING PAD!

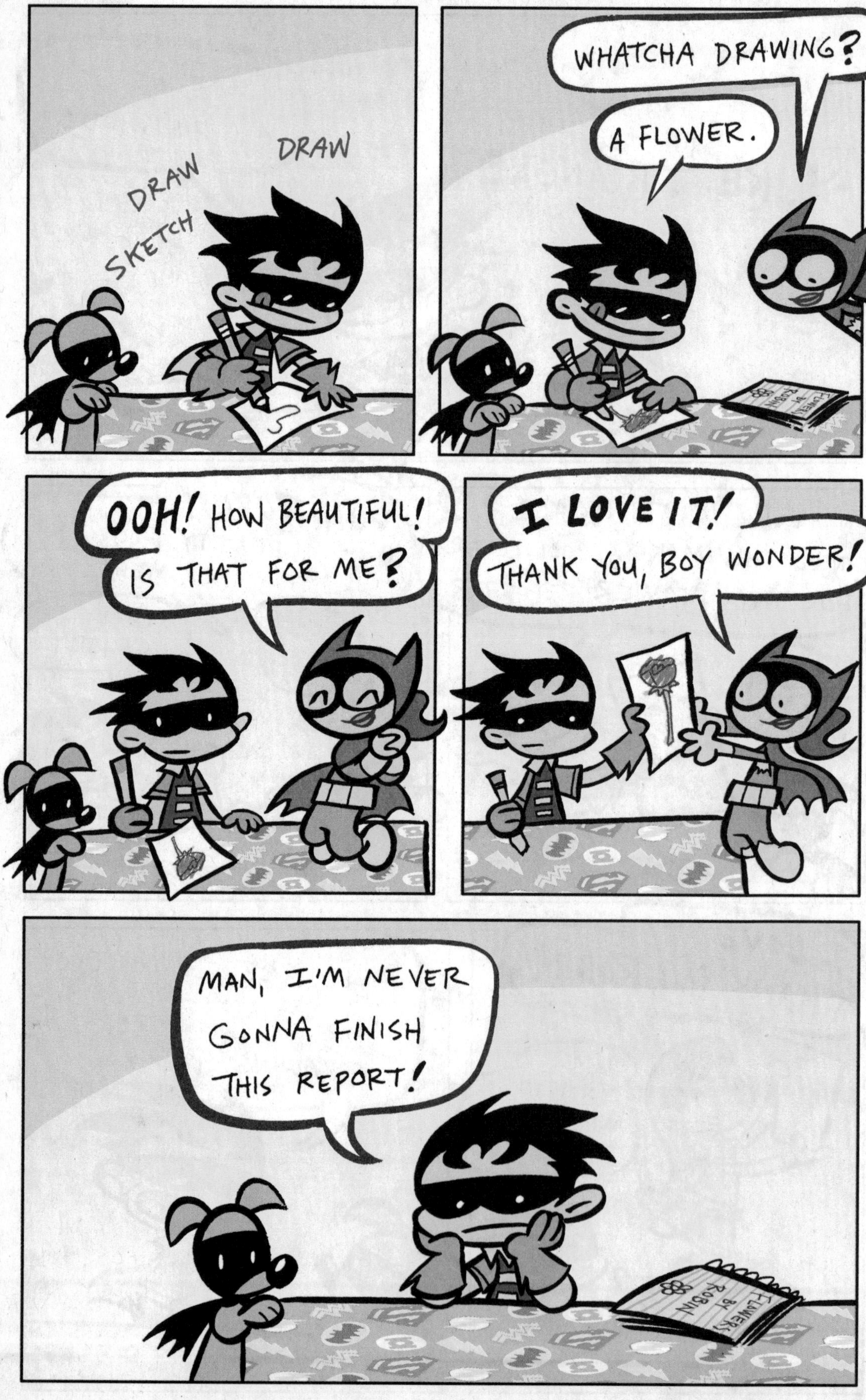
DRAW
DRAW
SKETCH
WHATCHA DRAWING?
A FLOWER.
FLOWERS BY ROBIN
OOH! HOW BEAUTIFUL! IS THAT FOR ME?
I LOVE IT! THANK YOU, BOY WONDER!
MAN, I'M NEVER GONNA FINISH THIS REPORT!
FLOWERS BY ROBIN

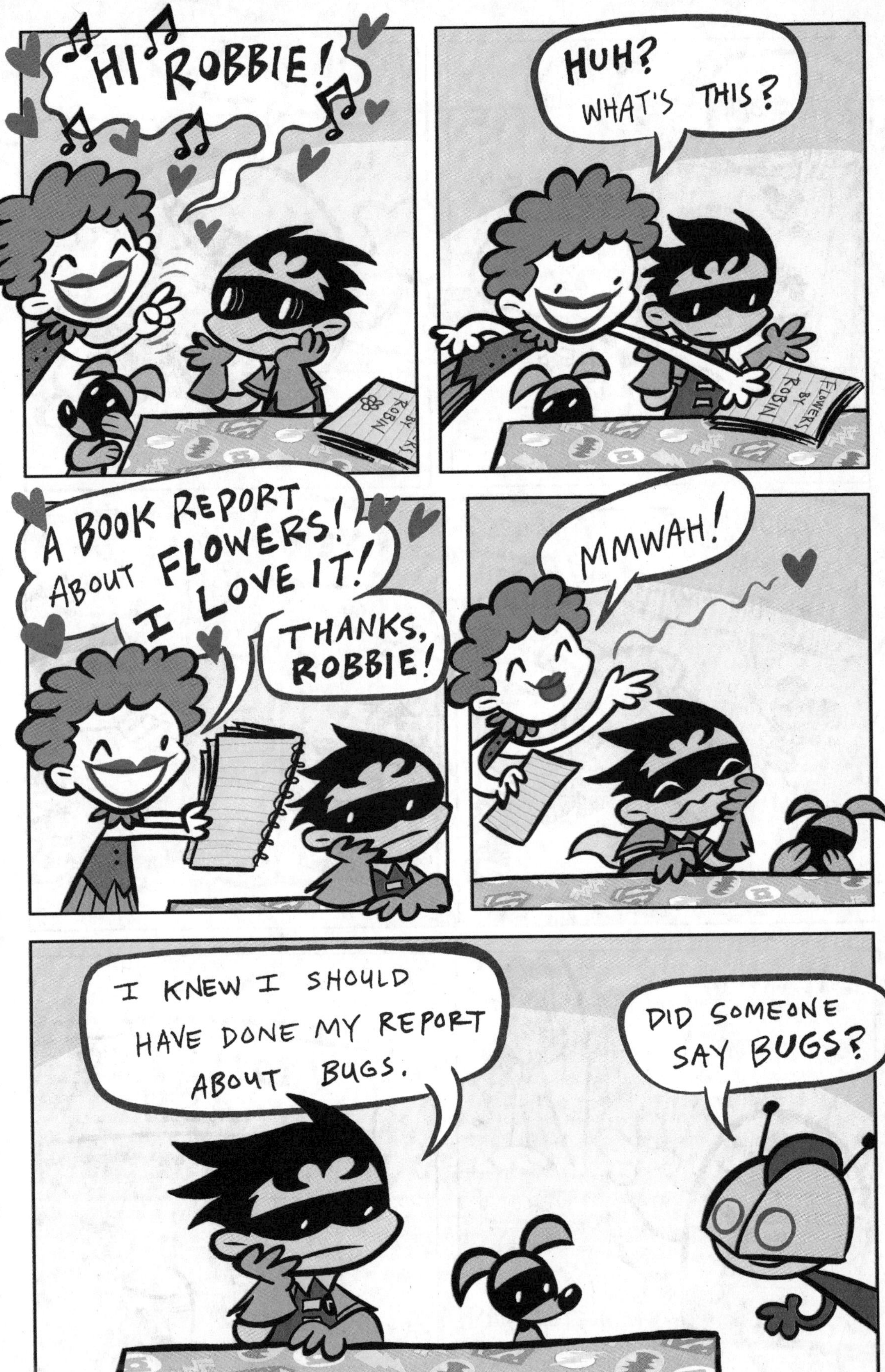
HI ROBBIE!
FLOWERS BY ROBIN
HUH? WHAT'S THIS?
FLOWERS BY ROBIN
A BOOK REPORT ABOUT FLOWERS! I LOVE IT!
THANKS, ROBBIE!
MMWAH!
I KNEW I SHOULD HAVE DONE MY REPORT ABOUT BUGS.
DID SOMEONE SAY BUGS?

—IT'S THE ANT!

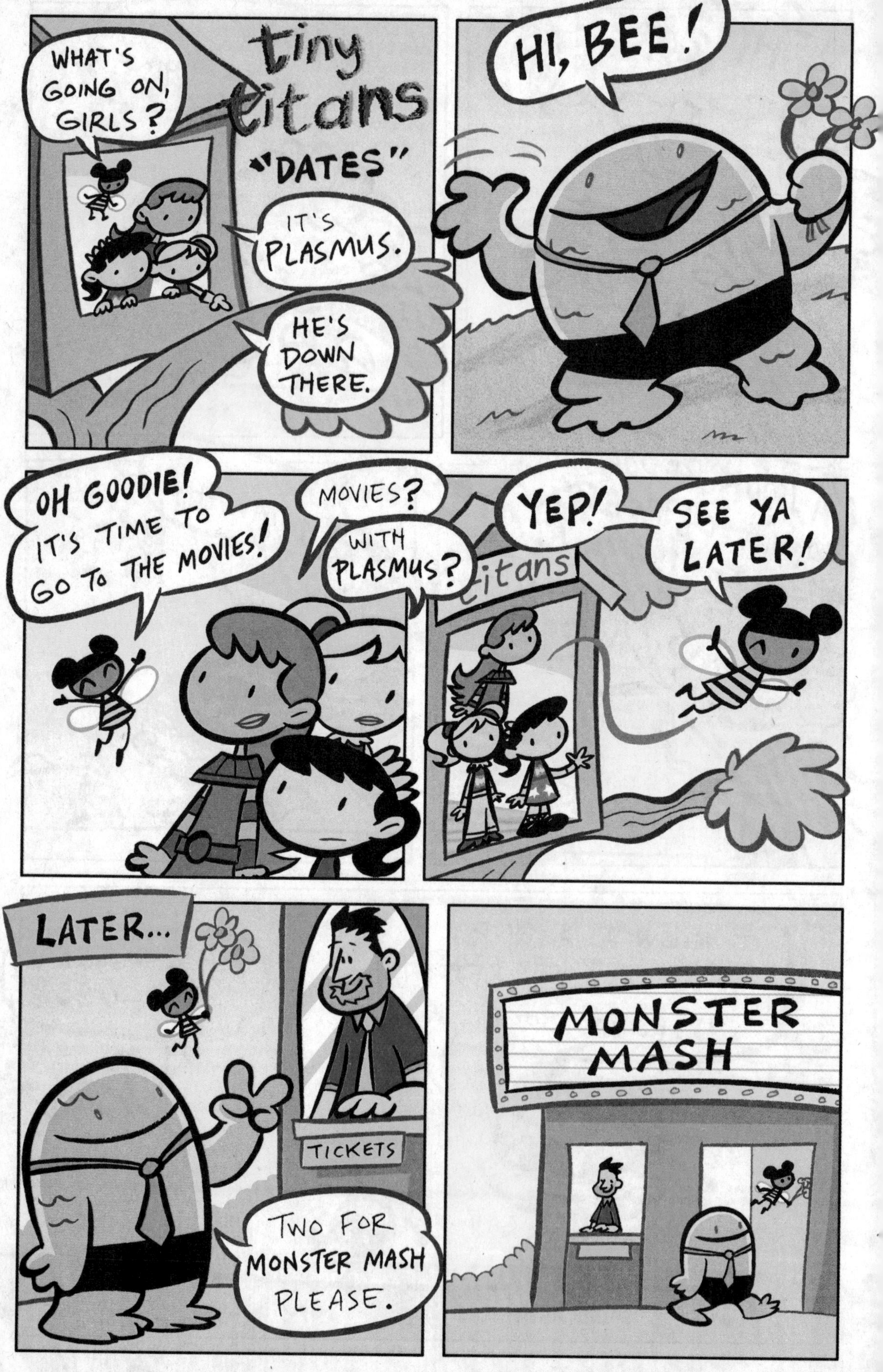
tiny titans
"DATES"
WHAT'S GOING ON, GIRLS?
IT'S PLASMUS.
HE'S DOWN THERE.
HI, BEE!
OH GOODIE! IT'S TIME TO GO TO THE MOVIES!
MOVIES?
WITH PLASMUS?
YEP!
SEE YA LATER!
titans
LATER...
TICKETS
TWO FOR MONSTER MASH PLEASE.
MONSTER MASH

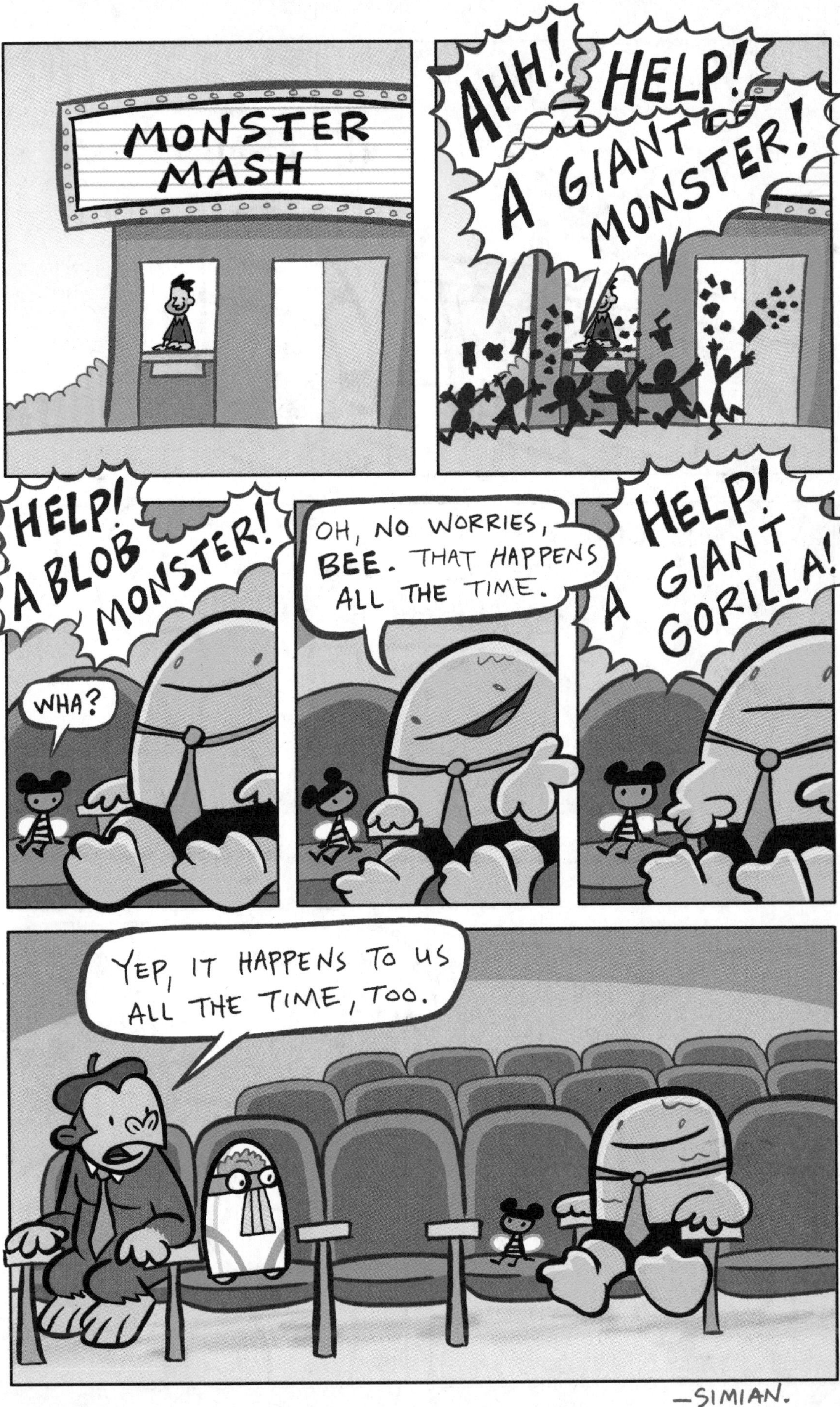
MONSTER MASH
AHH!
HELP!
A GIANT MONSTER!
HELP! A BLOB MONSTER!
WHA?
OH, NO WORRIES, BEE. THAT HAPPENS ALL THE TIME.
HELP! A GIANT GORILLA!
YEP, IT HAPPENS TO US ALL THE TIME, TOO.

—SIMIAN.

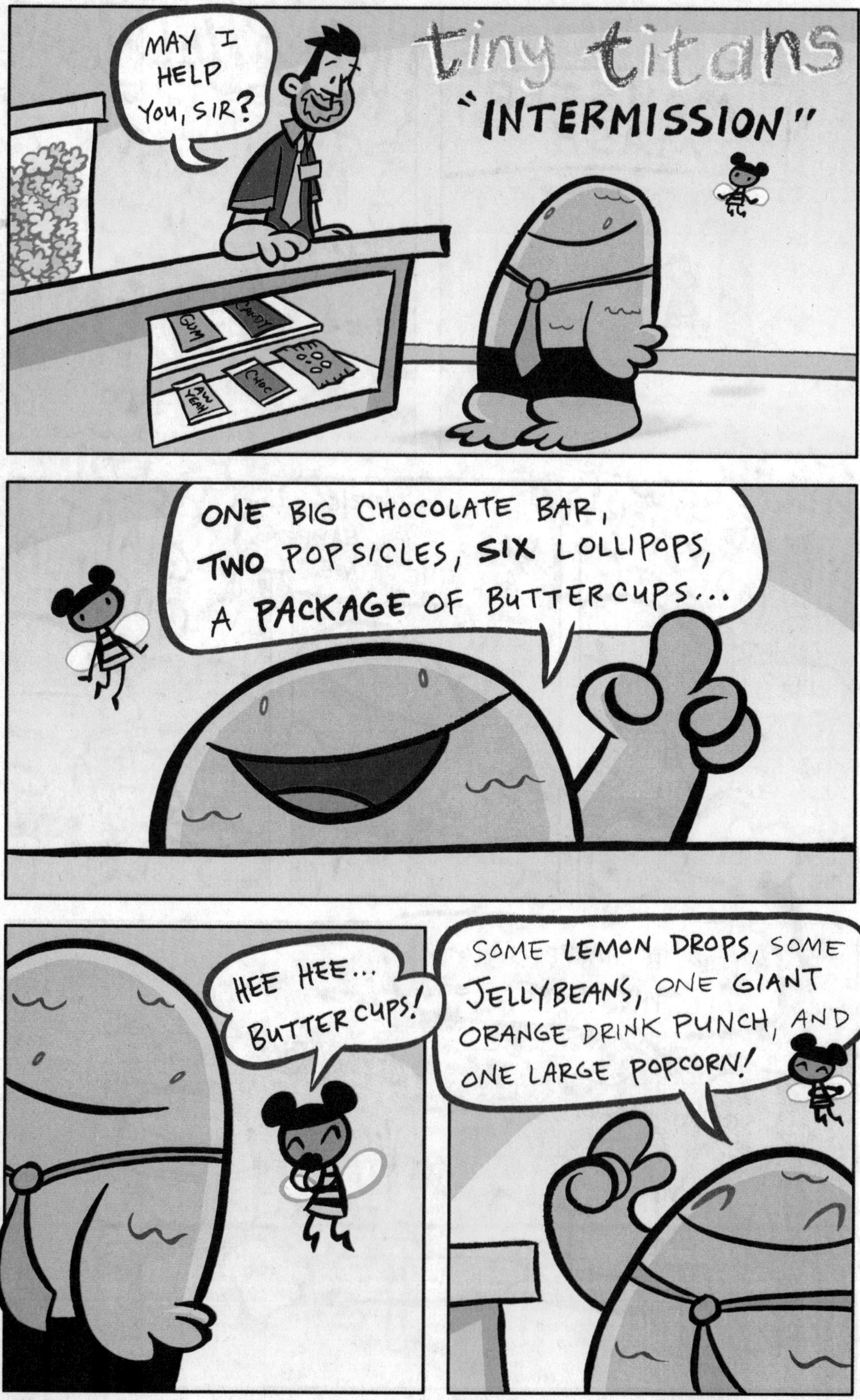
tiny titans
"INTERMISSION"
MAY I HELP YOU, SIR?
GUM
CANDY
CHOC
AW YEAH
ONE BIG CHOCOLATE BAR, TWO POPSICLES, SIX LOLLIPOPS, A PACKAGE OF BUTTERCUPS...
HEE HEE... BUTTERCUPS!
SOME LEMON DROPS, SOME JELLYBEANS, ONE GIANT ORANGE DRINK PUNCH, AND ONE LARGE POPCORN!

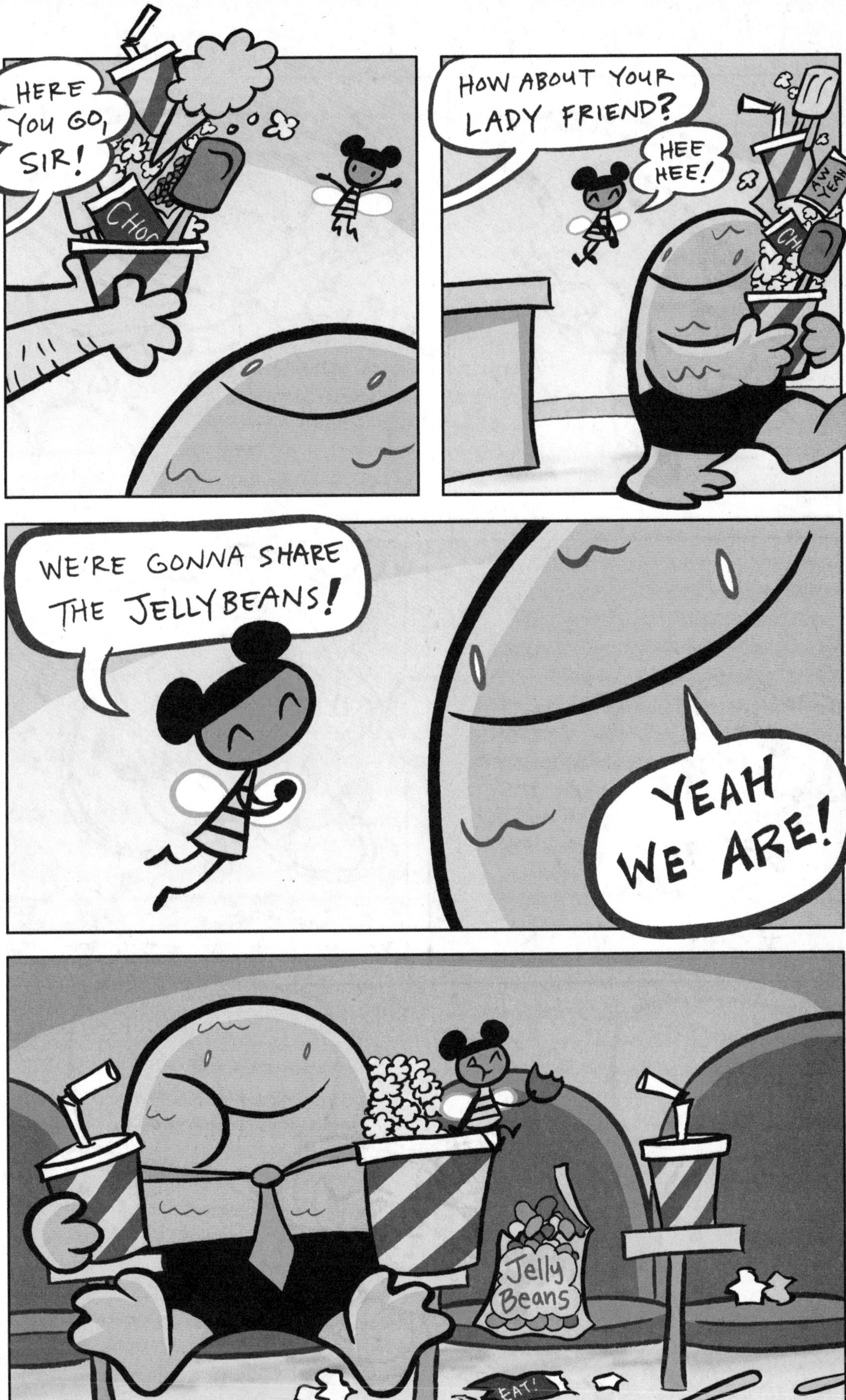
HERE YOU GO, SIR!
HOW ABOUT YOUR LADY FRIEND?
HEE HEE!
AW YEAH
WE'RE GONNA SHARE THE JELLYBEANS!
YEAH WE ARE!
Jelly Beans
EAT!

—SNACK TIME!

tiny titans in "JUMPROPE"

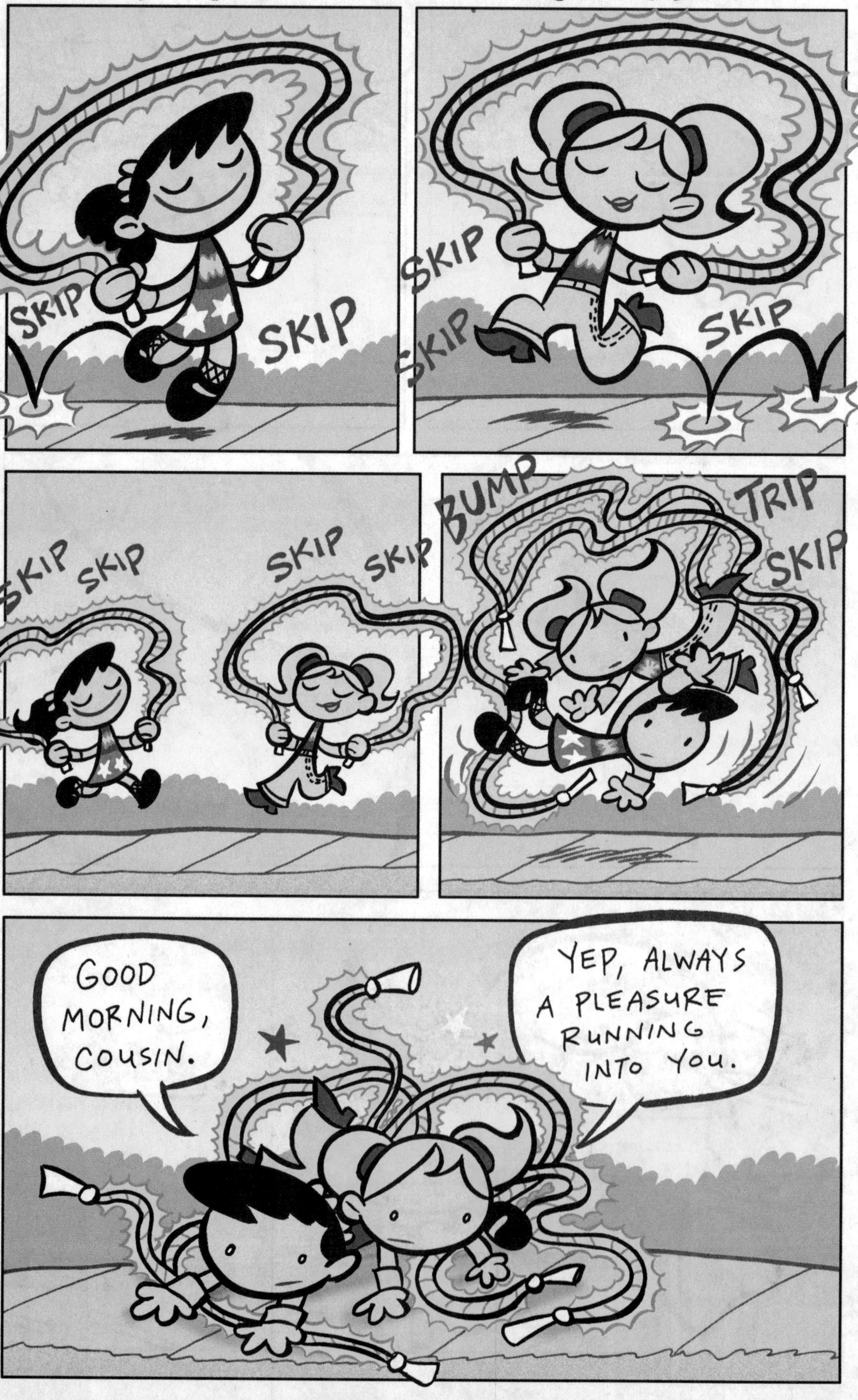
SKIP
SKIP
SKIP
SKIP
SKIP
SKIP
SKIP
SKIP
SKIP
BUMP
TRIP
SKIP
GOOD MORNING, COUSIN.
YEP, ALWAYS A PLEASURE RUNNING INTO YOU.

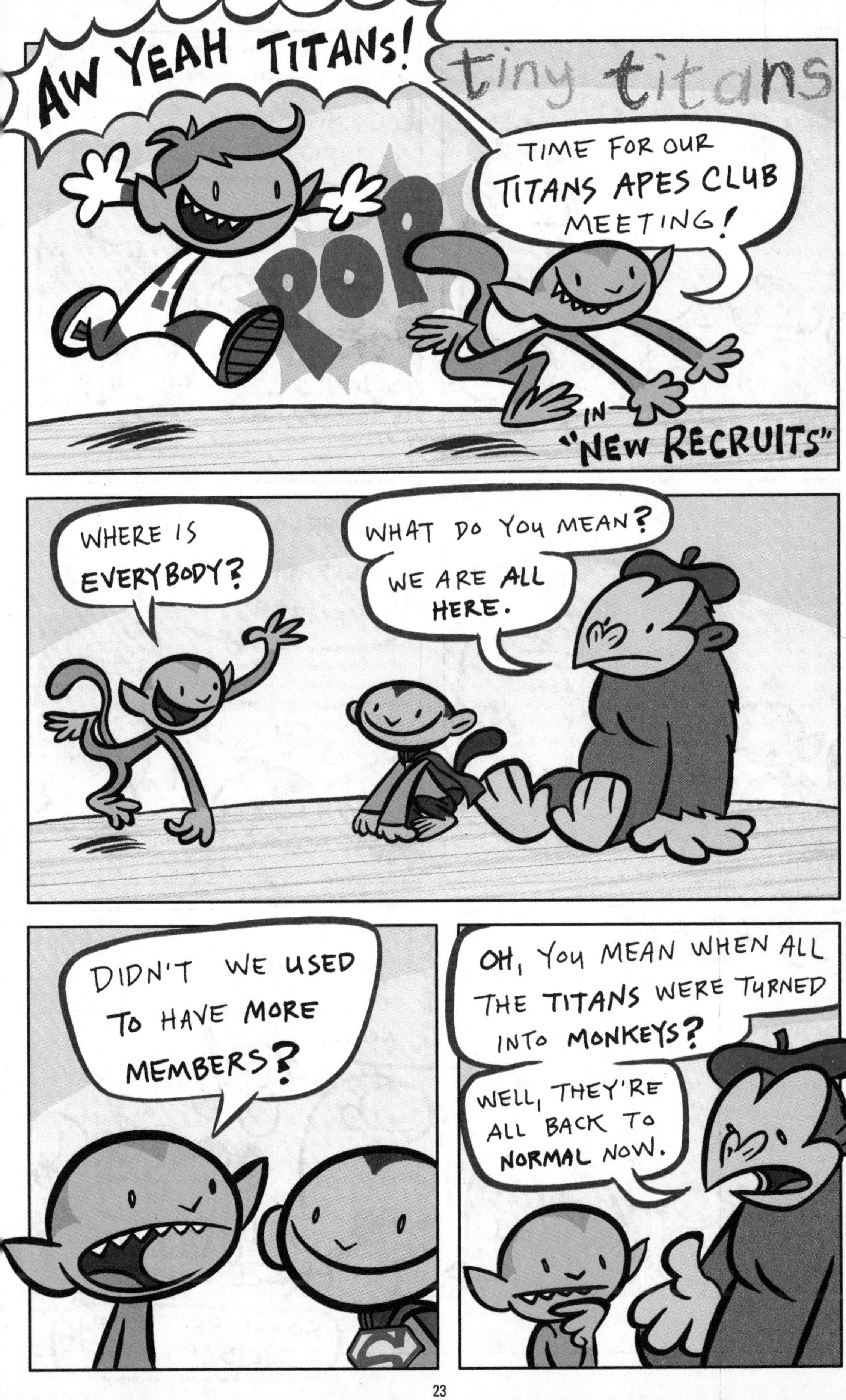
AW YEAH TITANS!
tiny titans
POP
TIME FOR OUR TITANS APES CLUB MEETING!
IN "NEW RECRUITS"
WHERE IS EVERYBODY?
WHAT DO YOU MEAN?
WE ARE ALL HERE.
DIDN'T WE USED TO HAVE MORE MEMBERS?
OH, YOU MEAN WHEN ALL THE TITANS WERE TURNED INTO MONKEYS?
WELL, THEY'RE ALL BACK TO NORMAL NOW.

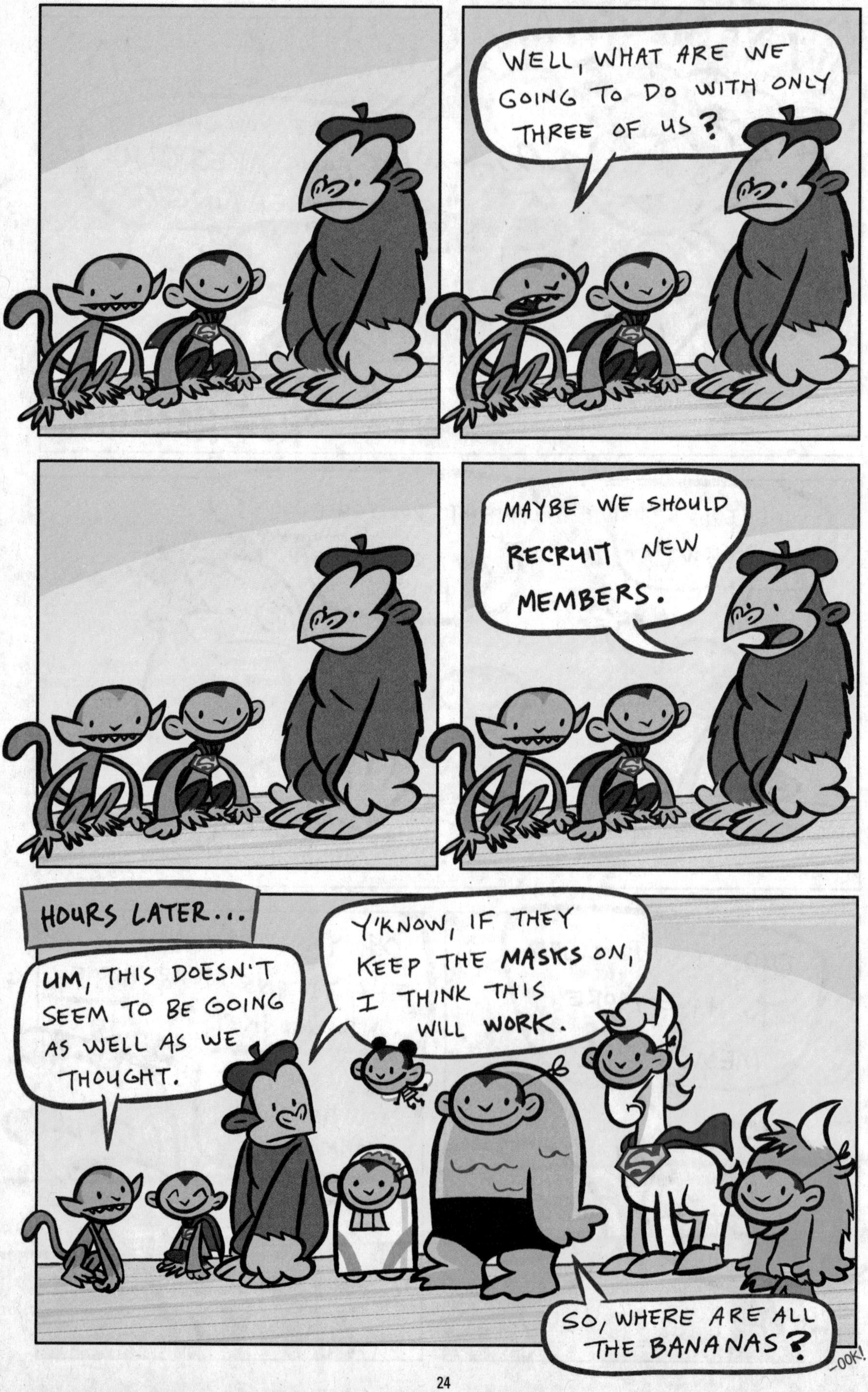
WELL, WHAT ARE WE GOING TO DO WITH ONLY THREE OF US?
MAYBE WE SHOULD RECRUIT NEW MEMBERS.
HOURS LATER...
UM, THIS DOESN'T SEEM TO BE GOING AS WELL AS WE THOUGHT.
Y'KNOW, IF THEY KEEP THE MASKS ON, I THINK THIS WILL WORK.
SO, WHERE ARE ALL THE BANANAS?
-OOK!

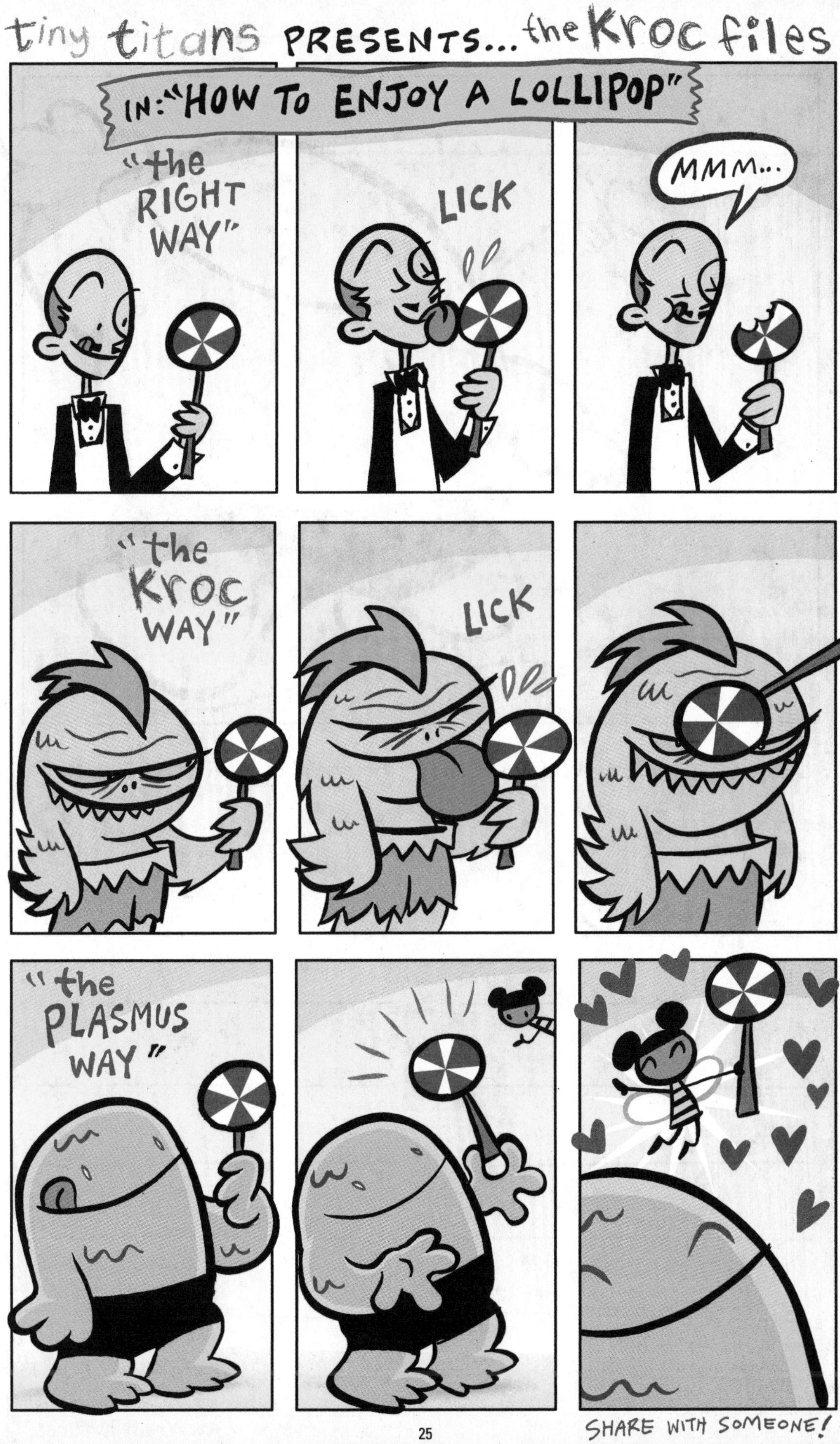
tiny titans PRESENTS... the Kroc files
IN: "HOW TO ENJOY A LOLLIPOP"
"the RIGHT WAY"
LICK
MMM...
"the Kroc WAY"
LICK
"the PLASMUS WAY"
SHARE WITH SOMEONE!

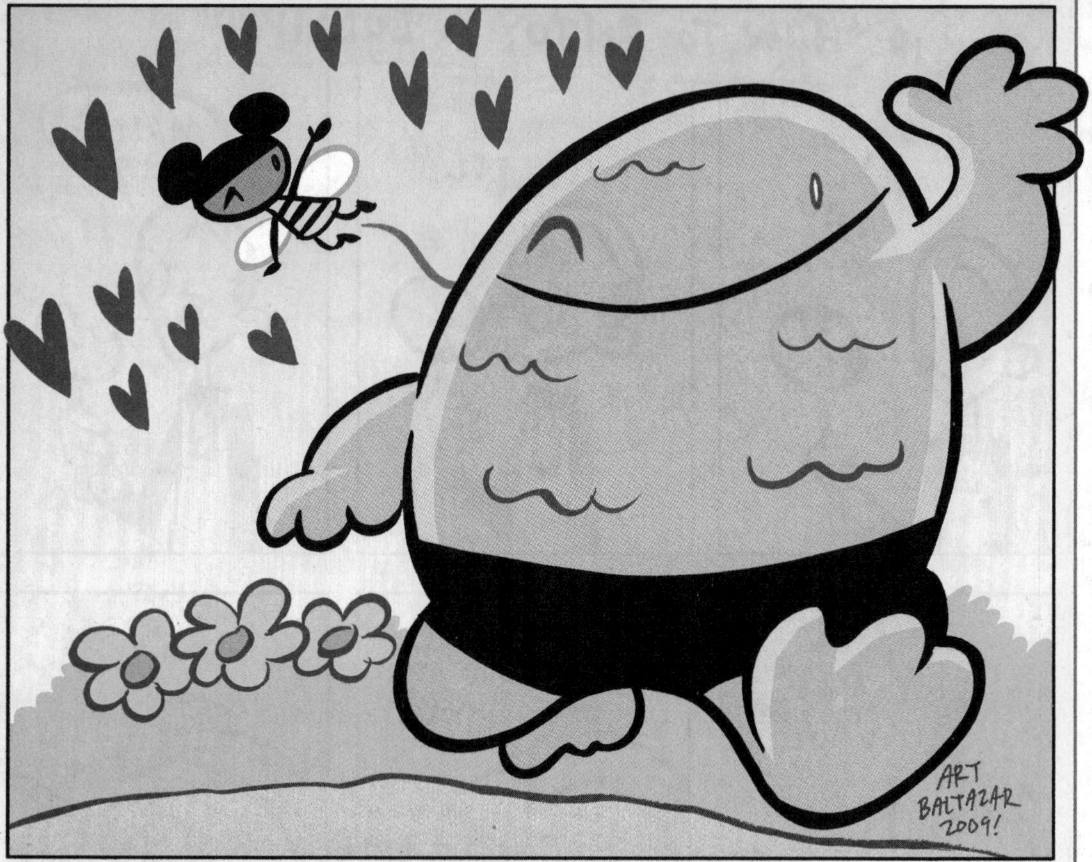
ART BALTAZAR 2009!

HOW MANY NEW WORDS CAN YOU MAKE WITH THE WORD

FRIENDSHIP?

FIND

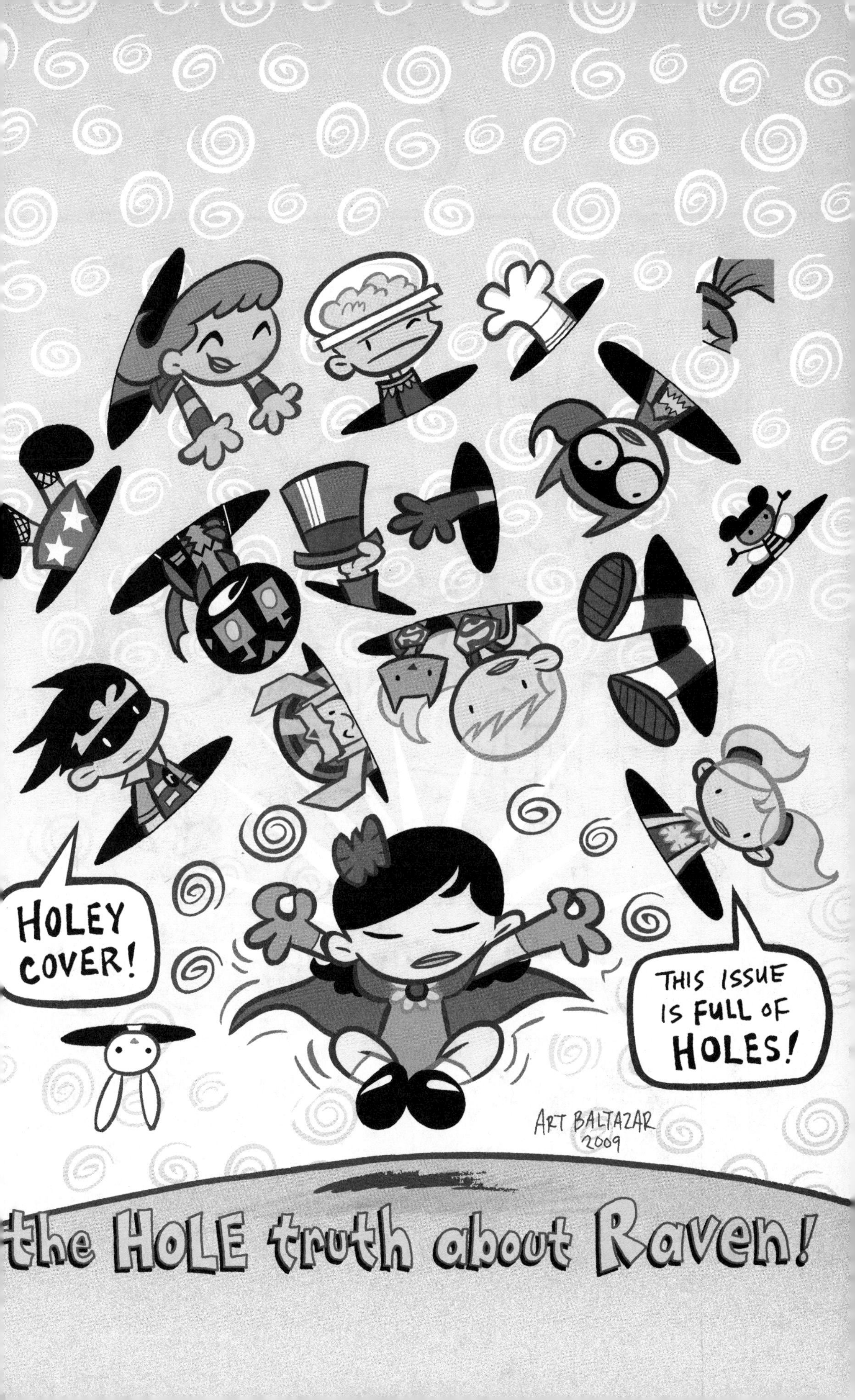
HOLEY COVER!
THIS ISSUE IS FULL OF HOLES!
ART BALTAZAR 2009
the HOLE truth about Raven!

tiny titans

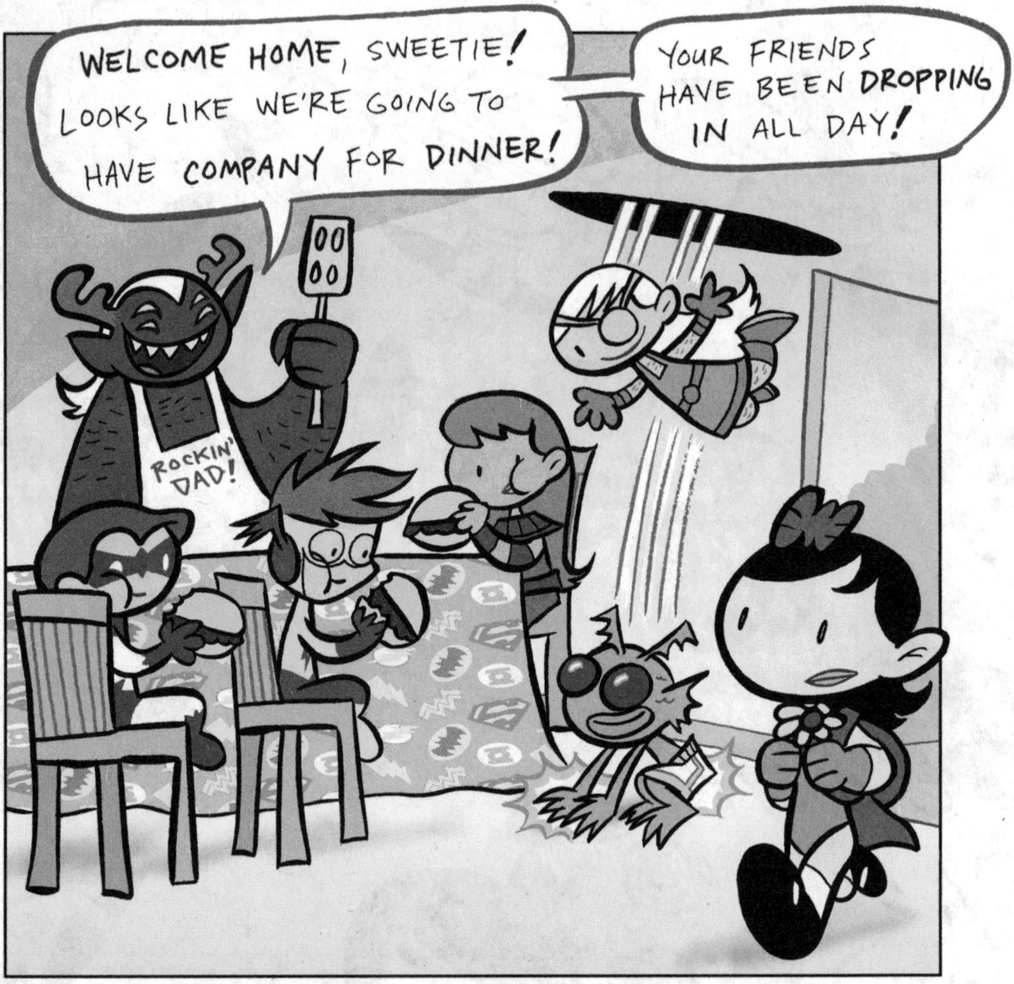

WELCOME HOME, SWEETIE! LOOKS LIKE WE'RE GOING TO HAVE COMPANY FOR DINNER!
YOUR FRIENDS HAVE BEEN DROPPING IN ALL DAY!
ROCKIN' DAD!

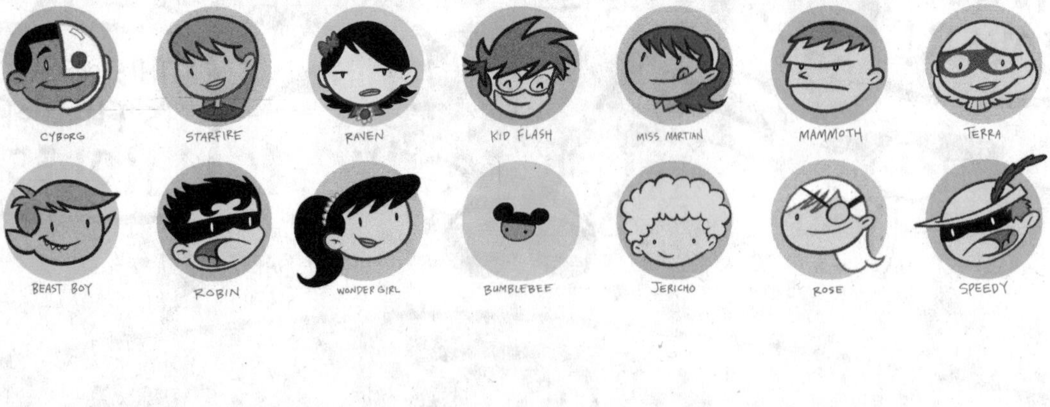

CYBORG
STARFIRE
RAVEN
KID FLASH
MISS MARTIAN
MAMMOTH
TERRA
BEAST BOY
ROBIN
WONDER GIRL
BUMBLEBEE
JERICHO
ROSE
SPEEDY

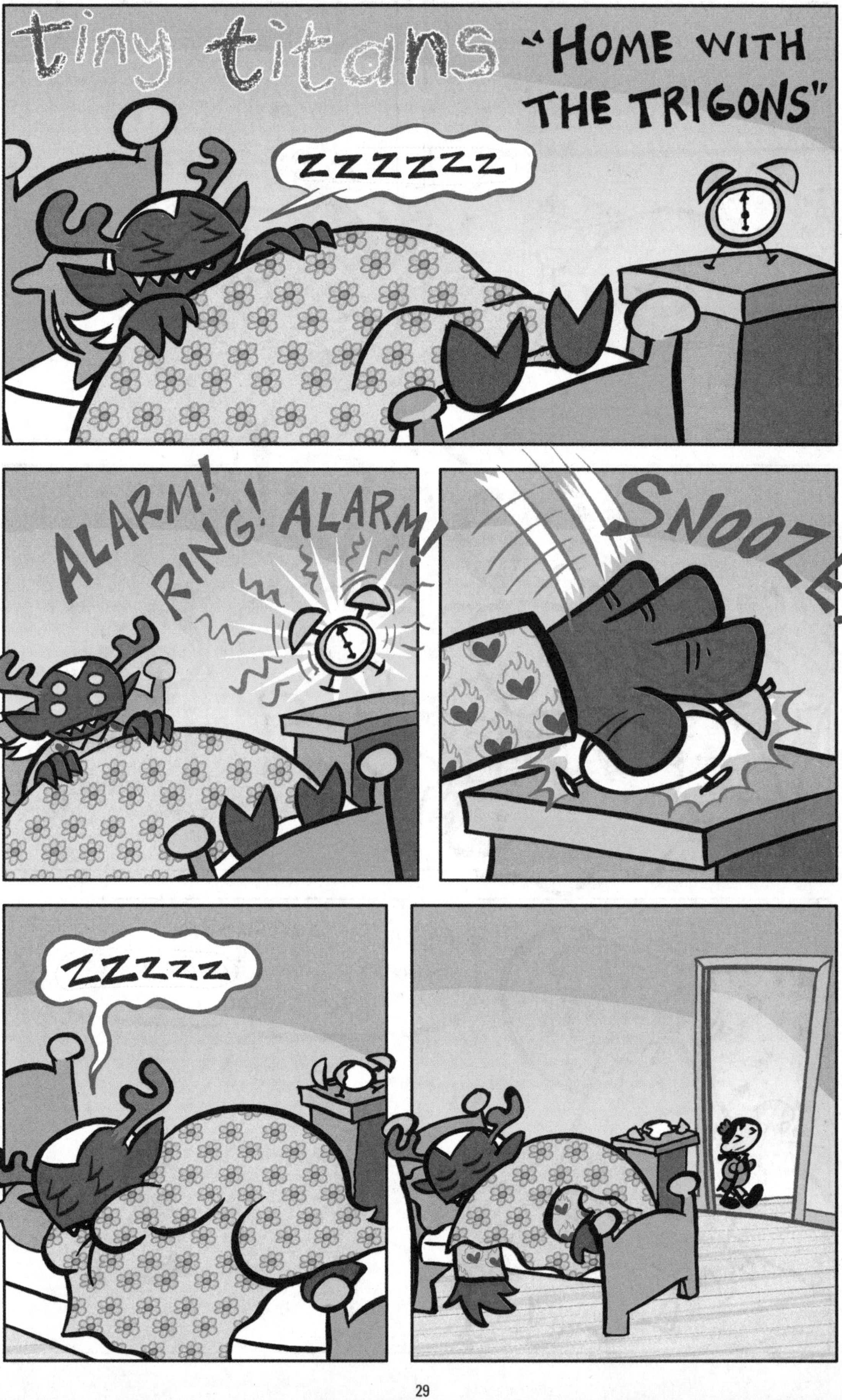
tiny titans
"HOME WITH THE TRIGONS"
ZZZZZZZ
ALARM! RING! ALARM!
SNOOZE!
ZZZZZ

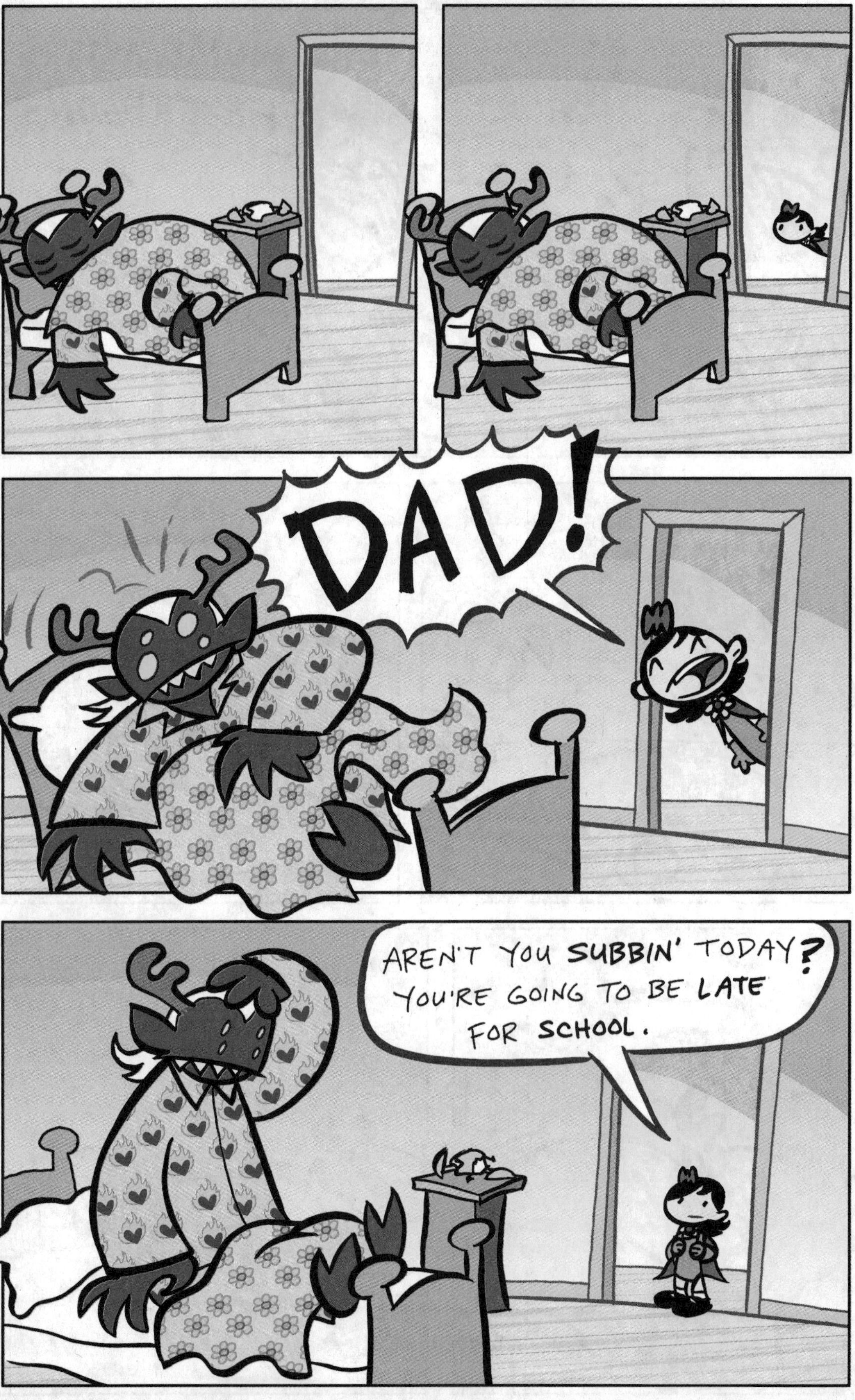
DAD!
AREN'T YOU SUBBIN' TODAY? YOU'RE GOING TO BE LATE FOR SCHOOL.

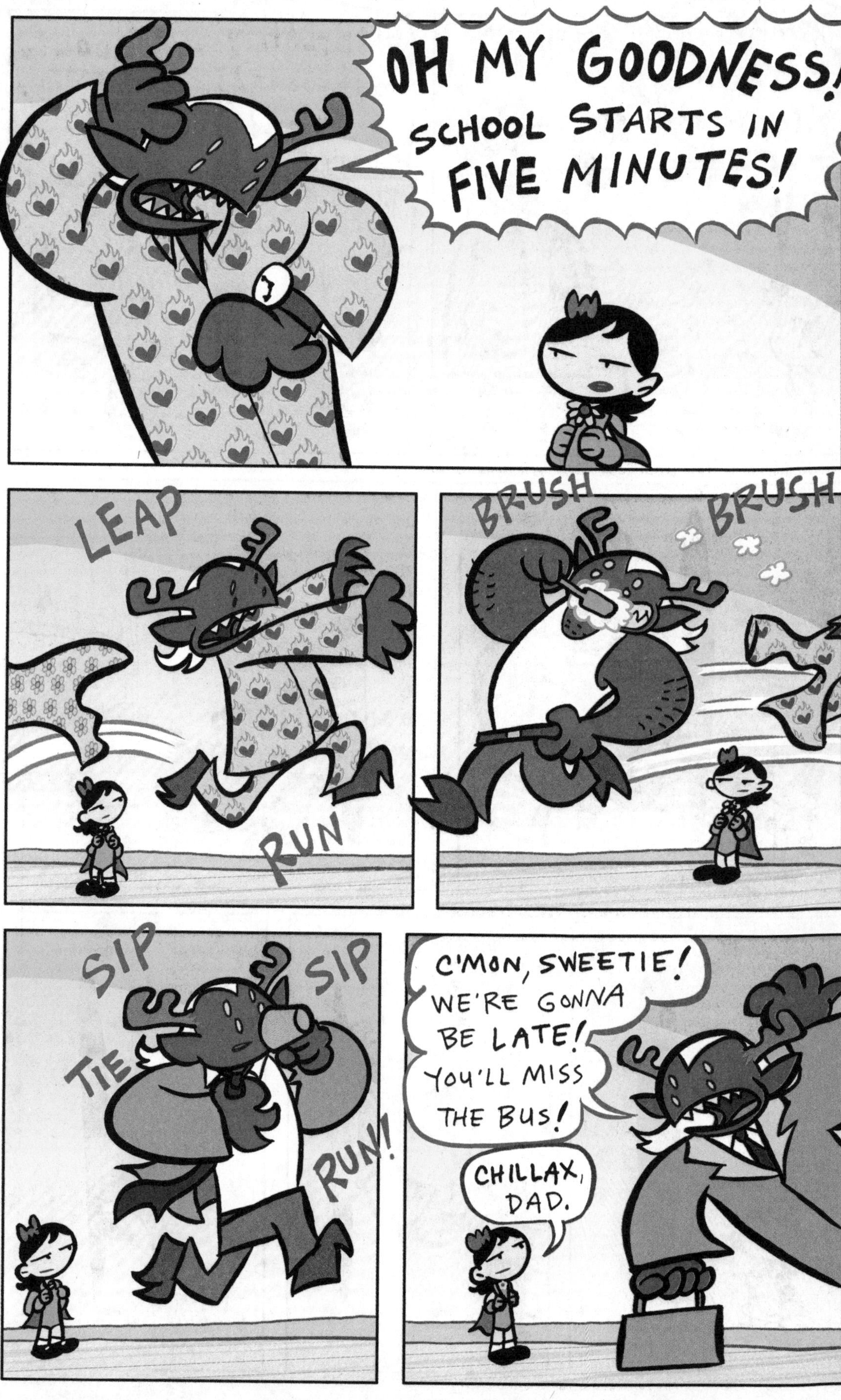
OH MY GOODNESS!
SCHOOL STARTS IN FIVE MINUTES!
LEAP
RUN
BRUSH
BRUSH
SIP
SIP
TIE
RUN!
C'MON, SWEETIE! WE'RE GONNA BE LATE! YOU'LL MISS THE BUS!
CHILLAX, DAD.

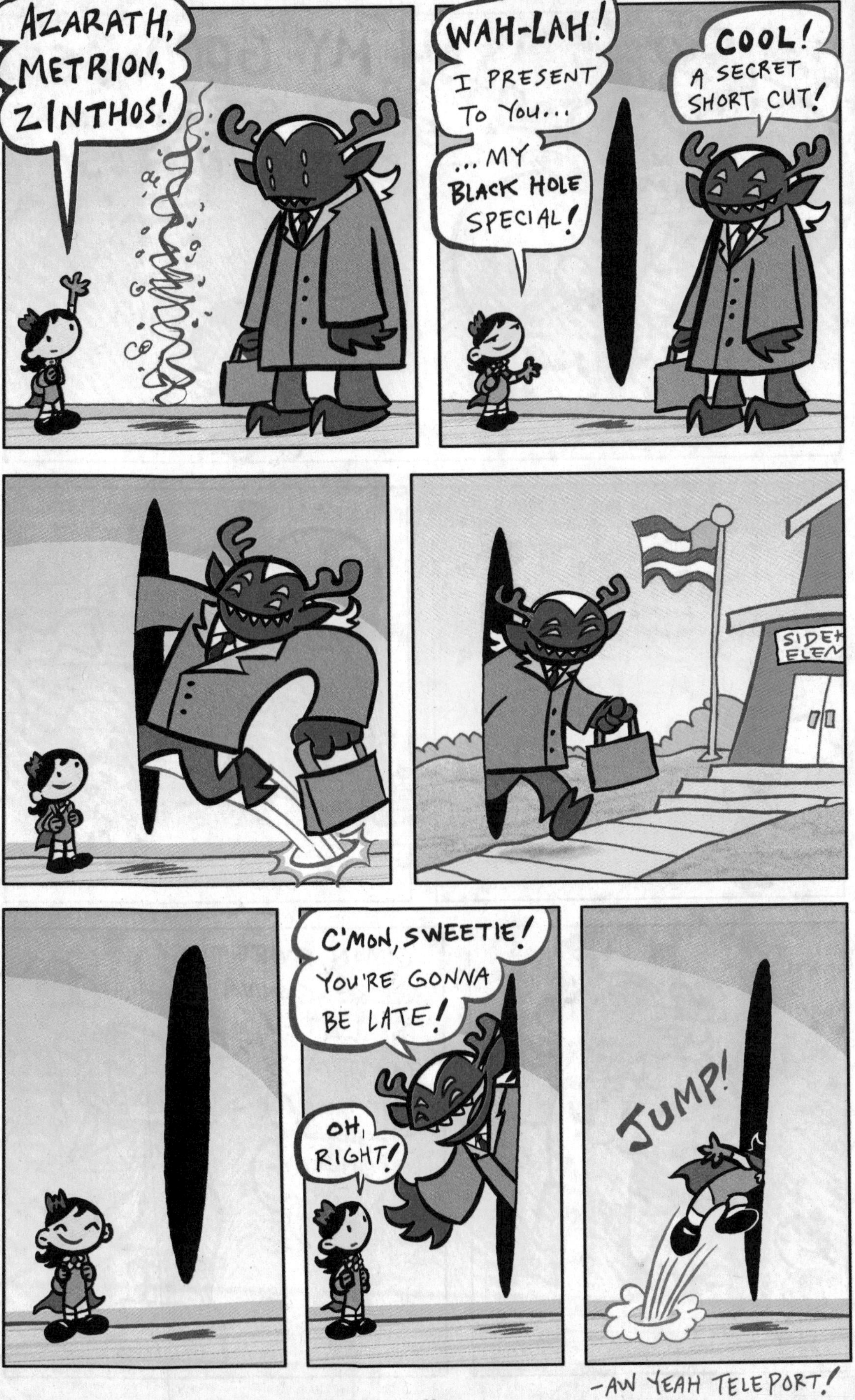
AZARATH, METRION, ZINTHOS!
WAH-LAH! I PRESENT TO YOU...
... MY BLACK HOLE SPECIAL!
COOL! A SECRET SHORT CUT!
C'MON, SWEETIE! YOU'RE GONNA BE LATE!
OH, RIGHT!
JUMP!
-AW YEAH TELEPORT!

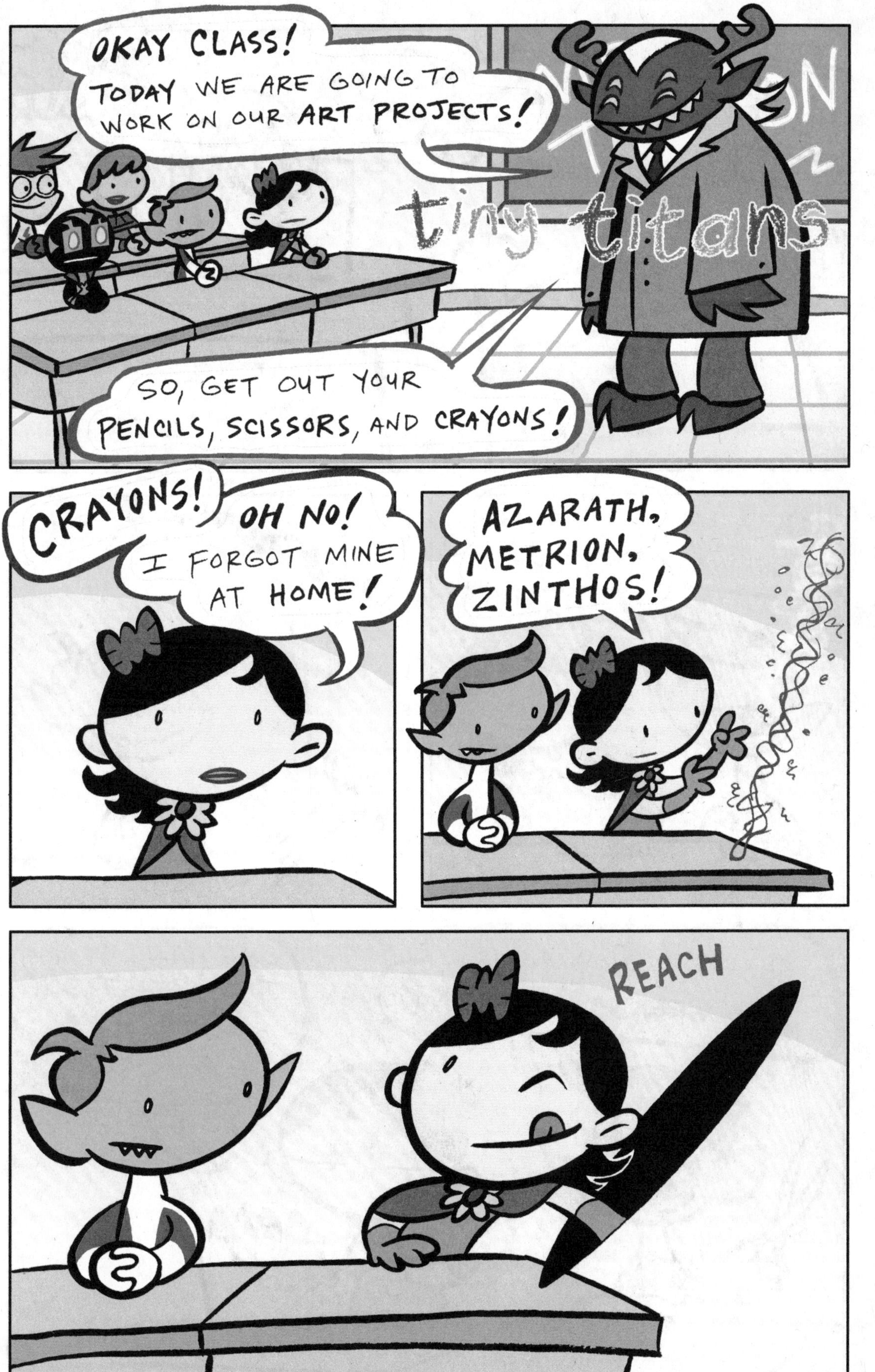
OKAY CLASS! TODAY WE ARE GOING TO WORK ON OUR ART PROJECTS!
tiny titans
SO, GET OUT YOUR PENCILS, SCISSORS, AND CRAYONS!
CRAYONS!
OH NO! I FORGOT MINE AT HOME!
AZARATH, METRION, ZINTHOS!
REACH

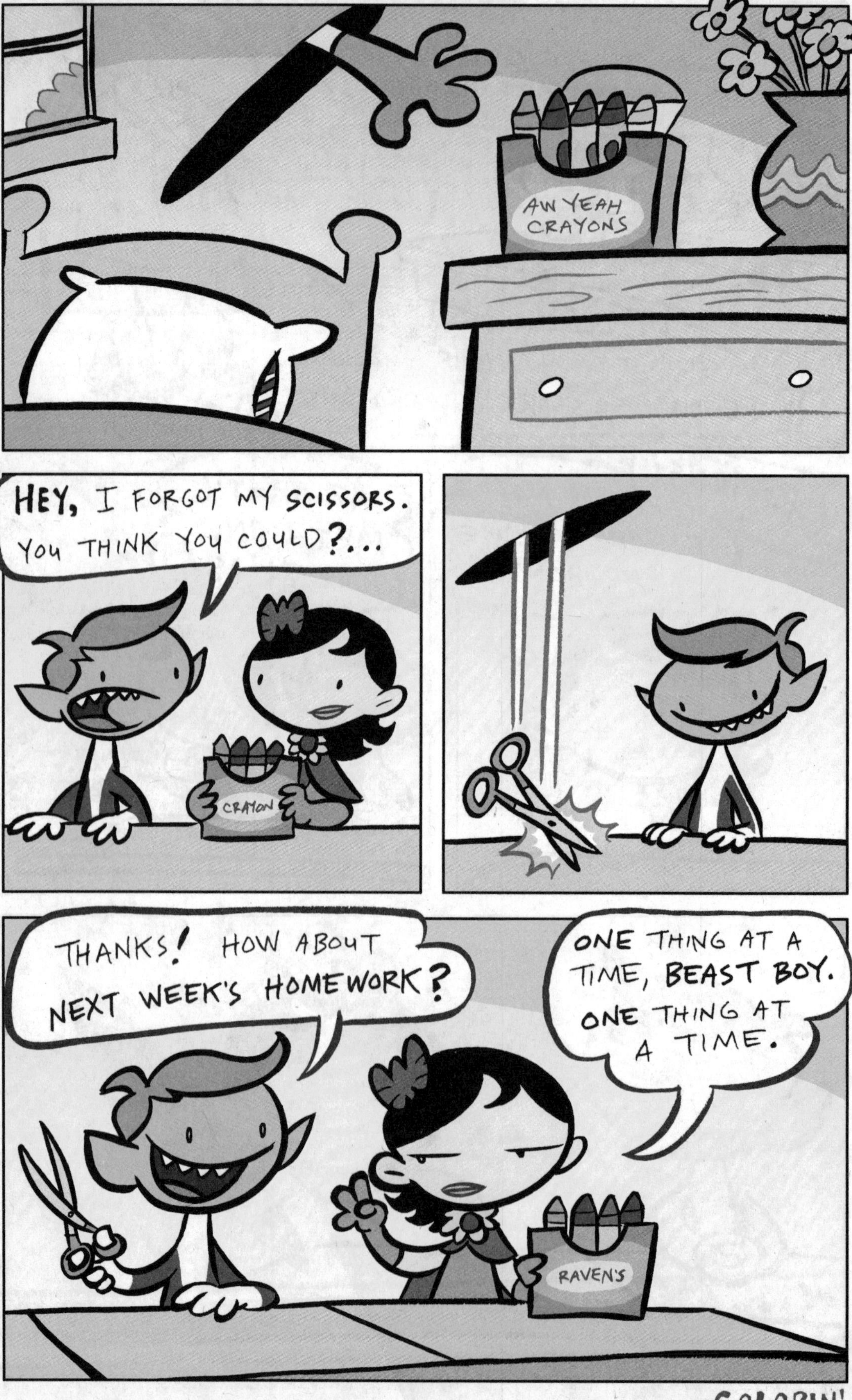
AW YEAH CRAYONS
HEY, I FORGOT MY SCISSORS. YOU THINK YOU COULD?...
CRAYON
THANKS! HOW ABOUT NEXT WEEK'S HOMEWORK?
ONE THING AT A TIME, BEAST BOY. ONE THING AT A TIME.
RAVEN'S

—COLORIN'

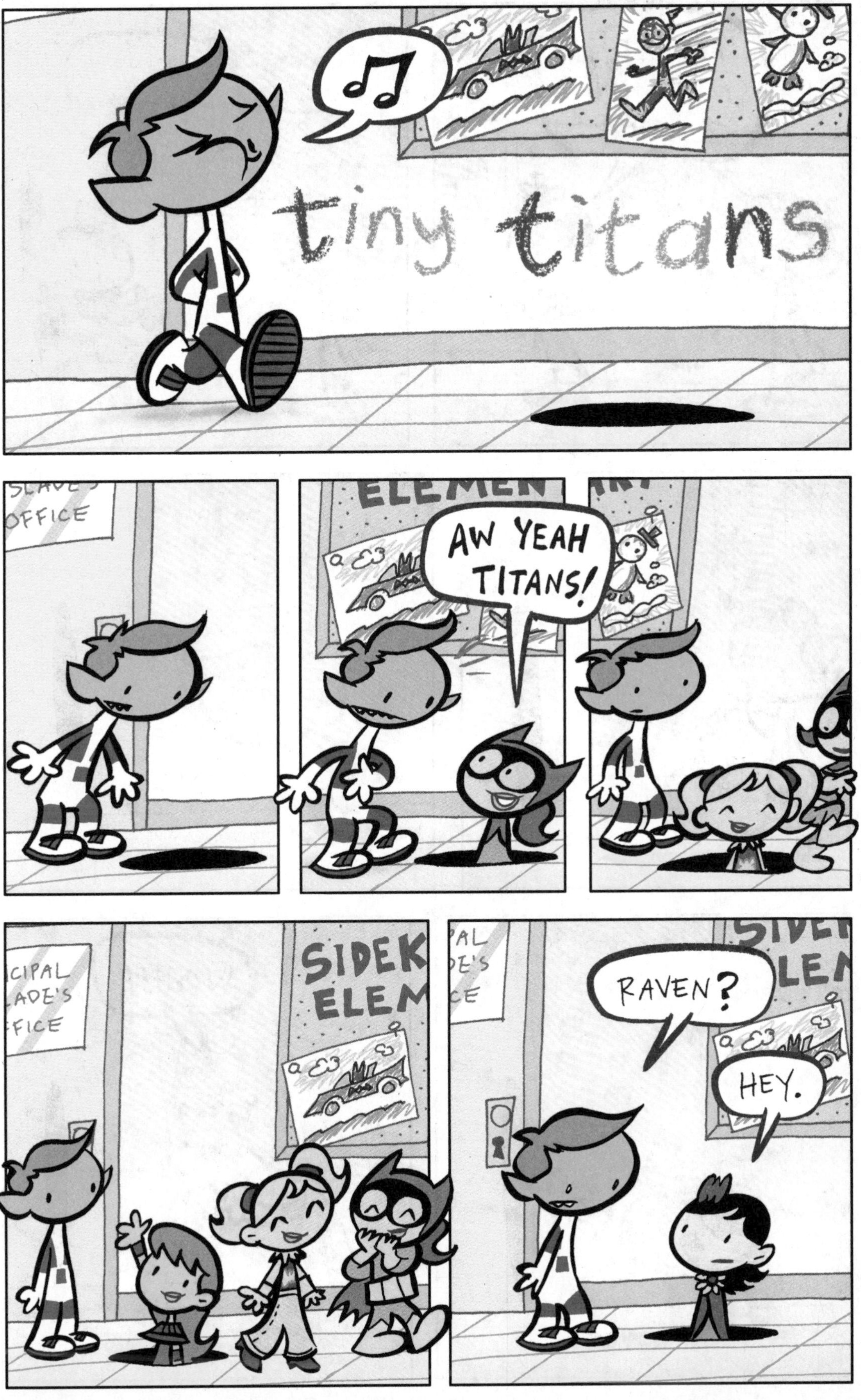
tiny titans
AW YEAH TITANS!
RAVEN?
HEY.

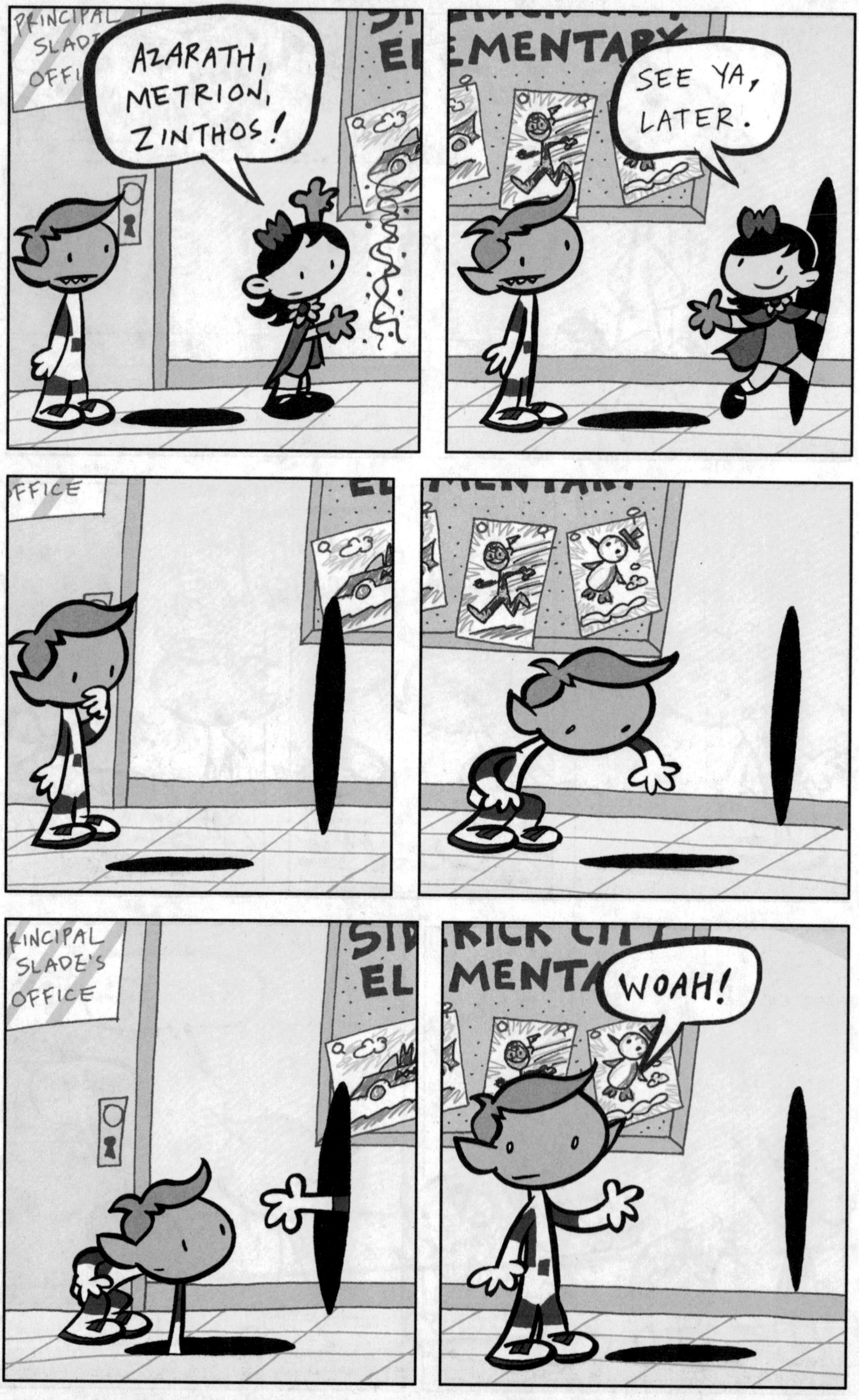
AZARATH, METRION, ZINTHOS!
SEE YA, LATER.
SLADE'S
OFFICE
WOAH!

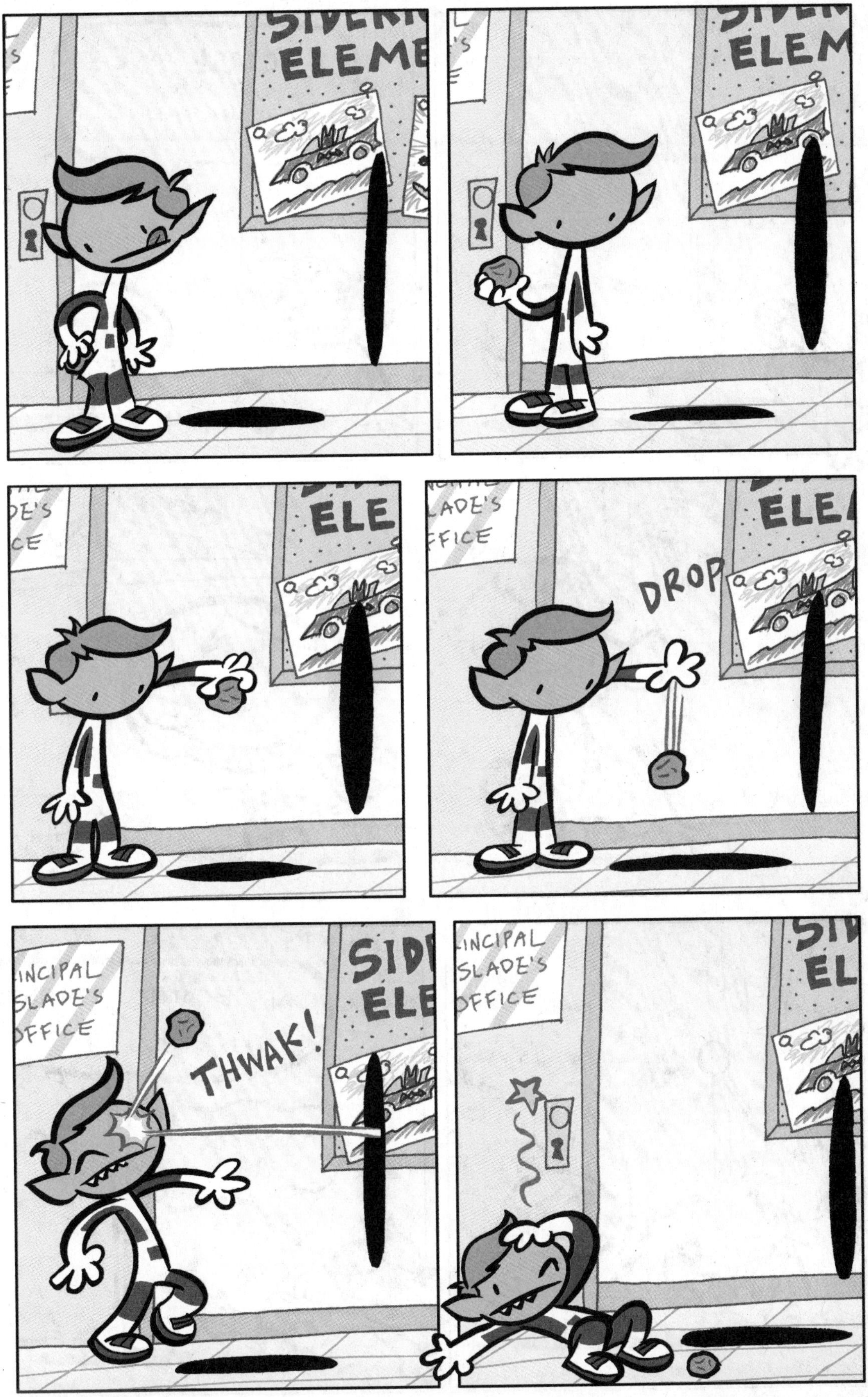
DROP
THWAK!

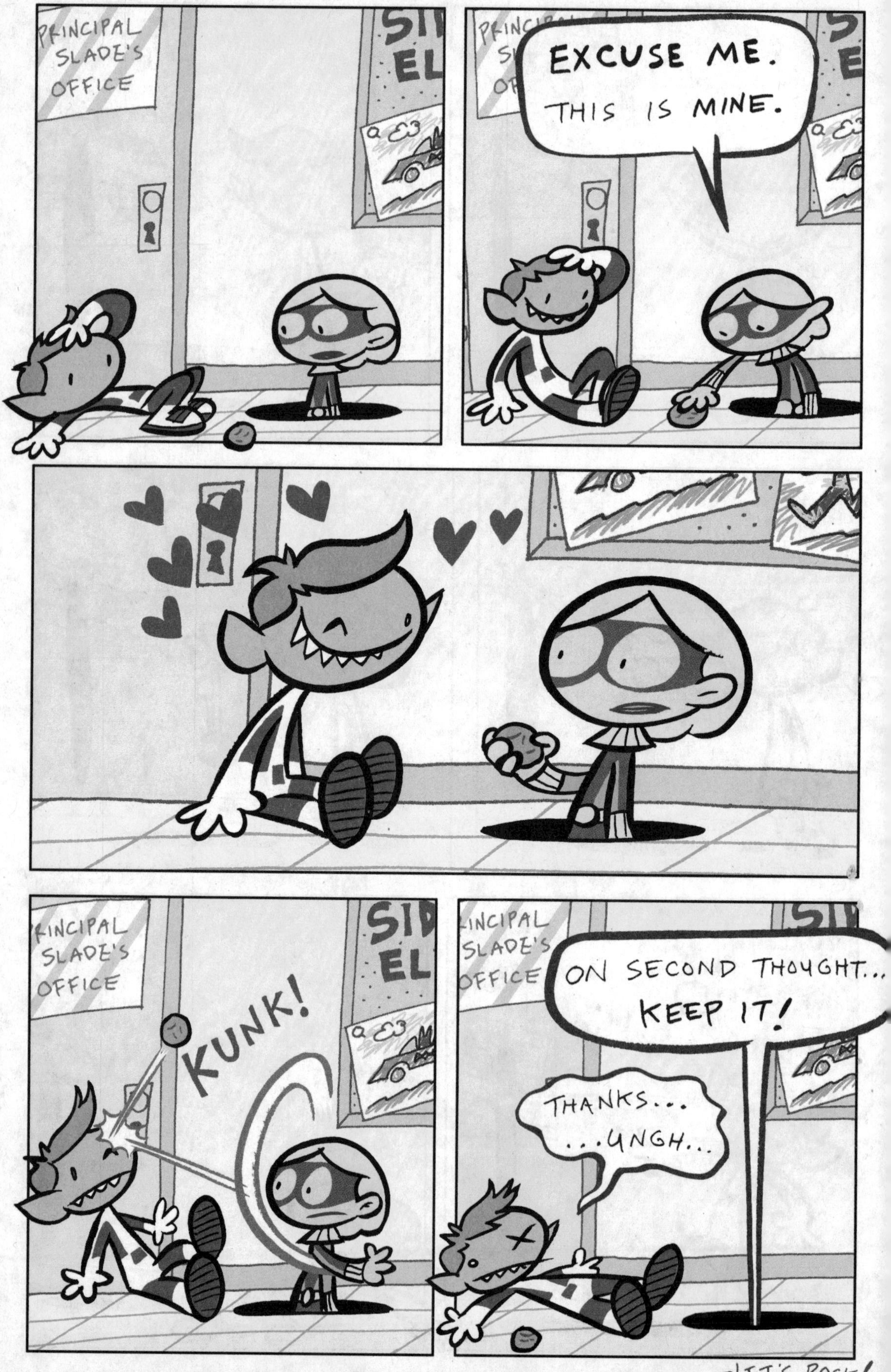
PRINCIPAL SLADE'S OFFICE
EXCUSE ME.
THIS IS MINE.
RINCIPAL SLADE'S OFFICE
KUNK!
INCIPAL SLADE'S OFFICE
ON SECOND THOUGHT... KEEP IT!
THANKS... ...UNGH...

—LET'S ROCK!

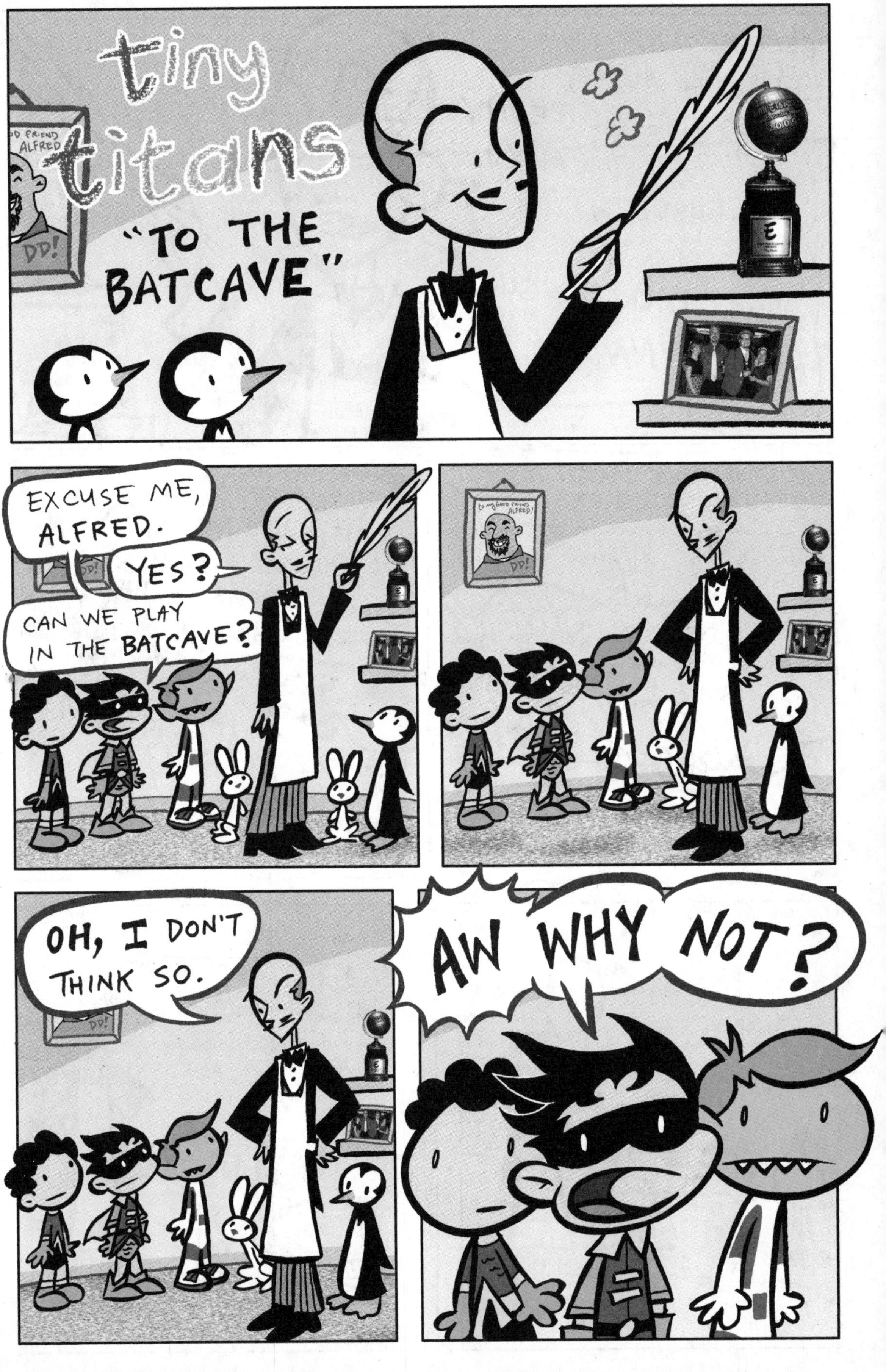
tiny titans
"TO THE BATCAVE"
EXCUSE ME, ALFRED.
YES?
CAN WE PLAY IN THE BATCAVE?
OH, I DON'T THINK SO.
AW WHY NOT?

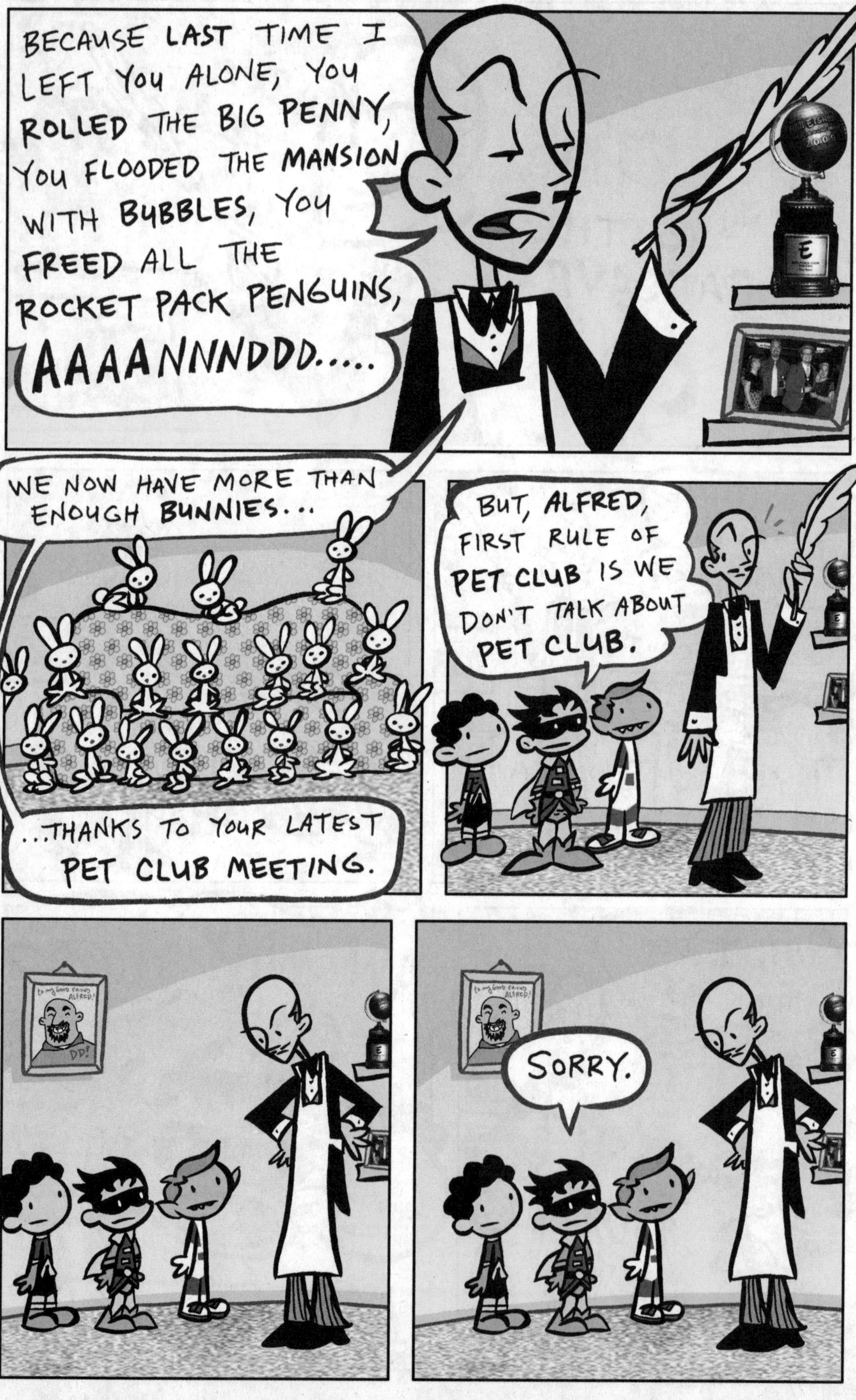
BECAUSE LAST TIME I LEFT YOU ALONE, YOU ROLLED THE BIG PENNY, YOU FLOODED THE MANSION WITH BUBBLES, YOU FREED ALL THE ROCKET PACK PENGUINS, AAAANNNDDD.....
WE NOW HAVE MORE THAN ENOUGH BUNNIES...
...THANKS TO YOUR LATEST PET CLUB MEETING.
BUT, ALFRED, FIRST RULE OF PET CLUB IS WE DON'T TALK ABOUT PET CLUB.
SORRY.

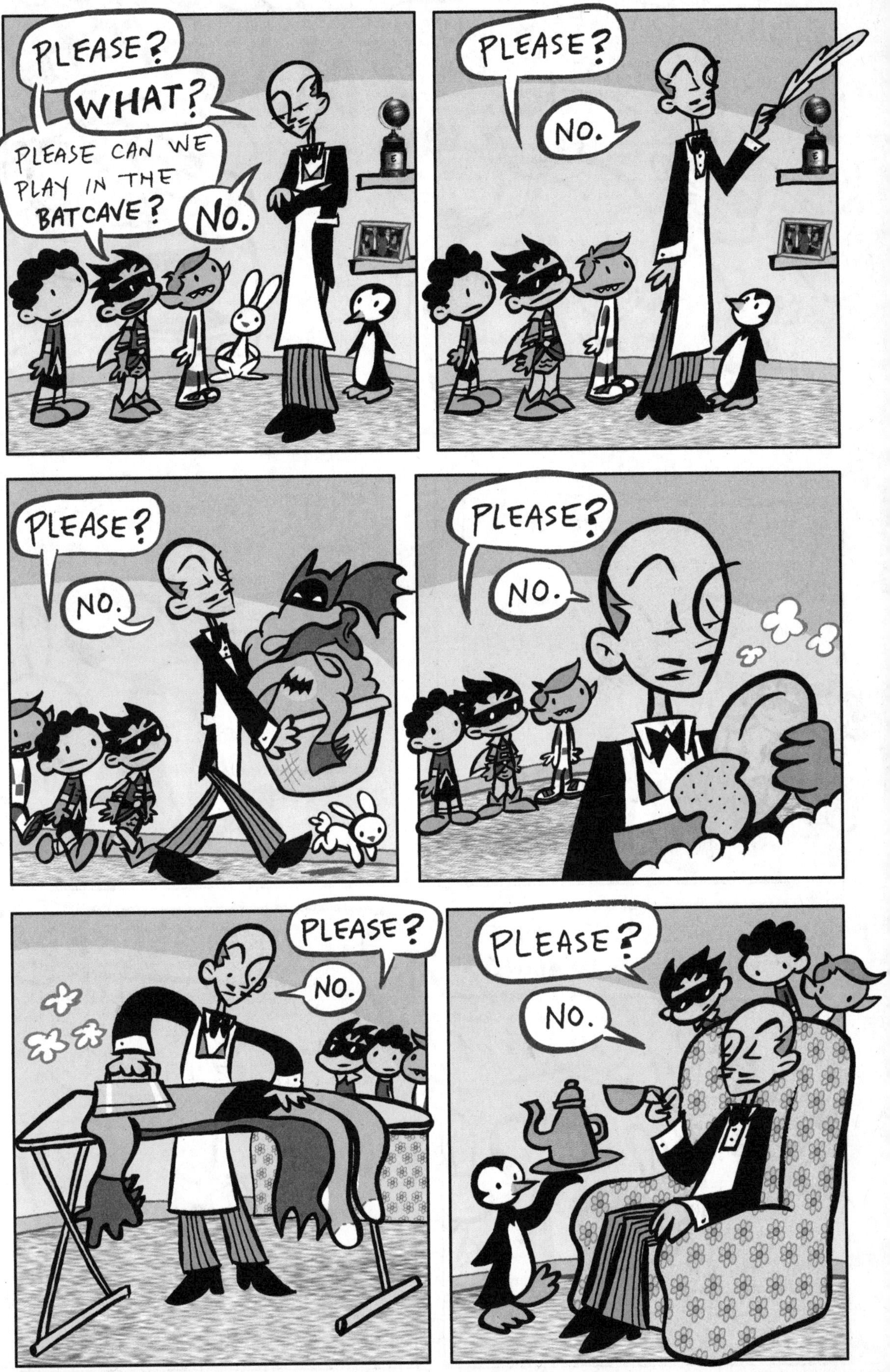
PLEASE?
WHAT?
PLEASE CAN WE PLAY IN THE BATCAVE?
NO.
PLEASE?
NO.
PLEASE?
NO.
PLEASE?
NO.
PLEASE?
NO.
PLEASE?
NO.

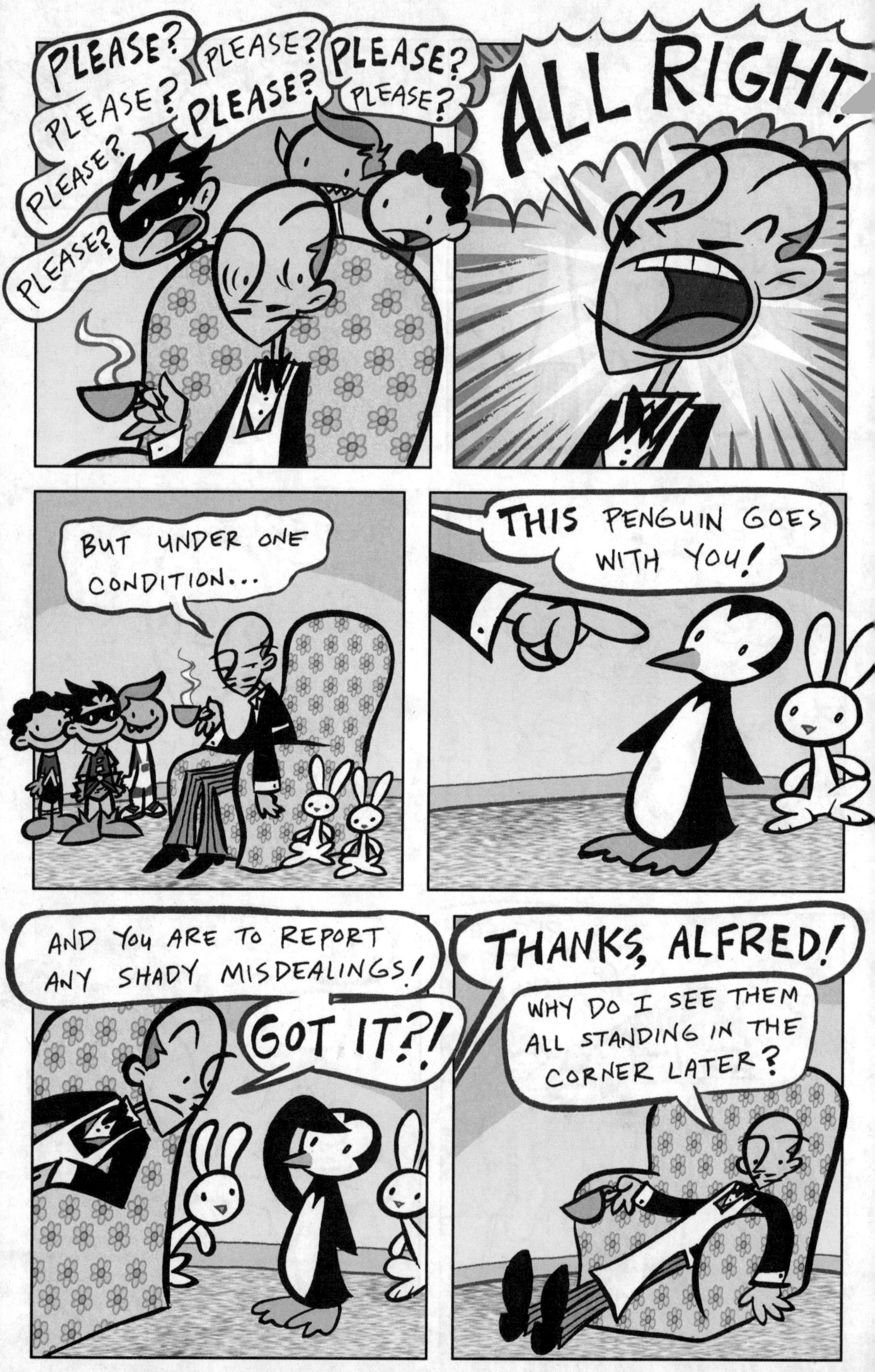
PLEASE?
PLEASE?
PLEASE?
PLEASE?
PLEASE?
PLEASE?
PLEASE?
PLEASE?
ALL RIGHT!
BUT UNDER ONE CONDITION...
THIS PENGUIN GOES WITH YOU!
AND YOU ARE TO REPORT ANY SHADY MISDEALINGS!
GOT IT?!
THANKS, ALFRED!
WHY DO I SEE THEM ALL STANDING IN THE CORNER LATER?

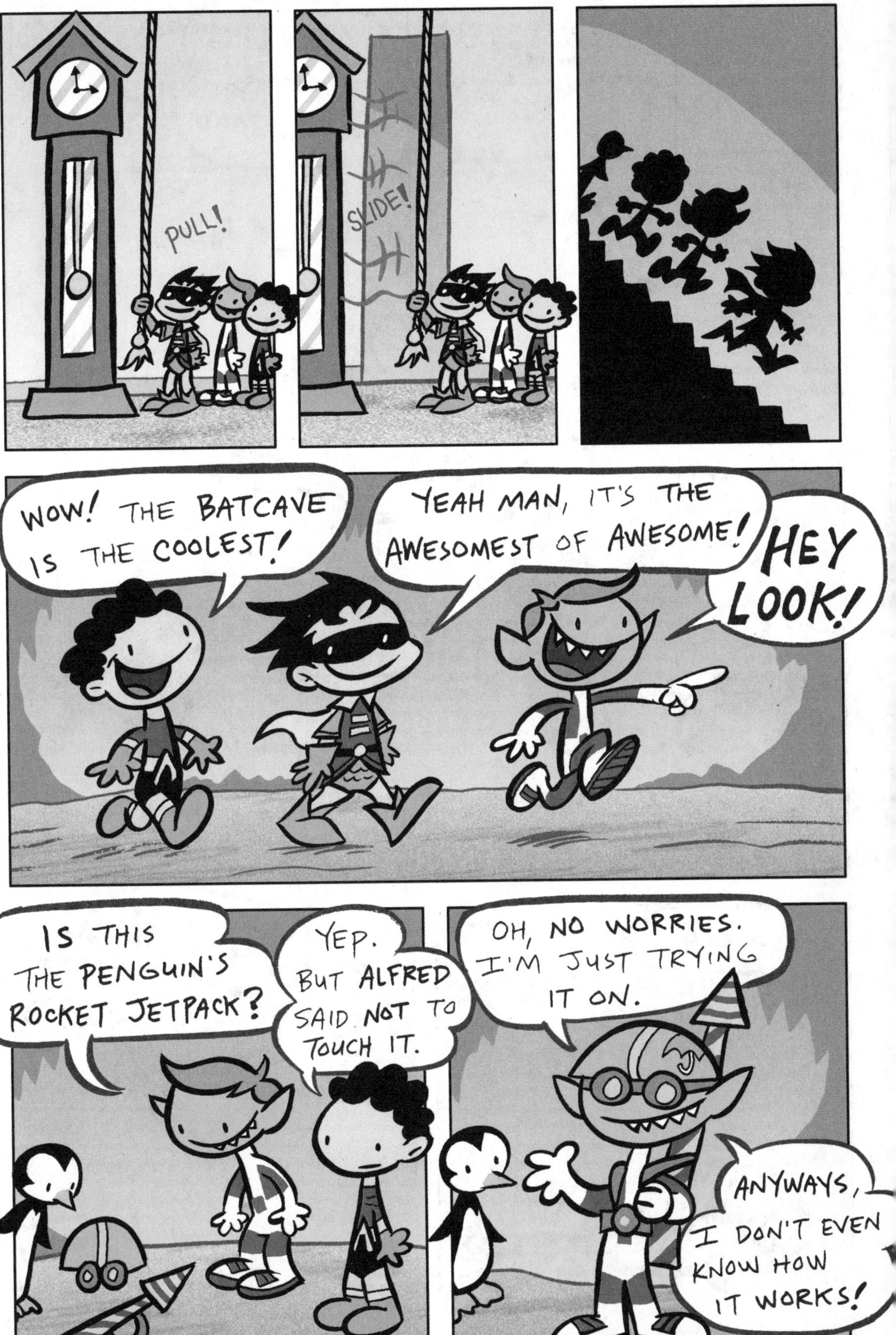
PULL!
SLIDE!
WOW! THE BATCAVE IS THE COOLEST!
YEAH MAN, IT'S THE AWESOMEST OF AWESOME!
HEY LOOK!
IS THIS THE PENGUIN'S ROCKET JETPACK?
YEP. BUT ALFRED SAID NOT TO TOUCH IT.
OH, NO WORRIES. I'M JUST TRYING IT ON.
ANYWAYS, I DON'T EVEN KNOW HOW IT WORKS!

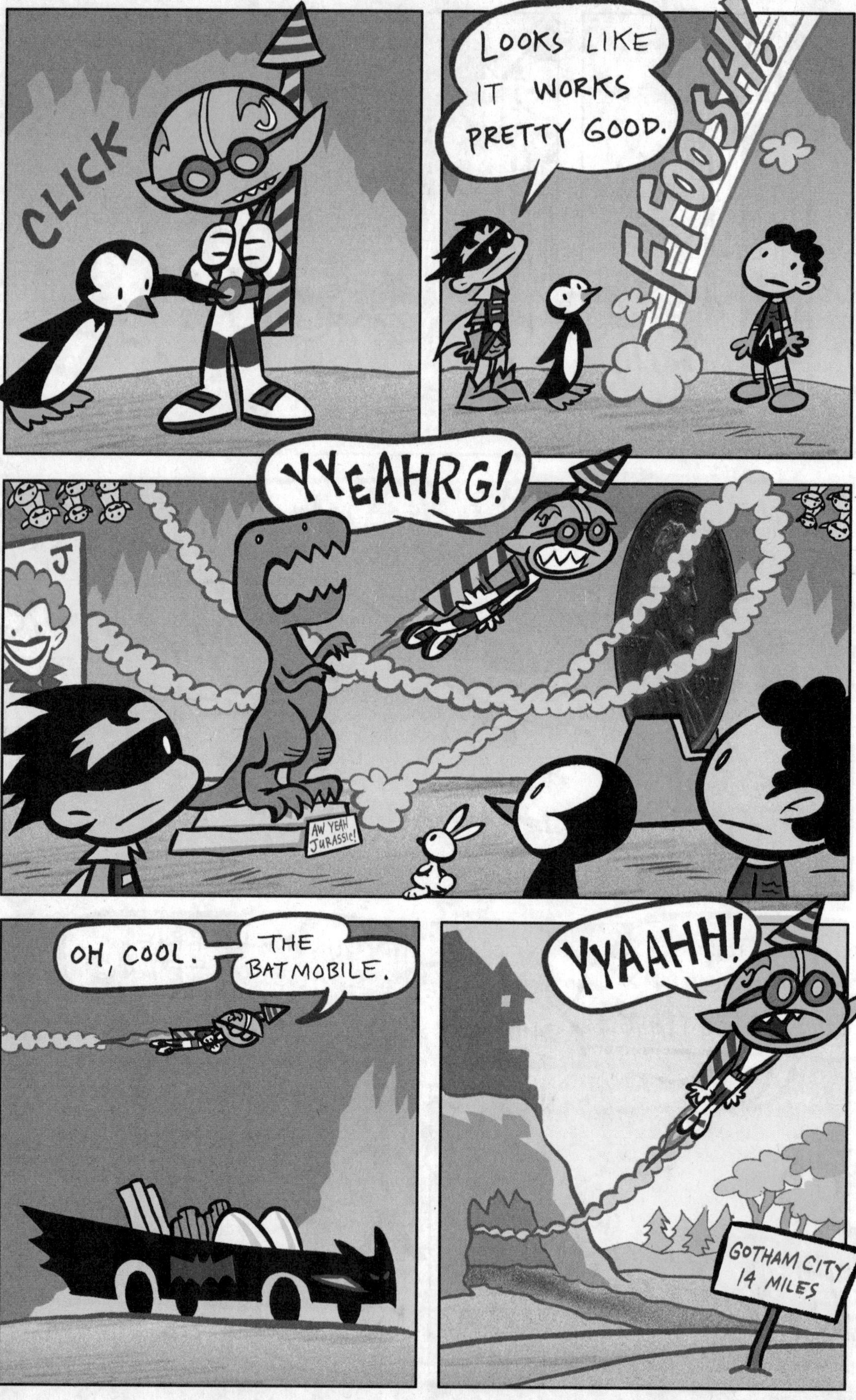
CLICK
LOOKS LIKE IT WORKS PRETTY GOOD.
FFOOSH!
YYEAHRG!
AW YEAH JURASSIC!
OH, COOL.
THE BATMOBILE.
YYAAHH!
GOTHAM CITY 14 MILES

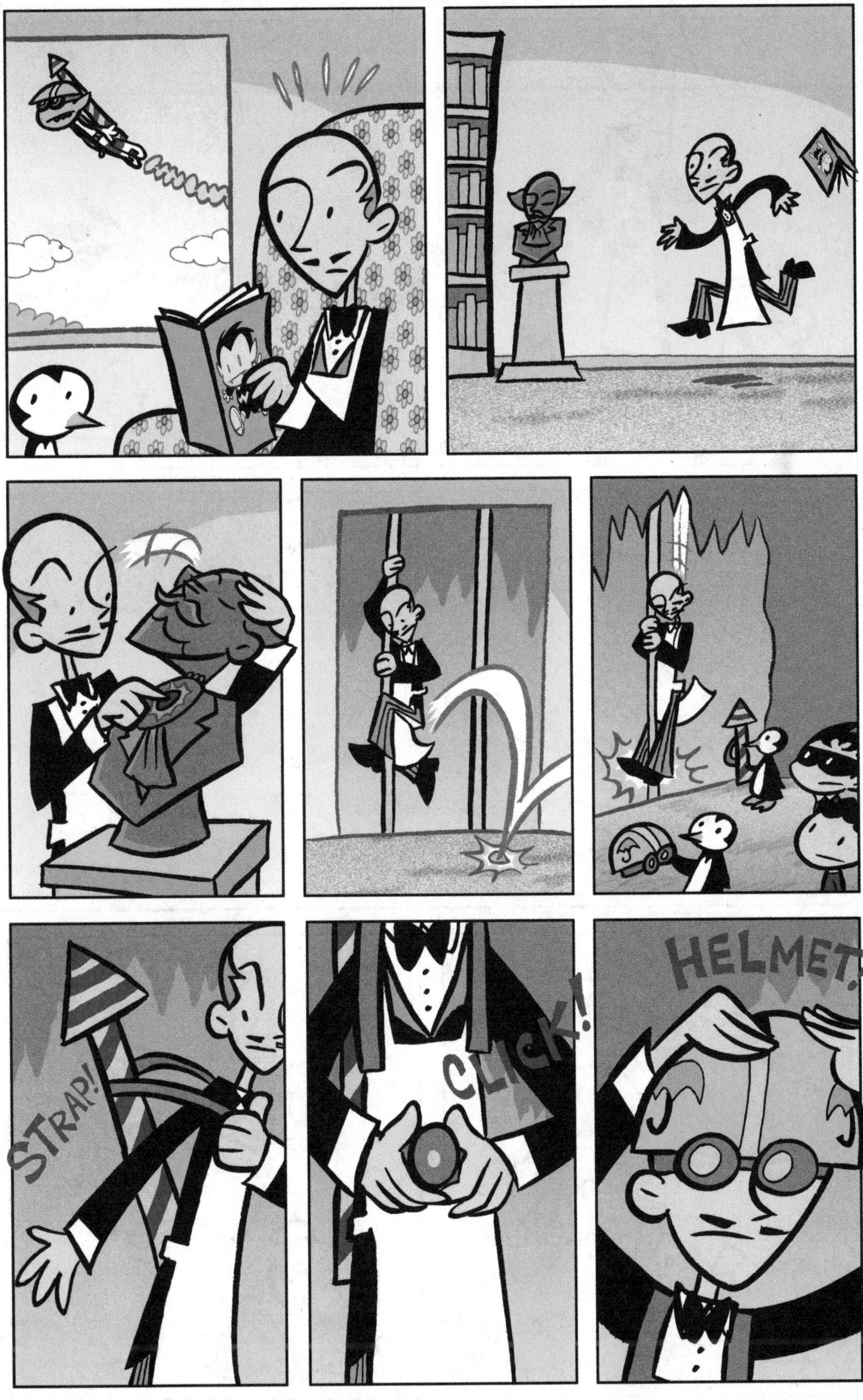
STRAP!
CLICK!
HELMET!

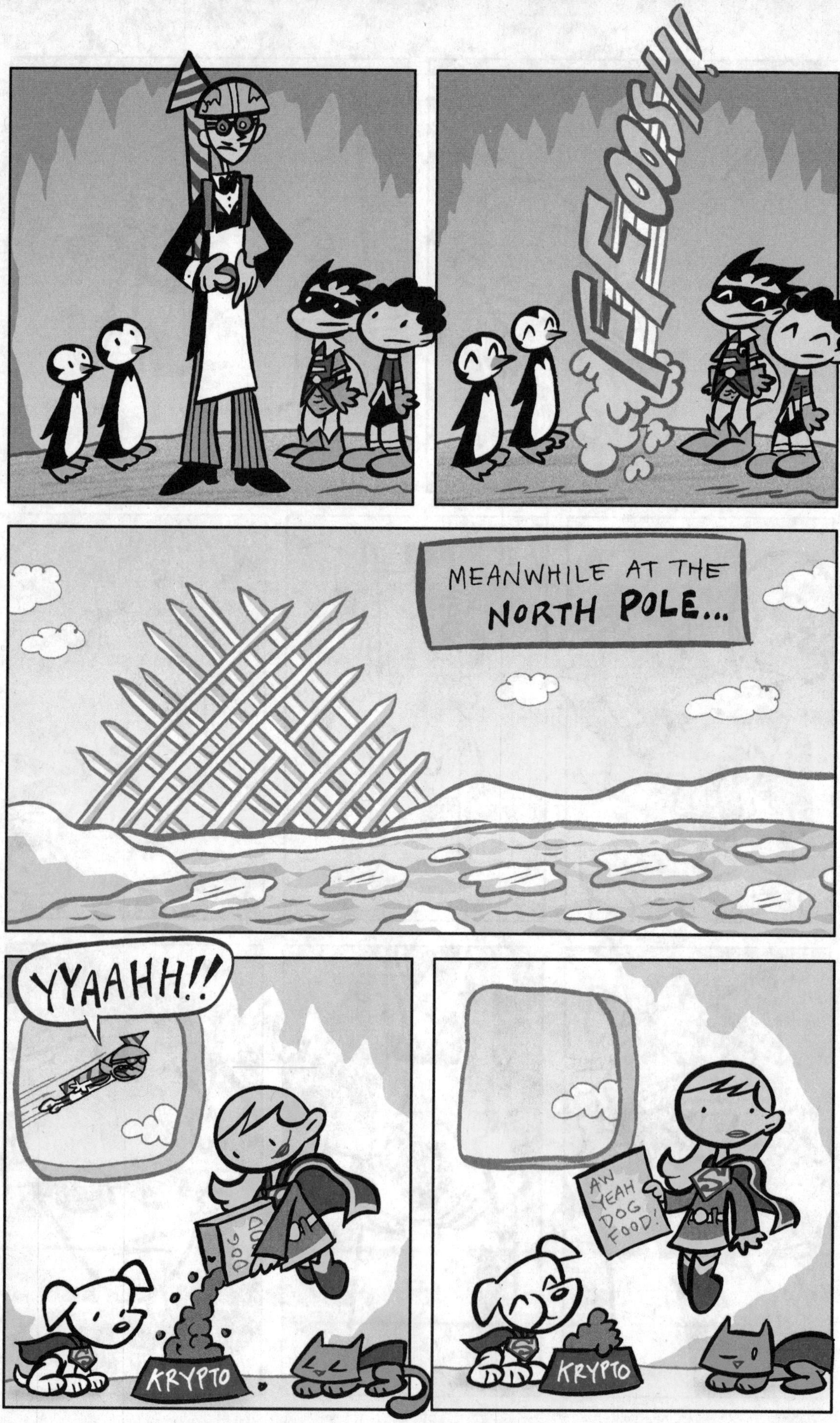
FOOSH!
MEANWHILE AT THE NORTH POLE...
YYAAHH!!
DOG FOOD
KRYPTO
AW YEAH DOG FOOD!
KRYPTO

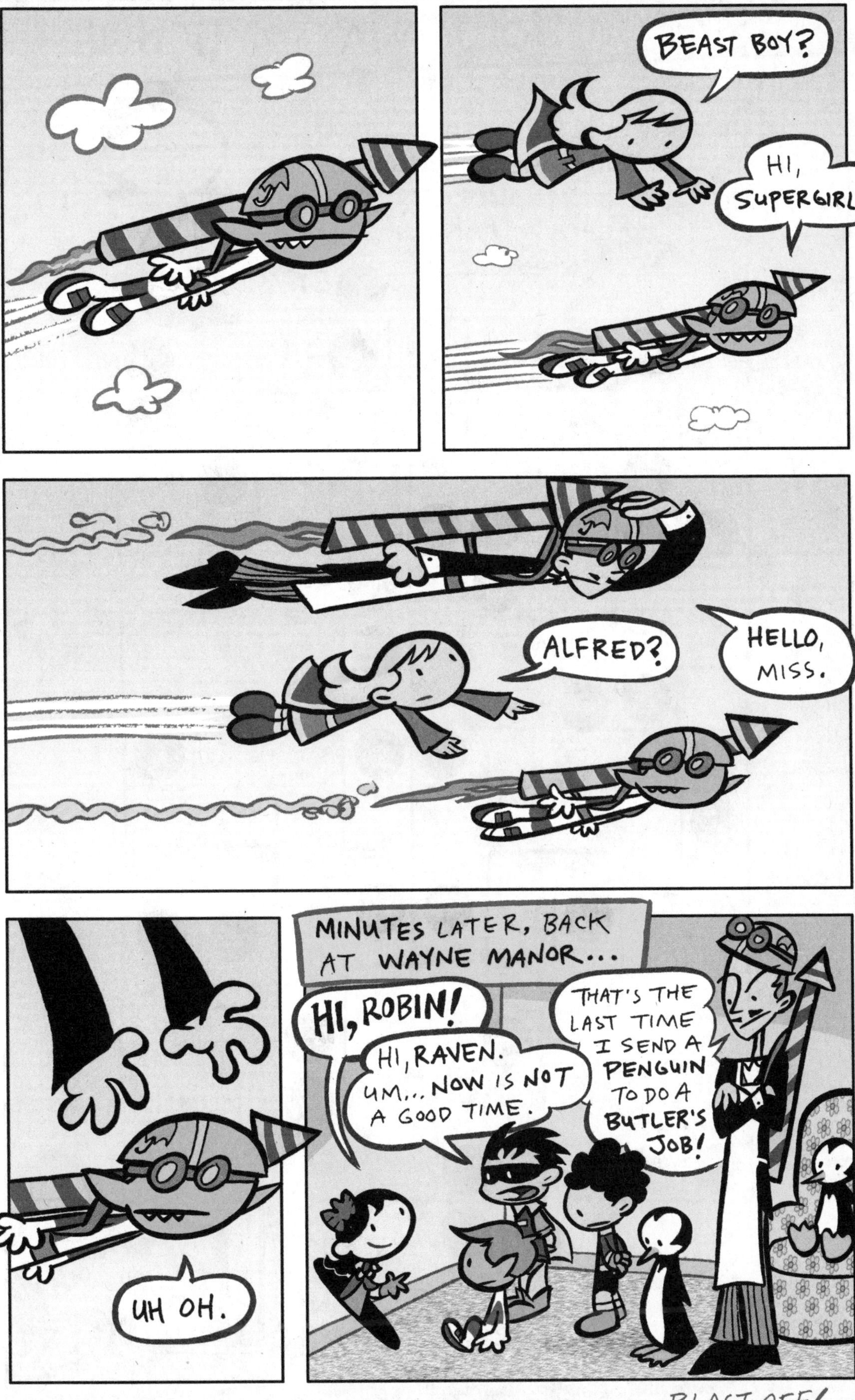
BEAST BOY?
HI, SUPERGIRL.
ALFRED?
HELLO, MISS.
UH OH.
MINUTES LATER, BACK AT WAYNE MANOR...
HI, ROBIN!
HI, RAVEN. UM... NOW IS NOT A GOOD TIME.
THAT'S THE LAST TIME I SEND A PENGUIN TO DO A BUTLER'S JOB!

—BLAST OFF!

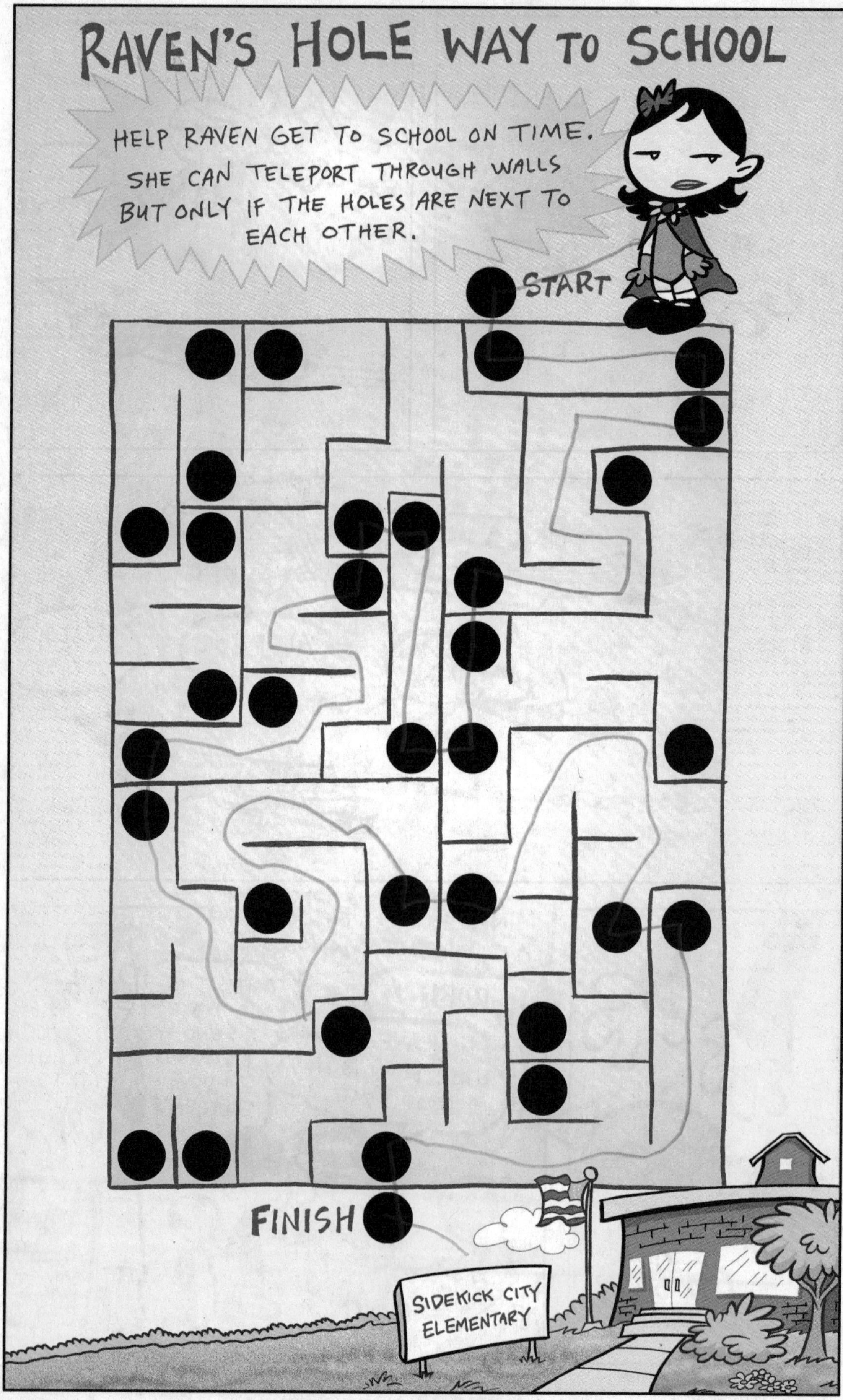
RAVEN'S HOLE WAY TO SCHOOL
HELP RAVEN GET TO SCHOOL ON TIME. SHE CAN TELEPORT THROUGH WALLS BUT ONLY IF THE HOLES ARE NEXT TO EACH OTHER.
START
FINISH
SIDEKICK CITY ELEMENTARY

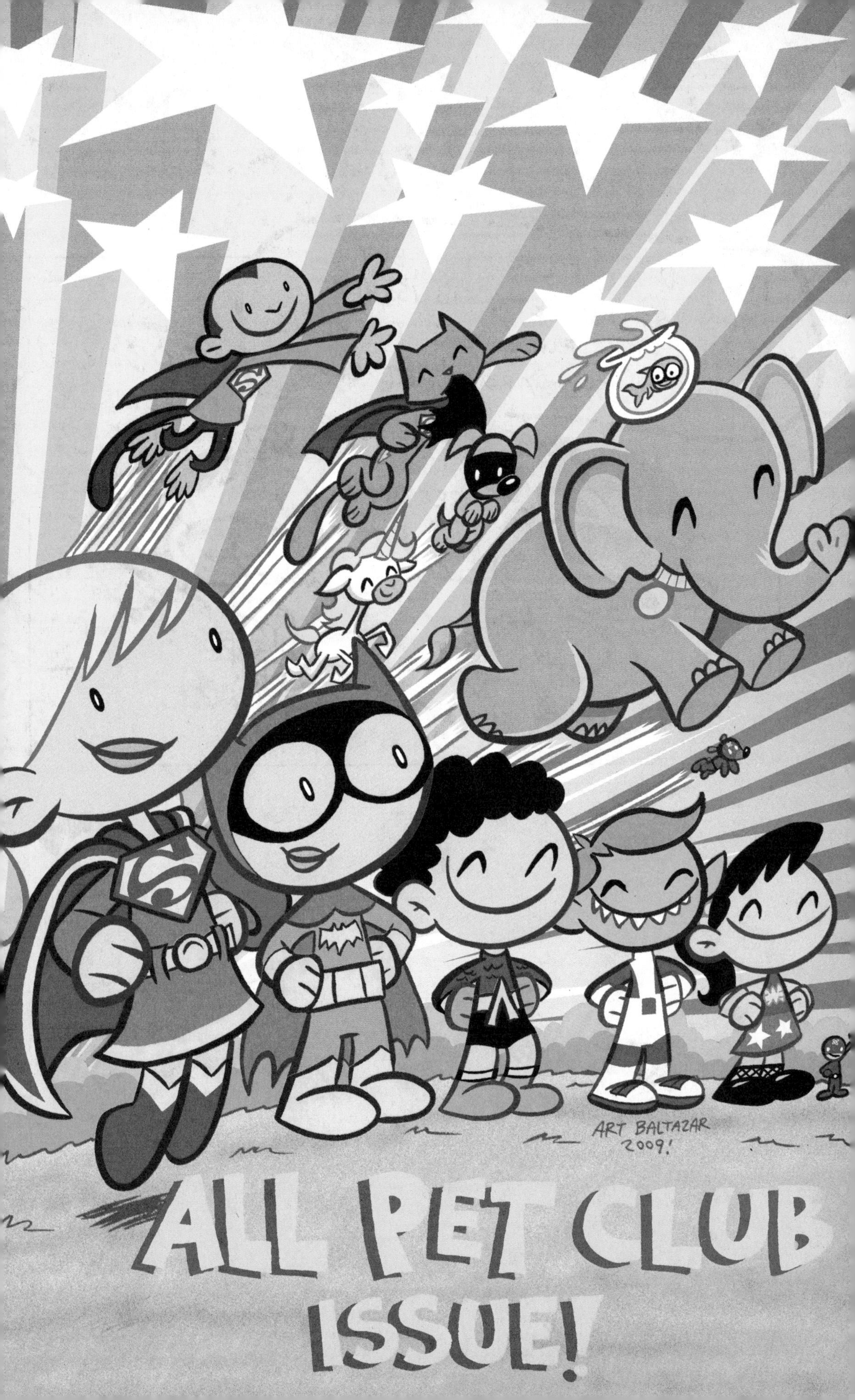
ART BALTAZAR
2009!
ALL PET CLUB
ISSUE!

tiny titans

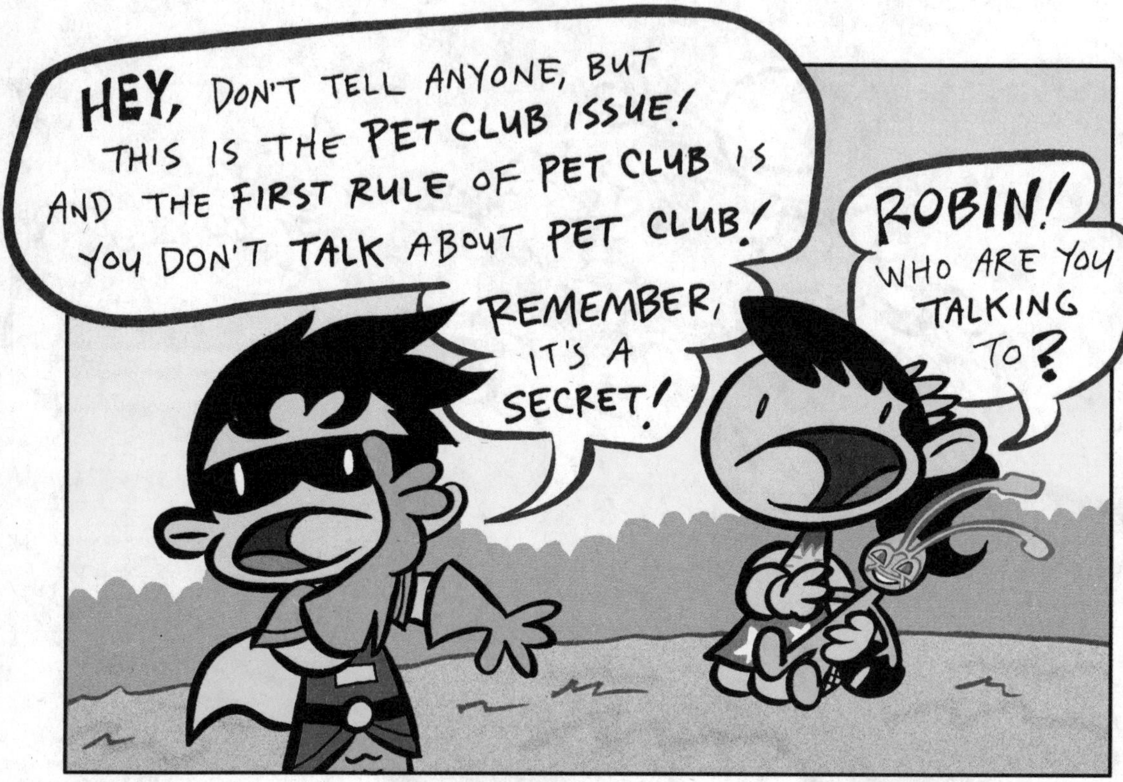
HEY, DON'T TELL ANYONE, BUT THIS IS THE PET CLUB ISSUE! AND THE FIRST RULE OF PET CLUB IS YOU DON'T TALK ABOUT PET CLUB!
REMEMBER, IT'S A SECRET!
ROBIN!
WHO ARE YOU TALKING TO?

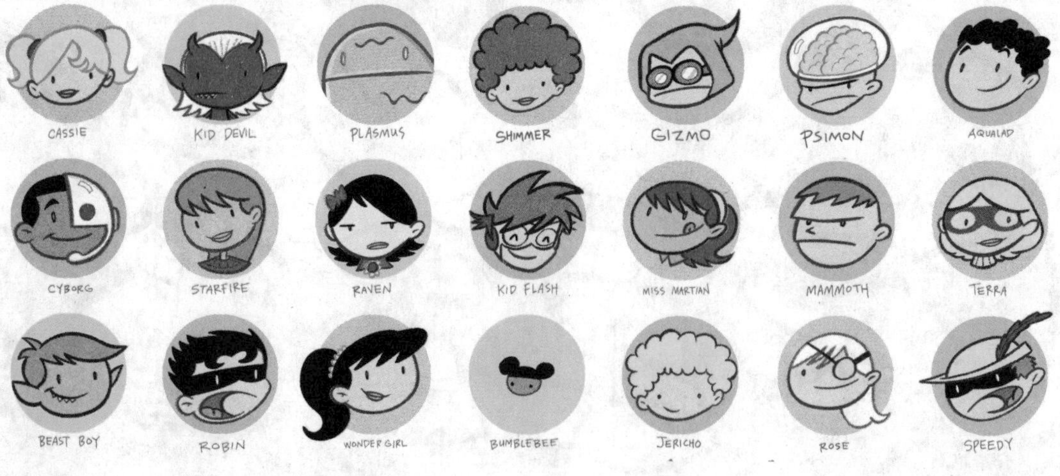
CASSIE
KID DEVIL
PLASMUS
SHIMMER
GIZMO
PSIMON
AQUALAD
CYBORG
STARFIRE
RAVEN
KID FLASH
MISS MARTIAN
MAMMOTH
TERRA
BEAST BOY
ROBIN
WONDER GIRL
BUMBLEBEE
JERICHO
ROSE
SPEEDY

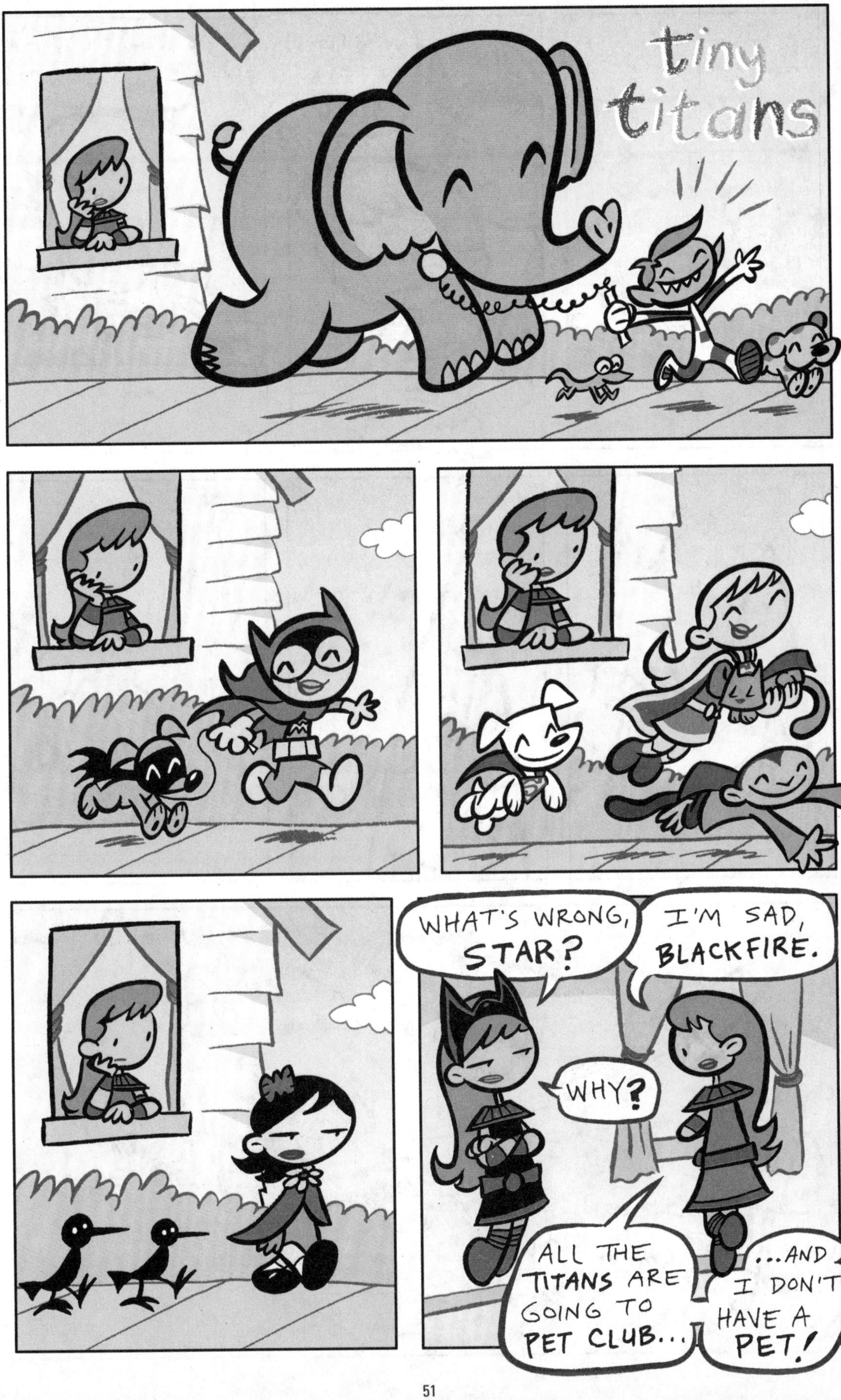
tiny titans
WHAT'S WRONG, STAR?
I'M SAD, BLACKFIRE.
WHY?
ALL THE TITANS ARE GOING TO PET CLUB...
...AND I DON'T HAVE A PET!

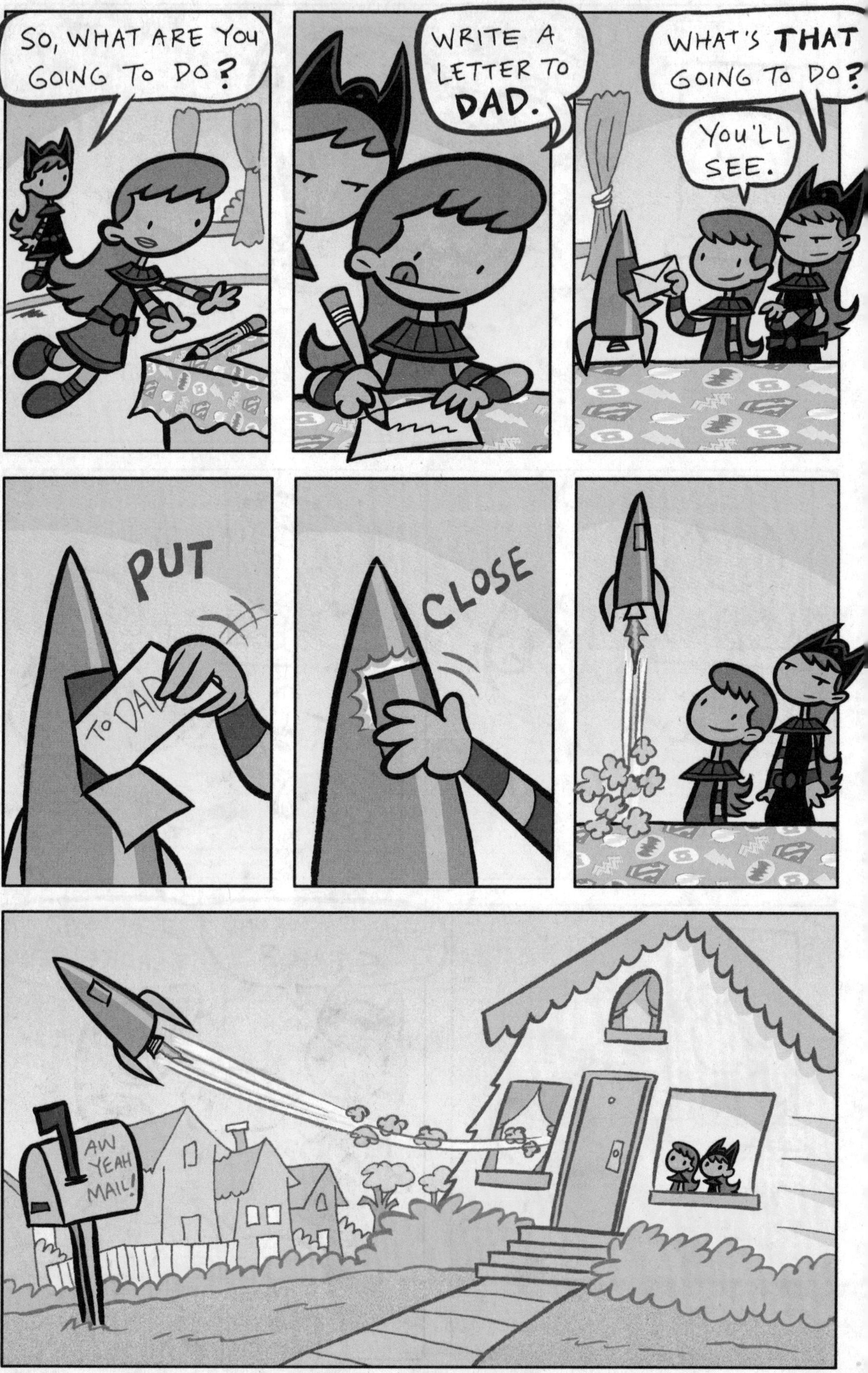
SO, WHAT ARE YOU GOING TO DO?
WRITE A LETTER TO DAD.
WHAT'S THAT GOING TO DO?
YOU'LL SEE.
PUT
TO DAD
CLOSE
AW YEAH MAIL!

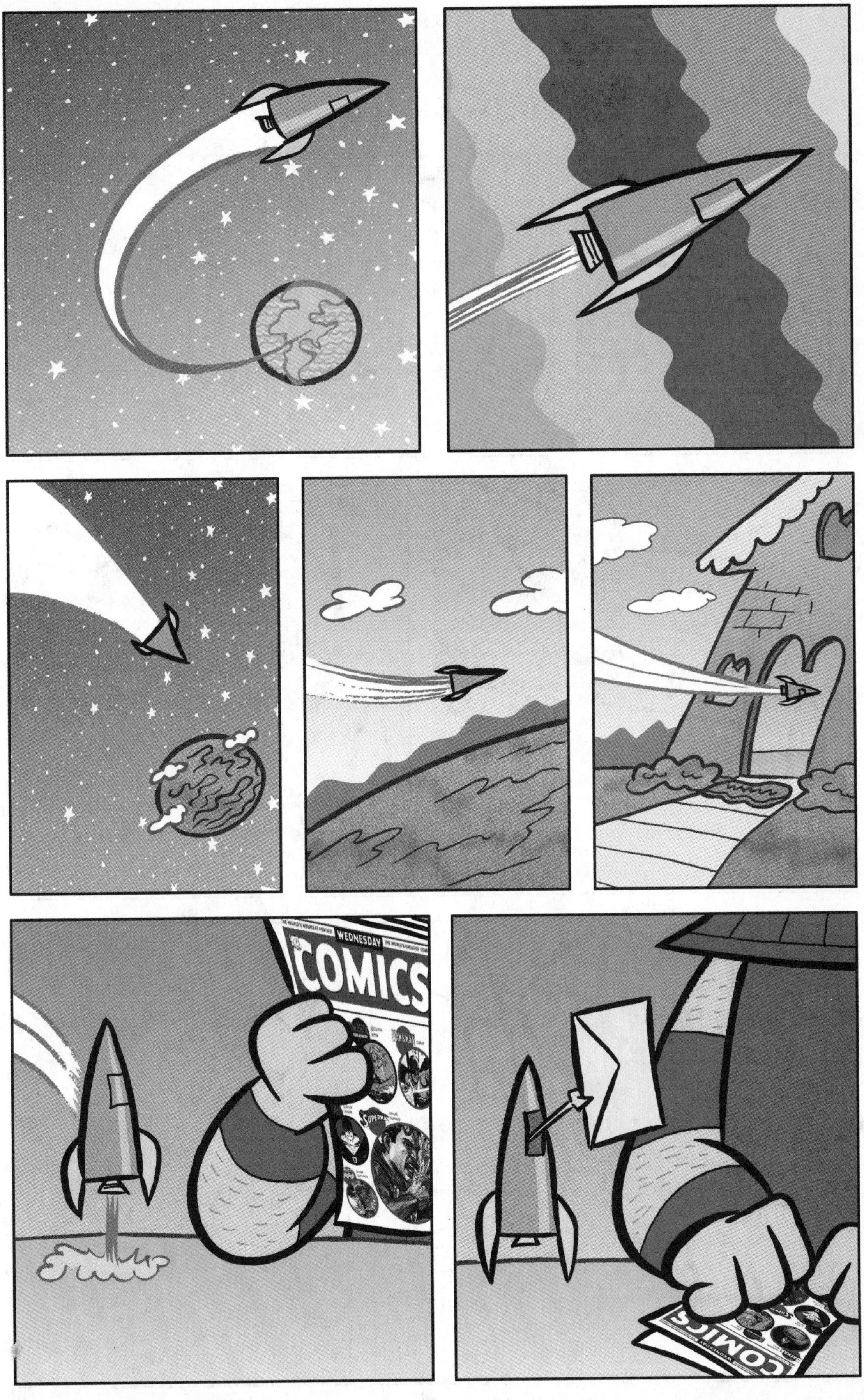
WEDNESDAY
COMICS

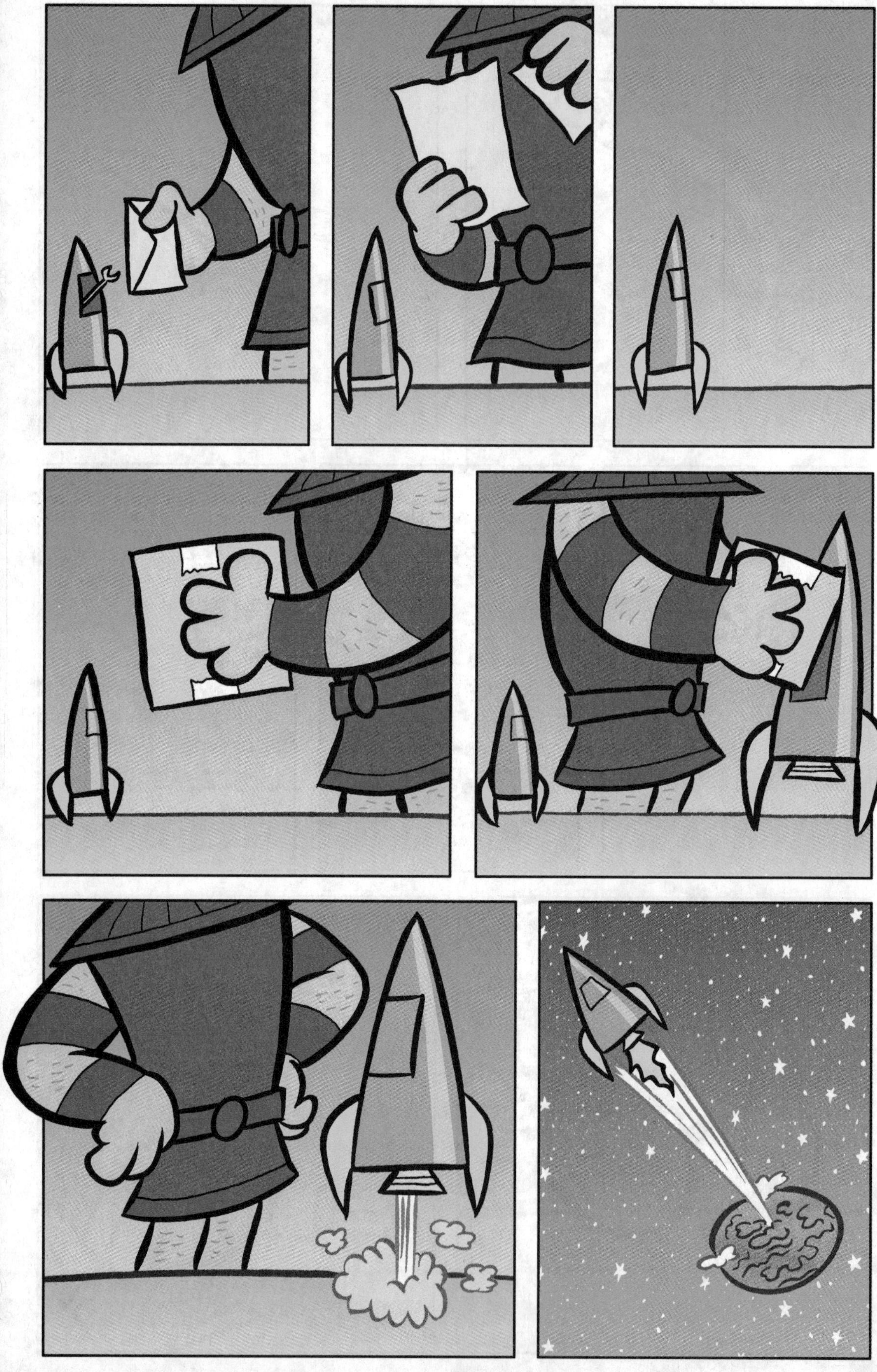

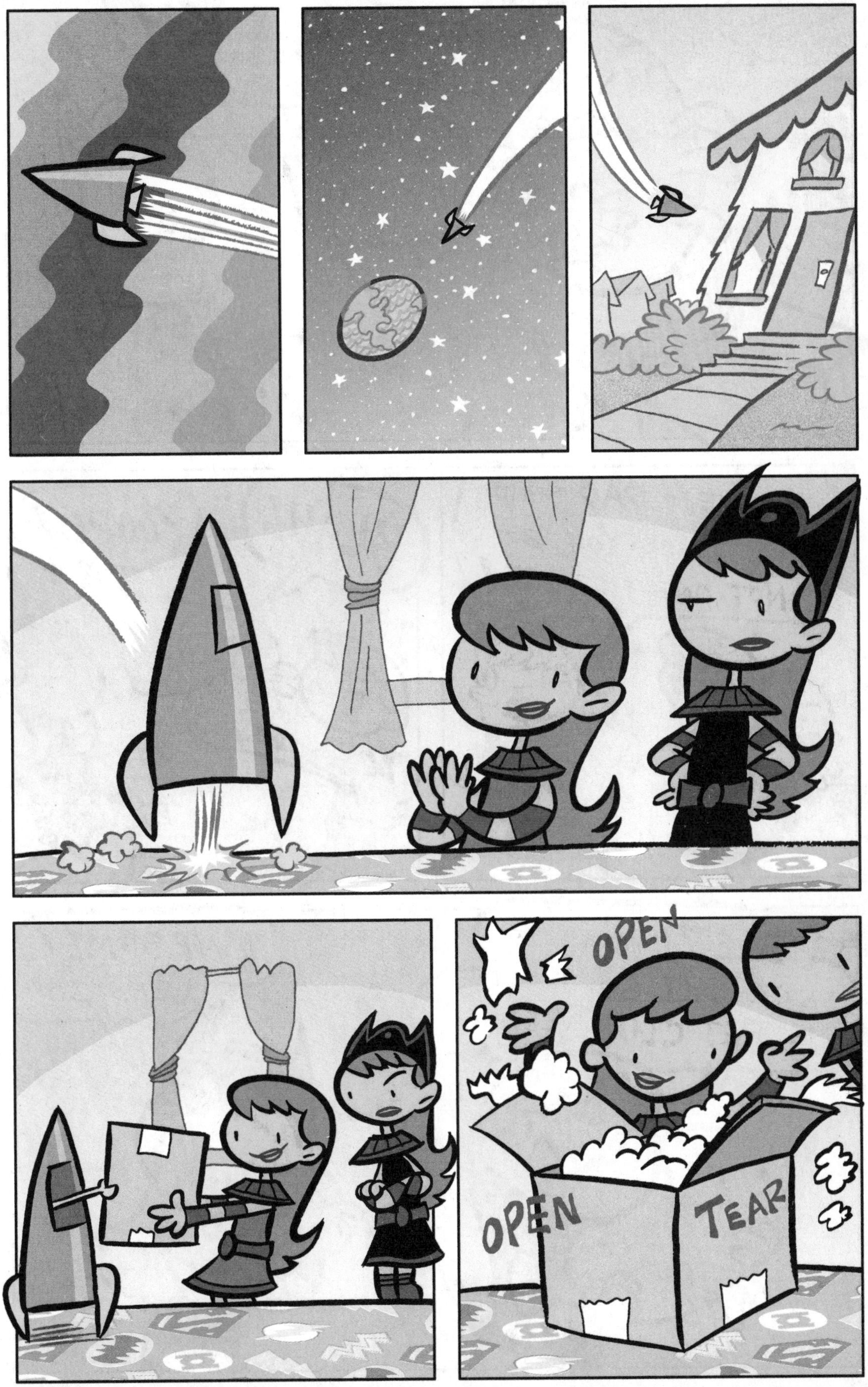
OPEN
OPEN
TEAR

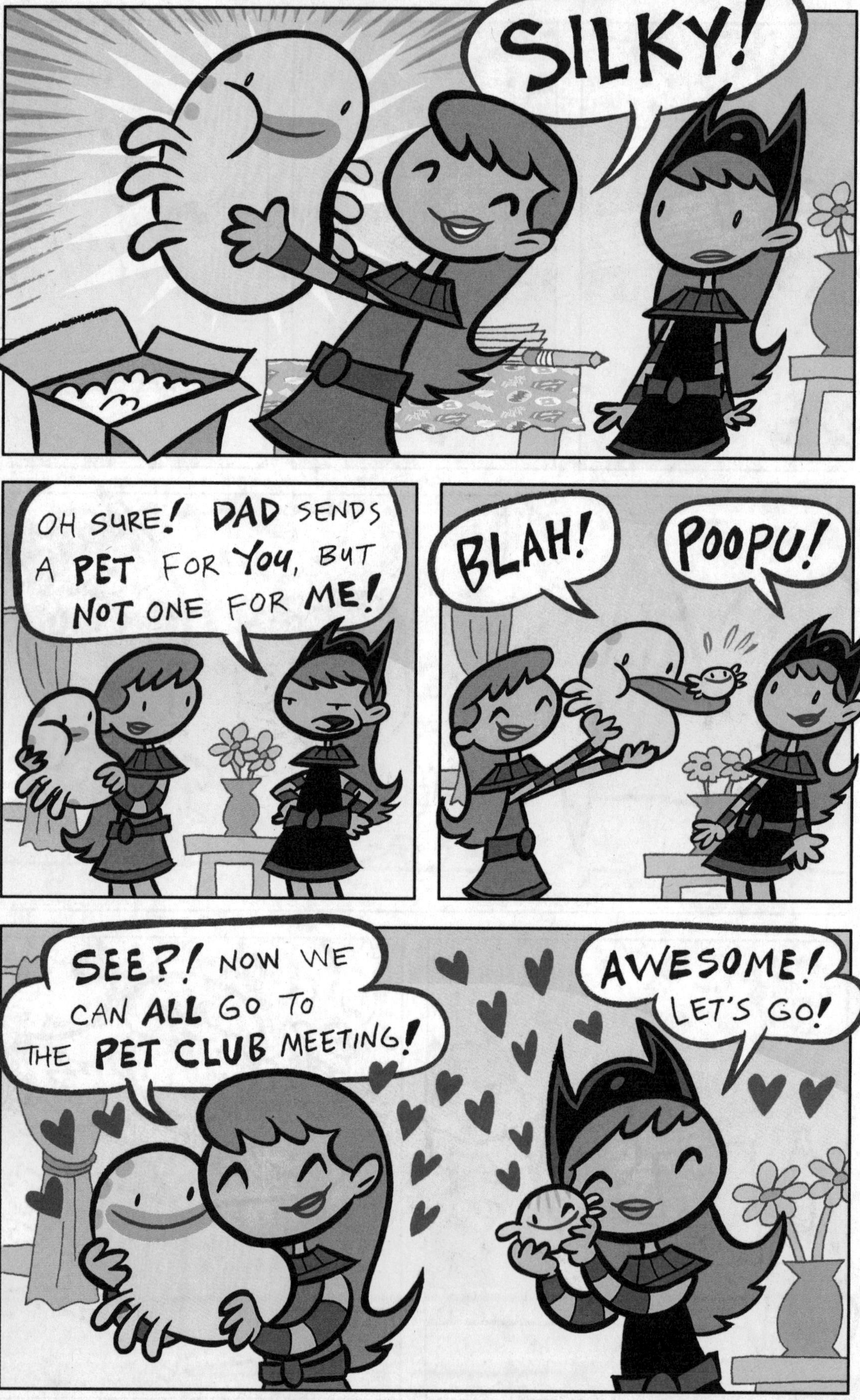
SILKY!
OH SURE! DAD SENDS A PET FOR YOU, BUT NOT ONE FOR ME!
BLAH!
POOPU!
SEE?! NOW WE CAN ALL GO TO THE PET CLUB MEETING!
AWESOME! LET'S GO!

–AW YEAH ALIEN PETS!

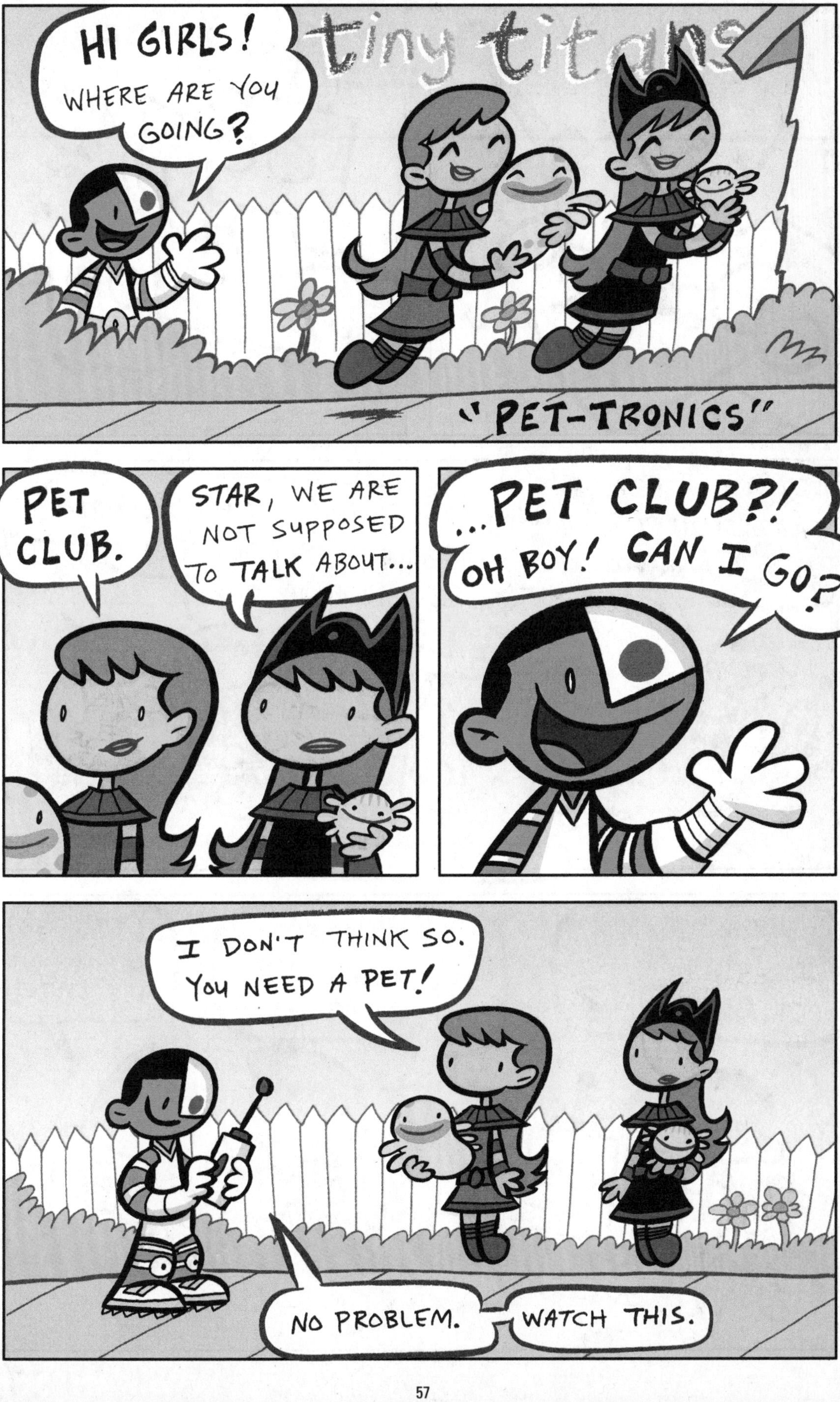
tiny titans
HI GIRLS! WHERE ARE YOU GOING?
"PET-TRONICS"
PET CLUB.
STAR, WE ARE NOT SUPPOSED TO TALK ABOUT...
...PET CLUB?! OH BOY! CAN I GO?
I DON'T THINK SO. YOU NEED A PET!
NO PROBLEM.
WATCH THIS.

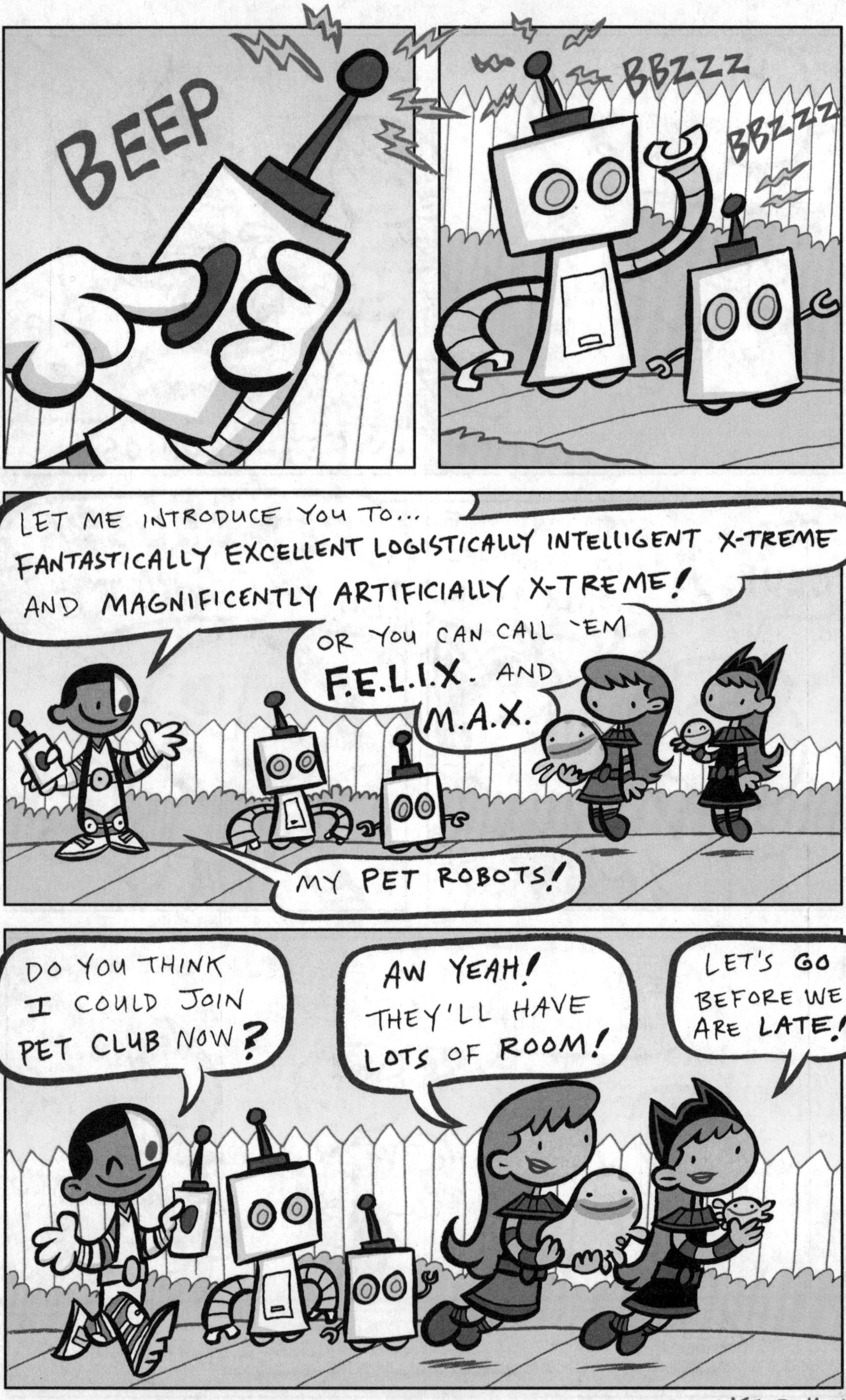
BEEP
BBZZZ
BBZZZ
LET ME INTRODUCE YOU TO... FANTASTICALLY EXCELLENT LOGISTICALLY INTELLIGENT X-TREME AND MAGNIFICENTLY ARTIFICIALLY X-TREME!
OR YOU CAN CALL 'EM F.E.L.I.X. AND M.A.X.
MY PET ROBOTS!
DO YOU THINK I COULD JOIN PET CLUB NOW?
AW YEAH! THEY'LL HAVE LOTS OF ROOM!
LET'S GO BEFORE WE ARE LATE!

–KEEP ON KEEPIN' ON

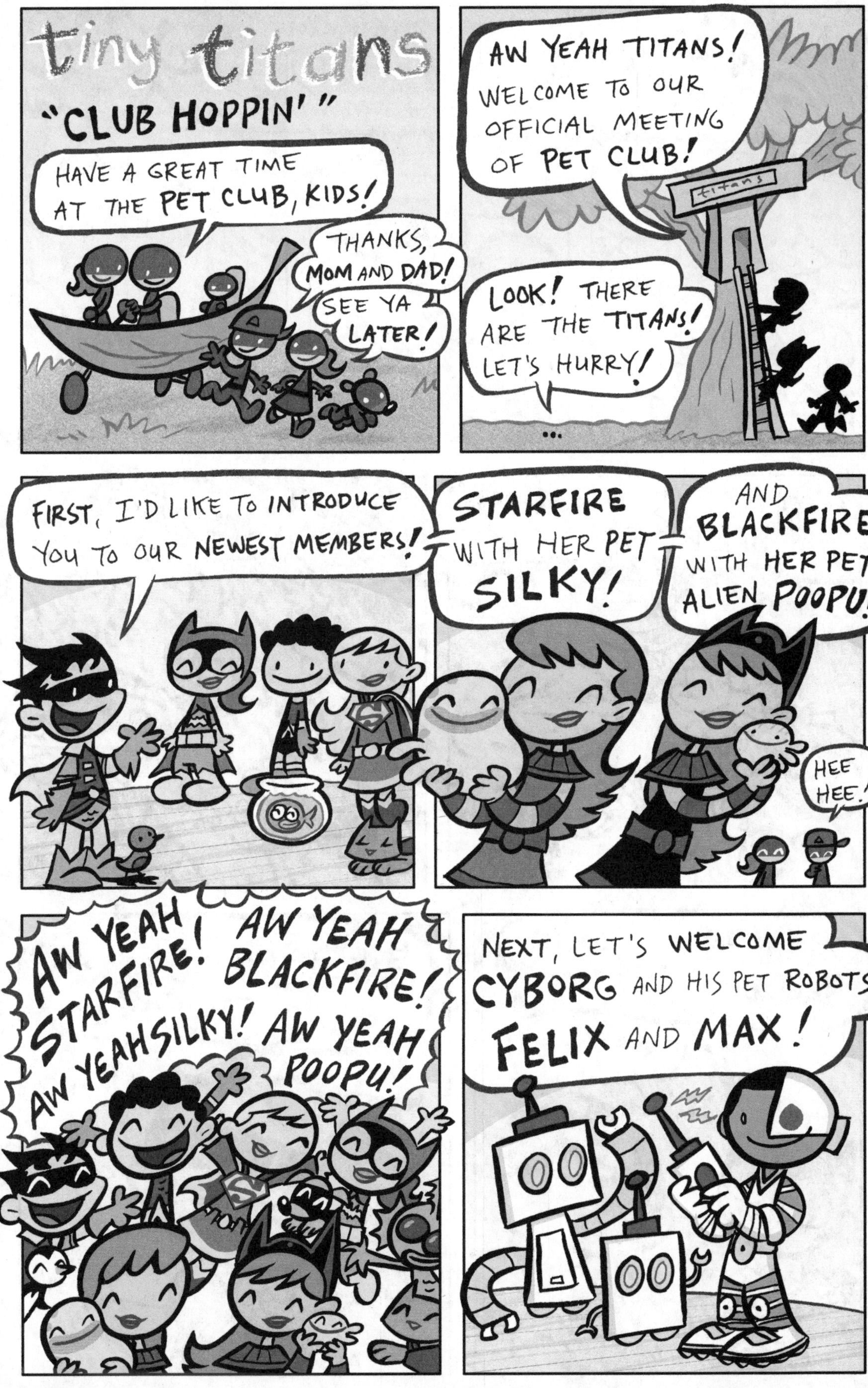
tiny titans
"CLUB HOPPIN'"
HAVE A GREAT TIME AT THE PET CLUB, KIDS!
THANKS, MOM AND DAD!
SEE YA LATER!
AW YEAH TITANS! WELCOME TO OUR OFFICIAL MEETING OF PET CLUB!
titans
LOOK! THERE ARE THE TITANS! LET'S HURRY!
...
FIRST, I'D LIKE TO INTRODUCE YOU TO OUR NEWEST MEMBERS!
STARFIRE WITH HER PET SILKY!
AND BLACKFIRE WITH HER PET ALIEN POOPU!
HEE HEE!
AW YEAH STARFIRE! AW YEAH BLACKFIRE! AW YEAH SILKY! AW YEAH POOPU!
NEXT, LET'S WELCOME CYBORG AND HIS PET ROBOTS FELIX AND MAX!

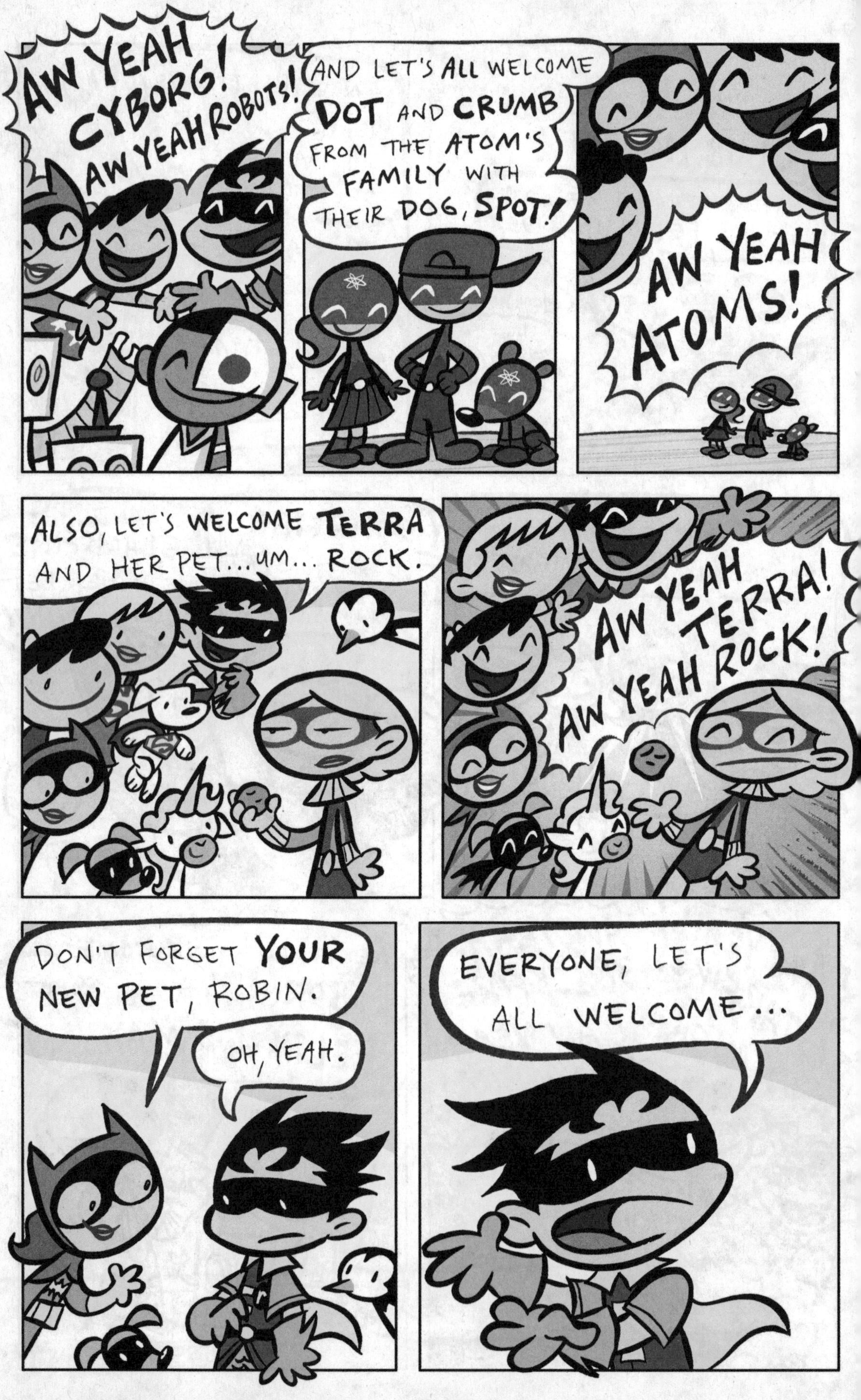
AW YEAH CYBORG!
AW YEAH ROBOTS!
AND LET'S ALL WELCOME DOT AND CRUMB FROM THE ATOM'S FAMILY WITH THEIR DOG, SPOT!
AW YEAH ATOMS!
ALSO, LET'S WELCOME TERRA AND HER PET... UM... ROCK.
AW YEAH TERRA!
AW YEAH ROCK!
DON'T FORGET YOUR NEW PET, ROBIN.
OH, YEAH.
EVERYONE, LET'S ALL WELCOME...

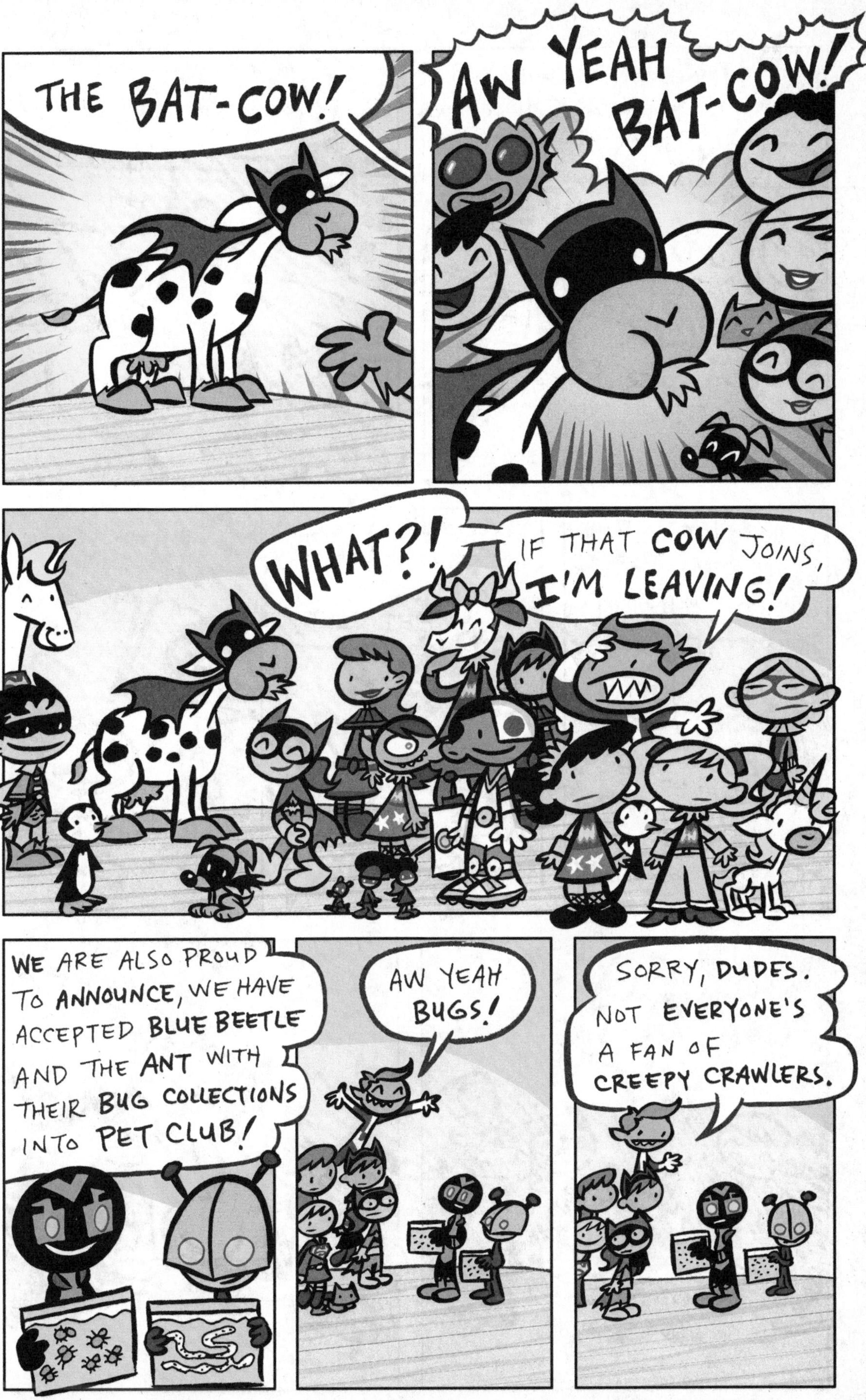

THE BAT-COW!
AW YEAH BAT-COW!
WHAT?!
IF THAT COW JOINS, I'M LEAVING!
WE ARE ALSO PROUD TO ANNOUNCE, WE HAVE ACCEPTED BLUE BEETLE AND THE ANT WITH THEIR BUG COLLECTIONS INTO PET CLUB!
AW YEAH BUGS!
SORRY, DUDES. NOT EVERYONE'S A FAN OF CREEPY CRAWLERS.

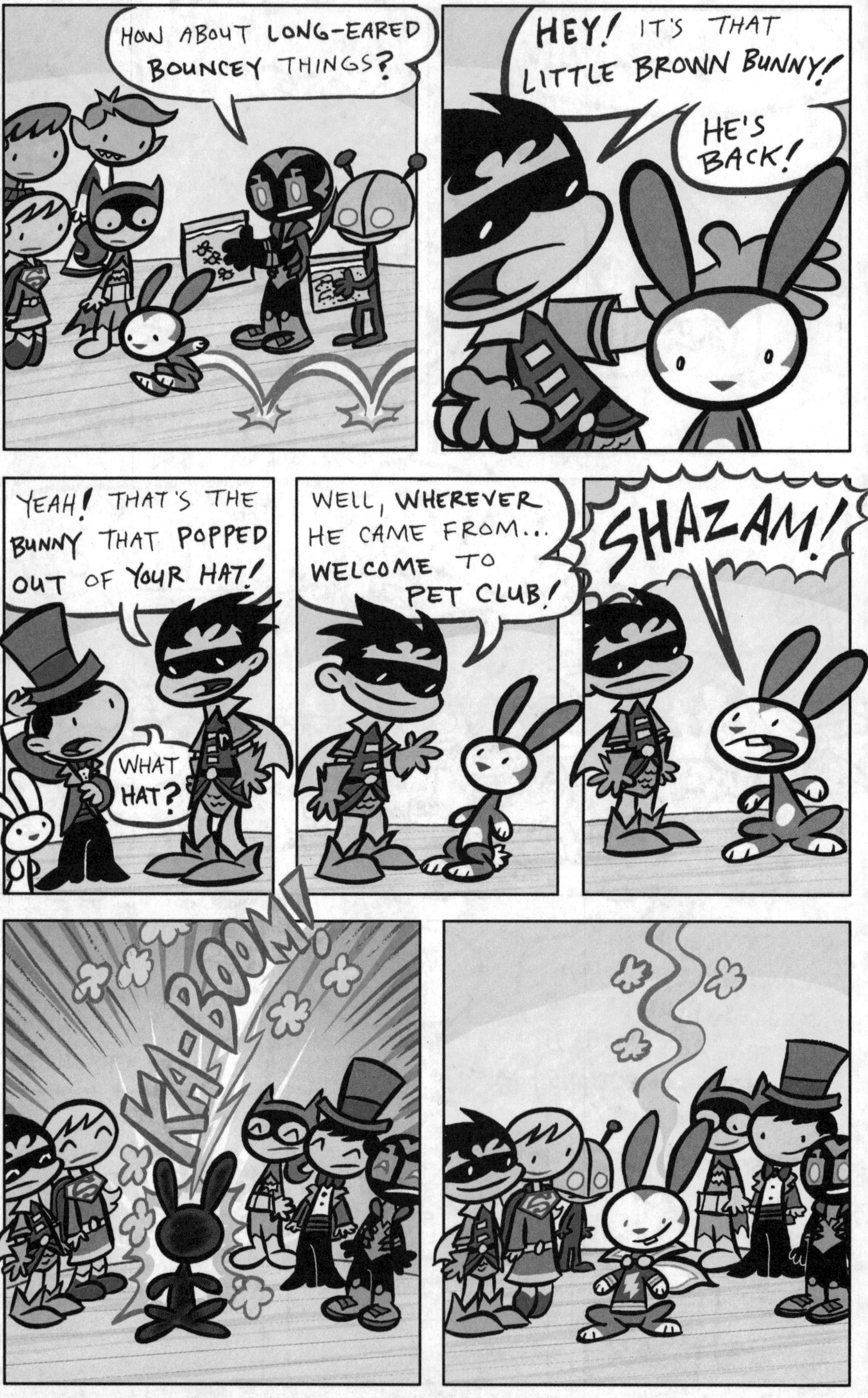
HOW ABOUT LONG-EARED BOUNCEY THINGS?
HEY! IT'S THAT LITTLE BROWN BUNNY!
HE'S BACK!
YEAH! THAT'S THE BUNNY THAT POPPED OUT OF YOUR HAT!
WHAT HAT?
WELL, WHEREVER HE CAME FROM... WELCOME TO PET CLUB!
SHAZAM!
KA-BOOM!

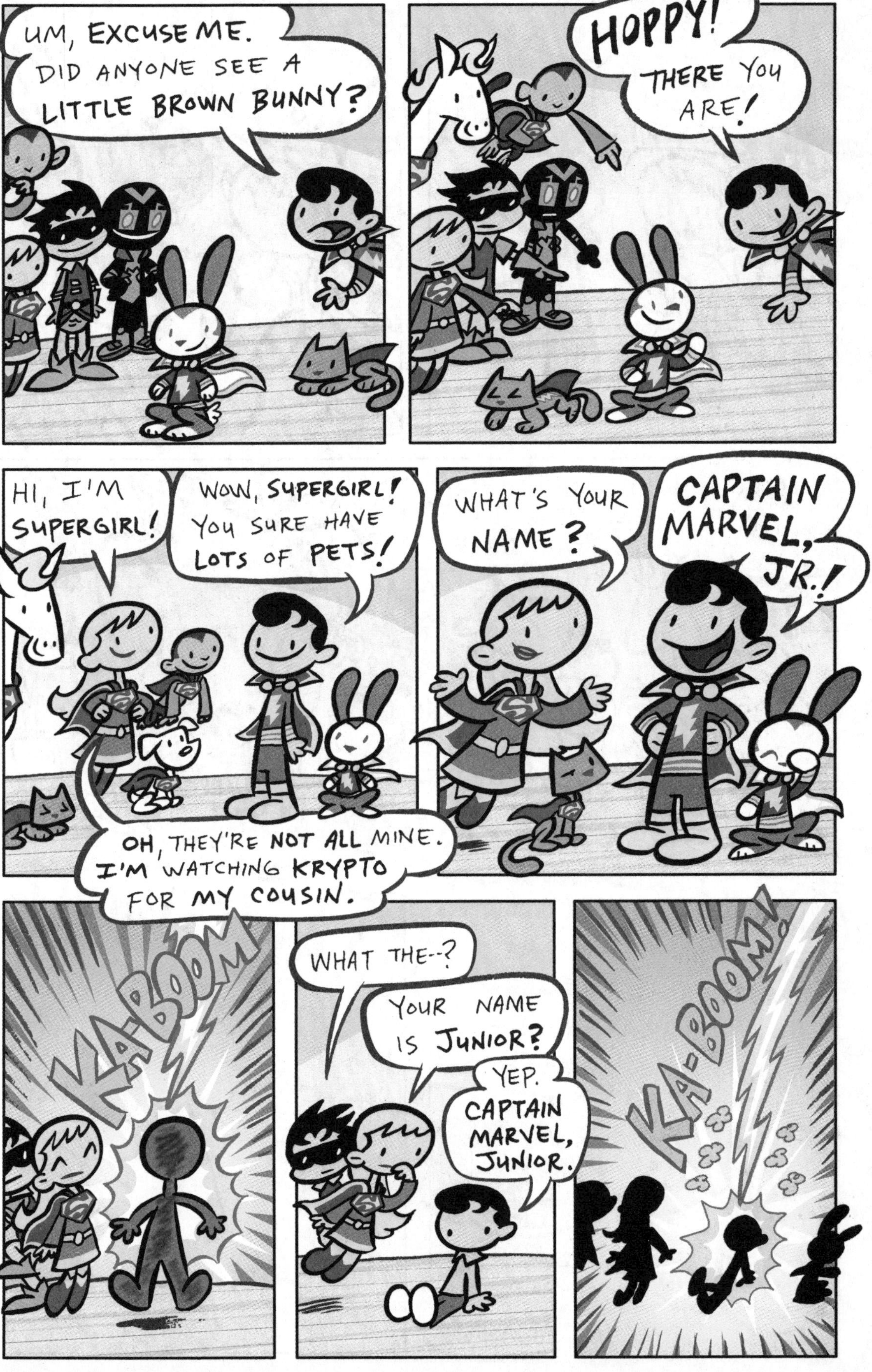
UM, EXCUSE ME. DID ANYONE SEE A LITTLE BROWN BUNNY?
HOPPY! THERE YOU ARE!
HI, I'M SUPERGIRL!
WOW, SUPERGIRL! YOU SURE HAVE LOTS OF PETS!
OH, THEY'RE NOT ALL MINE. I'M WATCHING KRYPTO FOR MY COUSIN.
WHAT'S YOUR NAME?
CAPTAIN MARVEL, JR.!
KA-BOOM
WHAT THE--?
YOUR NAME IS JUNIOR?
YEP. CAPTAIN MARVEL, JUNIOR.
KA-BOOM!

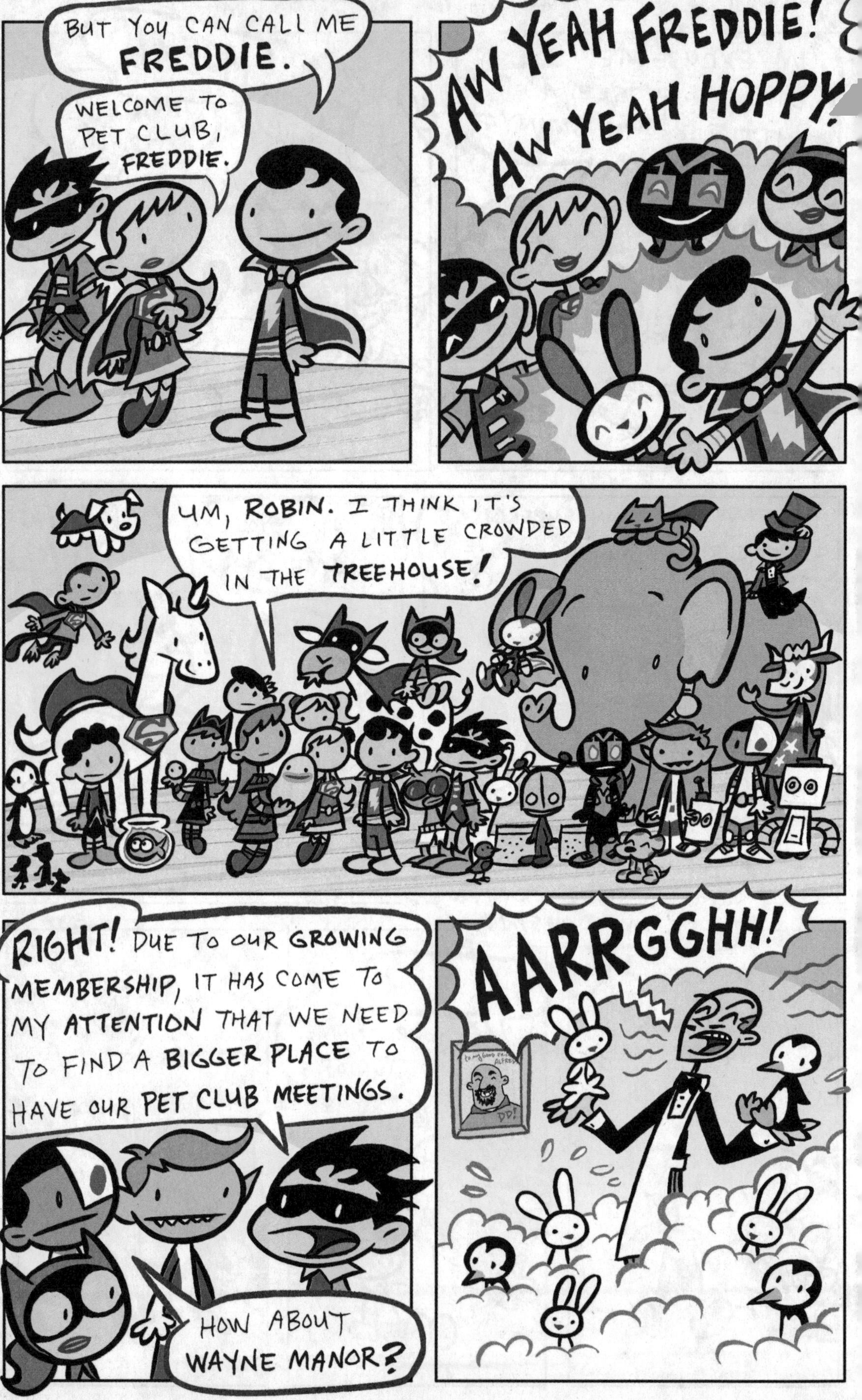
BUT YOU CAN CALL ME FREDDIE.
WELCOME TO PET CLUB, FREDDIE.
AW YEAH FREDDIE!
AW YEAH HOPPY!
UM, ROBIN. I THINK IT'S GETTING A LITTLE CROWDED IN THE TREEHOUSE!
RIGHT! DUE TO OUR GROWING MEMBERSHIP, IT HAS COME TO MY ATTENTION THAT WE NEED TO FIND A BIGGER PLACE TO HAVE OUR PET CLUB MEETINGS.
HOW ABOUT WAYNE MANOR?
AARRGGHH!

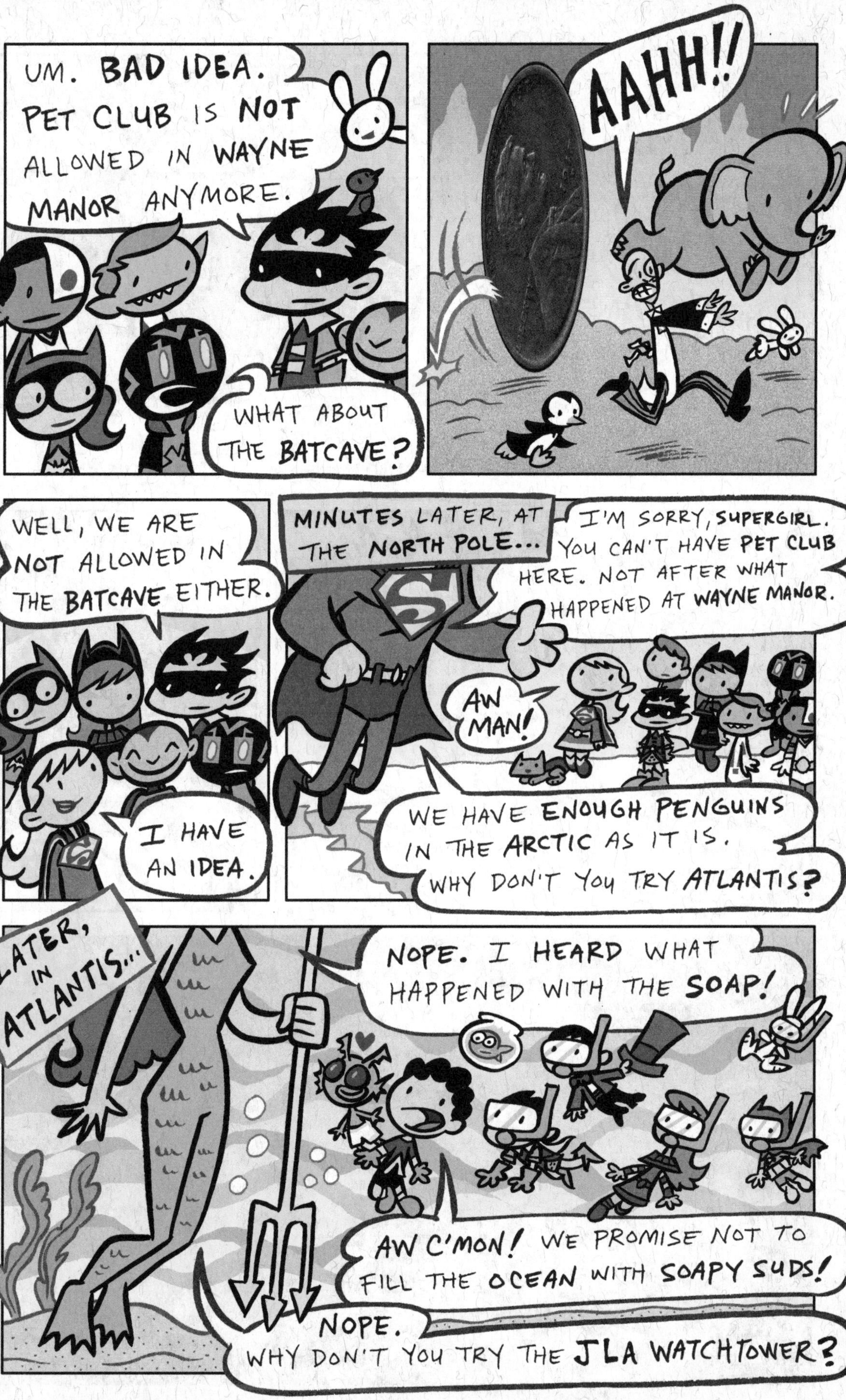
UM. BAD IDEA. PET CLUB IS NOT ALLOWED IN WAYNE MANOR ANYMORE.
WHAT ABOUT THE BATCAVE?
AAHH!!
WELL, WE ARE NOT ALLOWED IN THE BATCAVE EITHER.
I HAVE AN IDEA.
MINUTES LATER, AT THE NORTH POLE...
I'M SORRY, SUPERGIRL. YOU CAN'T HAVE PET CLUB HERE. NOT AFTER WHAT HAPPENED AT WAYNE MANOR.
AW MAN!
WE HAVE ENOUGH PENGUINS IN THE ARCTIC AS IT IS. WHY DON'T YOU TRY ATLANTIS?
LATER, IN ATLANTIS...
NOPE. I HEARD WHAT HAPPENED WITH THE SOAP!
AW C'MON! WE PROMISE NOT TO FILL THE OCEAN WITH SOAPY SUDS!
NOPE. WHY DON'T YOU TRY THE JLA WATCHTOWER?

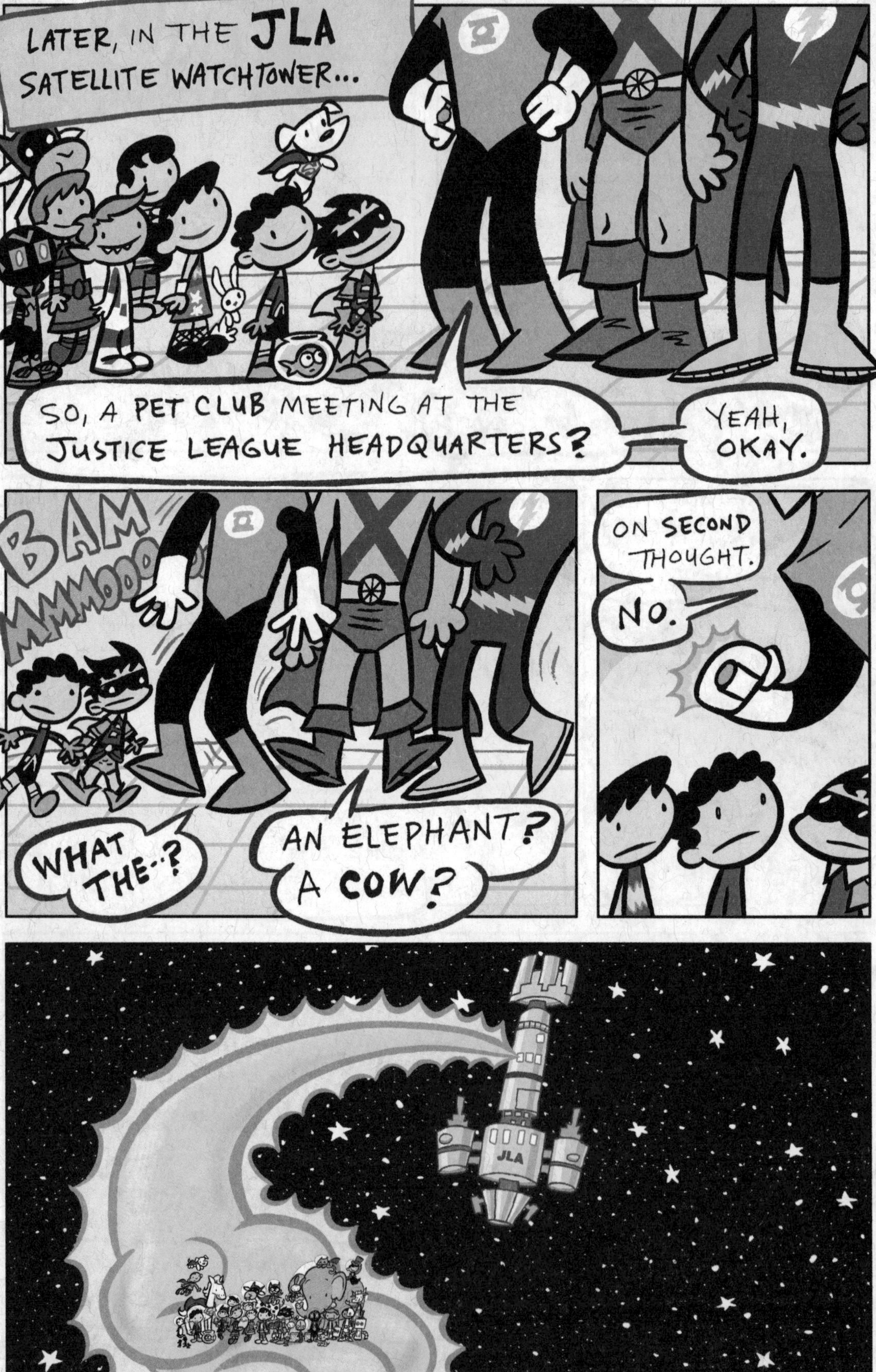
LATER, IN THE JLA SATELLITE WATCHTOWER...
SO, A PET CLUB MEETING AT THE JUSTICE LEAGUE HEADQUARTERS?
YEAH, OKAY.
BAM
MMMOOO
WHAT THE..?
AN ELEPHANT? A COW?
ON SECOND THOUGHT.
NO.
JLA

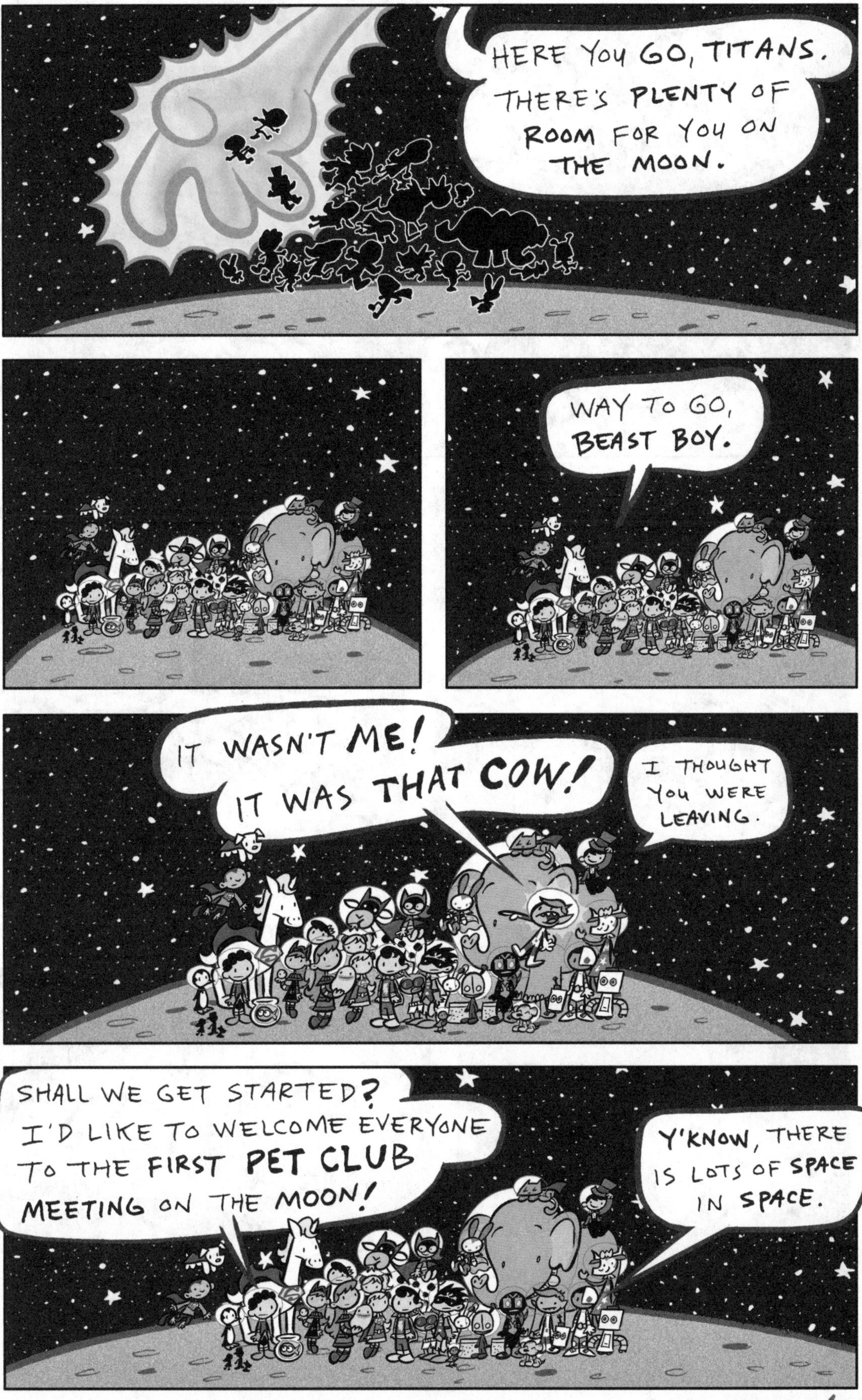
HERE YOU GO, TITANS. THERE'S PLENTY OF ROOM FOR YOU ON THE MOON.
WAY TO GO, BEAST BOY.
IT WASN'T ME! IT WAS THAT COW!
I THOUGHT YOU WERE LEAVING.
SHALL WE GET STARTED? I'D LIKE TO WELCOME EVERYONE TO THE FIRST PET CLUB MEETING ON THE MOON!
Y'KNOW, THERE IS LOTS OF SPACE IN SPACE.

-IT'S COSMIC!

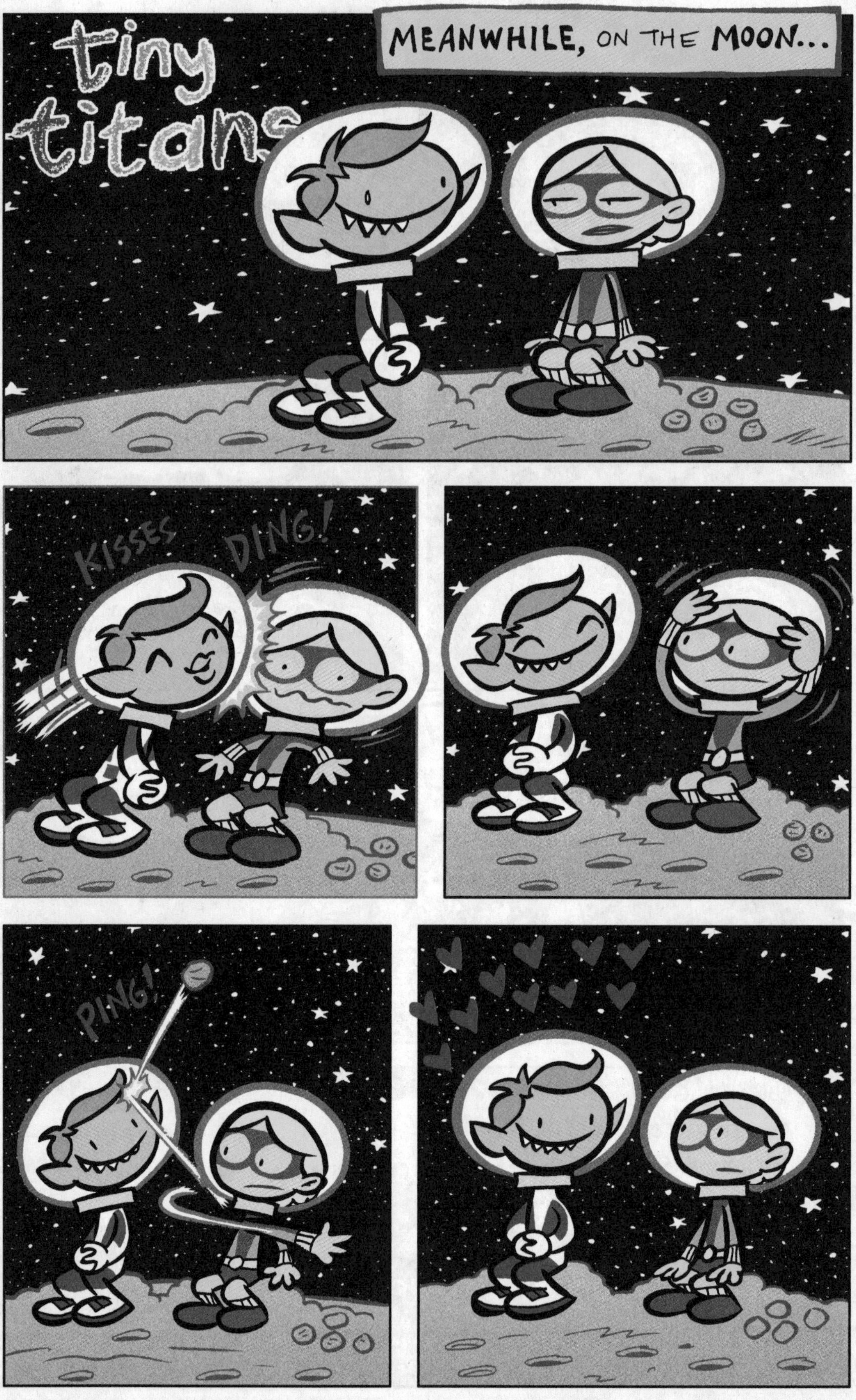
tiny titans
MEANWHILE, ON THE MOON...
KISSES
DING!
PING!

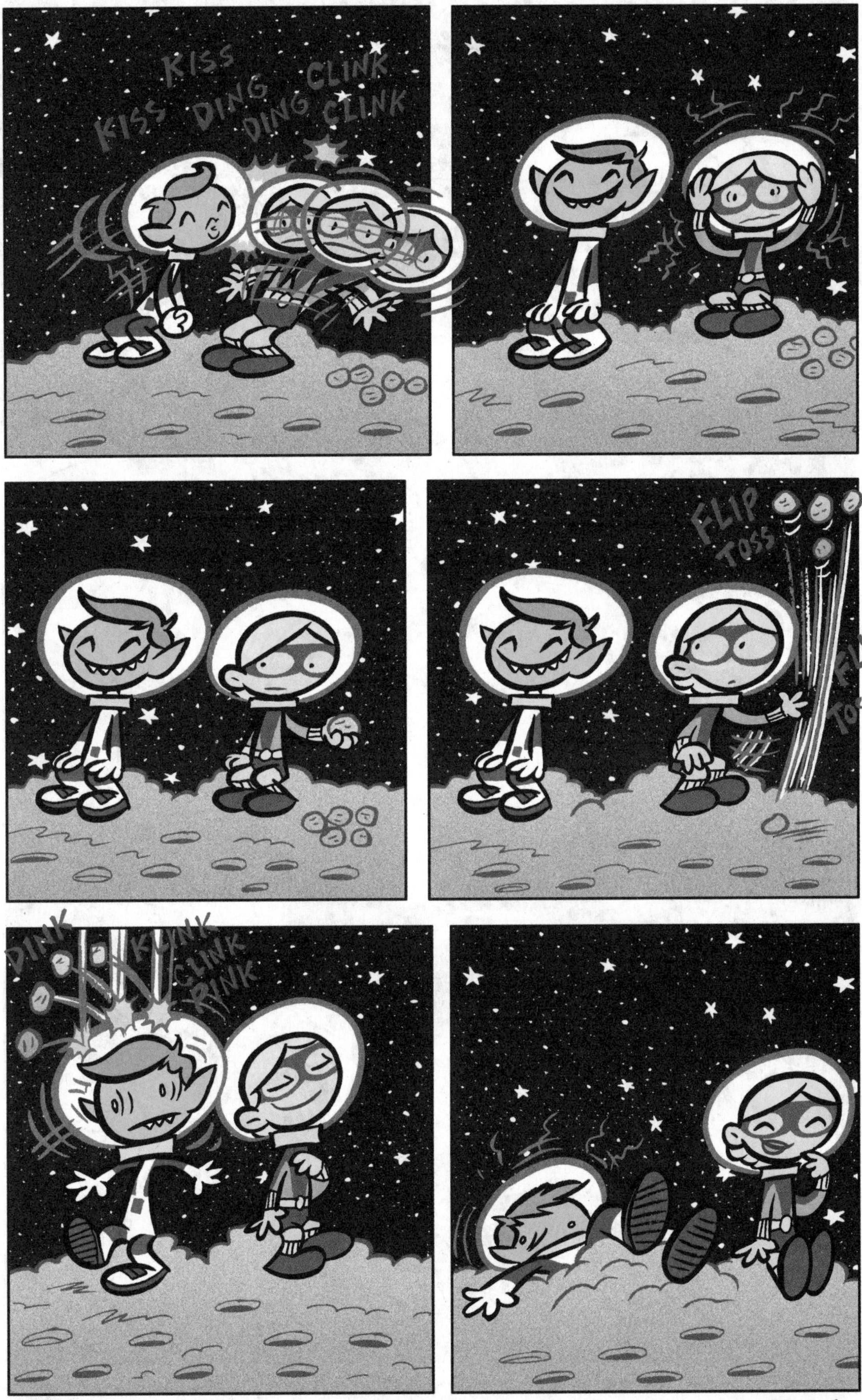
KISS
KISS
DING
DING
CLINK
CLINK
FLIP
TOSS
FLIP
TOSS
DINK
KLINK
CLINK
RINK

—MOON.

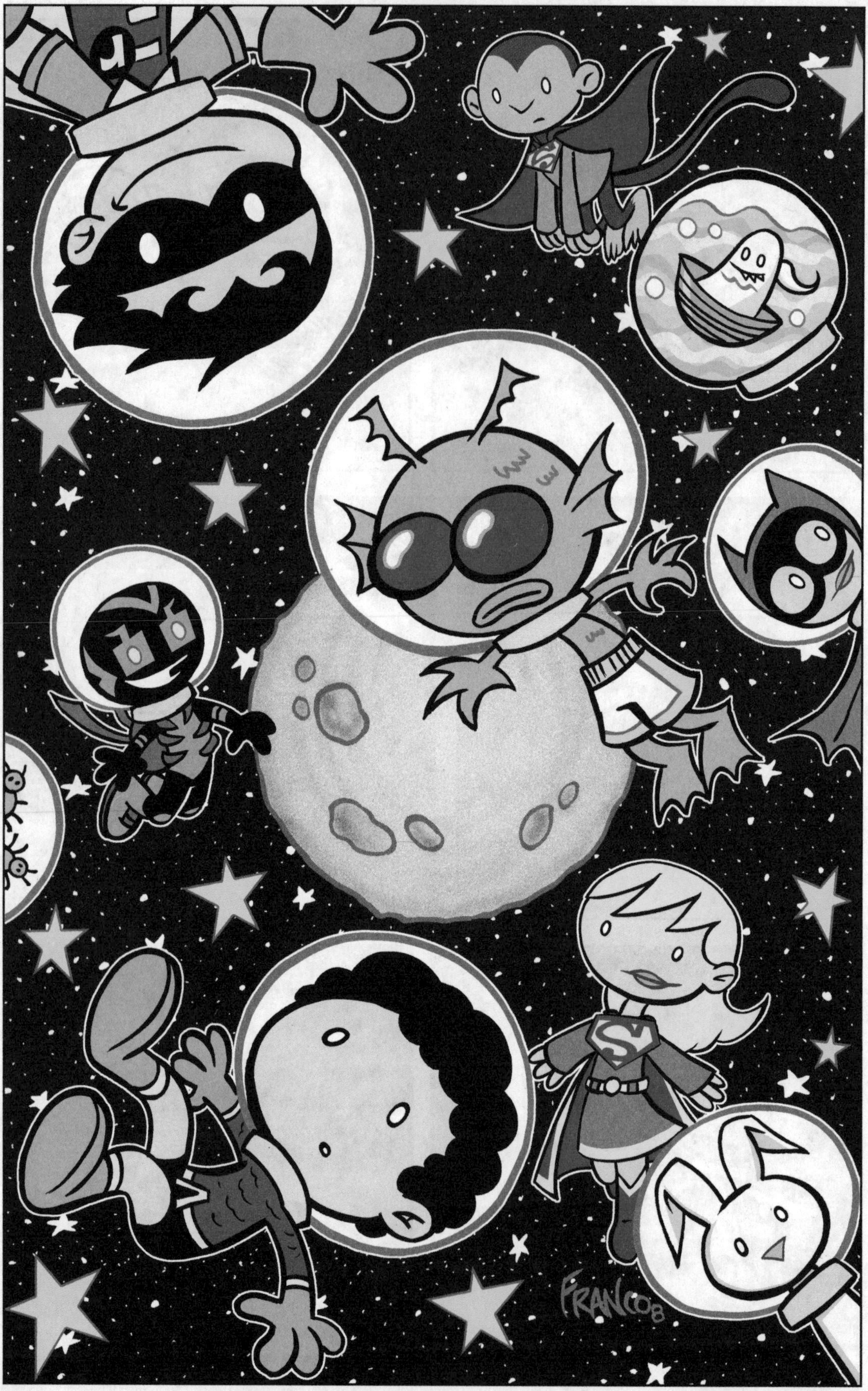
FRANCO8

TINY TITANS BONUS PIN-UP!

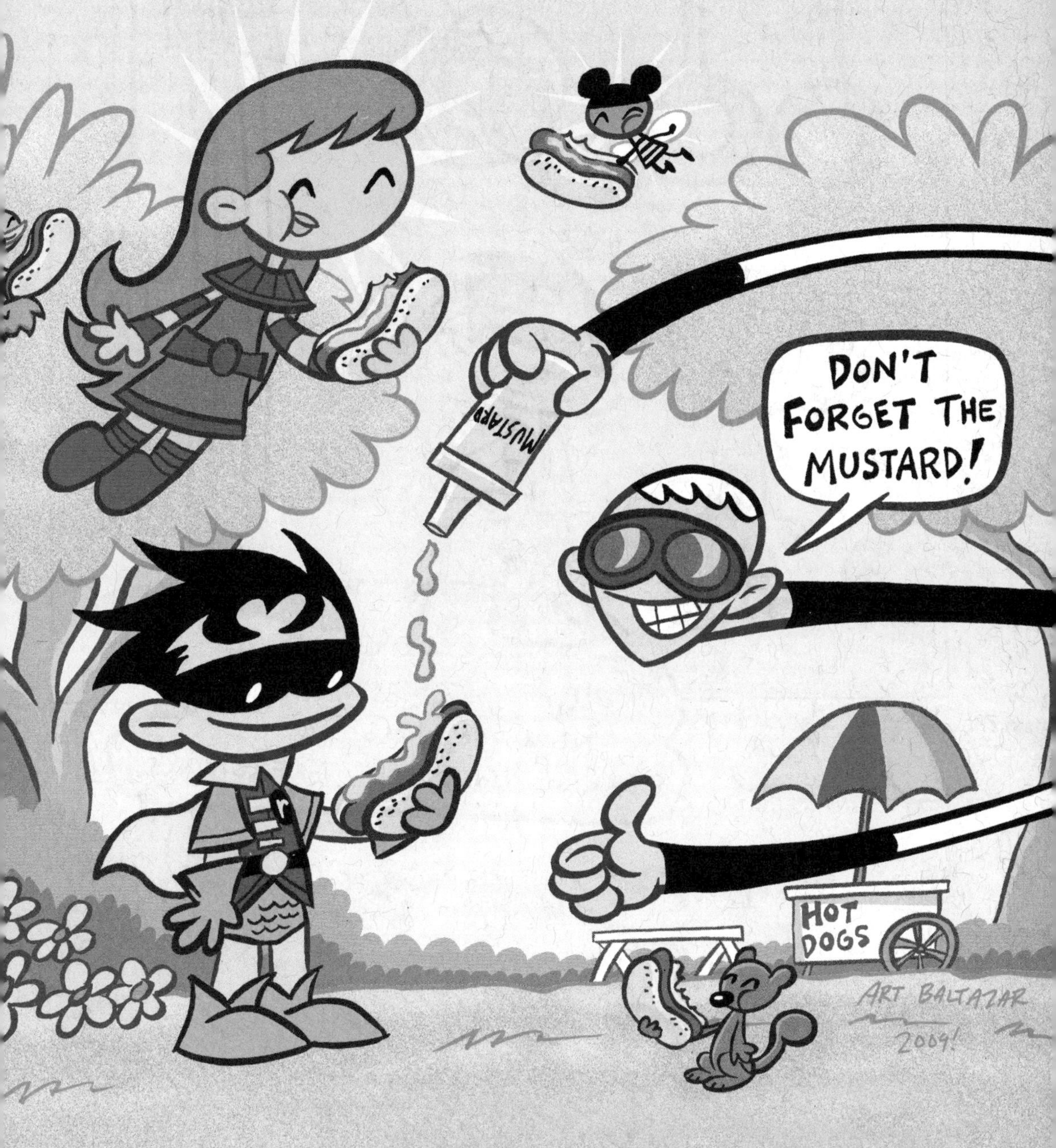
MUSTARD
DON'T FORGET THE MUSTARD!
HOT DOGS
ART BALTAZAR 2009!

HOT DOGS, TITANS, & STRETCHY GUYS!

tiny titans

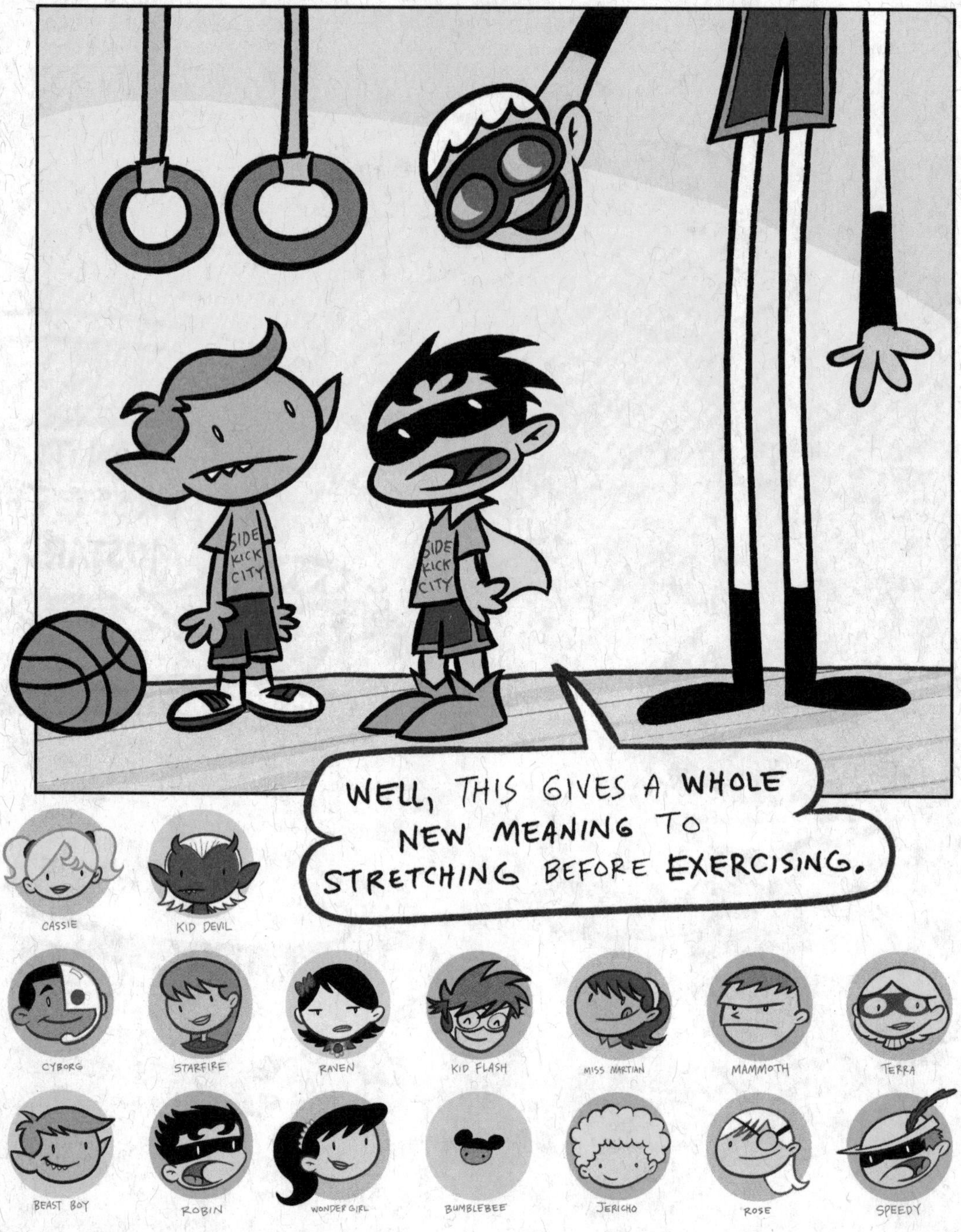
WELL, THIS GIVES A WHOLE NEW MEANING TO STRETCHING BEFORE EXERCISING.
SIDE KICK CITY
SIDE KICK CITY
CASSIE
KID DEVIL
CYBORG
STARFIRE
RAVEN
KID FLASH
MISS MARTIAN
MAMMOTH
TERRA
BEAST BOY
ROBIN
WONDER GIRL
BUMBLEBEE
JERICHO
ROSE
SPEEDY

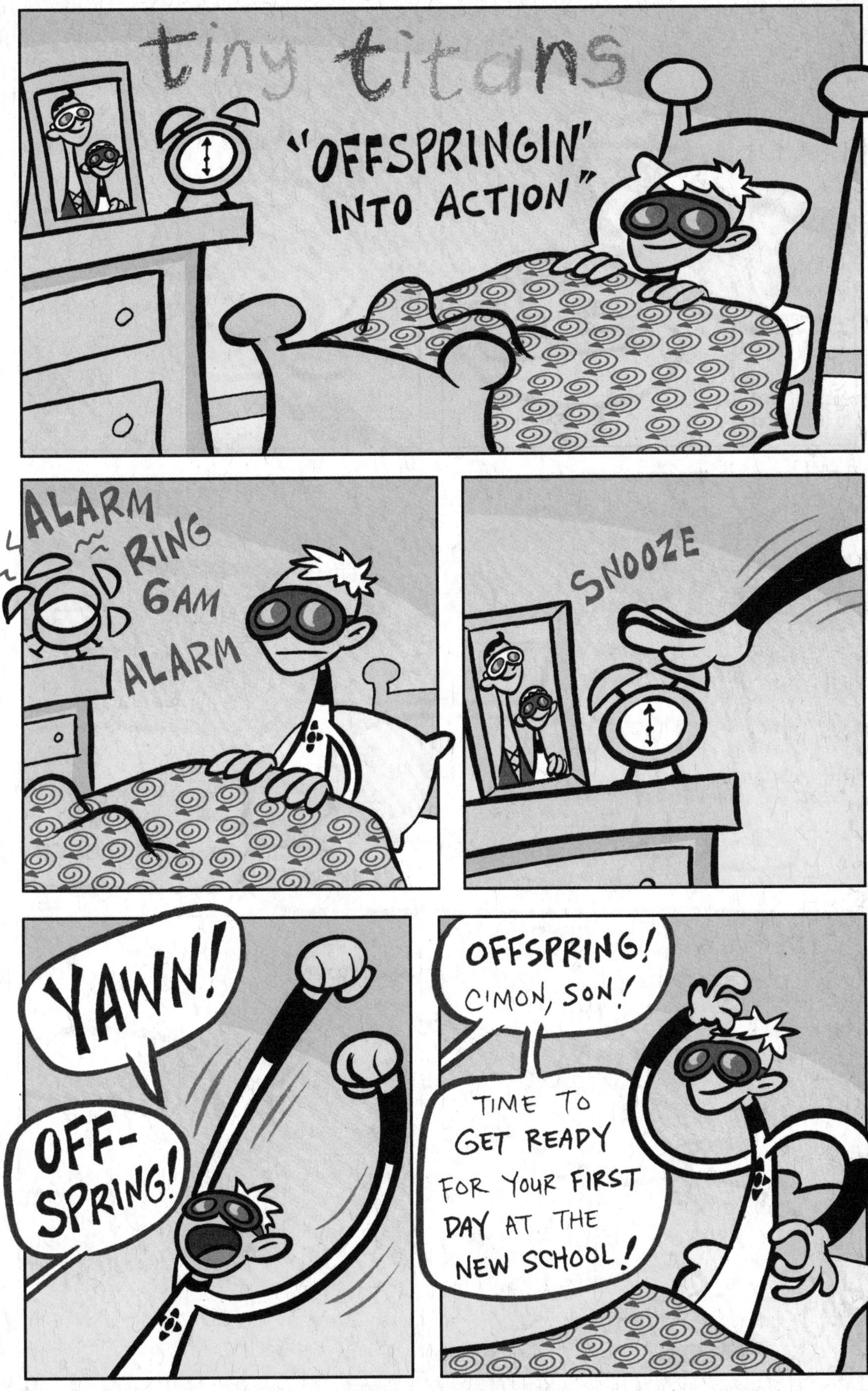
tiny titans
"OFFSPRINGIN' INTO ACTION"
ALARM RING 6AM ALARM
SNOOZE
YAWN!
OFF-SPRING!
OFFSPRING! C'MON, SON!
TIME TO GET READY FOR YOUR FIRST DAY AT THE NEW SCHOOL!

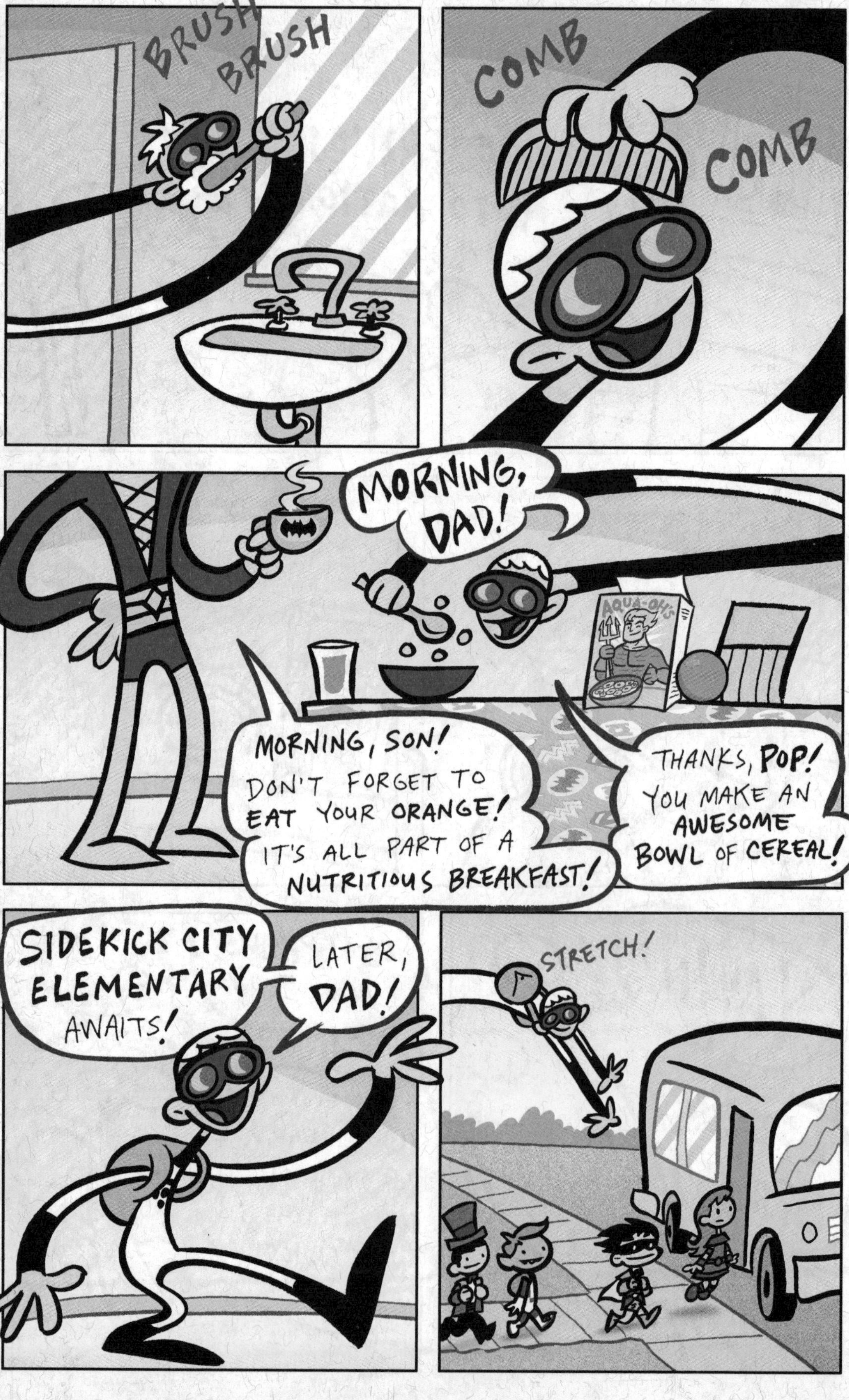
BRUSH
BRUSH
COMB
COMB
MORNING, DAD!
AQUA-OH'S
MORNING, SON! DON'T FORGET TO EAT YOUR ORANGE! IT'S ALL PART OF A NUTRITIOUS BREAKFAST!
THANKS, POP! YOU MAKE AN AWESOME BOWL OF CEREAL!
SIDEKICK CITY ELEMENTARY AWAITS!
LATER, DAD!
STRETCH!

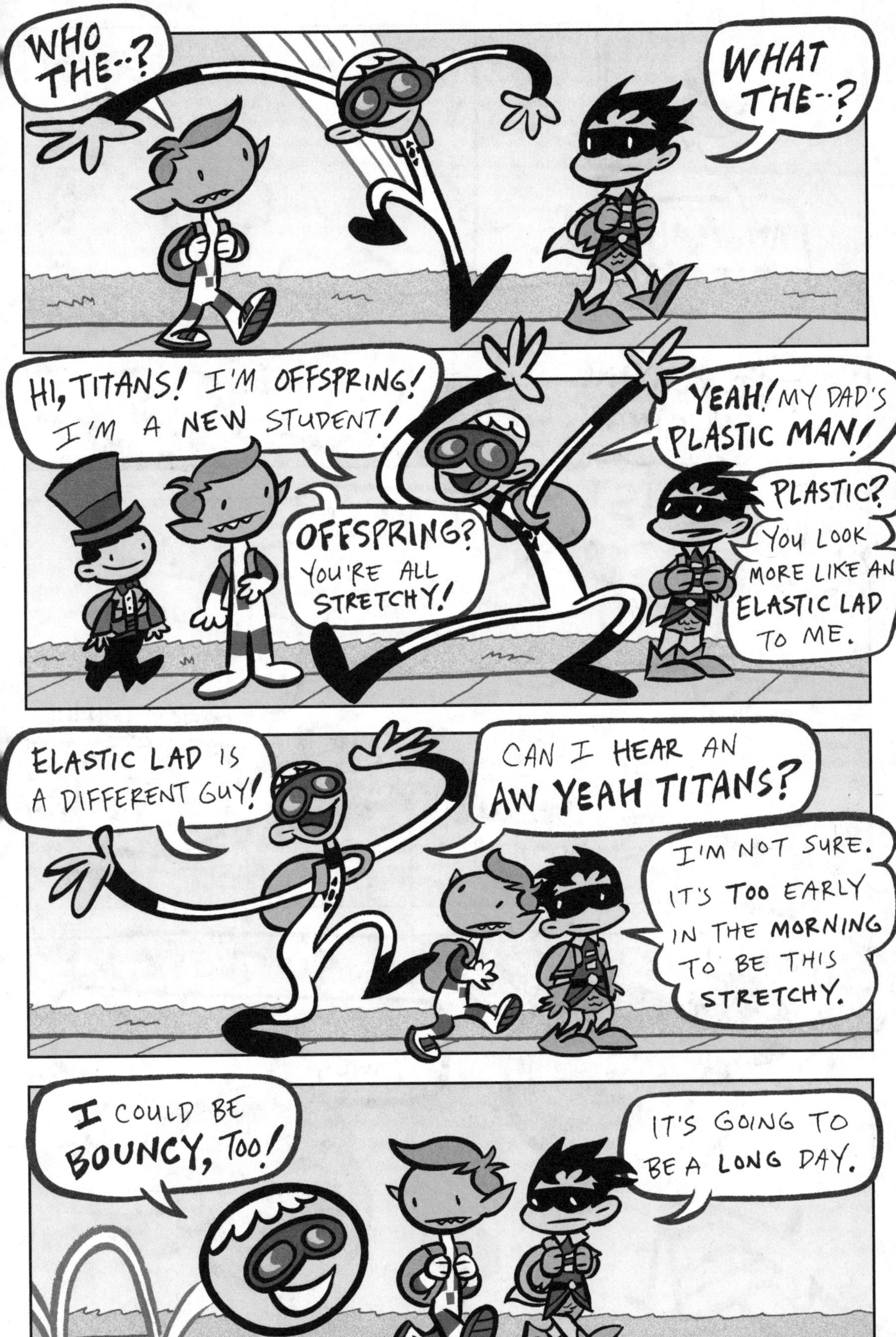
WHO THE..?
WHAT THE..?
HI, TITANS! I'M OFFSPRING! I'M A NEW STUDENT!
YEAH! MY DAD'S PLASTIC MAN!
OFFSPRING? YOU'RE ALL STRETCHY!
PLASTIC? YOU LOOK MORE LIKE AN ELASTIC LAD TO ME.
ELASTIC LAD IS A DIFFERENT GUY!
CAN I HEAR AN AW YEAH TITANS?
I'M NOT SURE. IT'S TOO EARLY IN THE MORNING TO BE THIS STRETCHY.
I COULD BE BOUNCY, TOO!
IT'S GOING TO BE A LONG DAY.

—SCHOOL BUS!

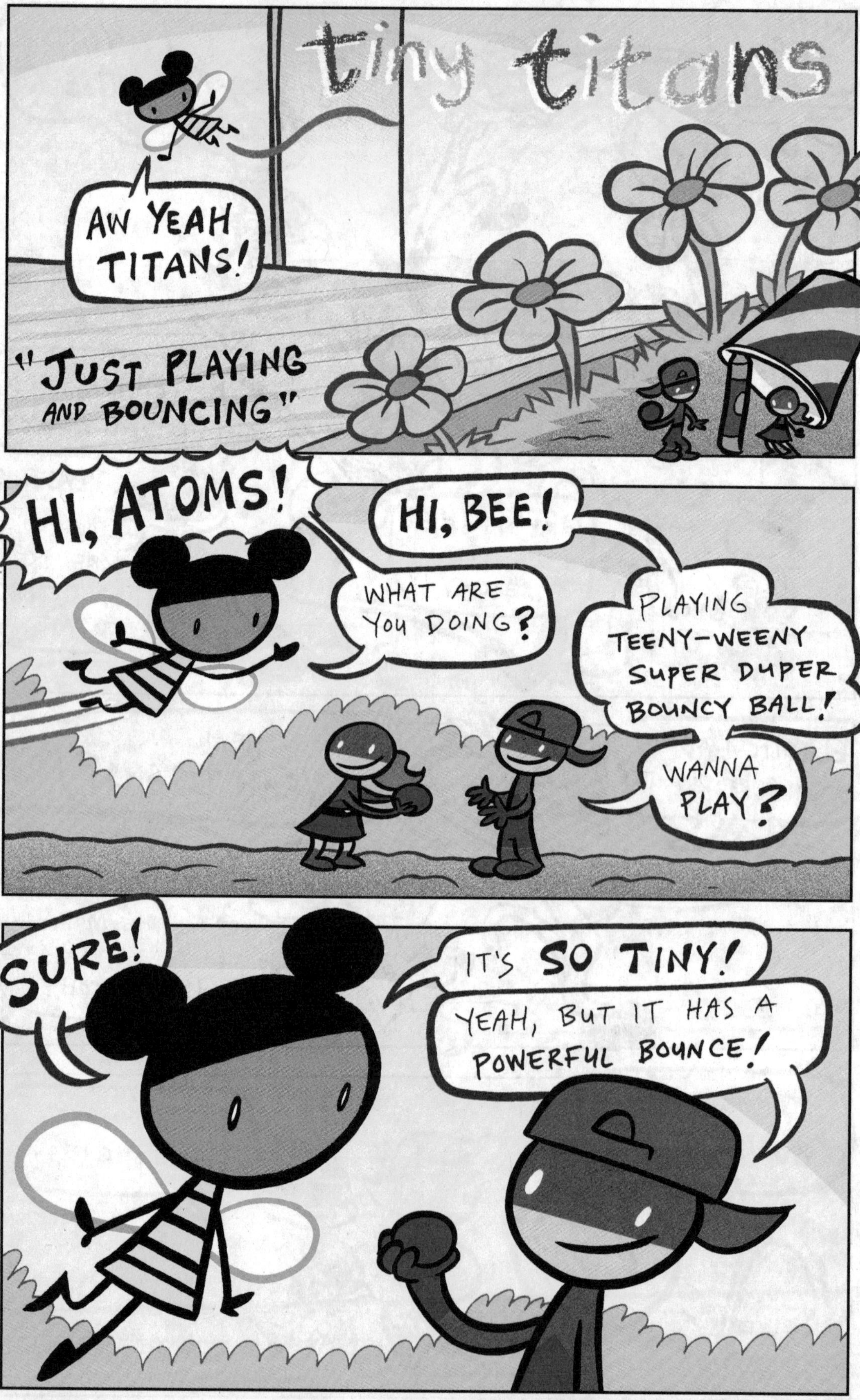
tiny titans
AW YEAH TITANS!
"JUST PLAYING AND BOUNCING"
HI, ATOMS!
HI, BEE!
WHAT ARE YOU DOING?
PLAYING TEENY-WEENY SUPER DUPER BOUNCY BALL!
WANNA PLAY?
SURE!
IT'S SO TINY!
YEAH, BUT IT HAS A POWERFUL BOUNCE!

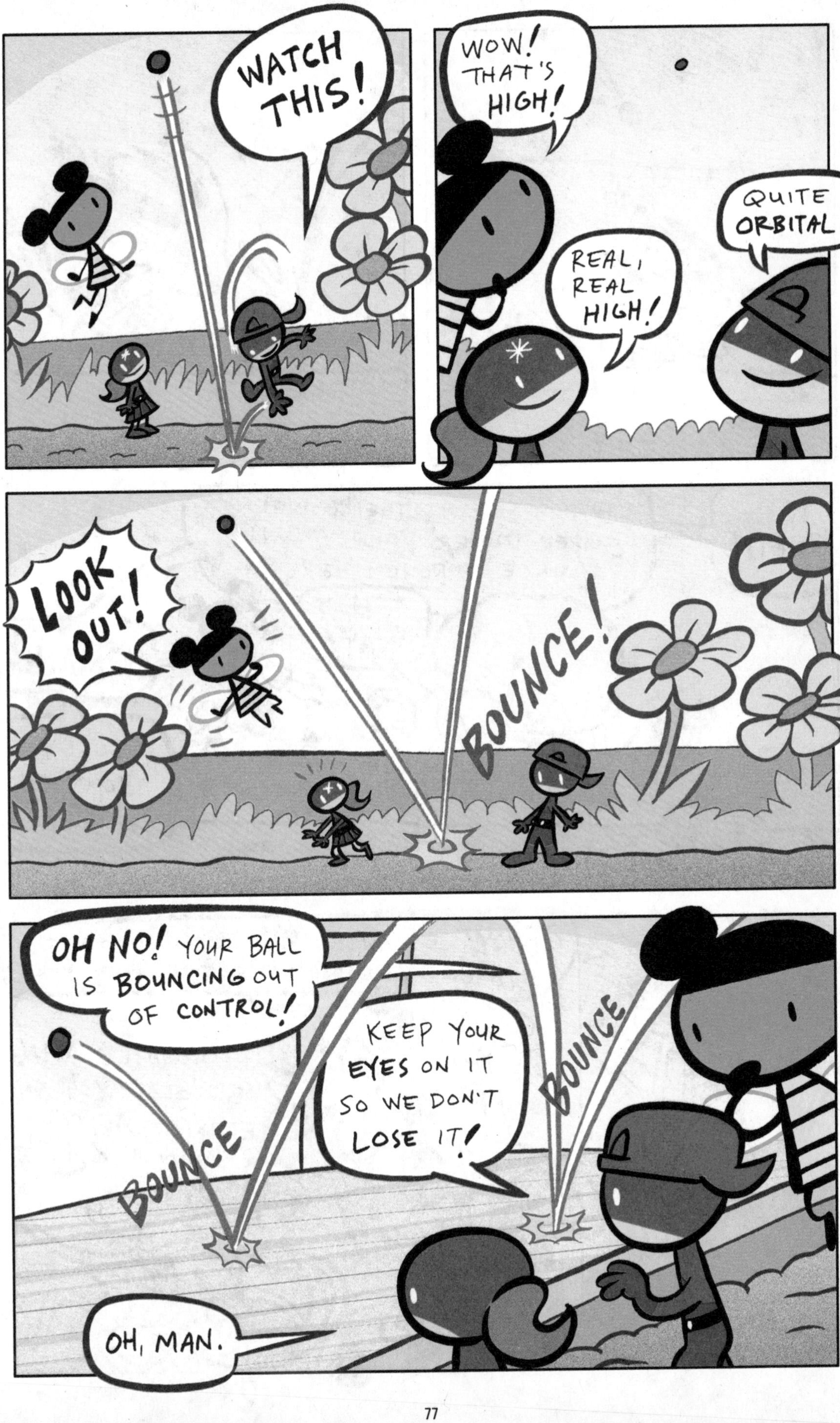
WATCH THIS!
WOW! THAT'S HIGH!
REAL, REAL HIGH!
QUITE ORBITAL.
LOOK OUT!
BOUNCE!
OH NO! YOUR BALL IS BOUNCING OUT OF CONTROL!
KEEP YOUR EYES ON IT SO WE DON'T LOSE IT!
BOUNCE
BOUNCE
OH, MAN.

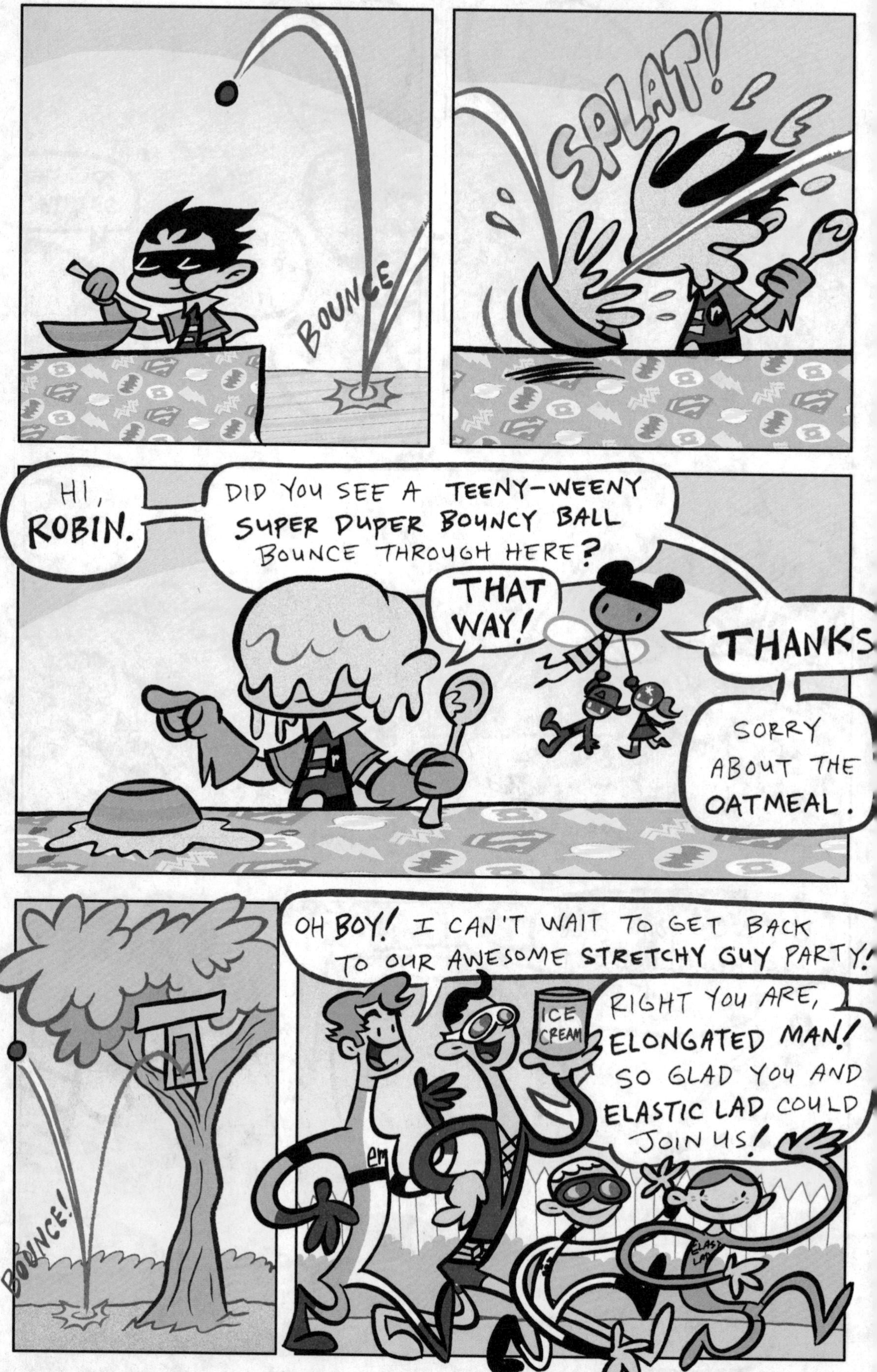
BOUNCE
SPLAT!
HI, ROBIN.
DID YOU SEE A TEENY-WEENY SUPER DUPER BOUNCY BALL BOUNCE THROUGH HERE?
THAT WAY!
THANKS
SORRY ABOUT THE OATMEAL.
BOUNCE!
OH BOY! I CAN'T WAIT TO GET BACK TO OUR AWESOME STRETCHY GUY PARTY!
ICE CREAM
RIGHT YOU ARE, ELONGATED MAN! SO GLAD YOU AND ELASTIC LAD COULD JOIN US!

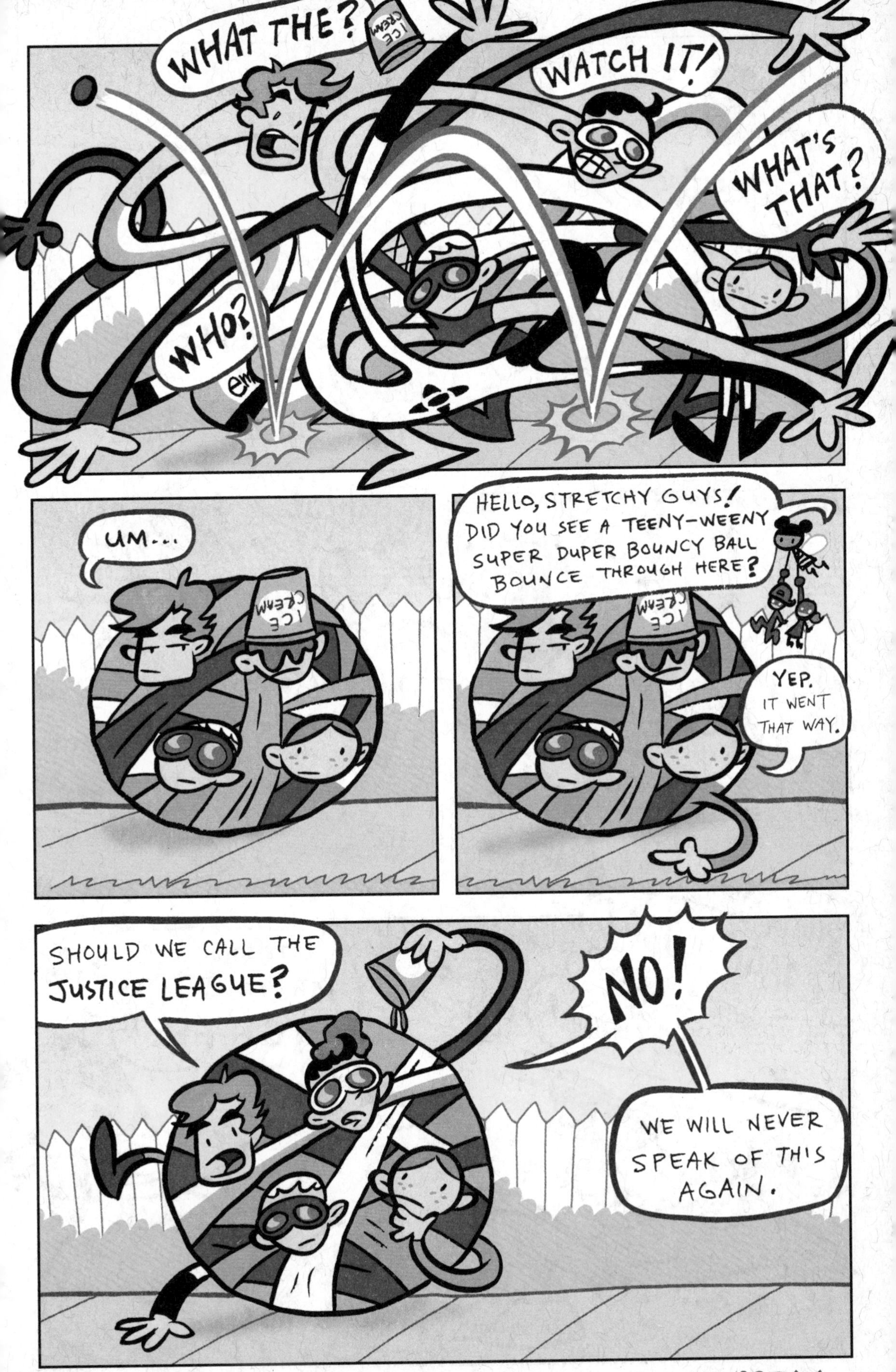
WHAT THE?
WATCH IT!
WHAT'S THAT?
WHO?
UM...
HELLO, STRETCHY GUYS! DID YOU SEE A TEENY-WEENY SUPER DUPER BOUNCY BALL BOUNCE THROUGH HERE?
YEP. IT WENT THAT WAY.
SHOULD WE CALL THE JUSTICE LEAGUE?
NO!
WE WILL NEVER SPEAK OF THIS AGAIN.

–ICE CREAM

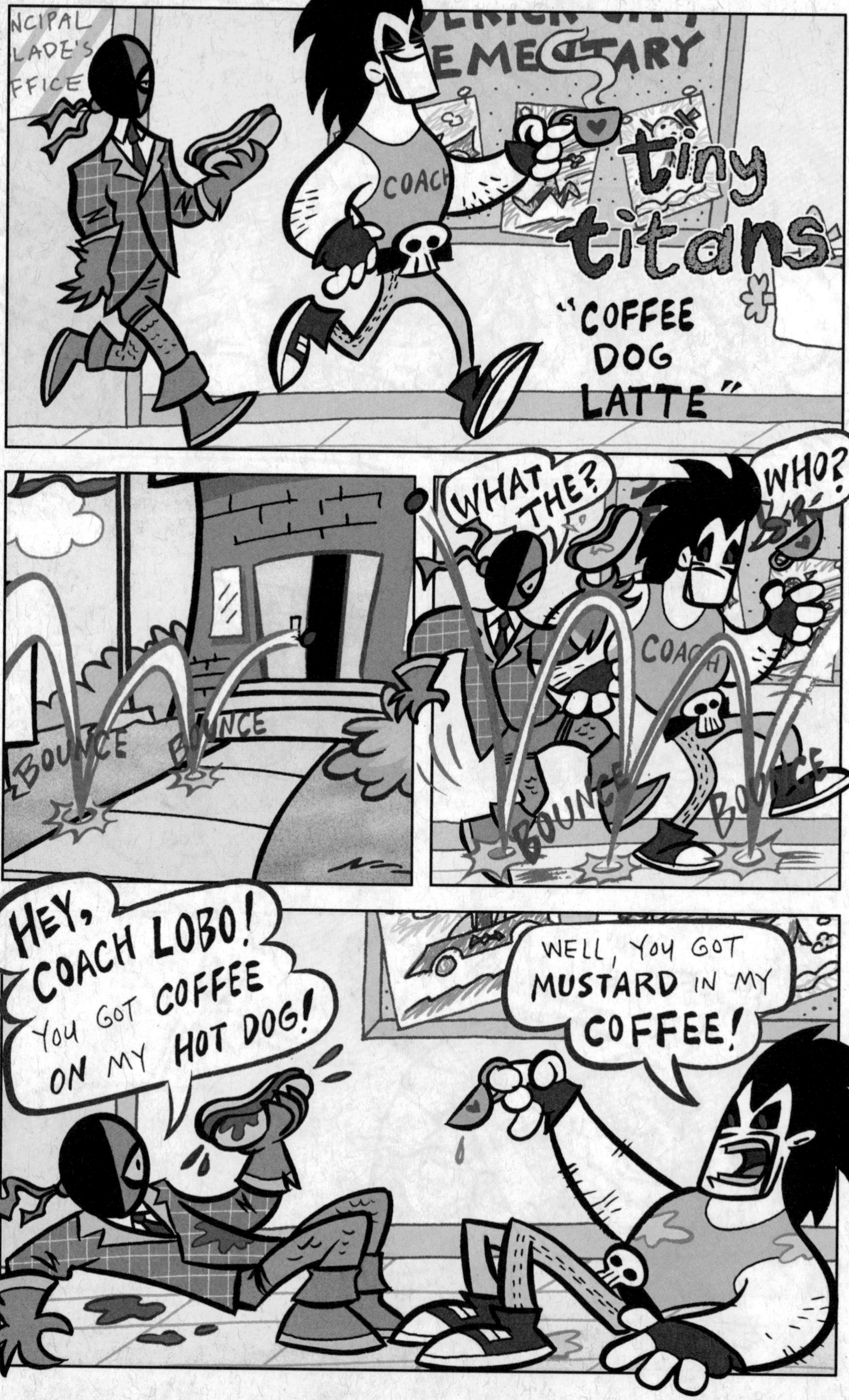
tiny titans
"COFFEE DOG LATTE"
BOUNCE
BOUNCE
WHAT THE?
WHO?
BOUNCE
BOUNCE
HEY, COACH LOBO! YOU GOT COFFEE ON MY HOT DOG!
WELL, YOU GOT MUSTARD IN MY COFFEE!

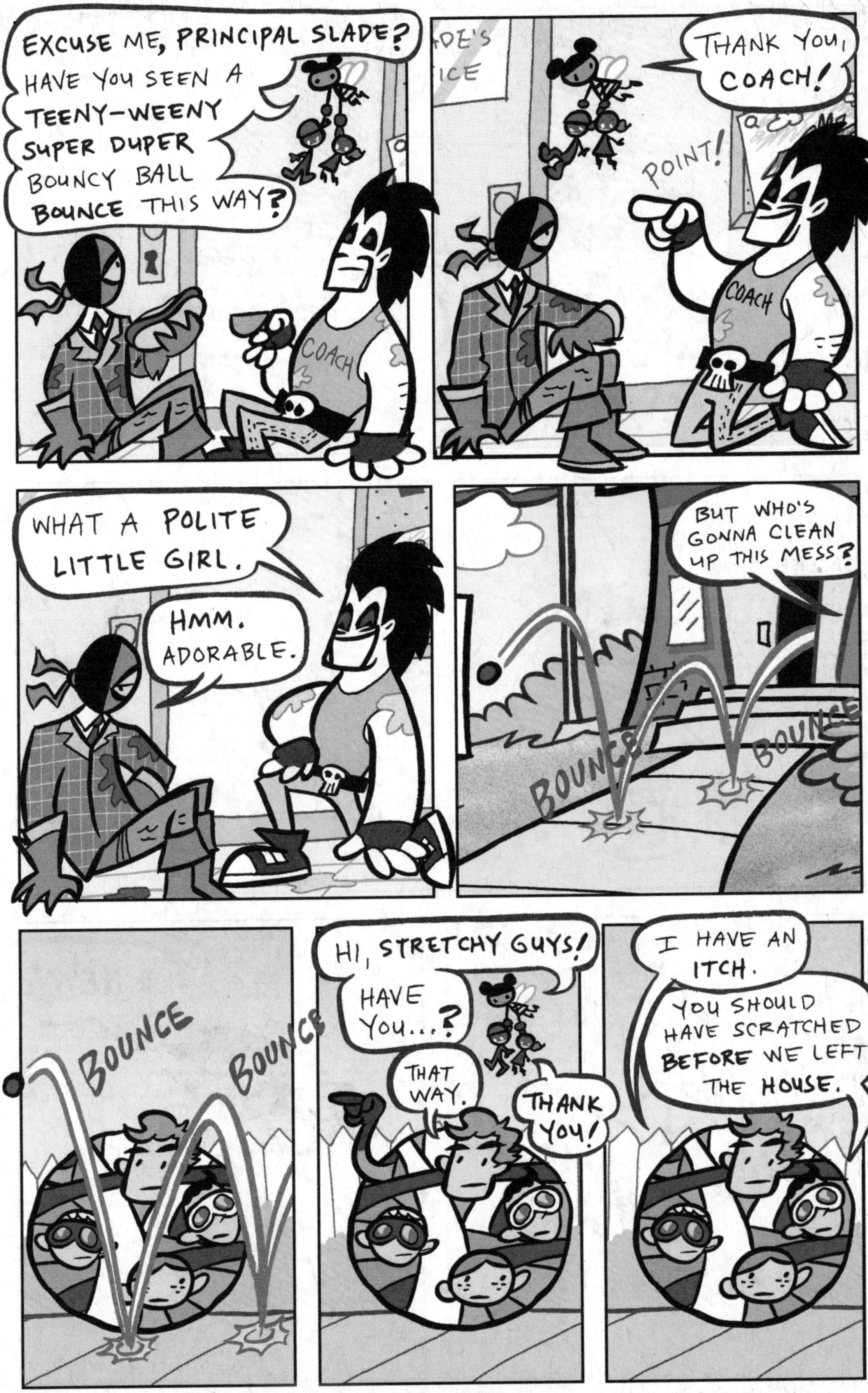
EXCUSE ME, PRINCIPAL SLADE? HAVE YOU SEEN A TEENY-WEENY SUPER DUPER BOUNCY BALL BOUNCE THIS WAY?
THANK YOU, COACH!
POINT!
COACH
COACH
WHAT A POLITE LITTLE GIRL.
HMM. ADORABLE.
BUT WHO'S GONNA CLEAN UP THIS MESS?
BOUNCE
BOUNCE
BOUNCE
BOUNCE
HI, STRETCHY GUYS!
HAVE YOU...?
THAT WAY.
THANK YOU!
I HAVE AN ITCH.
YOU SHOULD HAVE SCRATCHED BEFORE WE LEFT THE HOUSE.

-MUSTARD.

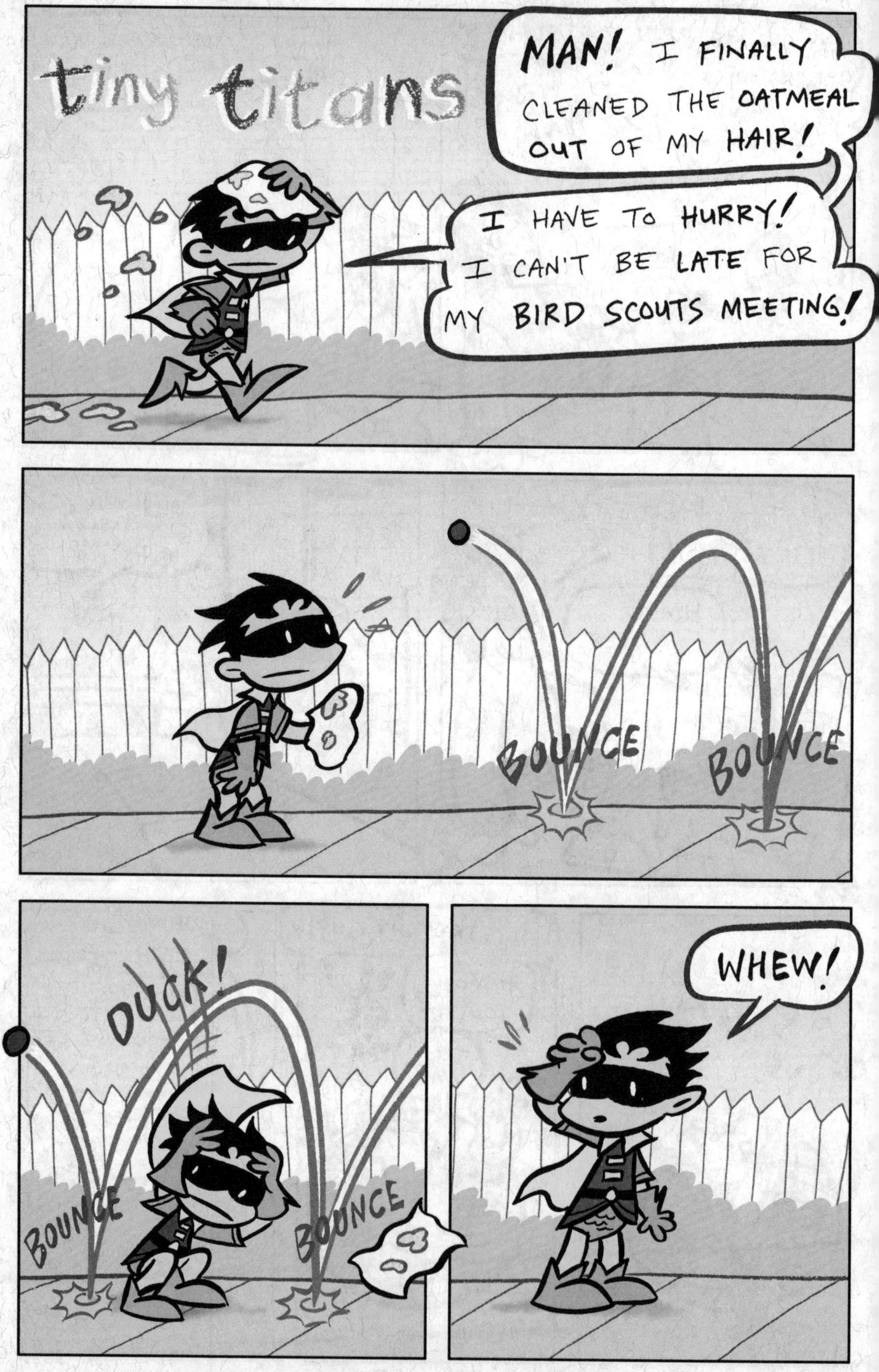
tiny titans
MAN! I FINALLY CLEANED THE OATMEAL OUT OF MY HAIR!
I HAVE TO HURRY! I CAN'T BE LATE FOR MY BIRD SCOUTS MEETING!
BOUNCE
BOUNCE
DUCK!
BOUNCE
BOUNCE
WHEW!

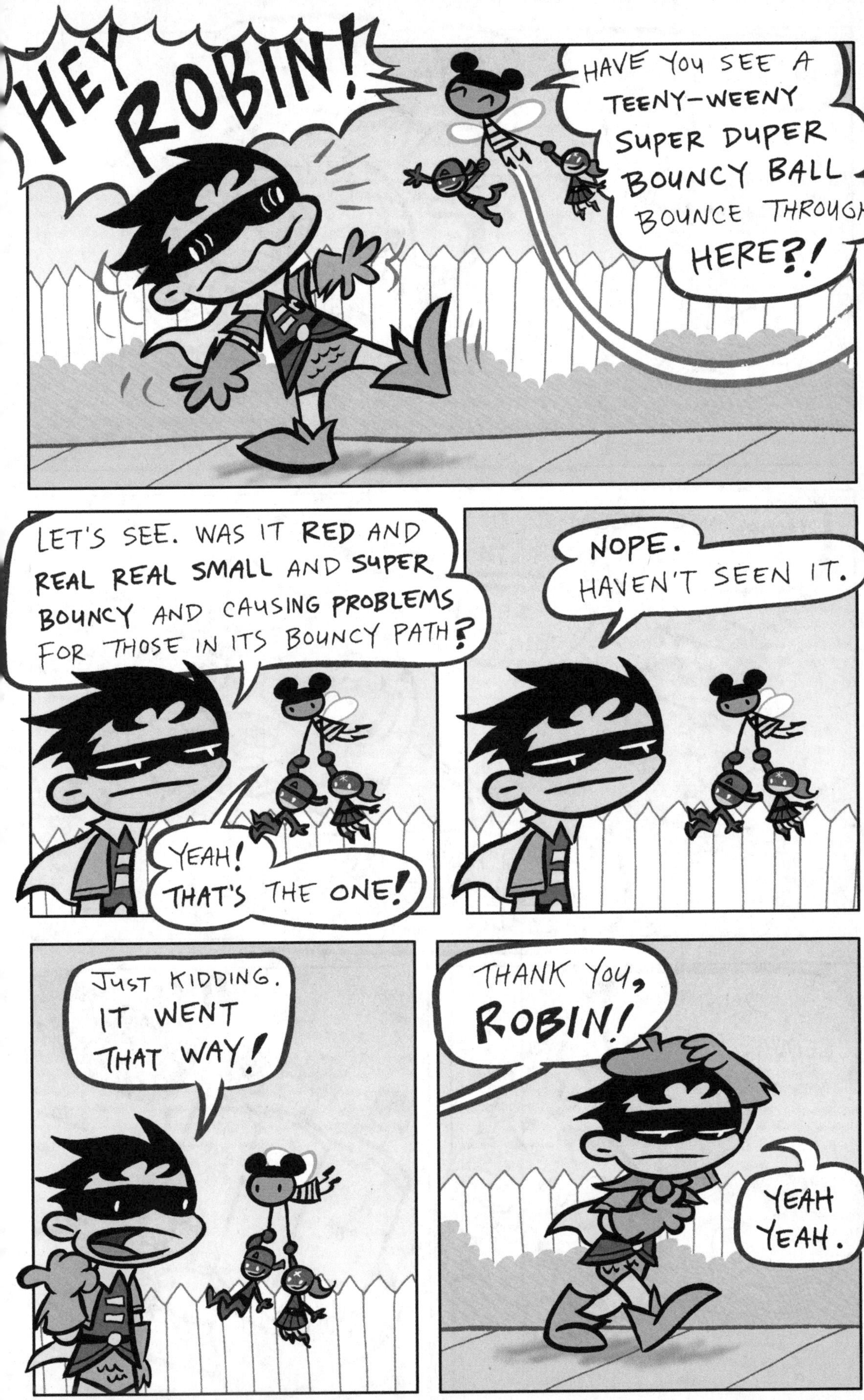
HEY ROBIN!
HAVE YOU SEE A TEENY-WEENY SUPER DUPER BOUNCY BALL BOUNCE THROUGH HERE?!
LET'S SEE. WAS IT RED AND REAL REAL SMALL AND SUPER BOUNCY AND CAUSING PROBLEMS FOR THOSE IN ITS BOUNCY PATH?
YEAH! THAT'S THE ONE!
NOPE. HAVEN'T SEEN IT.
JUST KIDDING. IT WENT THAT WAY!
THANK YOU, ROBIN!
YEAH YEAH.

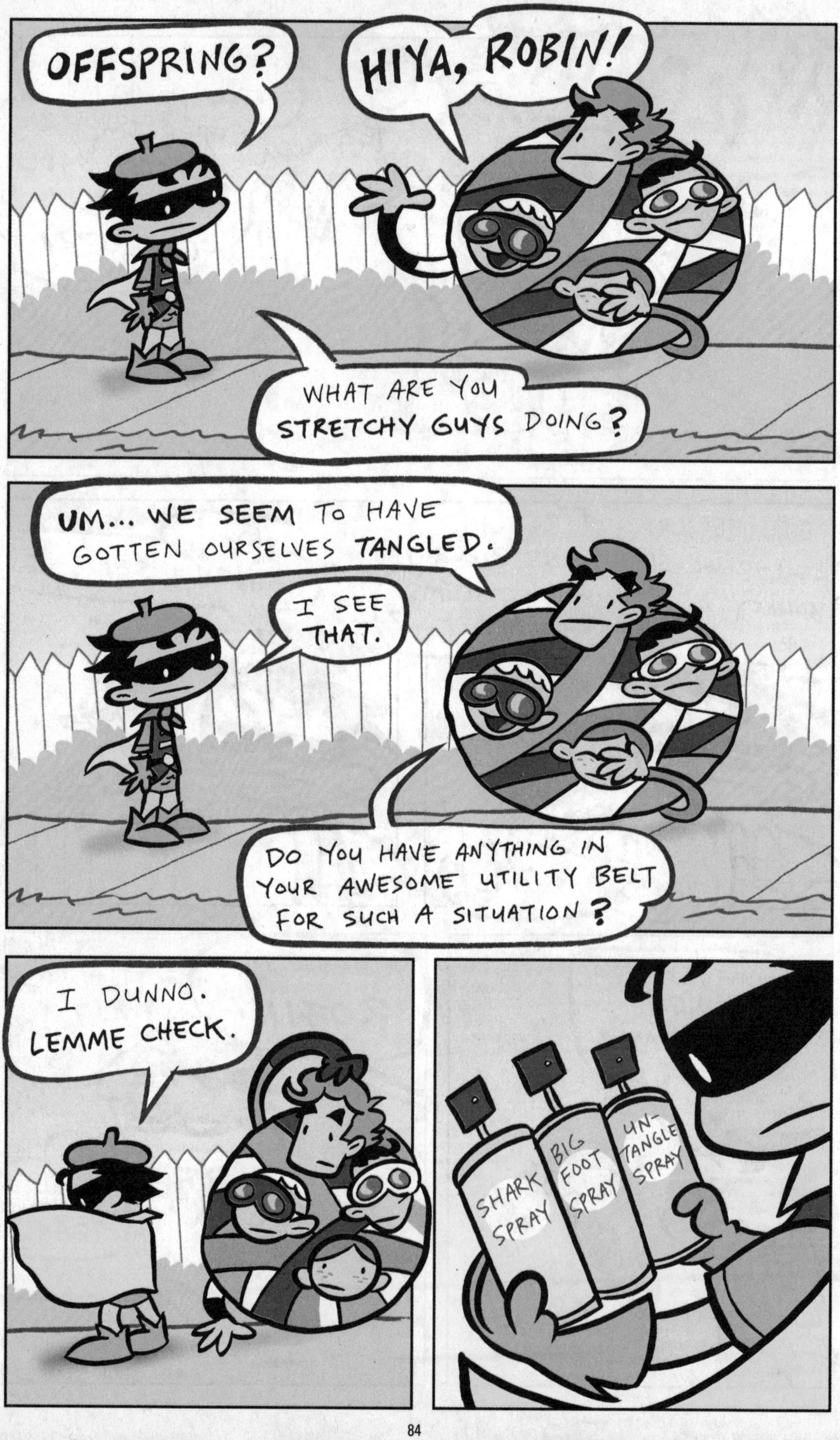
OFFSPRING?
HIYA, ROBIN!
WHAT ARE YOU STRETCHY GUYS DOING?
UM... WE SEEM TO HAVE GOTTEN OURSELVES TANGLED.
I SEE THAT.
DO YOU HAVE ANYTHING IN YOUR AWESOME UTILITY BELT FOR SUCH A SITUATION?
I DUNNO. LEMME CHECK.
SHARK SPRAY
BIG FOOT SPRAY
UN-TANGLE SPRAY

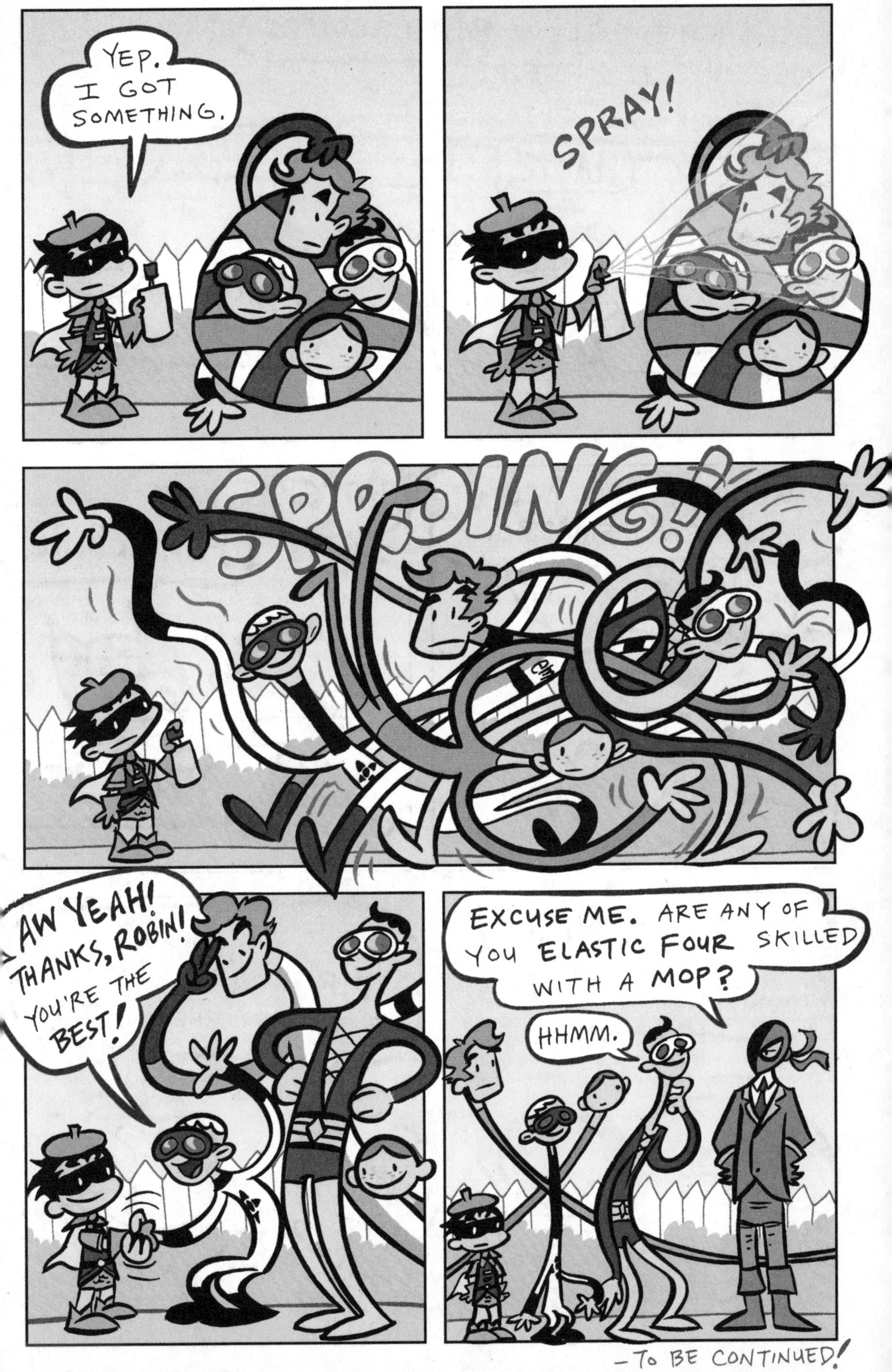
YEP. I GOT SOMETHING.
SPRAY!
SPROING!
AW YEAH! THANKS, ROBIN! YOU'RE THE BEST!
EXCUSE ME. ARE ANY OF YOU ELASTIC FOUR SKILLED WITH A MOP?
HHMM.

–TO BE CONTINUED!

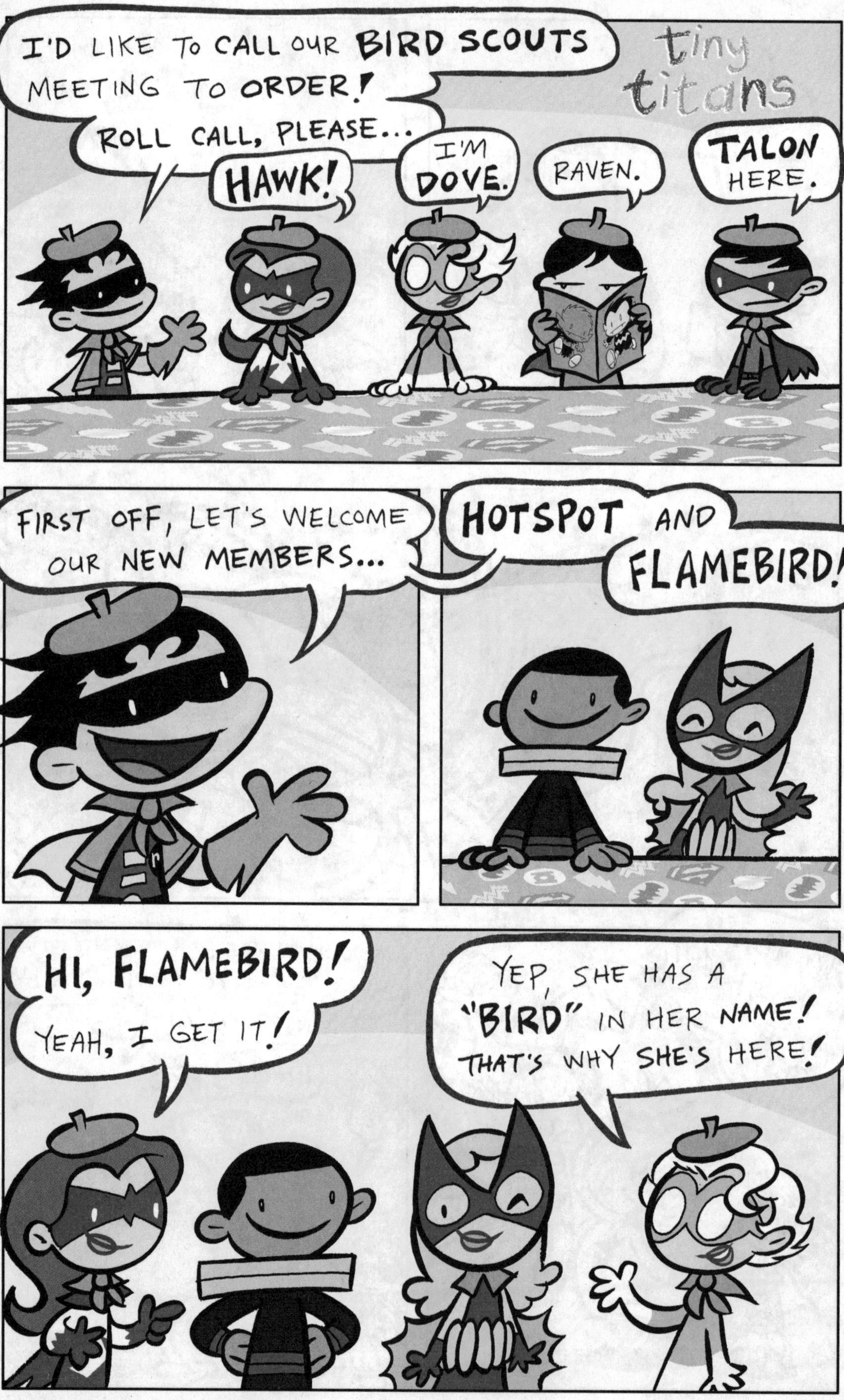
tiny titans
I'D LIKE TO CALL OUR BIRD SCOUTS MEETING TO ORDER!
ROLL CALL, PLEASE...
HAWK!
I'M DOVE.
RAVEN.
TALON HERE.
FIRST OFF, LET'S WELCOME OUR NEW MEMBERS...
HOTSPOT AND FLAMEBIRD!
HI, FLAMEBIRD!
YEAH, I GET IT!
YEP, SHE HAS A "BIRD" IN HER NAME!
THAT'S WHY SHE'S HERE!

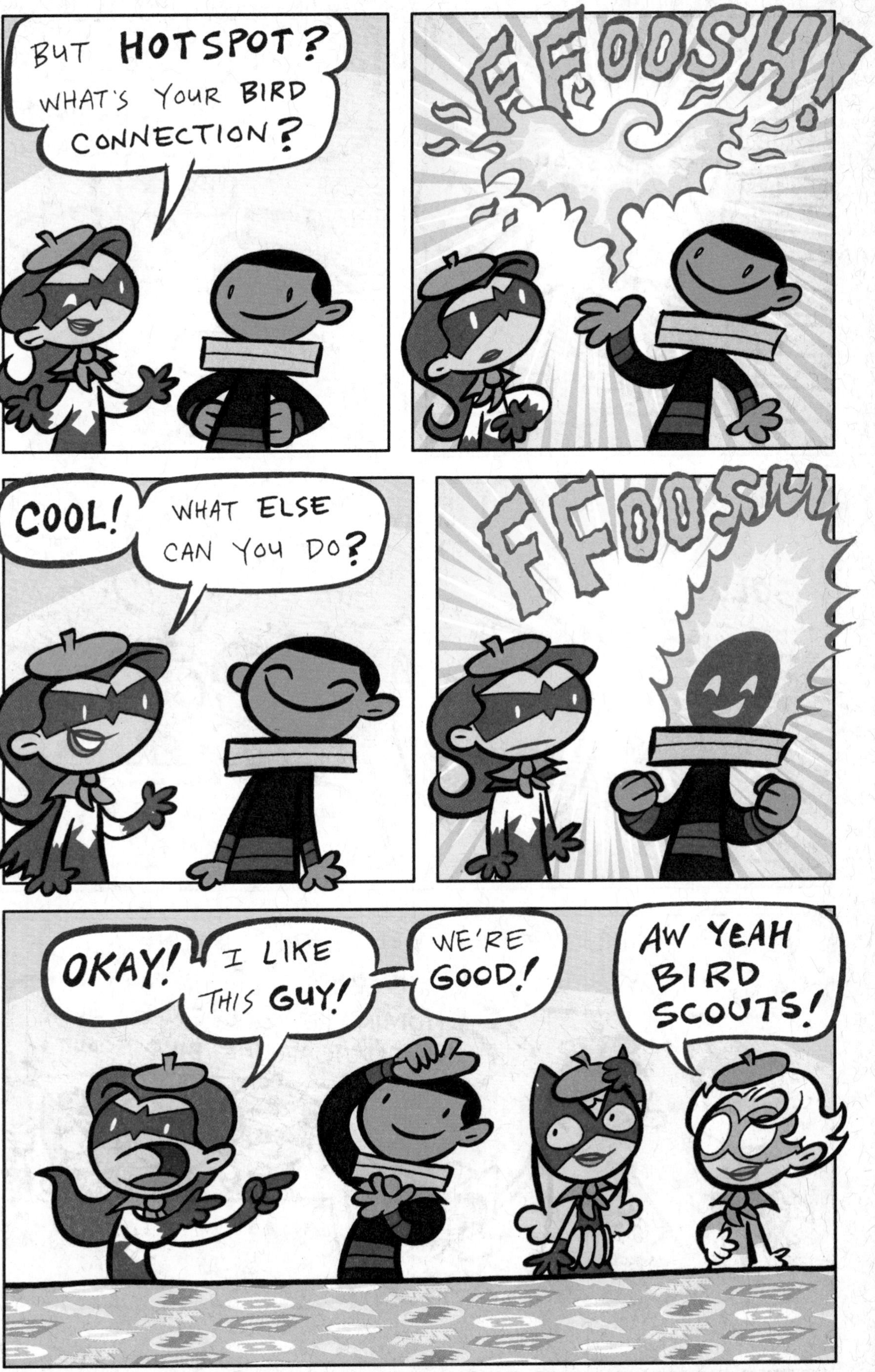
BUT HOTSPOT? WHAT'S YOUR BIRD CONNECTION?
FFOOSH!
COOL!
WHAT ELSE CAN YOU DO?
FFOOSH
OKAY!
I LIKE THIS GUY!
WE'RE GOOD!
AW YEAH BIRD SCOUTS!

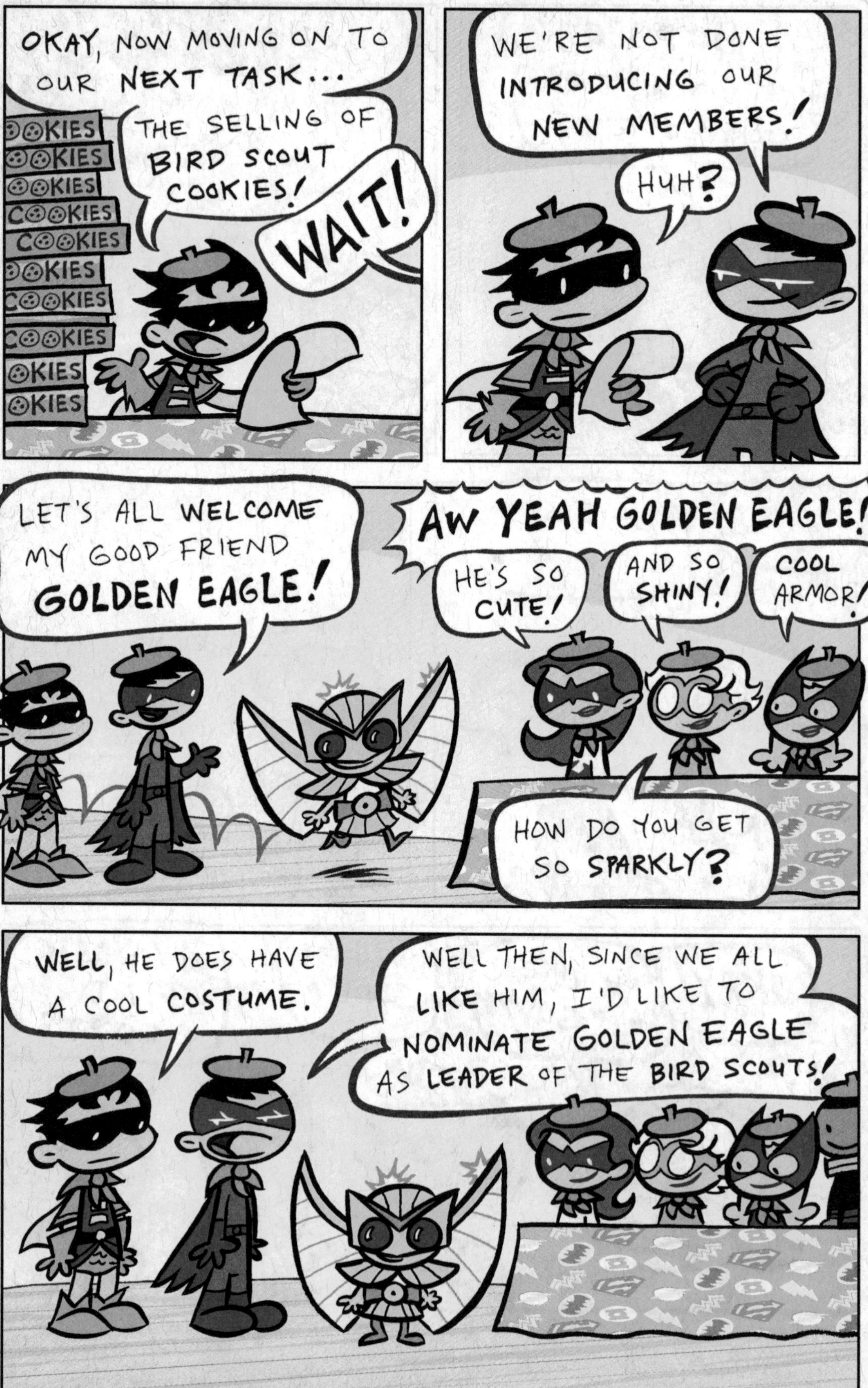
OKAY, NOW MOVING ON TO OUR NEXT TASK...
THE SELLING OF BIRD SCOUT COOKIES!
COOKIES
WAIT!
WE'RE NOT DONE INTRODUCING OUR NEW MEMBERS!
HUH?
LET'S ALL WELCOME MY GOOD FRIEND GOLDEN EAGLE!
AW YEAH GOLDEN EAGLE!
HE'S SO CUTE!
AND SO SHINY!
COOL ARMOR!
HOW DO YOU GET SO SPARKLY?
WELL, HE DOES HAVE A COOL COSTUME.
WELL THEN, SINCE WE ALL LIKE HIM, I'D LIKE TO NOMINATE GOLDEN EAGLE AS LEADER OF THE BIRD SCOUTS!

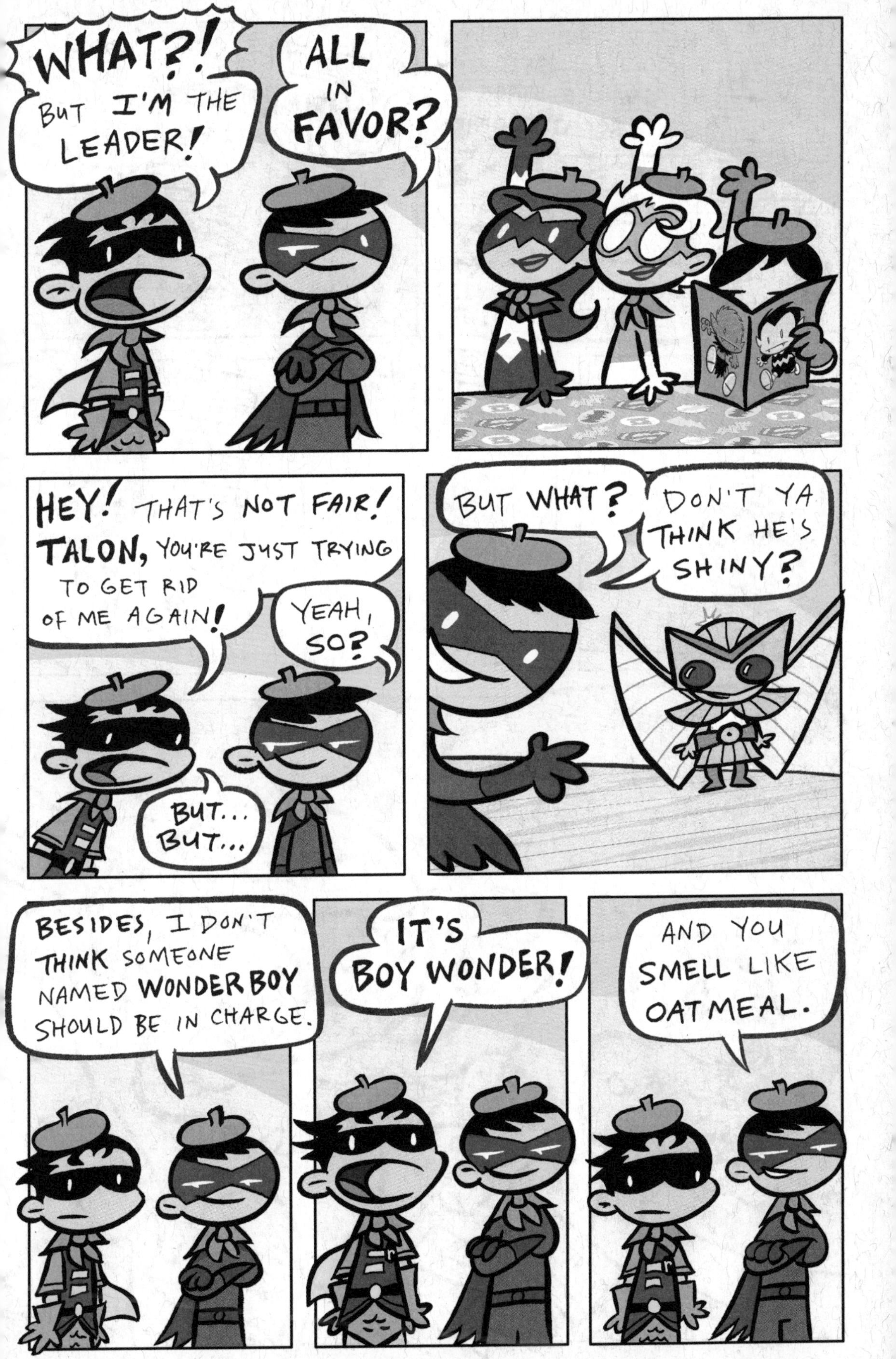
WHAT?! BUT I'M THE LEADER!
ALL IN FAVOR?
HEY! THAT'S NOT FAIR! TALON, YOU'RE JUST TRYING TO GET RID OF ME AGAIN!
YEAH, SO?
BUT... BUT...
BUT WHAT?
DON'T YA THINK HE'S SHINY?
BESIDES, I DON'T THINK SOMEONE NAMED WONDER BOY SHOULD BE IN CHARGE.
IT'S BOY WONDER!
AND YOU SMELL LIKE OATMEAL.

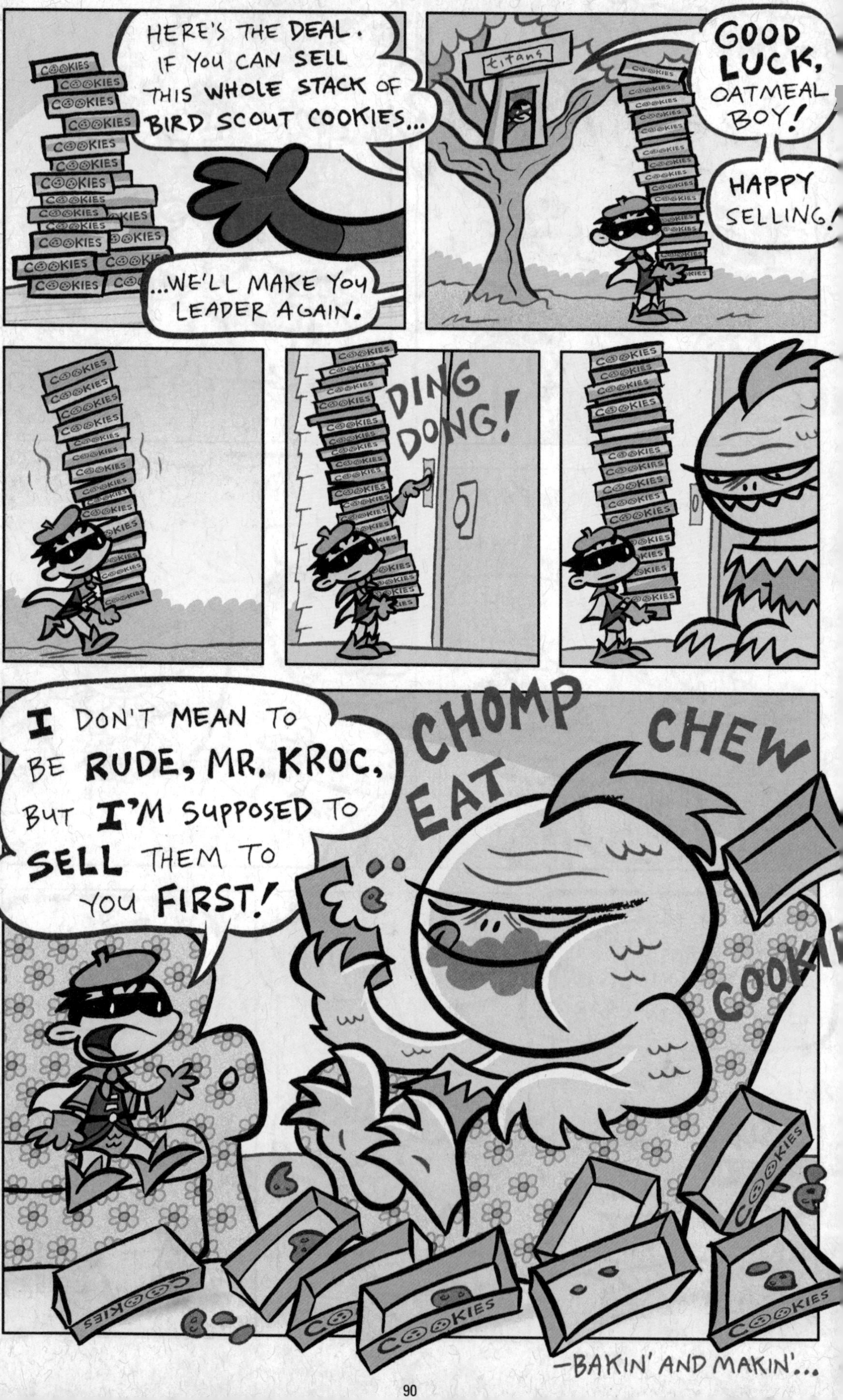
COOKIES
HERE'S THE DEAL. IF YOU CAN SELL THIS WHOLE STACK OF BIRD SCOUT COOKIES...
...WE'LL MAKE YOU LEADER AGAIN.
titans
GOOD LUCK, OATMEAL BOY!
HAPPY SELLING!
DING DONG!
I DON'T MEAN TO BE RUDE, MR. KROC, BUT I'M SUPPOSED TO SELL THEM TO YOU FIRST!
CHOMP
CHEW
EAT
COOKIE
—BAKIN' AND MAKIN'...

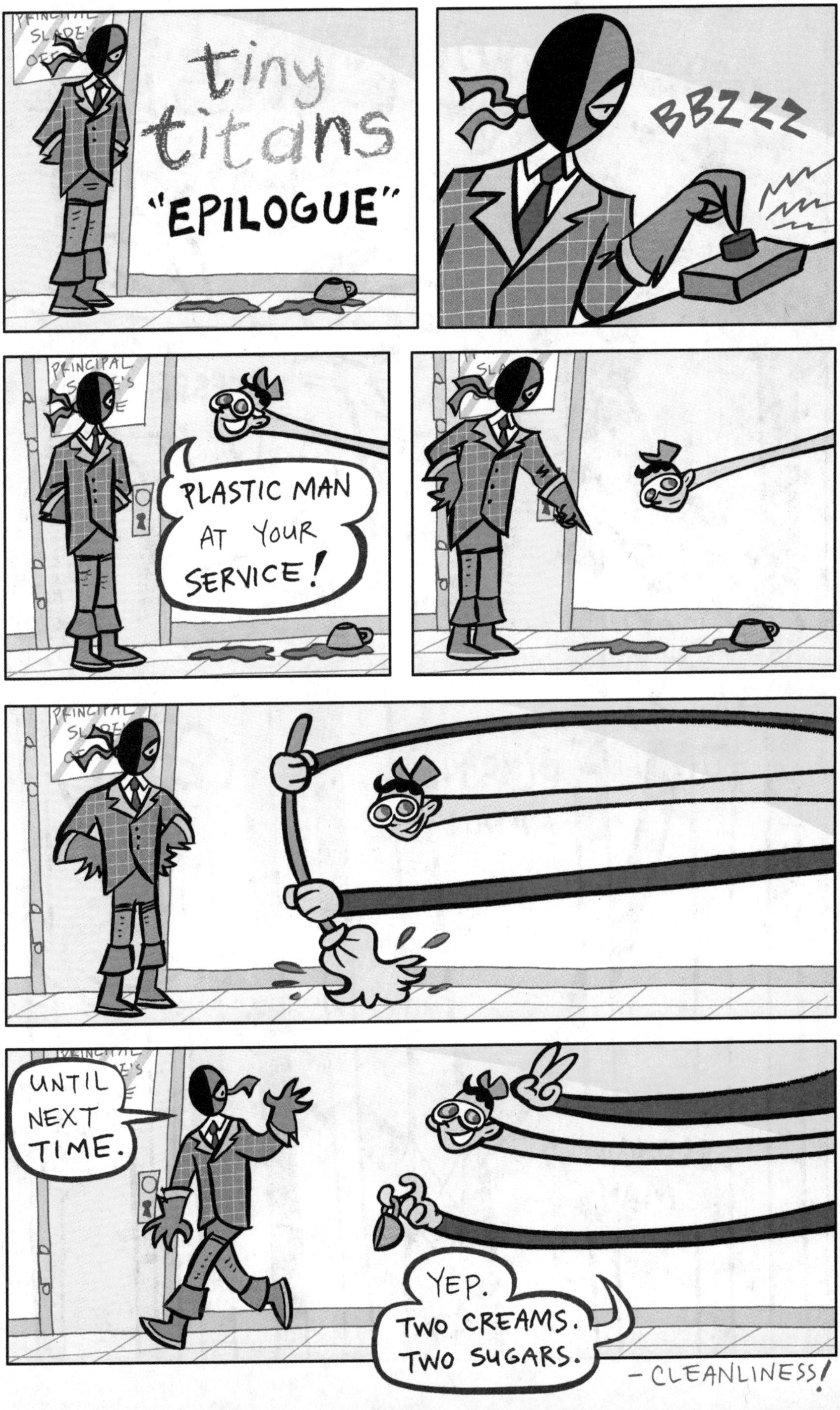
tiny titans
"EPILOGUE"
BBZZZ
PLASTIC MAN AT YOUR SERVICE!
UNTIL NEXT TIME.
YEP. TWO CREAMS. TWO SUGARS.
-CLEANLINESS!

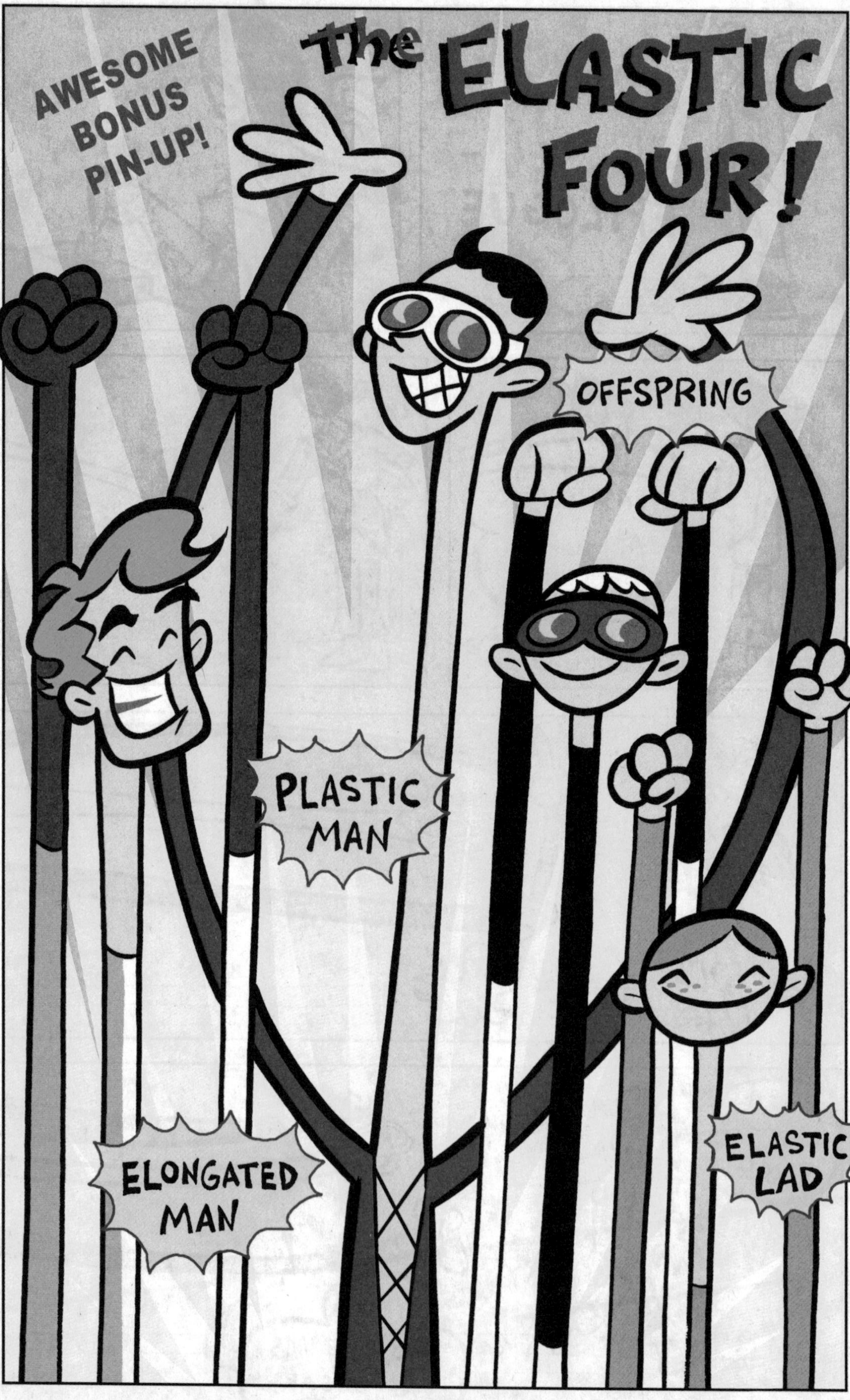
AWESOME BONUS PIN-UP!
The ELASTIC FOUR!
OFFSPRING
PLASTIC MAN
ELONGATED MAN
ELASTIC LAD

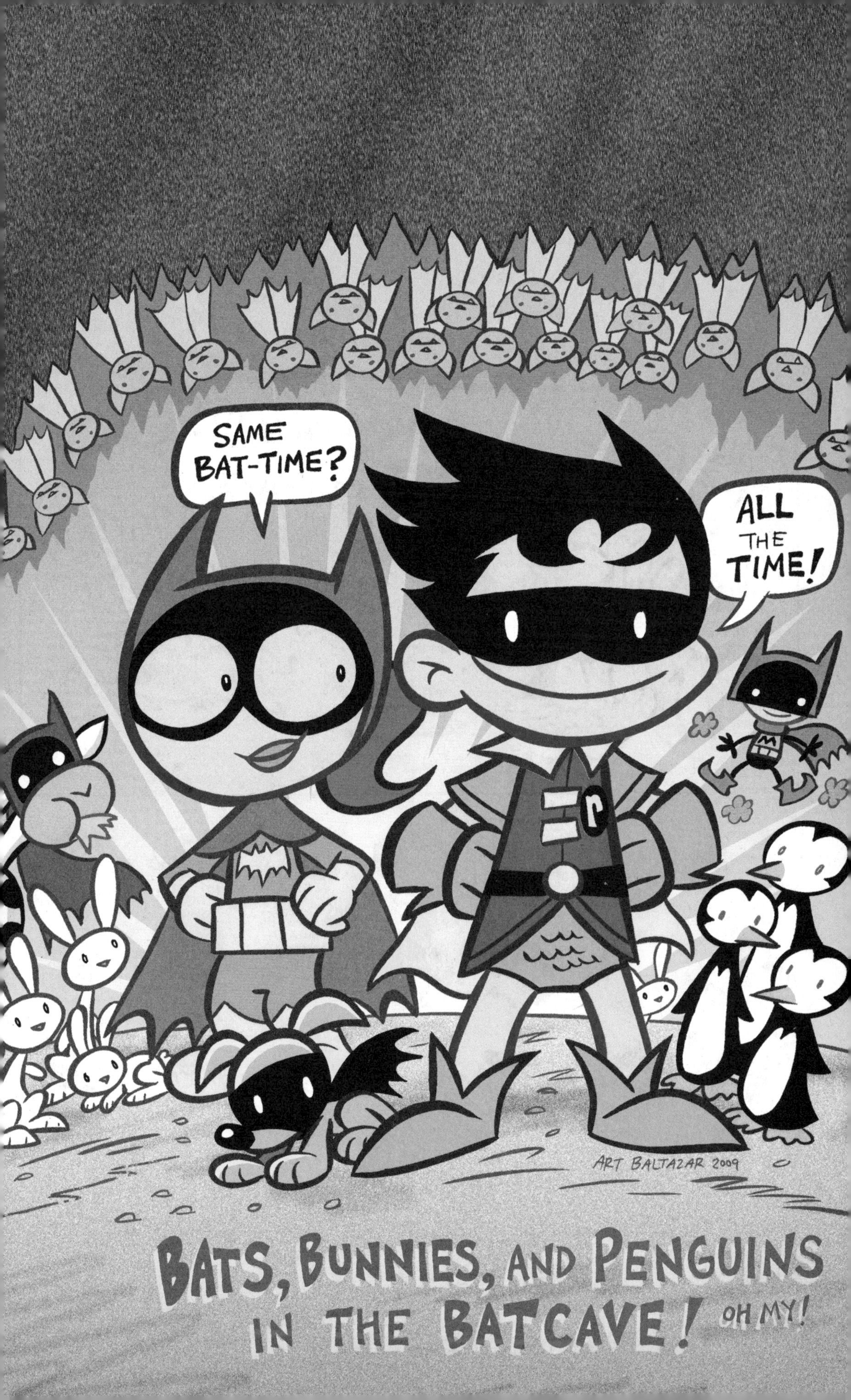
SAME
BAT-TIME?
ALL
THE
TIME!
ART BALTAZAR 2009
BATS, BUNNIES, AND PENGUINS
IN THE BATCAVE! OH MY!

tiny titans

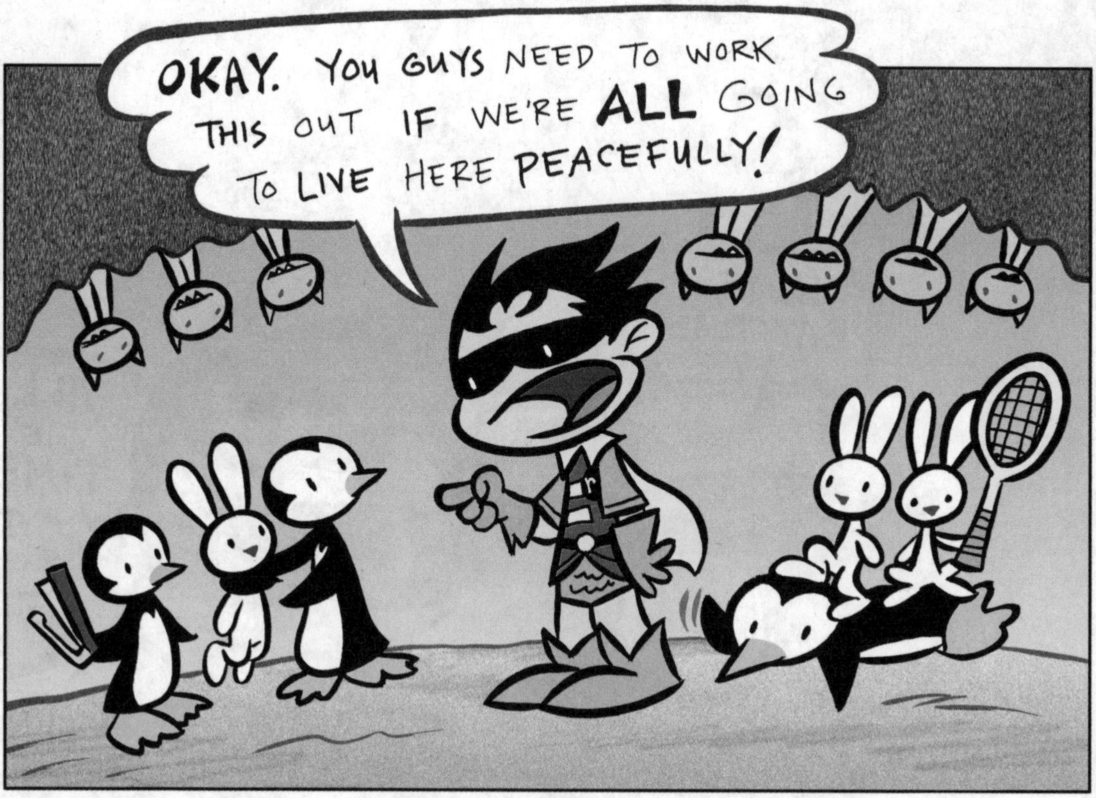
OKAY. YOU GUYS NEED TO WORK THIS OUT IF WE'RE ALL GOING TO LIVE HERE PEACEFULLY!

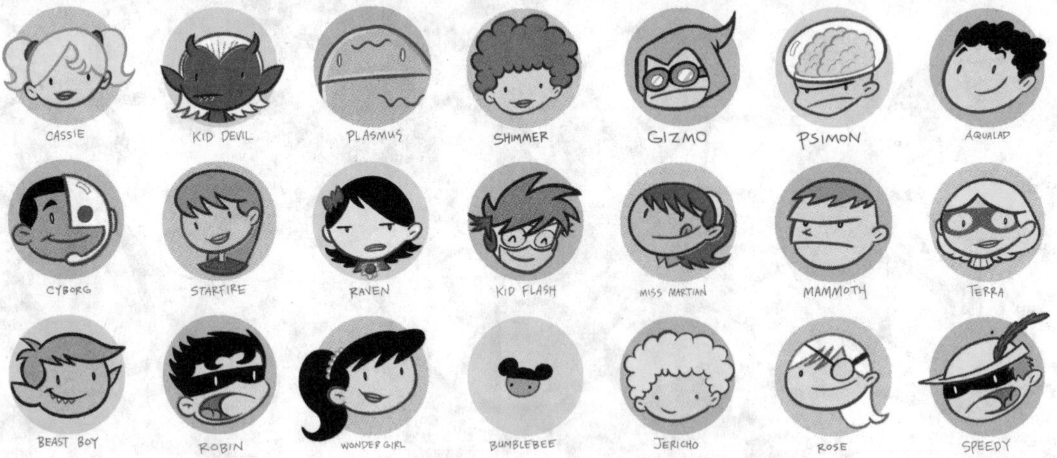
CASSIE
KID DEVIL
PLASMUS
SHIMMER
GIZMO
PSIMON
AQUALAD
CYBORG
STARFIRE
RAVEN
KID FLASH
MISS MARTIAN
MAMMOTH
TERRA
BEAST BOY
ROBIN
WONDER GIRL
BUMBLEBEE
JERICHO
ROSE
SPEEDY

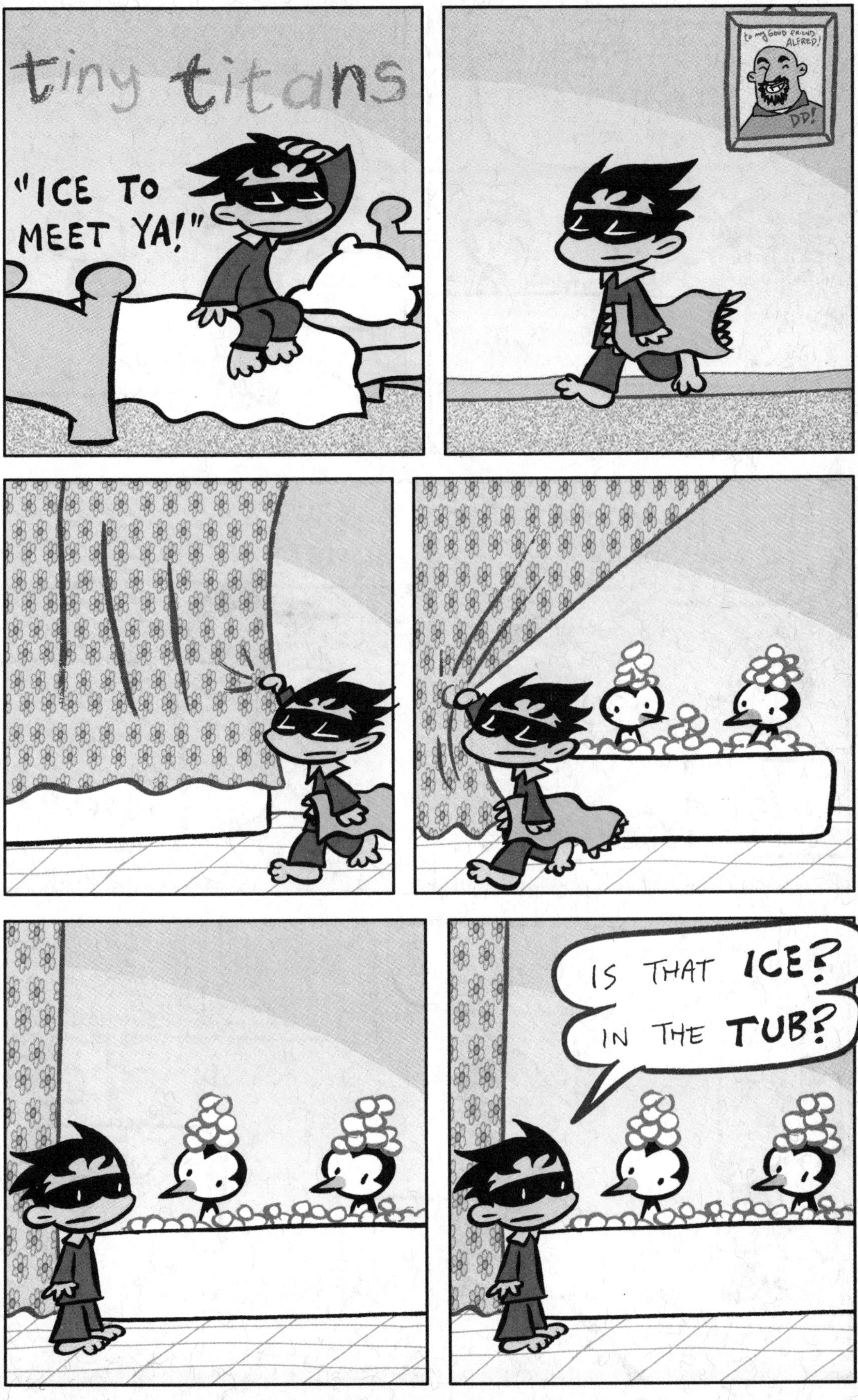
tiny titans
"ICE TO MEET YA!"
to my GOOD FRIEND ALFRED! DD!
IS THAT ICE? IN THE TUB?

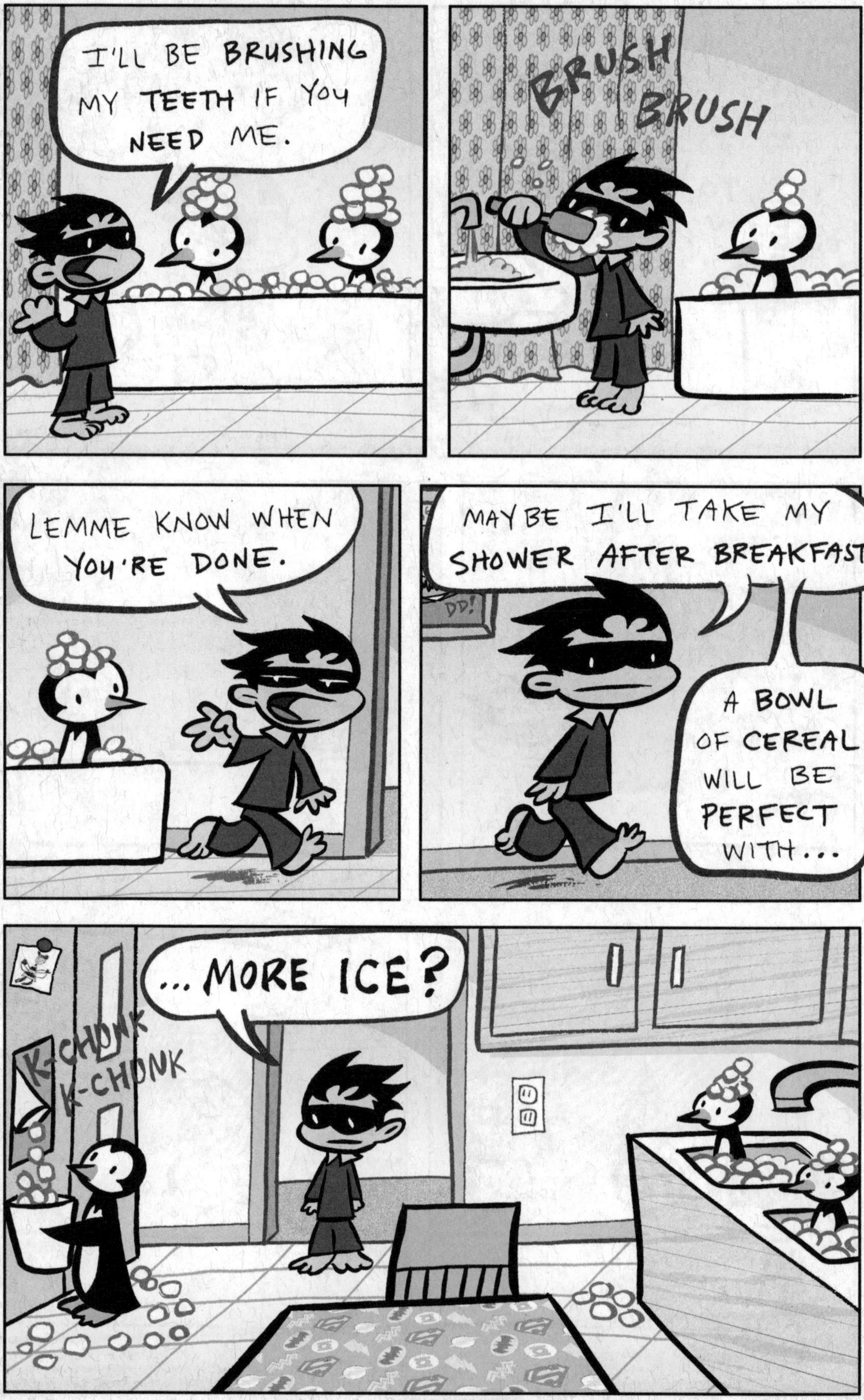
I'LL BE BRUSHING MY TEETH IF YOU NEED ME.
BRUSH BRUSH
LEMME KNOW WHEN YOU'RE DONE.
MAYBE I'LL TAKE MY SHOWER AFTER BREAKFAST.
A BOWL OF CEREAL WILL BE PERFECT WITH...
...MORE ICE?
K-CHONK K-CHONK

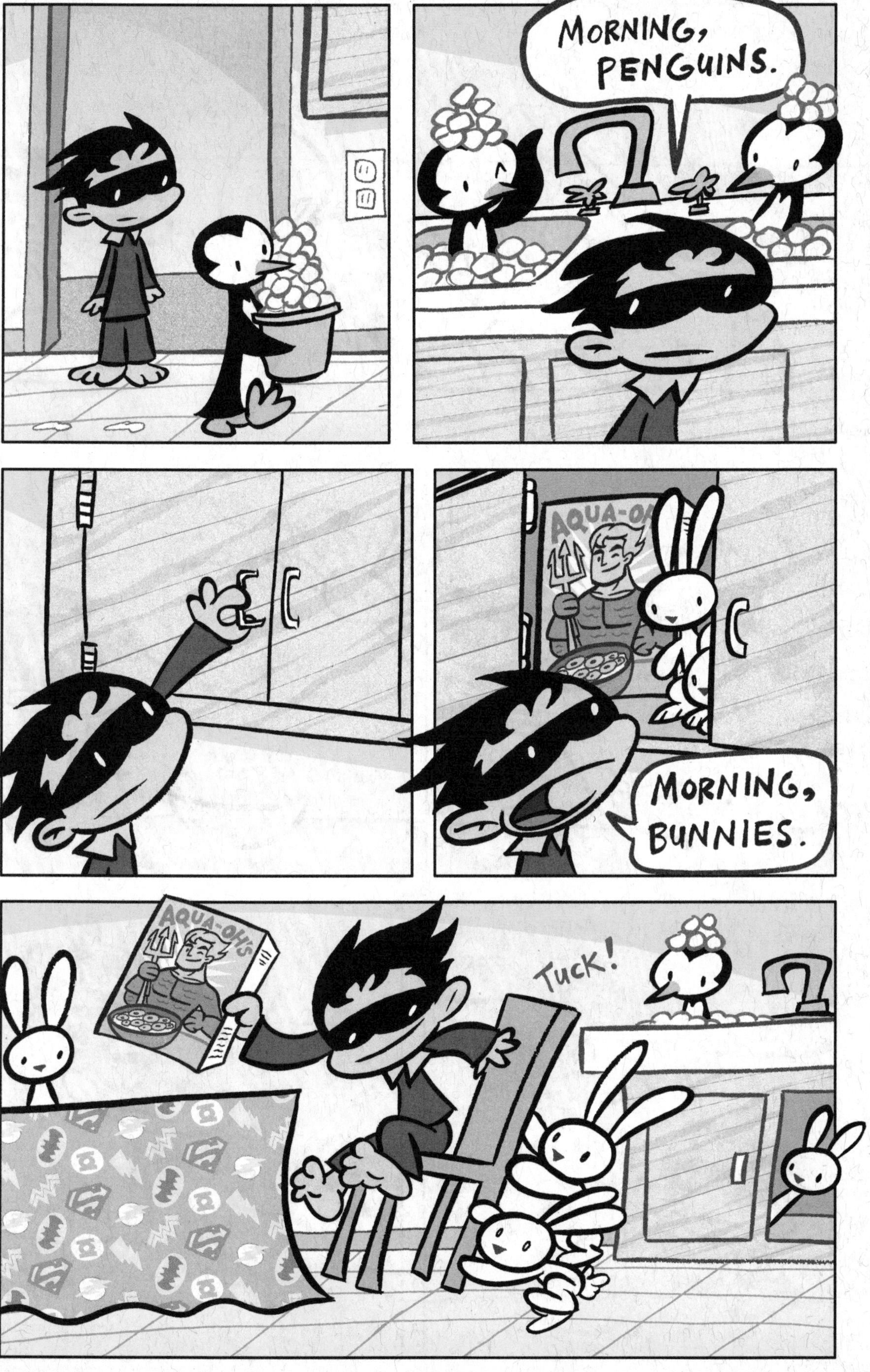
MORNING, PENGUINS.
AQUA-OH'S
MORNING, BUNNIES.
AQUA-OH'S
TUCK!

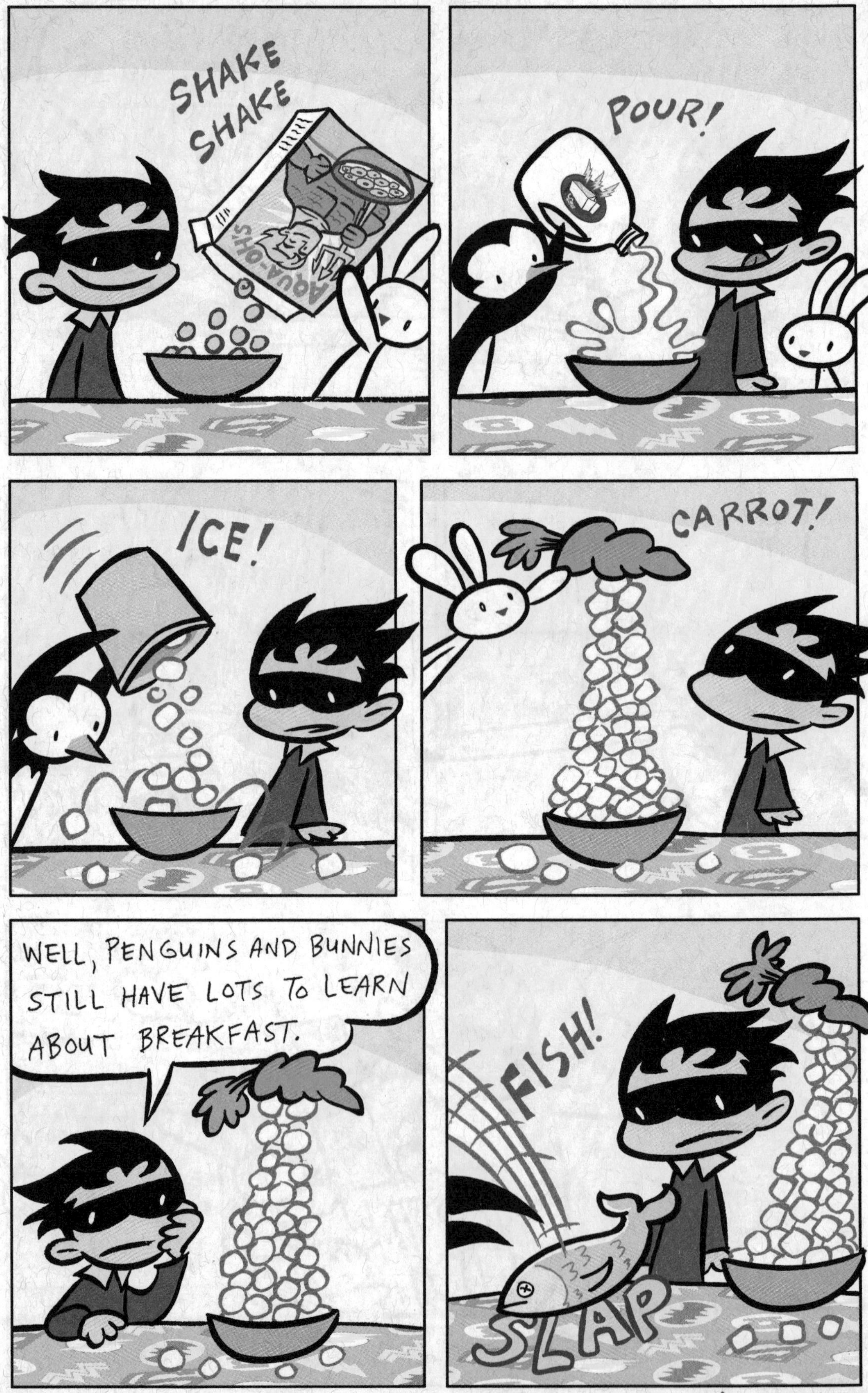
SHAKE
SHAKE
AQUA-OHS
POUR!
ICE!
CARROT!
WELL, PENGUINS AND BUNNIES STILL HAVE LOTS TO LEARN ABOUT BREAKFAST.
FISH!
SLAP
-NO THANKS

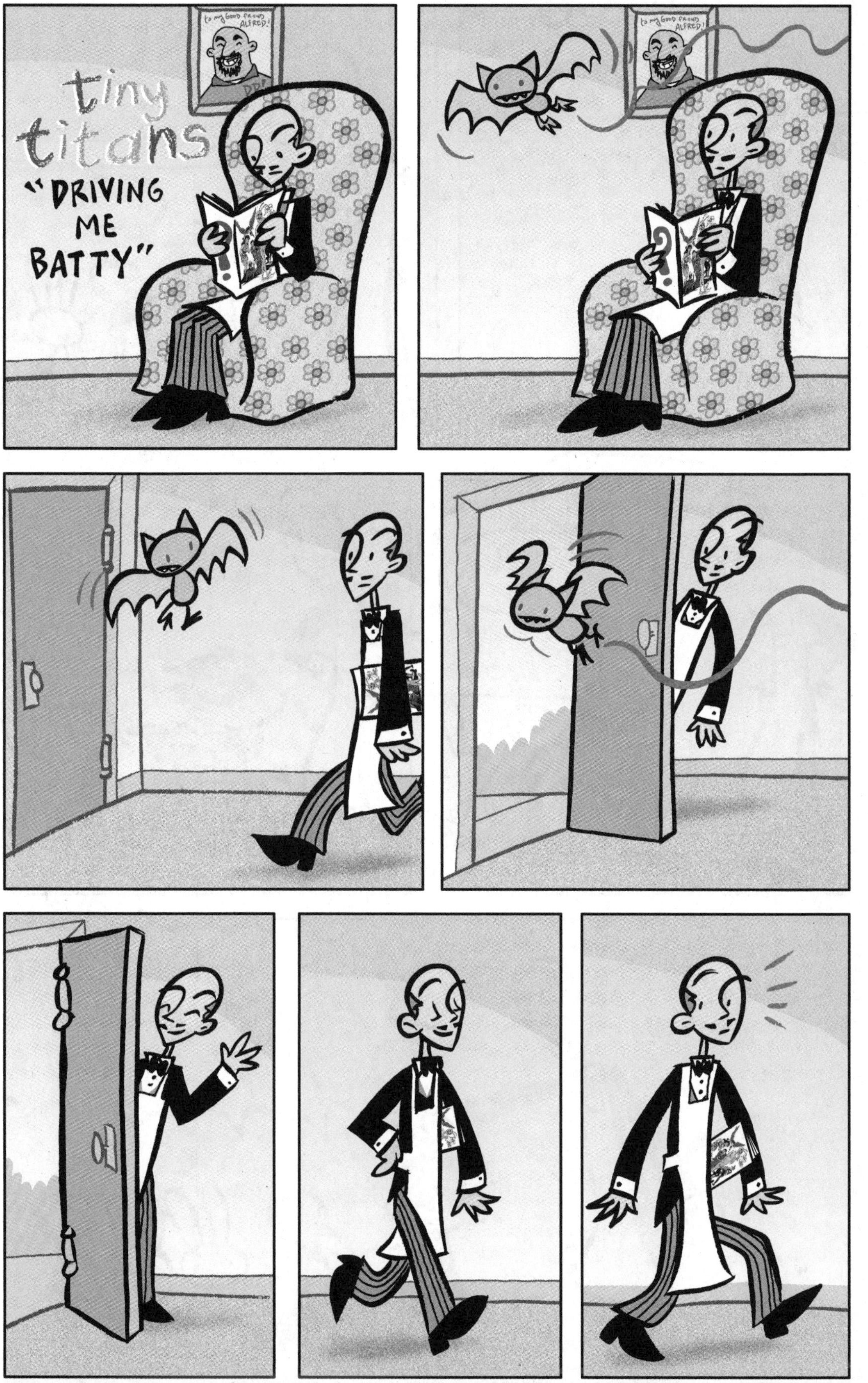
tiny titans
"DRIVING ME BATTY"
to my GOOD FRIEND ALFRED!

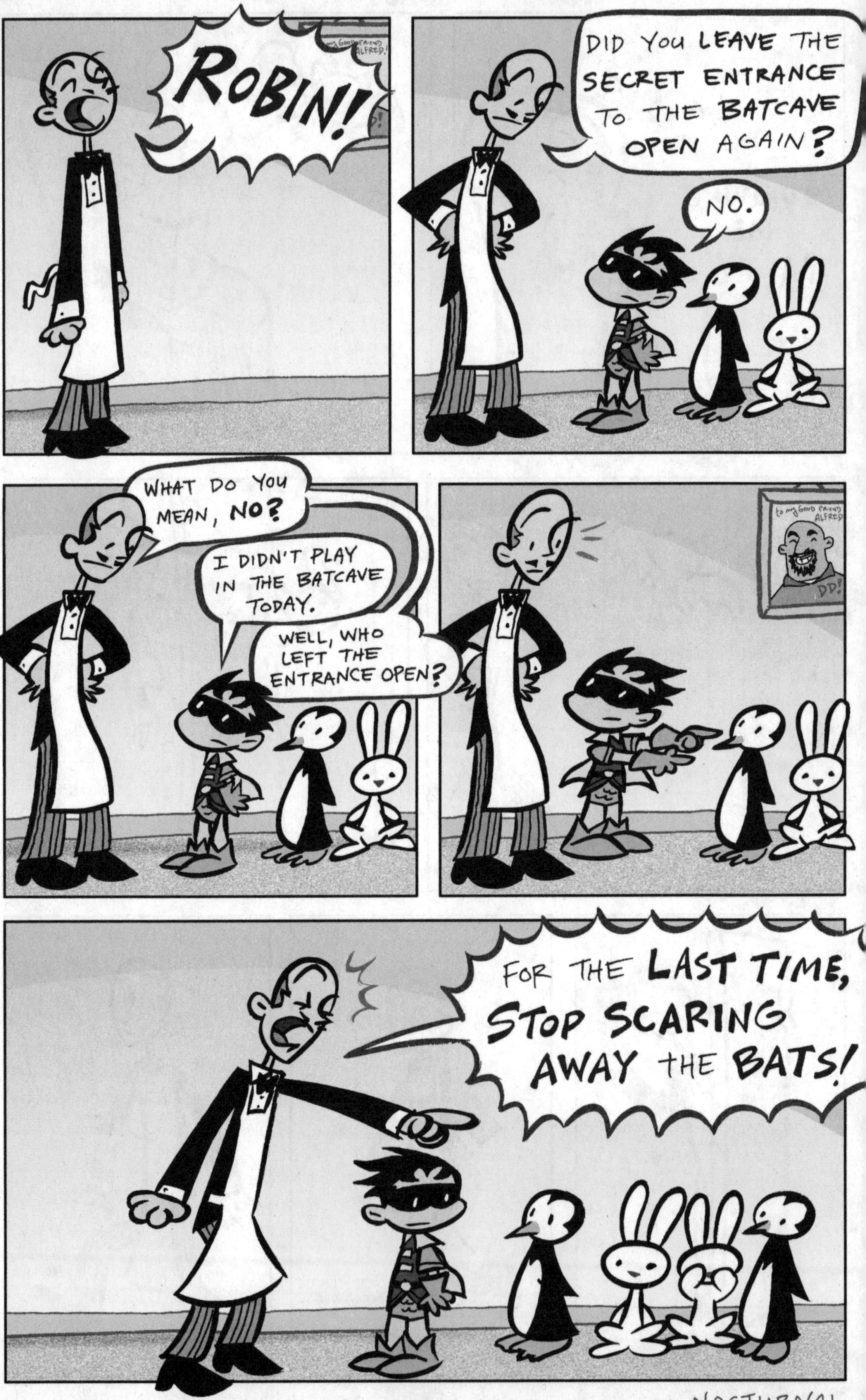
ROBIN!
DID YOU LEAVE THE SECRET ENTRANCE TO THE BATCAVE OPEN AGAIN?
NO.
WHAT DO YOU MEAN, NO?
I DIDN'T PLAY IN THE BATCAVE TODAY.
WELL, WHO LEFT THE ENTRANCE OPEN?
to my GOOD FRIEND ALFRED
DD!
FOR THE LAST TIME, STOP SCARING AWAY THE BATS!

—NOCTURNAL

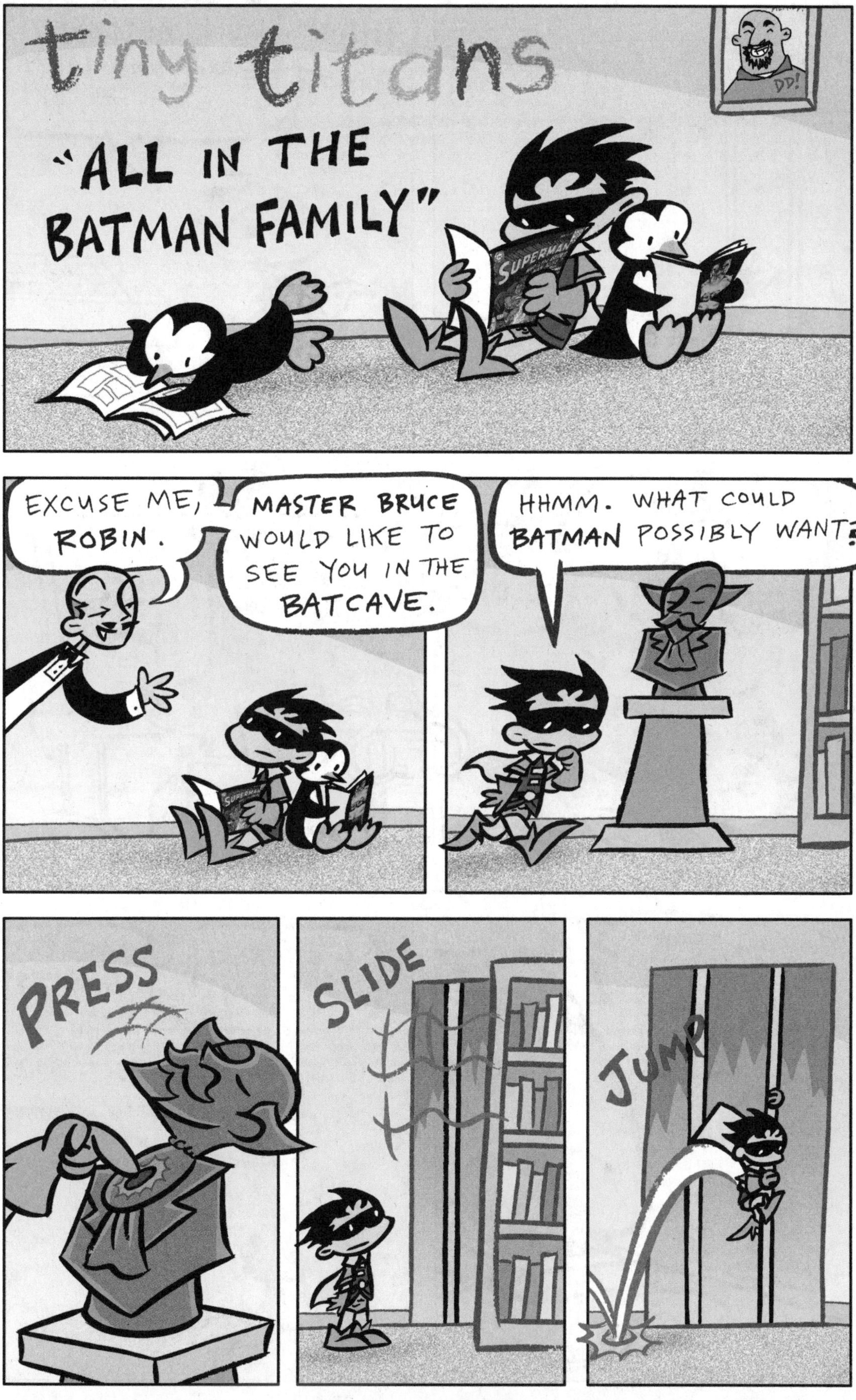
tiny titans
"ALL IN THE BATMAN FAMILY"
SUPERMAN
DD!
EXCUSE ME, ROBIN.
MASTER BRUCE WOULD LIKE TO SEE YOU IN THE BATCAVE.
HHMM. WHAT COULD BATMAN POSSIBLY WANT?
PRESS
SLIDE
JUMP

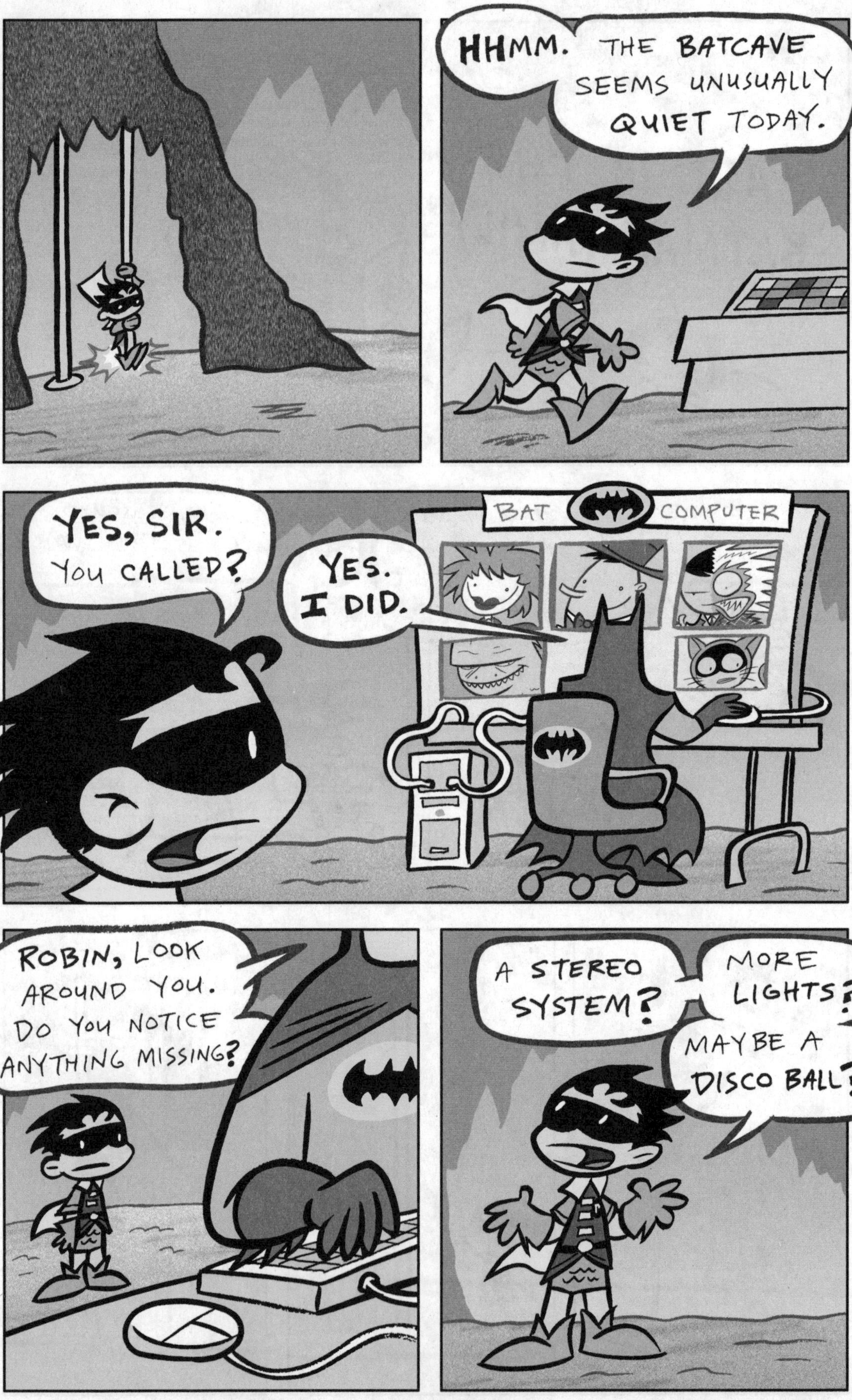

HHMM. THE BATCAVE SEEMS UNUSUALLY QUIET TODAY.
YES, SIR. YOU CALLED?
YES. I DID.
BAT COMPUTER
ROBIN, LOOK AROUND YOU. DO YOU NOTICE ANYTHING MISSING?
A STEREO SYSTEM?
MORE LIGHTS?
MAYBE A DISCO BALL?

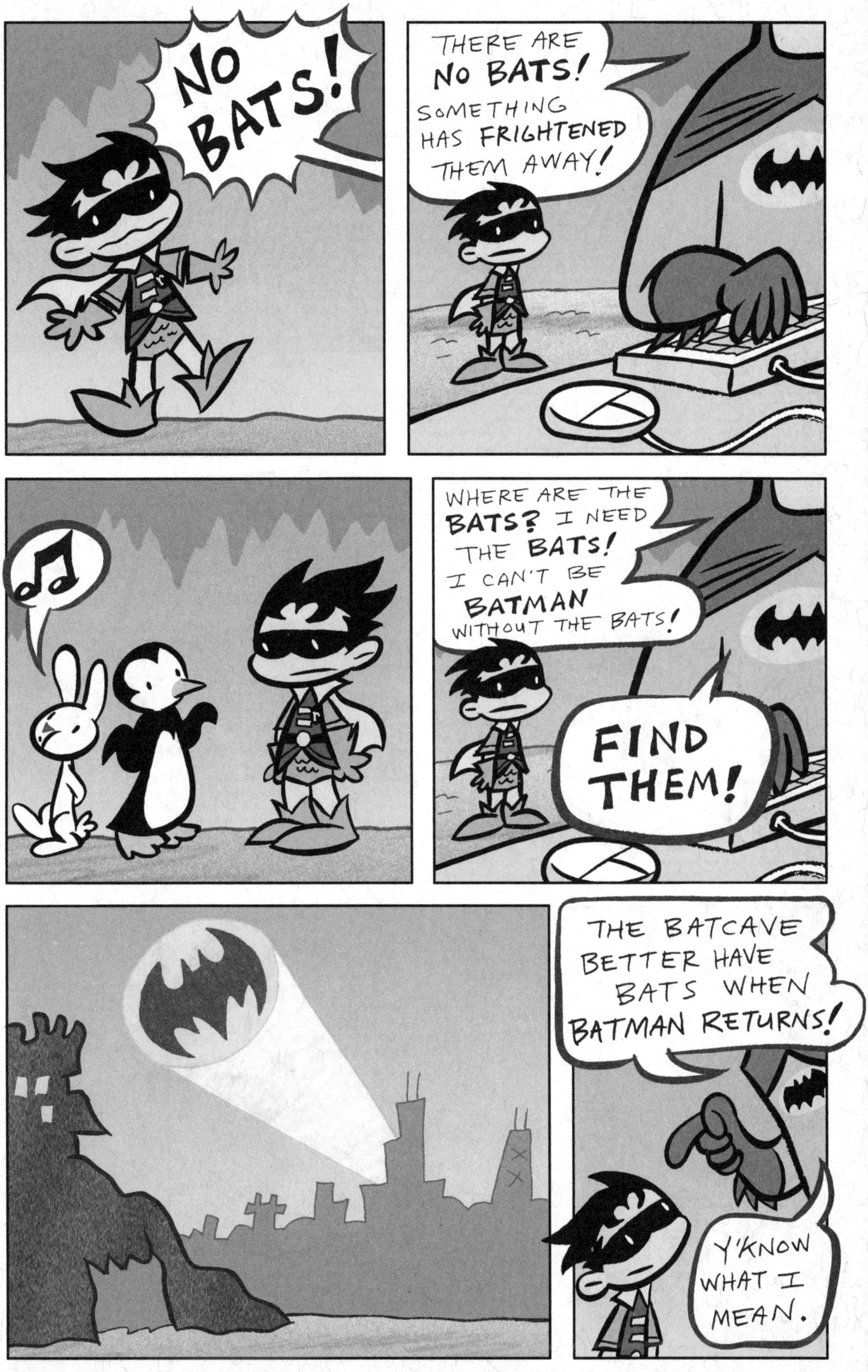
NO BATS!
THERE ARE NO BATS! SOMETHING HAS FRIGHTENED THEM AWAY!
WHERE ARE THE BATS? I NEED THE BATS! I CAN'T BE BATMAN WITHOUT THE BATS!
FIND THEM!
THE BATCAVE BETTER HAVE BATS WHEN BATMAN RETURNS!
Y'KNOW WHAT I MEAN.

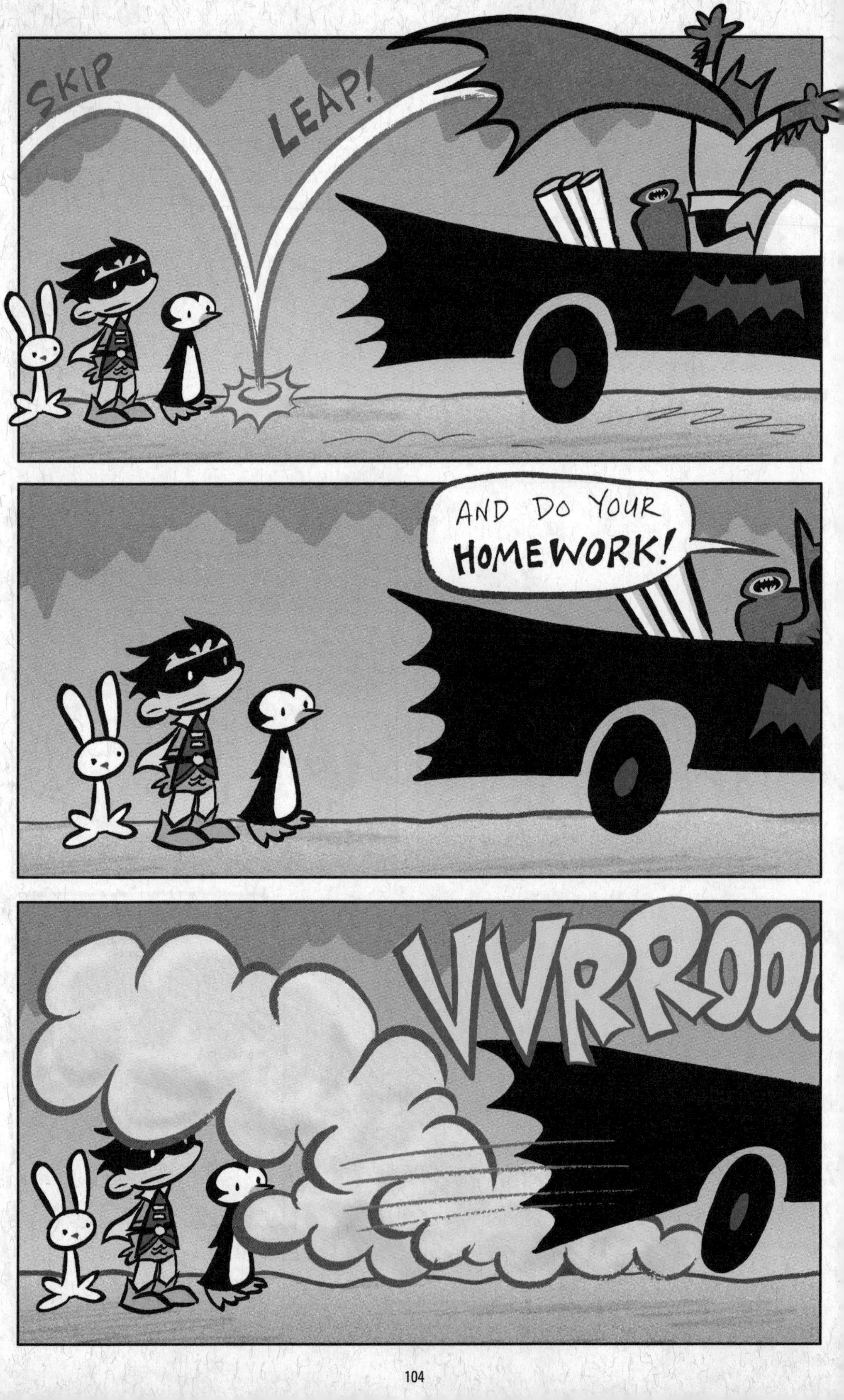
SKIP
LEAP!
AND DO YOUR HOMEWORK!
VVRROO

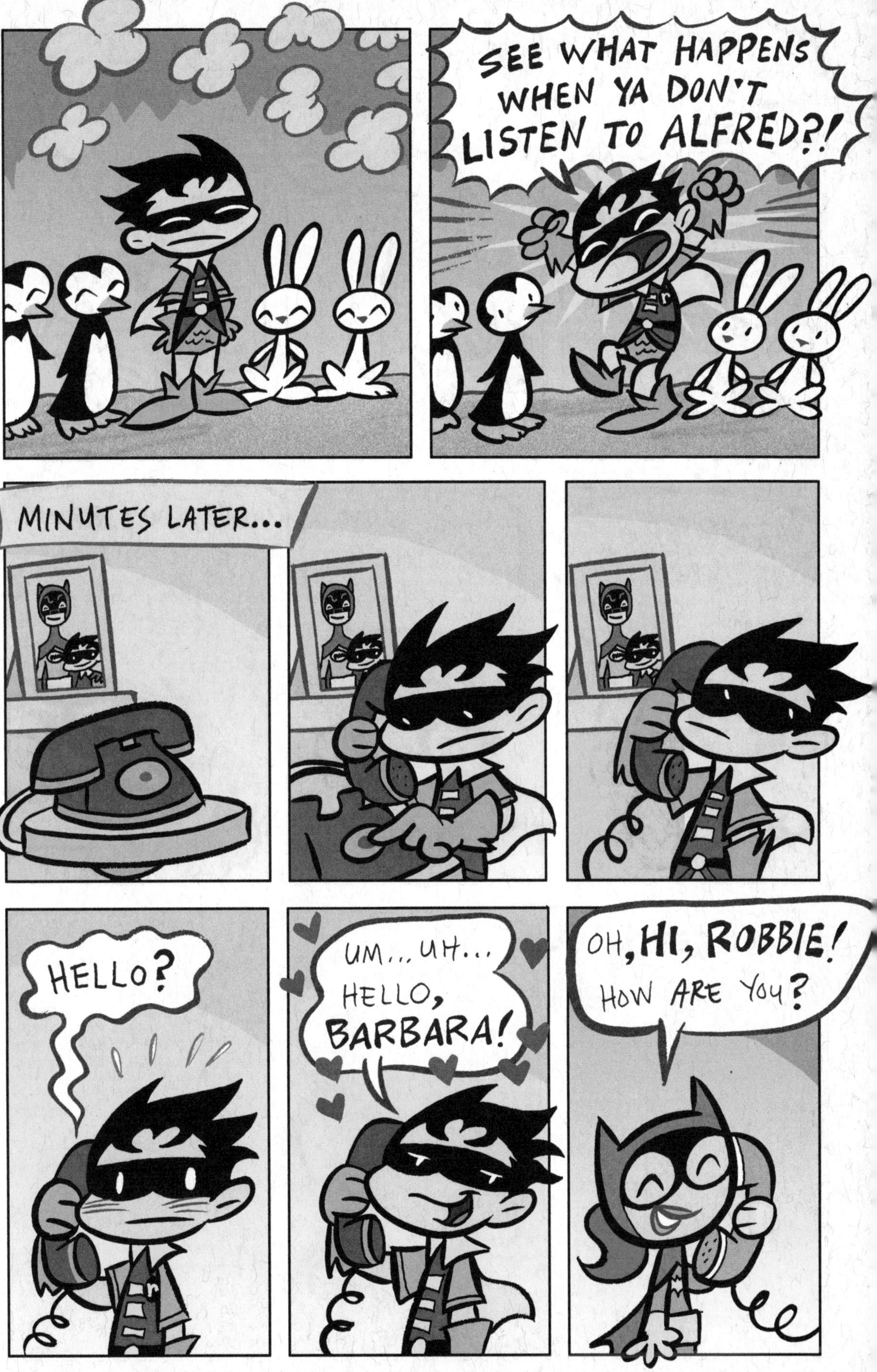
SEE WHAT HAPPENS WHEN YA DON'T LISTEN TO ALFRED?!
MINUTES LATER...
HELLO?
UM... UH... HELLO, BARBARA!
OH, HI, ROBBIE! HOW ARE YOU?

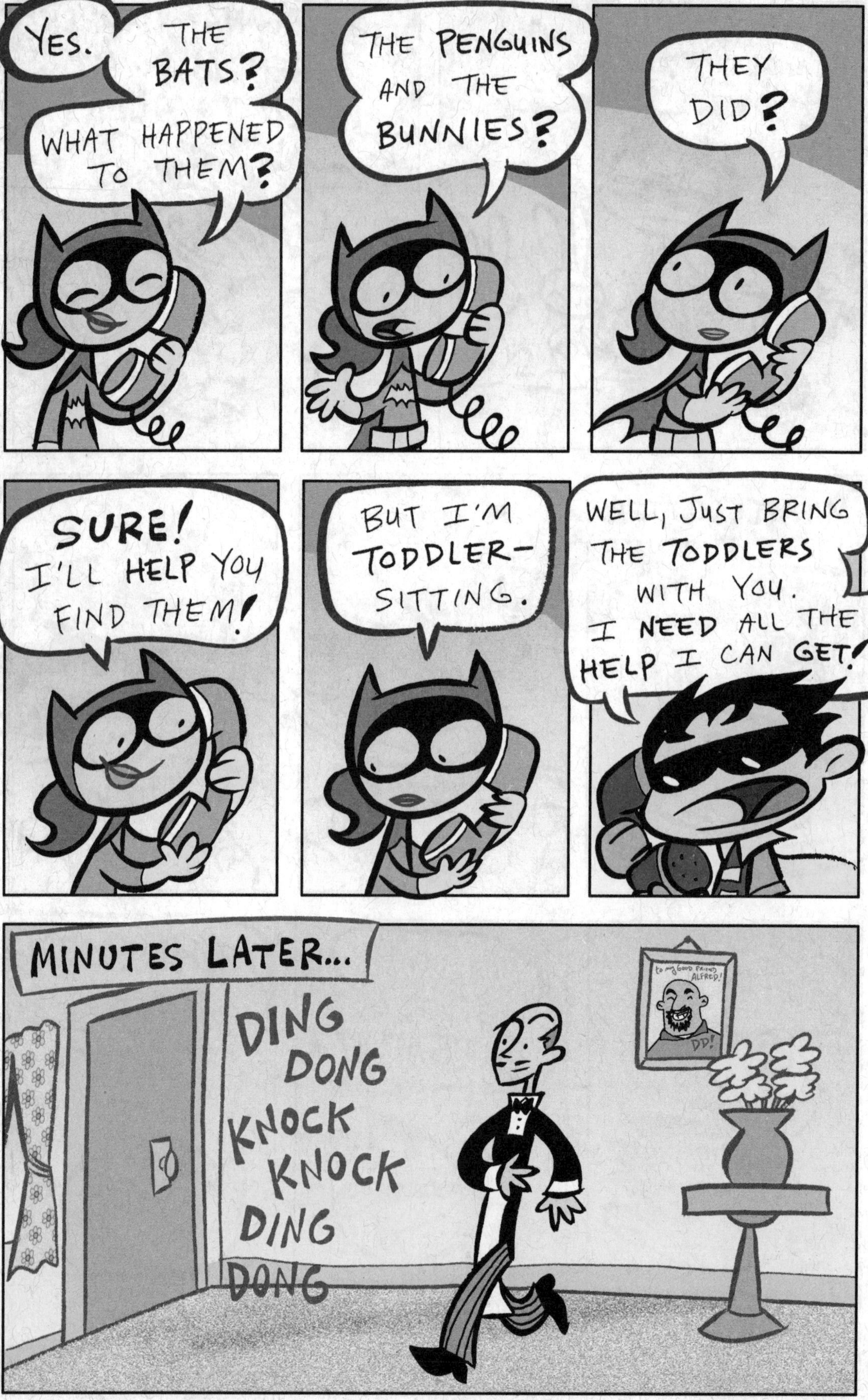
YES.
THE BATS?
WHAT HAPPENED TO THEM?
THE PENGUINS AND THE BUNNIES?
THEY DID?
SURE! I'LL HELP YOU FIND THEM!
BUT I'M TODDLER-SITTING.
WELL, JUST BRING THE TODDLERS WITH YOU. I NEED ALL THE HELP I CAN GET!
MINUTES LATER...
DING DONG KNOCK KNOCK DING DONG
to my GOOD FRIEND ALFRED!
DD!

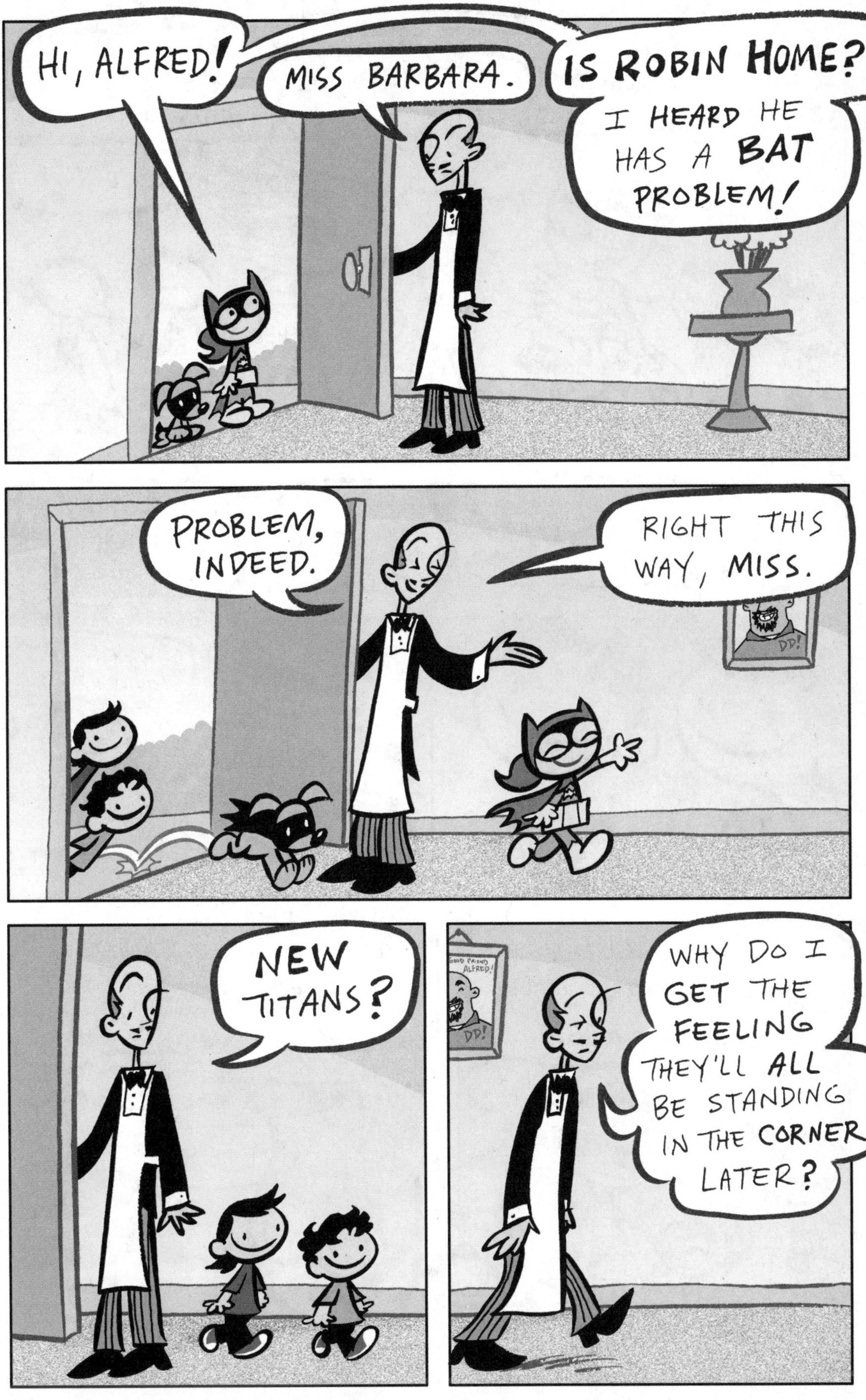
HI, ALFRED!
MISS BARBARA.
IS ROBIN HOME? I HEARD HE HAS A BAT PROBLEM!
PROBLEM, INDEED.
RIGHT THIS WAY, MISS.
NEW TITANS?
WHY DO I GET THE FEELING THEY'LL ALL BE STANDING IN THE CORNER LATER?

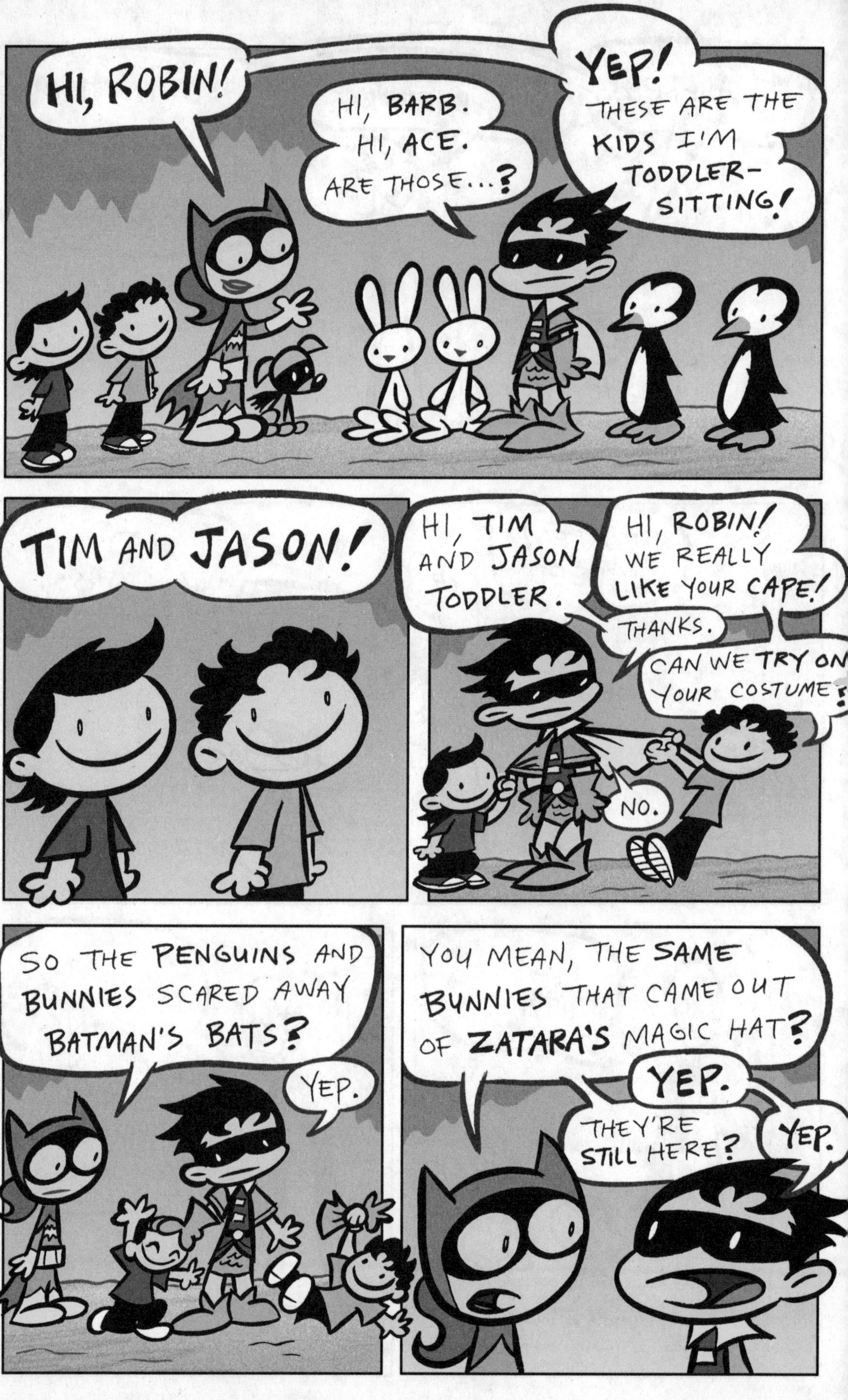
HI, ROBIN!
HI, BARB. HI, ACE. ARE THOSE...?
YEP! THESE ARE THE KIDS I'M TODDLER-SITTING!
TIM AND JASON!
HI, TIM AND JASON TODDLER.
HI, ROBIN! WE REALLY LIKE YOUR CAPE!
THANKS.
CAN WE TRY ON YOUR COSTUME?
NO.
SO THE PENGUINS AND BUNNIES SCARED AWAY BATMAN'S BATS?
YEP.
YOU MEAN, THE SAME BUNNIES THAT CAME OUT OF ZATARA'S MAGIC HAT?
YEP.
THEY'RE STILL HERE?
YEP.

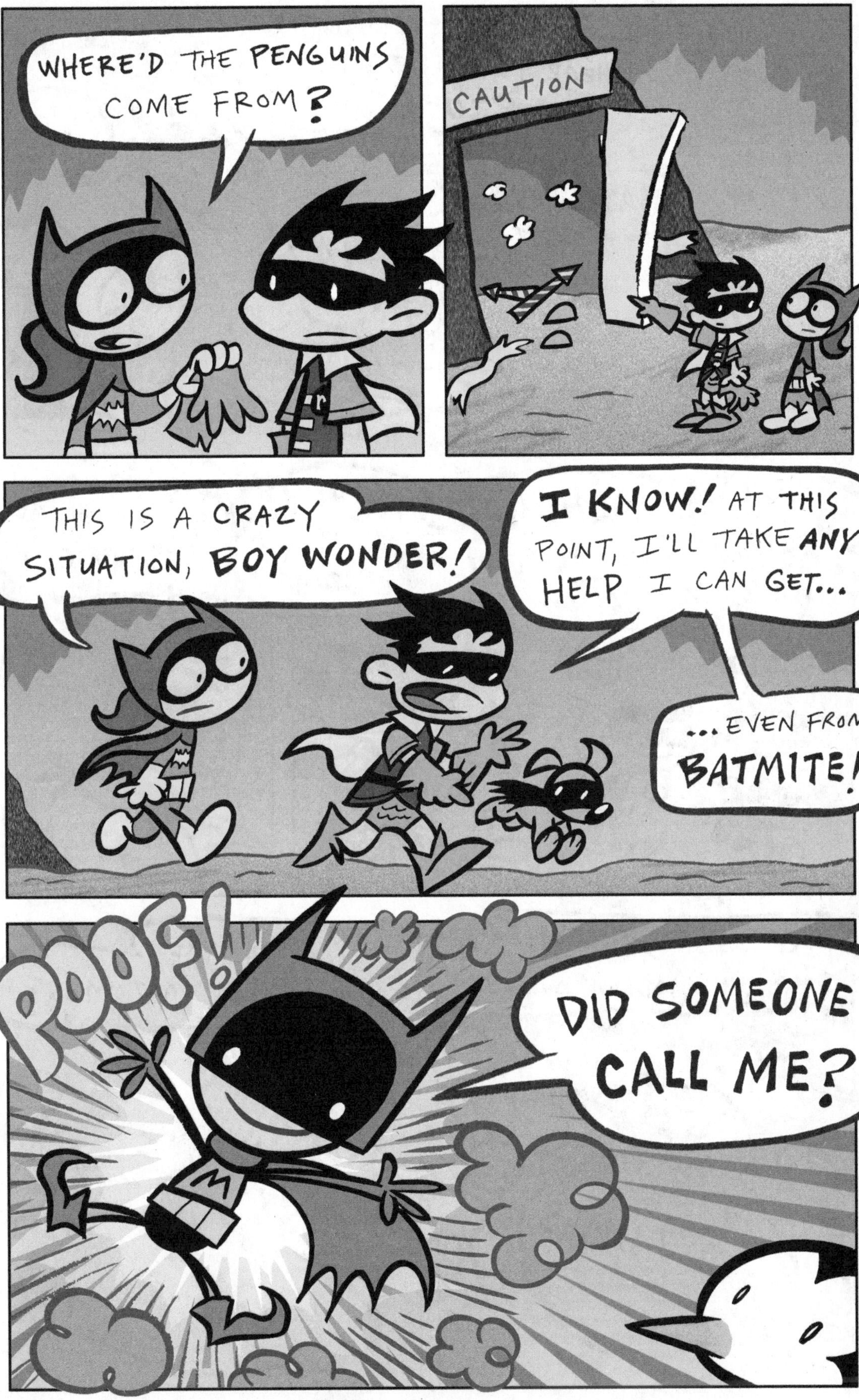
WHERE'D THE PENGUINS COME FROM?
CAUTION
THIS IS A CRAZY SITUATION, BOY WONDER!
I KNOW! AT THIS POINT, I'LL TAKE ANY HELP I CAN GET...
...EVEN FROM BATMITE!
POOF!
DID SOMEONE CALL ME?

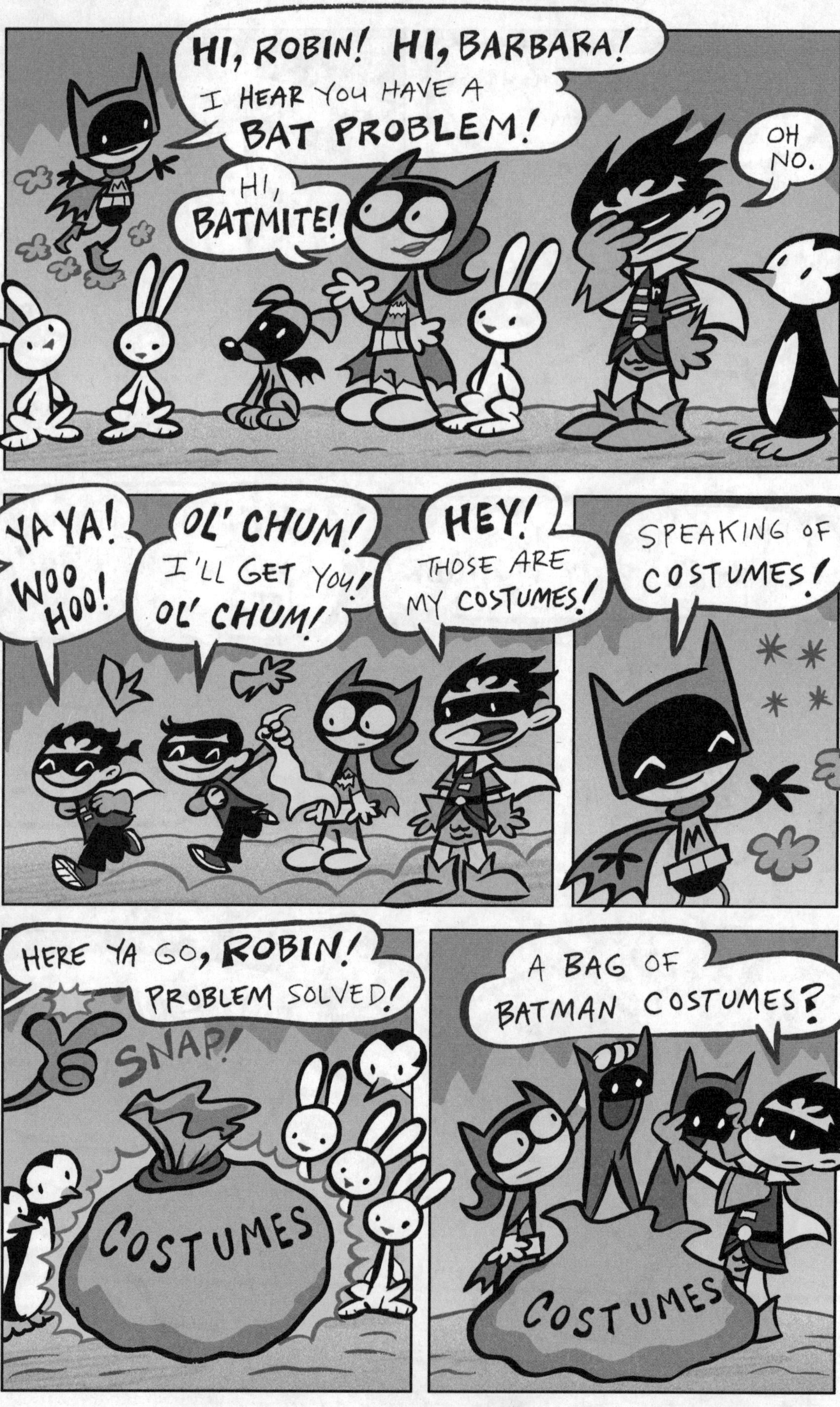
HI, ROBIN! HI, BARBARA! I HEAR YOU HAVE A BAT PROBLEM!
HI, BATMITE!
OH NO.
YAYA! WOO HOO!
OL' CHUM! I'LL GET YOU! OL' CHUM!
HEY! THOSE ARE MY COSTUMES!
SPEAKING OF COSTUMES!
HERE YA GO, ROBIN! PROBLEM SOLVED!
SNAP!
COSTUMES
A BAG OF BATMAN COSTUMES?
COSTUMES

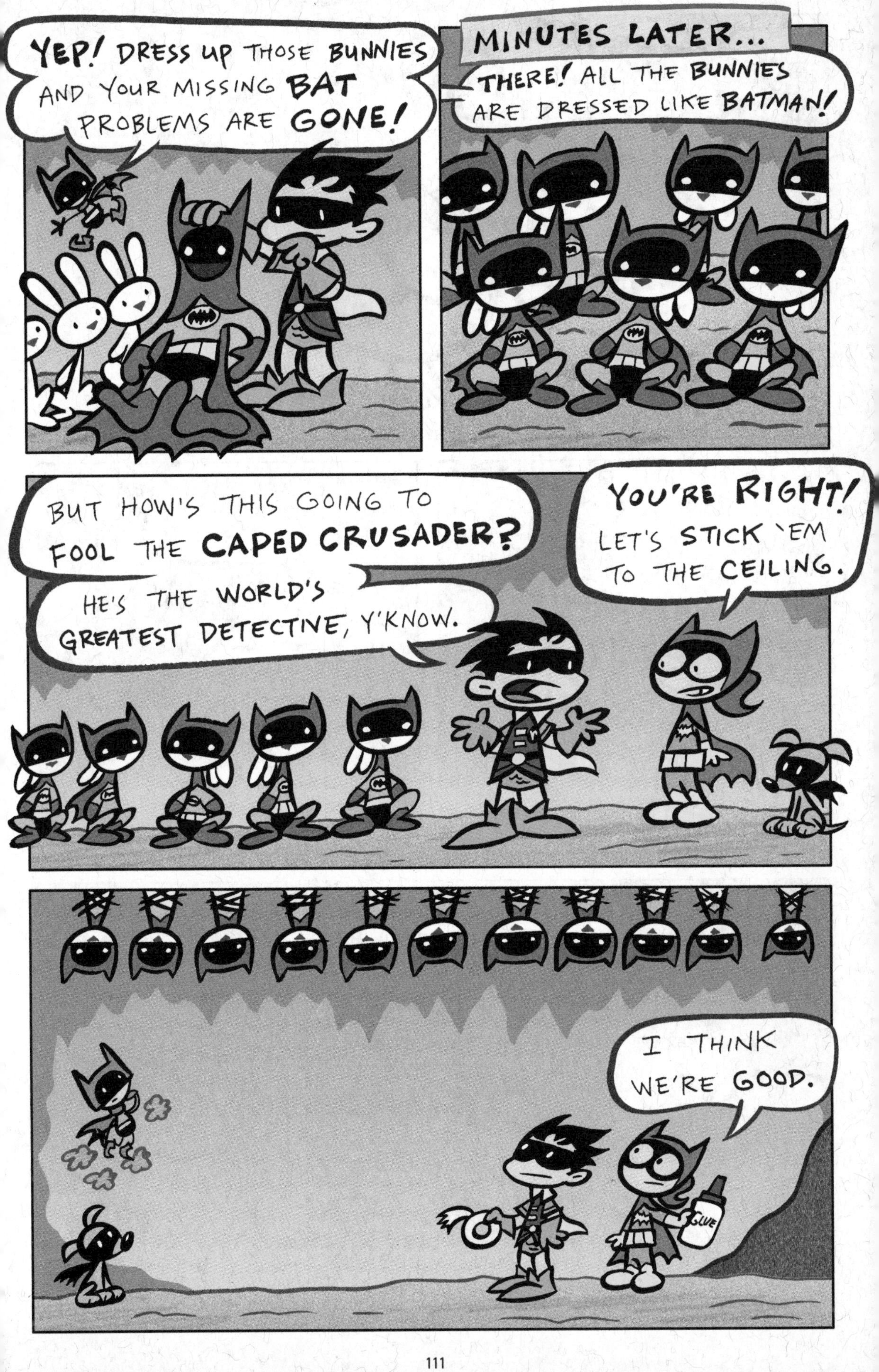
YEP! DRESS UP THOSE BUNNIES AND YOUR MISSING BAT PROBLEMS ARE GONE!
MINUTES LATER...
THERE! ALL THE BUNNIES ARE DRESSED LIKE BATMAN!
BUT HOW'S THIS GOING TO FOOL THE CAPED CRUSADER?
HE'S THE WORLD'S GREATEST DETECTIVE, Y'KNOW.
YOU'RE RIGHT! LET'S STICK 'EM TO THE CEILING.
I THINK WE'RE GOOD.
GLUE

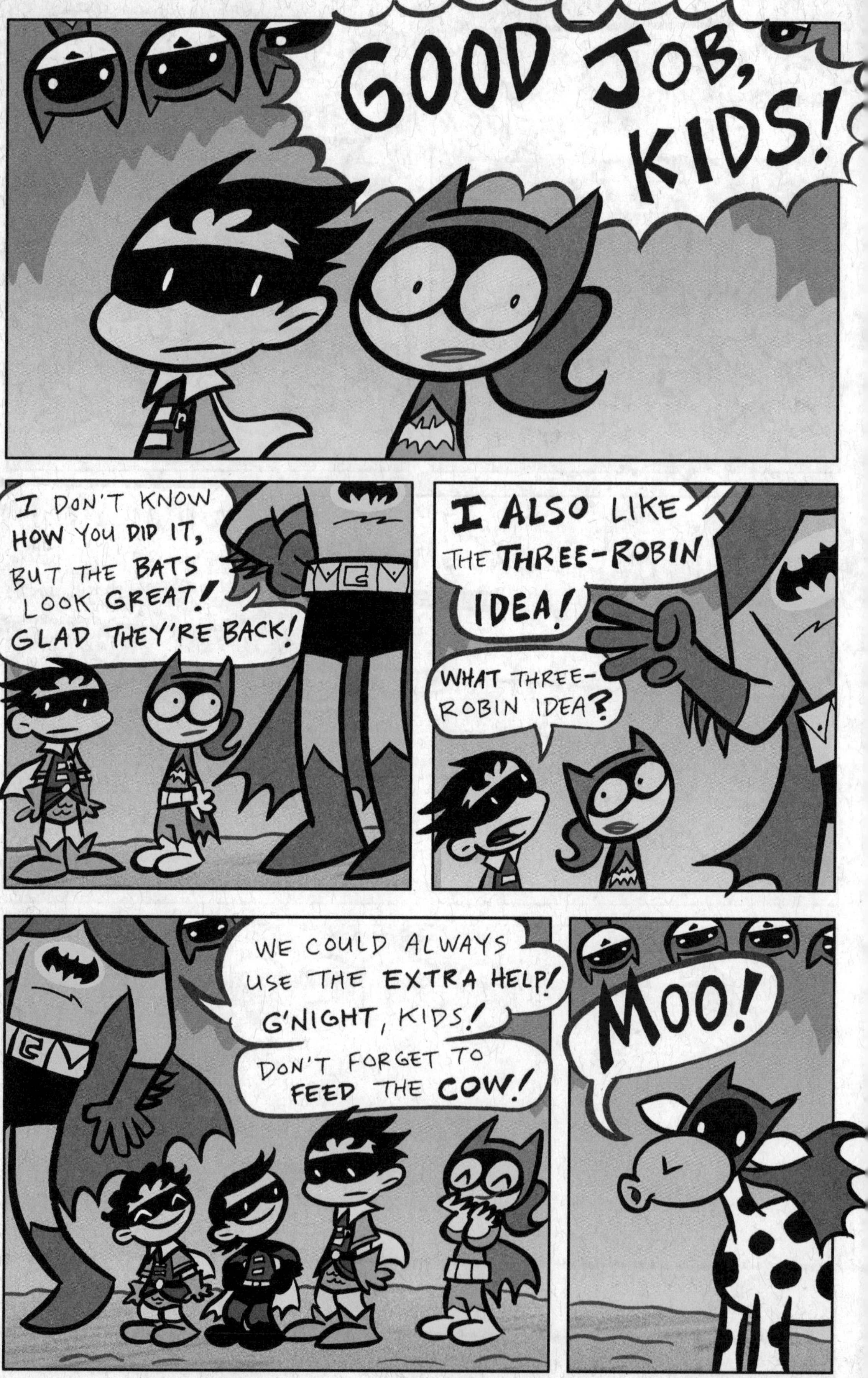
GOOD JOB, KIDS!
I DON'T KNOW HOW YOU DID IT, BUT THE BATS LOOK GREAT! GLAD THEY'RE BACK!
I ALSO LIKE THE THREE-ROBIN IDEA!
WHAT THREE-ROBIN IDEA?
WE COULD ALWAYS USE THE EXTRA HELP! G'NIGHT, KIDS!
DON'T FORGET TO FEED THE COW!
MOO!

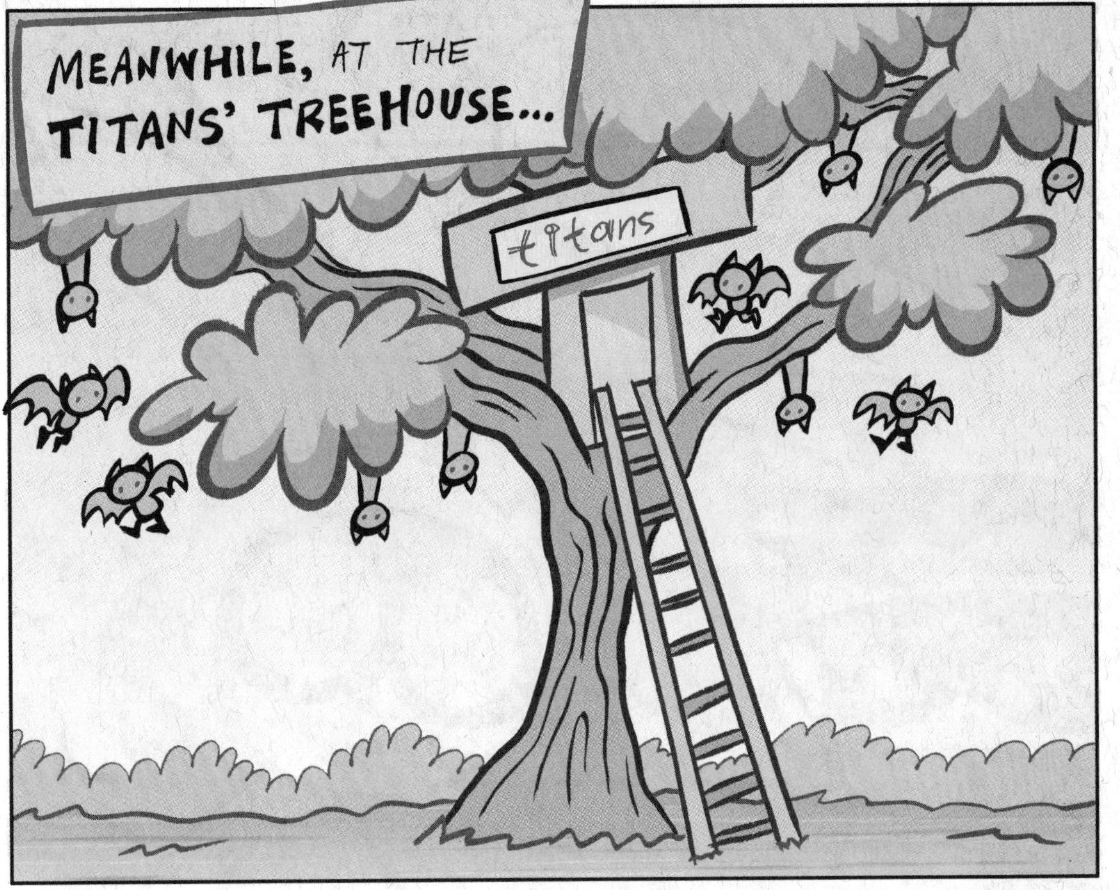
MEANWHILE, AT THE TITANS' TREEHOUSE...
titans

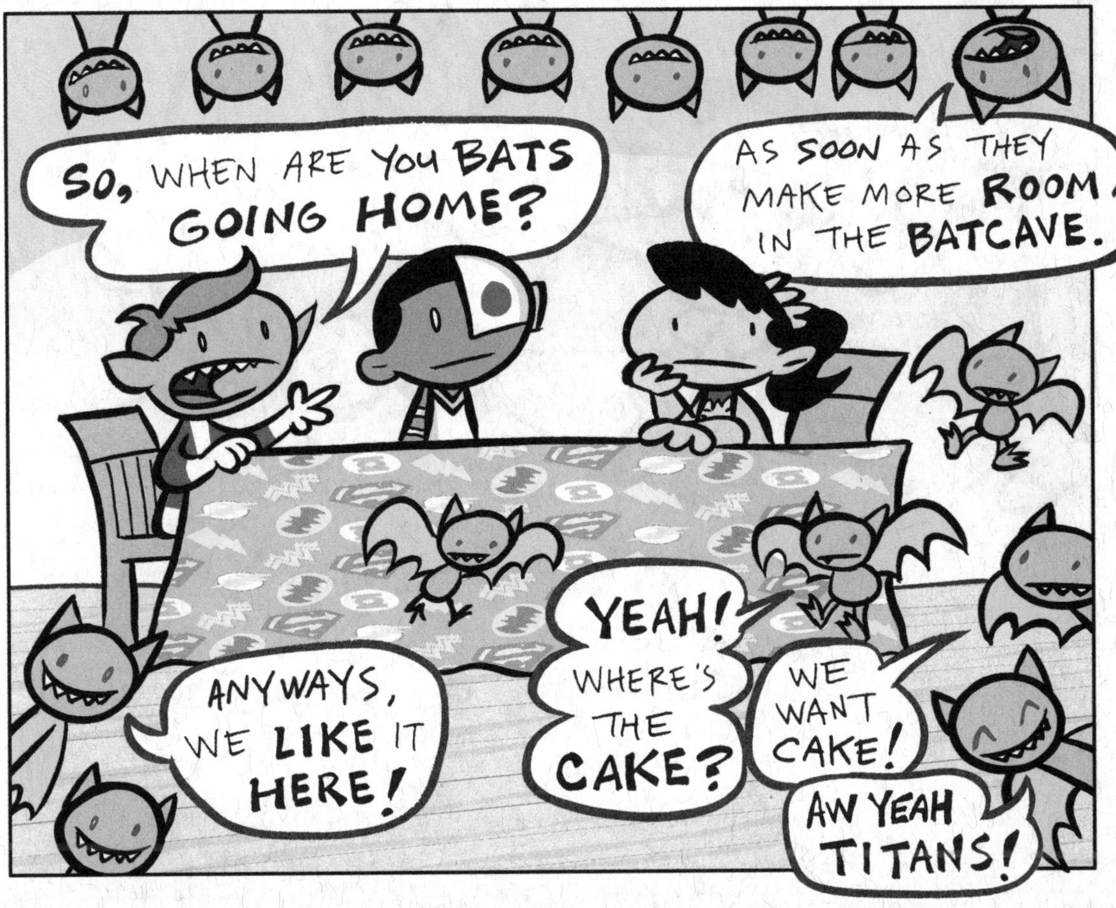
SO, WHEN ARE YOU BATS GOING HOME?
AS SOON AS THEY MAKE MORE ROOM IN THE BATCAVE.
ANYWAYS, WE LIKE IT HERE!
YEAH!
WHERE'S THE CAKE?
WE WANT CAKE!
AW YEAH TITANS!

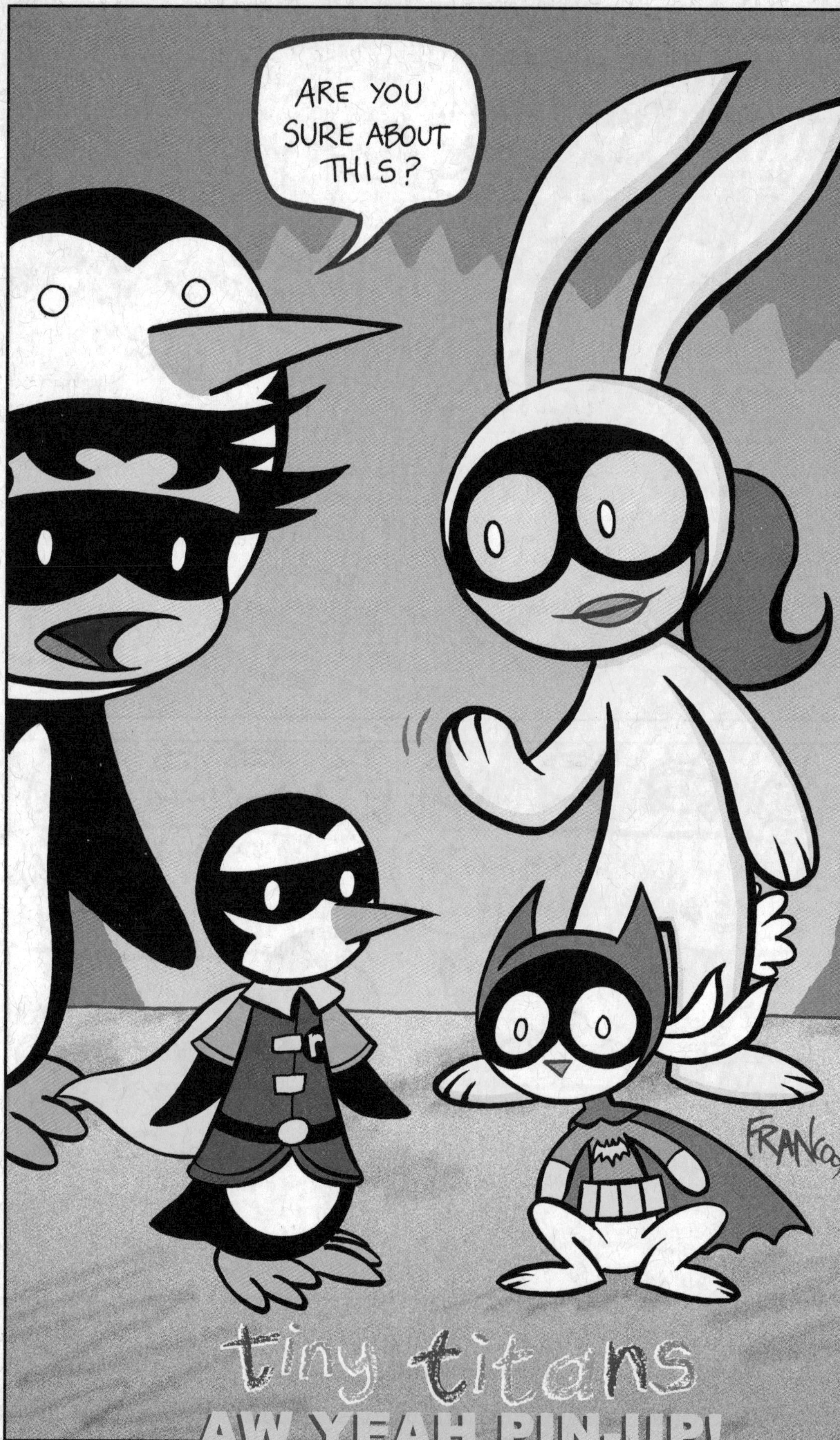
ARE YOU SURE ABOUT THIS?
FRANCO9
tiny titans
AW YEAH PIN-UP!

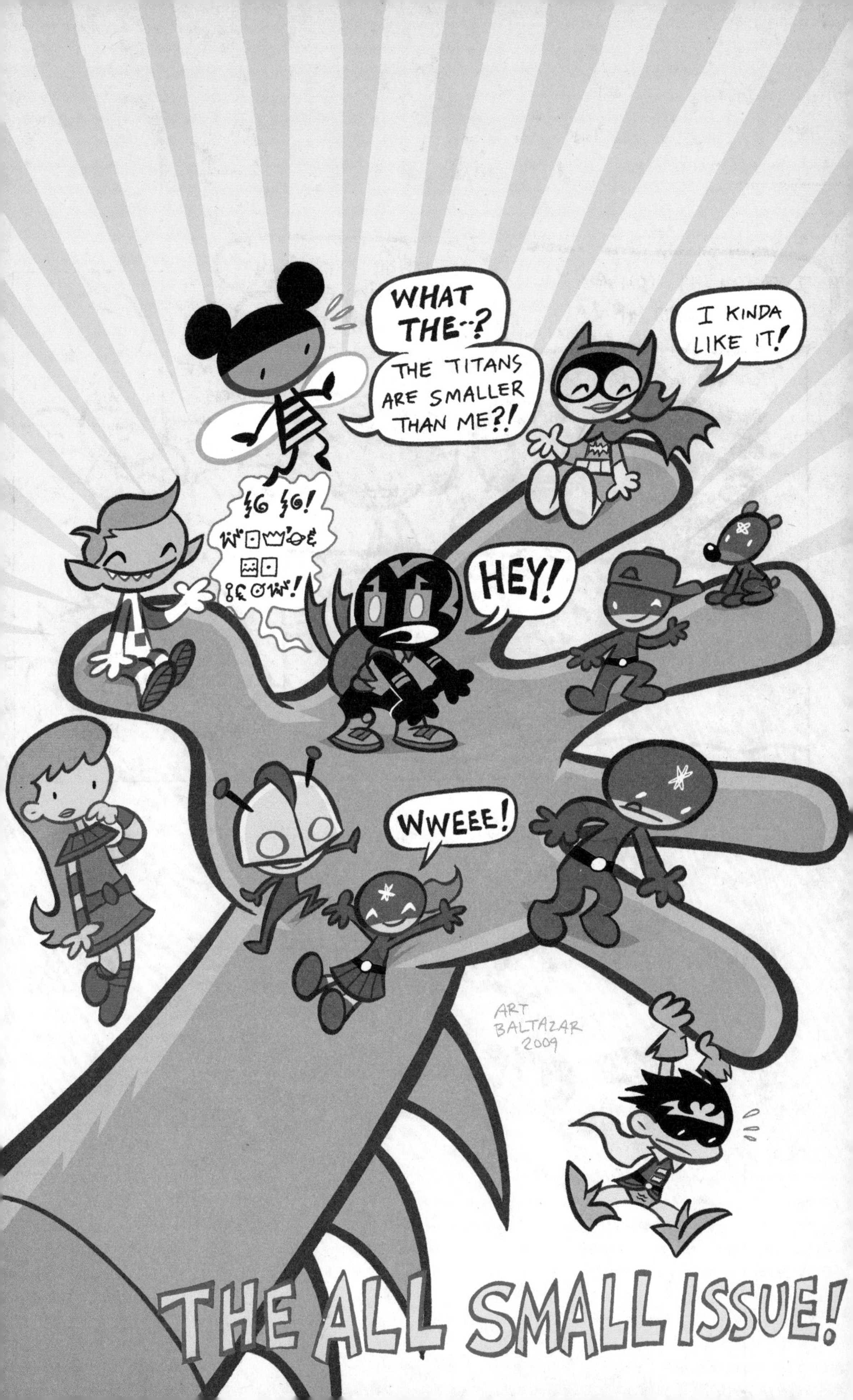

WHAT THE--?
THE TITANS ARE SMALLER THAN ME?!
I KINDA LIKE IT!
HEY!
WWEEE!
ART BALTAZAR 2009
THE ALL SMALL ISSUE!

tiny titans

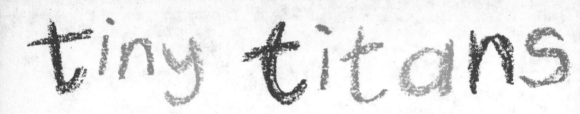

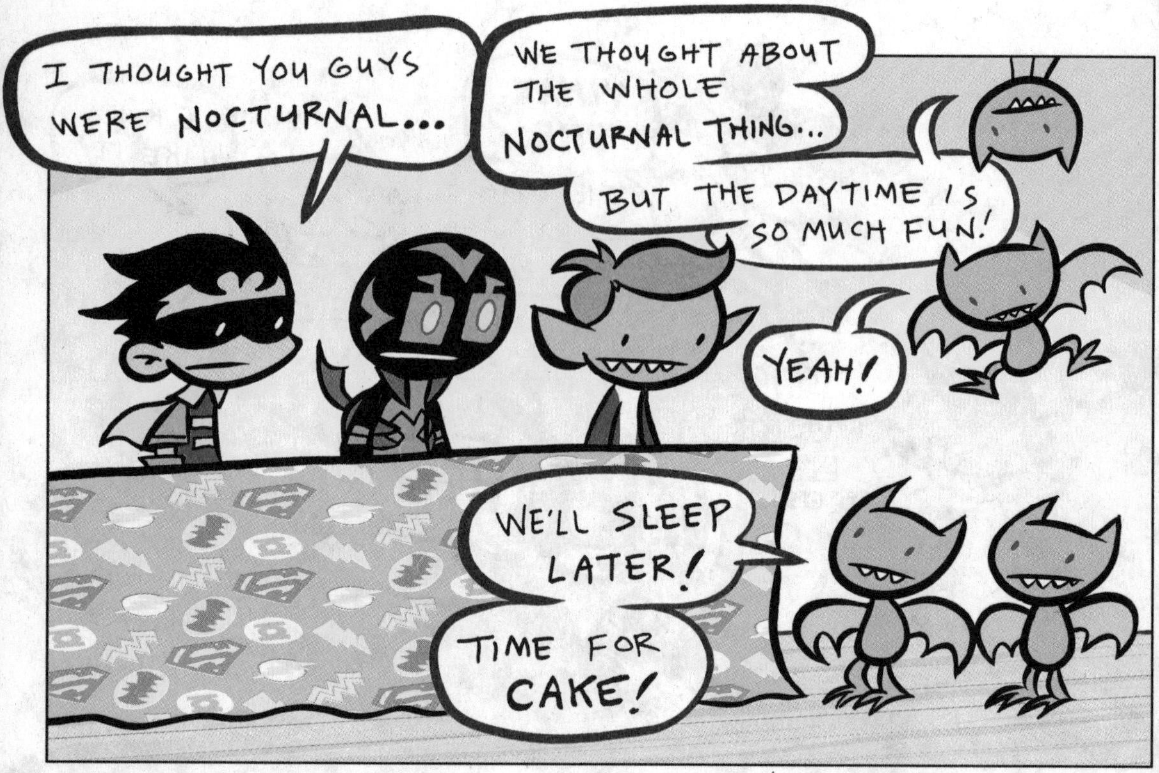
I THOUGHT YOU GUYS WERE NOCTURNAL...
WE THOUGHT ABOUT THE WHOLE NOCTURNAL THING...
BUT THE DAYTIME IS SO MUCH FUN!
YEAH!
WE'LL SLEEP LATER!
TIME FOR CAKE!

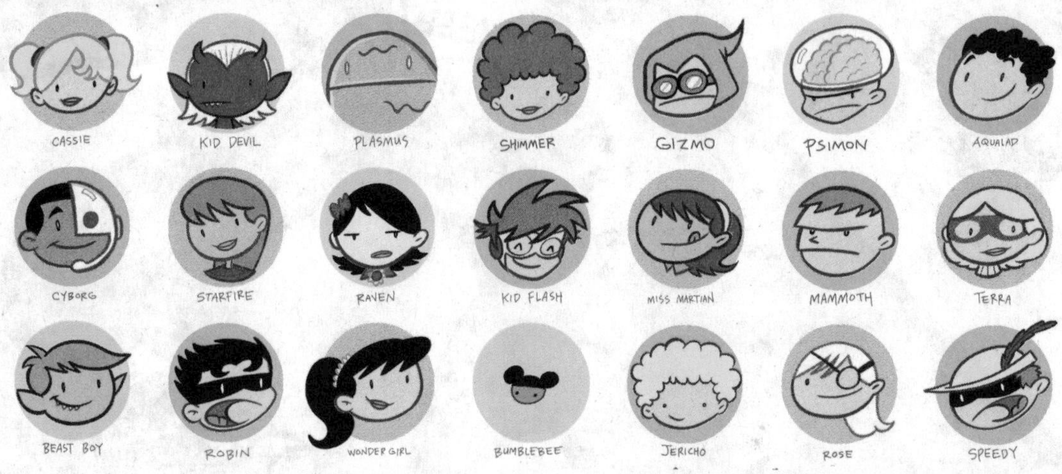
CASSIE
KID DEVIL
PLASMUS
SHIMMER
GIZMO
PSIMON
AQUALAD
CYBORG
STARFIRE
RAVEN
KID FLASH
MISS MARTIAN
MAMMOTH
TERRA
BEAST BOY
ROBIN
WONDER GIRL
BUMBLEBEE
JERICHO
ROSE
SPEEDY

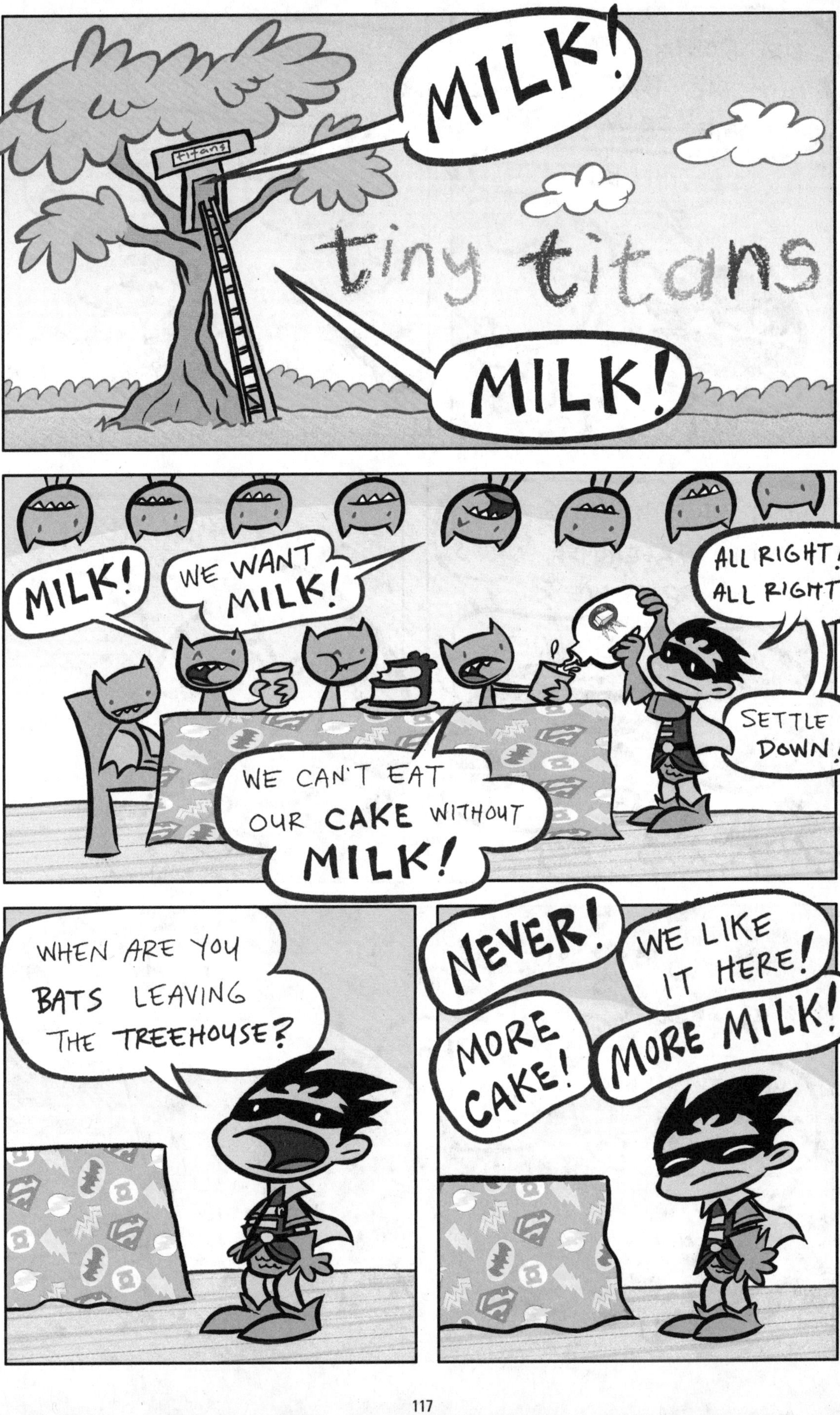
MILK!
titans
tiny titans
MILK!
MILK!
WE WANT MILK!
ALL RIGHT! ALL RIGHT!
SETTLE DOWN!
WE CAN'T EAT OUR CAKE WITHOUT MILK!
WHEN ARE YOU BATS LEAVING THE TREEHOUSE?
NEVER!
WE LIKE IT HERE!
MORE CAKE!
MORE MILK!

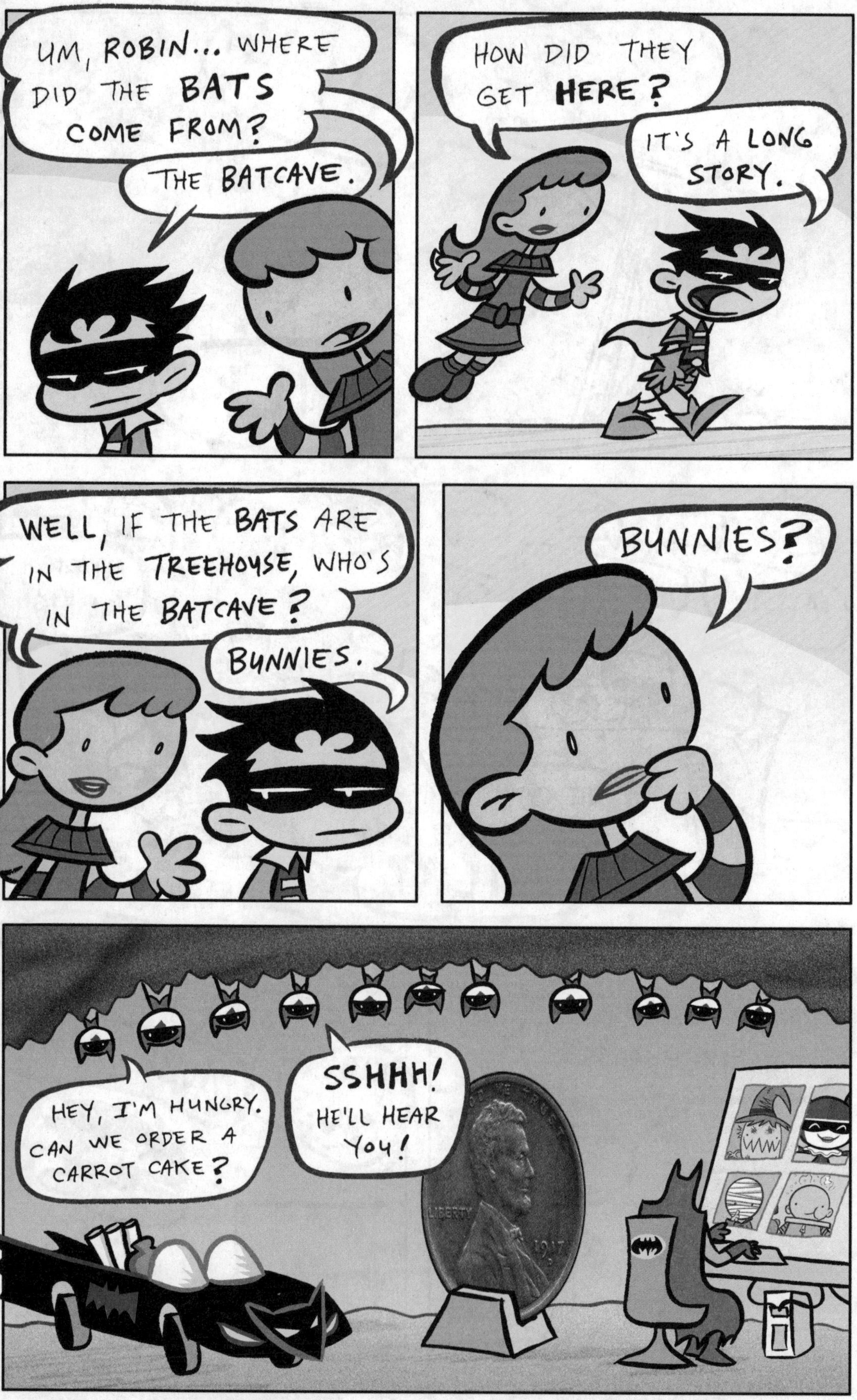
UM, ROBIN... WHERE DID THE BATS COME FROM?
THE BATCAVE.
HOW DID THEY GET HERE?
IT'S A LONG STORY.
WELL, IF THE BATS ARE IN THE TREEHOUSE, WHO'S IN THE BATCAVE?
BUNNIES.
BUNNIES?
HEY, I'M HUNGRY. CAN WE ORDER A CARROT CAKE?
SSHHH! HE'LL HEAR YOU!
LIBERTY
1917

-WHISPERIN'-

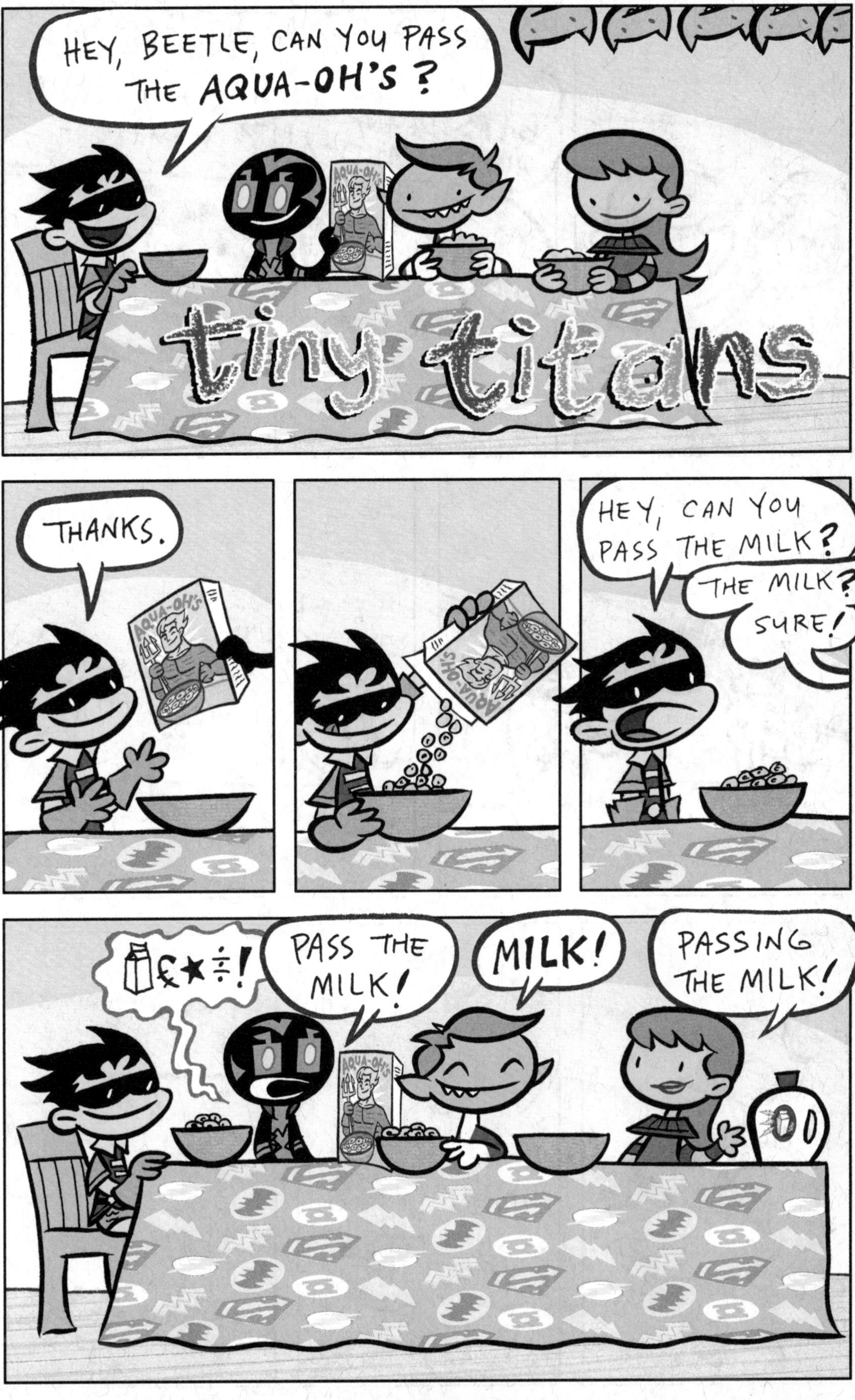
HEY, BEETLE, CAN YOU PASS THE AQUA-OH'S?
AQUA-OH'S
tiny titans
THANKS.
AQUA-OH'S
AQUA-OH'S
HEY, CAN YOU PASS THE MILK?
THE MILK? SURE!
£★÷!
PASS THE MILK!
MILK!
PASSING THE MILK!
AQUA-OH'S

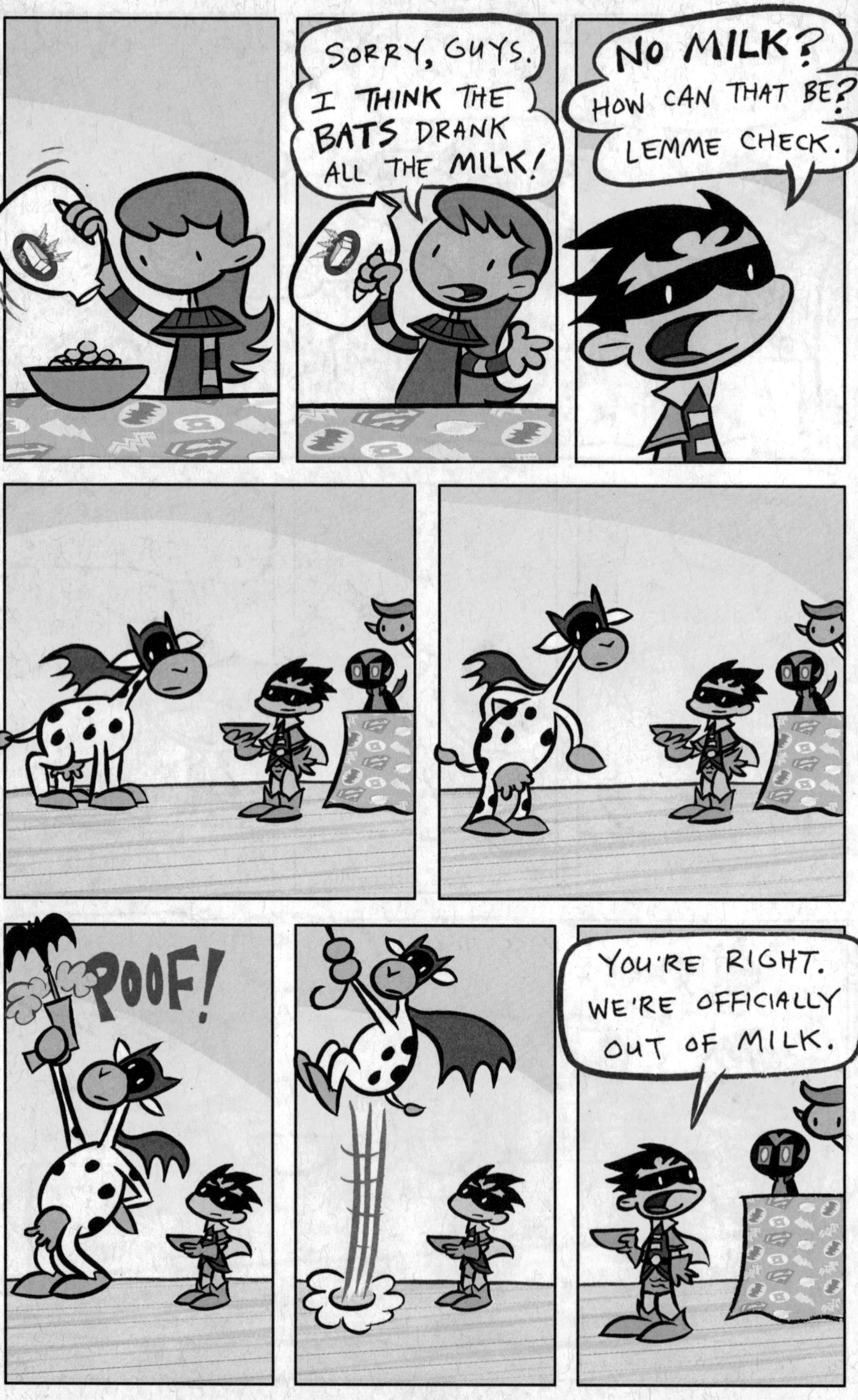
SORRY, GUYS. I THINK THE BATS DRANK ALL THE MILK!
NO MILK? HOW CAN THAT BE? LEMME CHECK.
POOF!
YOU'RE RIGHT. WE'RE OFFICIALLY OUT OF MILK.

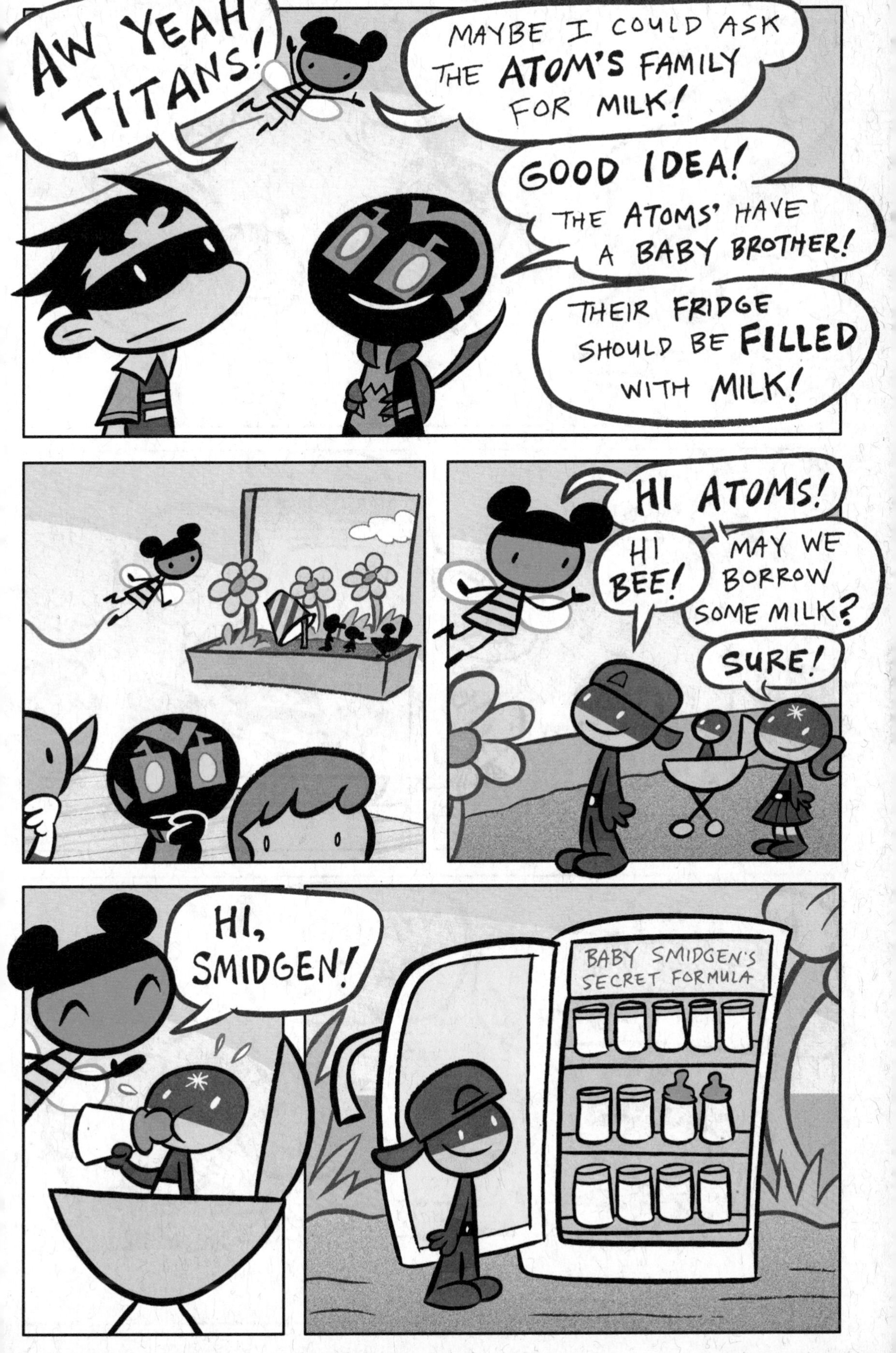

AW YEAH TITANS!
MAYBE I COULD ASK THE ATOM'S FAMILY FOR MILK!
GOOD IDEA!
THE ATOMS' HAVE A BABY BROTHER!
THEIR FRIDGE SHOULD BE FILLED WITH MILK!
HI ATOMS!
HI BEE!
MAY WE BORROW SOME MILK?
SURE!
HI, SMIDGEN!
BABY SMIDGEN'S SECRET FORMULA

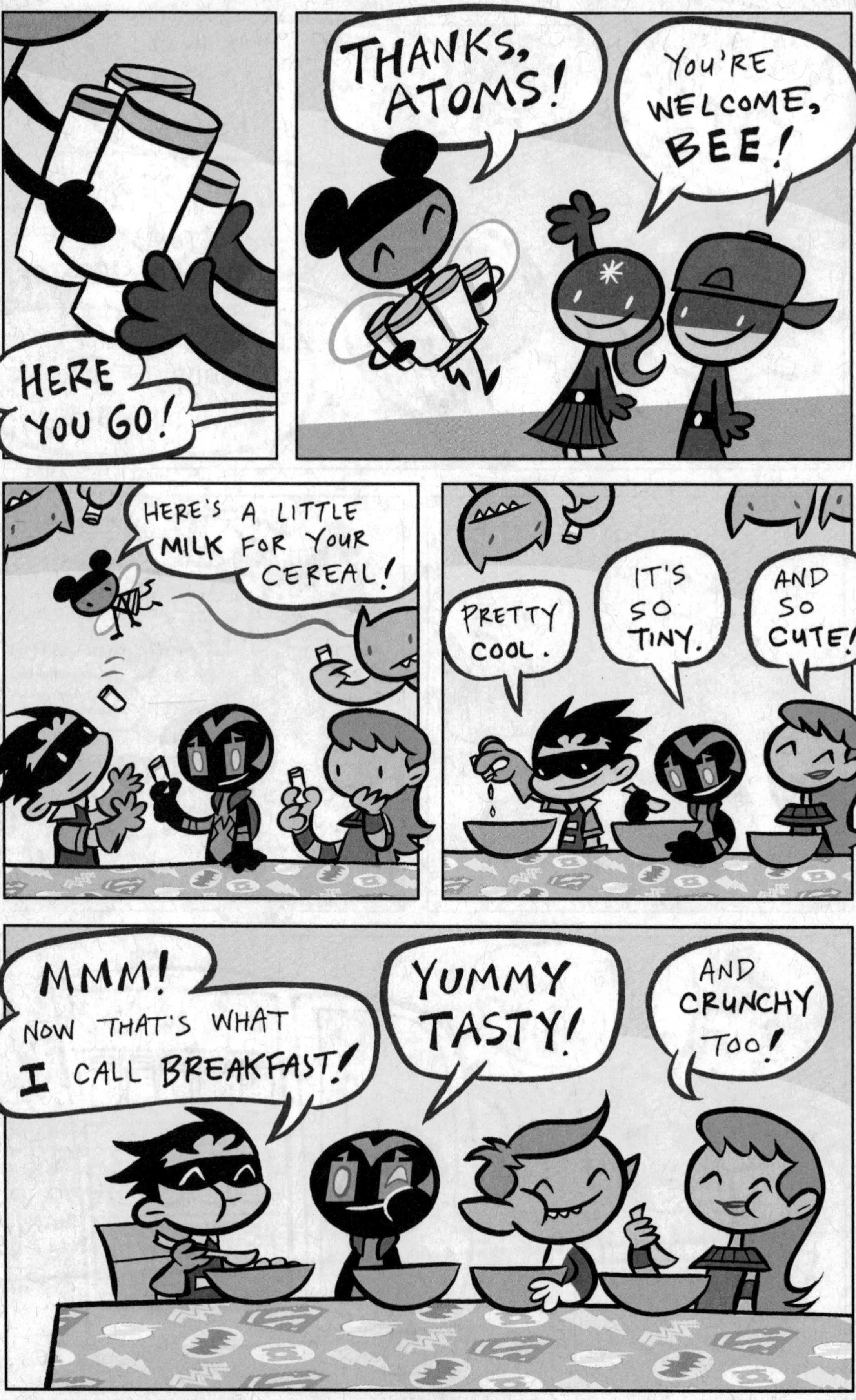
HERE YOU GO!
THANKS, ATOMS!
YOU'RE WELCOME, BEE!
HERE'S A LITTLE MILK FOR YOUR CEREAL!
PRETTY COOL.
IT'S SO TINY.
AND SO CUTE!
MMM! NOW THAT'S WHAT I CALL BREAKFAST!
YUMMY TASTY!
AND CRUNCHY TOO!

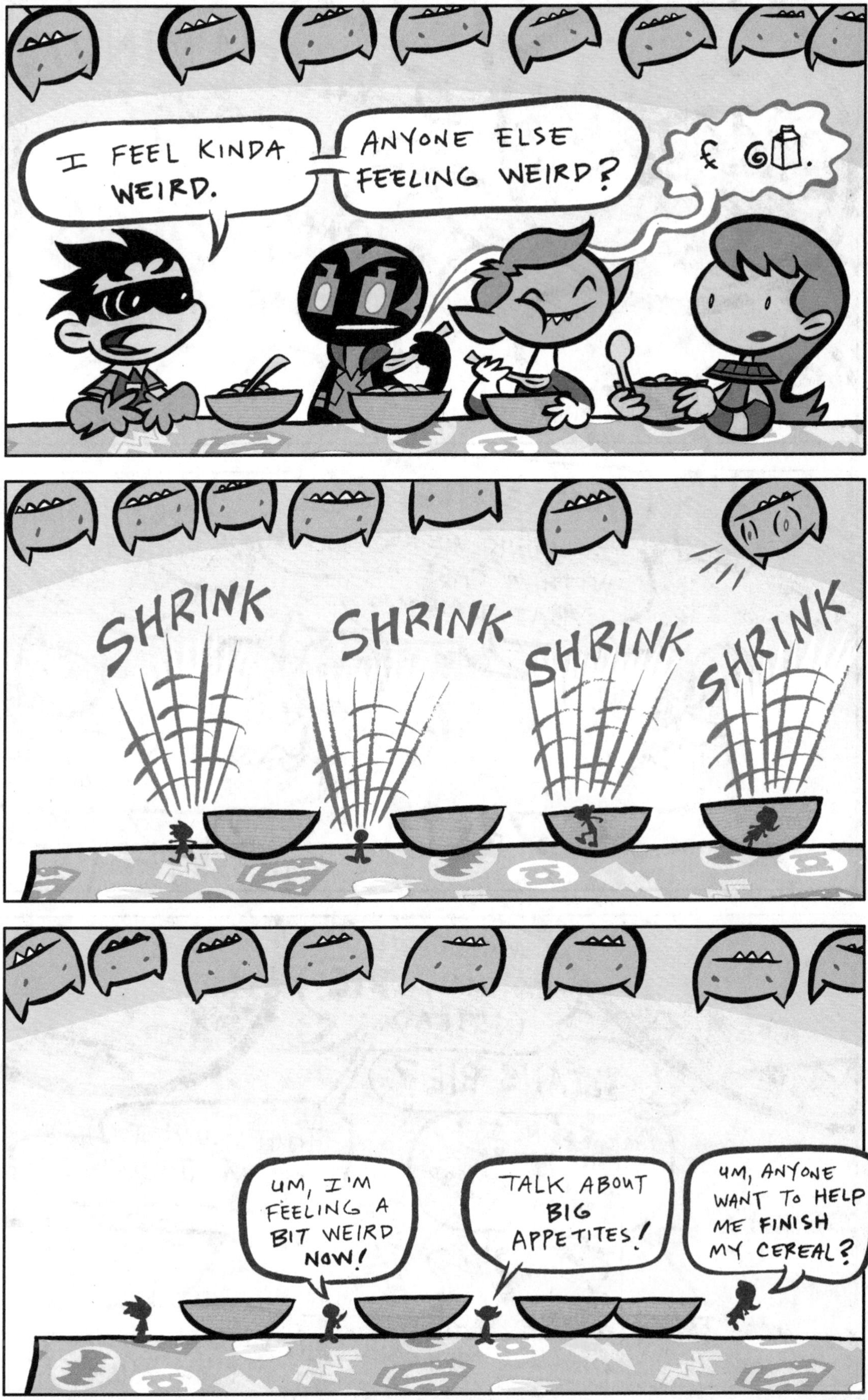
I FEEL KINDA WEIRD.
ANYONE ELSE FEELING WEIRD?
SHRINK
SHRINK
SHRINK
SHRINK
UM, I'M FEELING A BIT WEIRD NOW!
TALK ABOUT BIG APPETITES!
UM, ANYONE WANT TO HELP ME FINISH MY CEREAL?

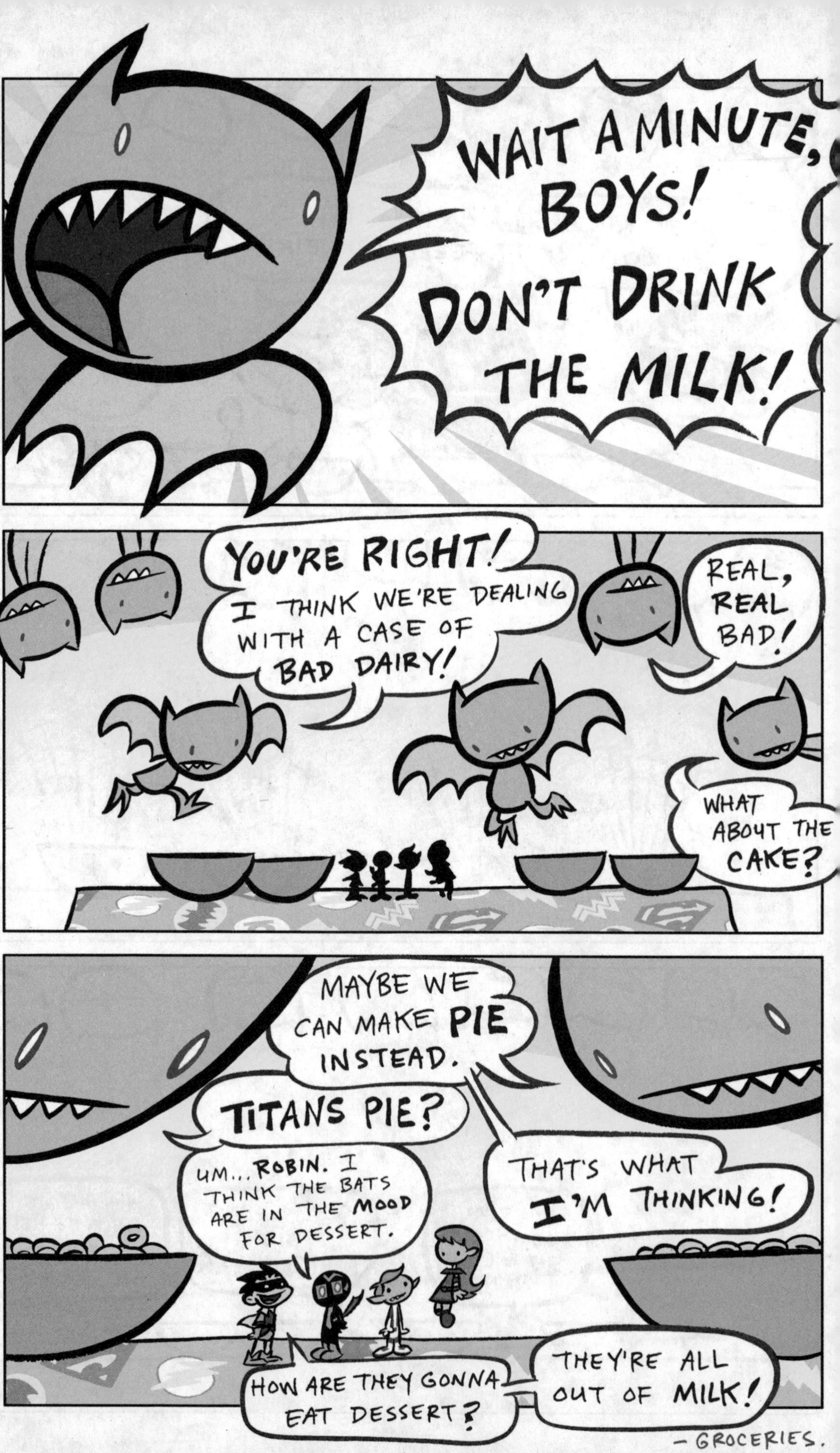
WAIT A MINUTE, BOYS!
DON'T DRINK THE MILK!
YOU'RE RIGHT!
I THINK WE'RE DEALING WITH A CASE OF BAD DAIRY!
REAL, REAL BAD!
WHAT ABOUT THE CAKE?
MAYBE WE CAN MAKE PIE INSTEAD.
TITANS PIE?
THAT'S WHAT I'M THINKING!
UM... ROBIN. I THINK THE BATS ARE IN THE MOOD FOR DESSERT.
HOW ARE THEY GONNA EAT DESSERT?
THEY'RE ALL OUT OF MILK!

– GROCERIES.

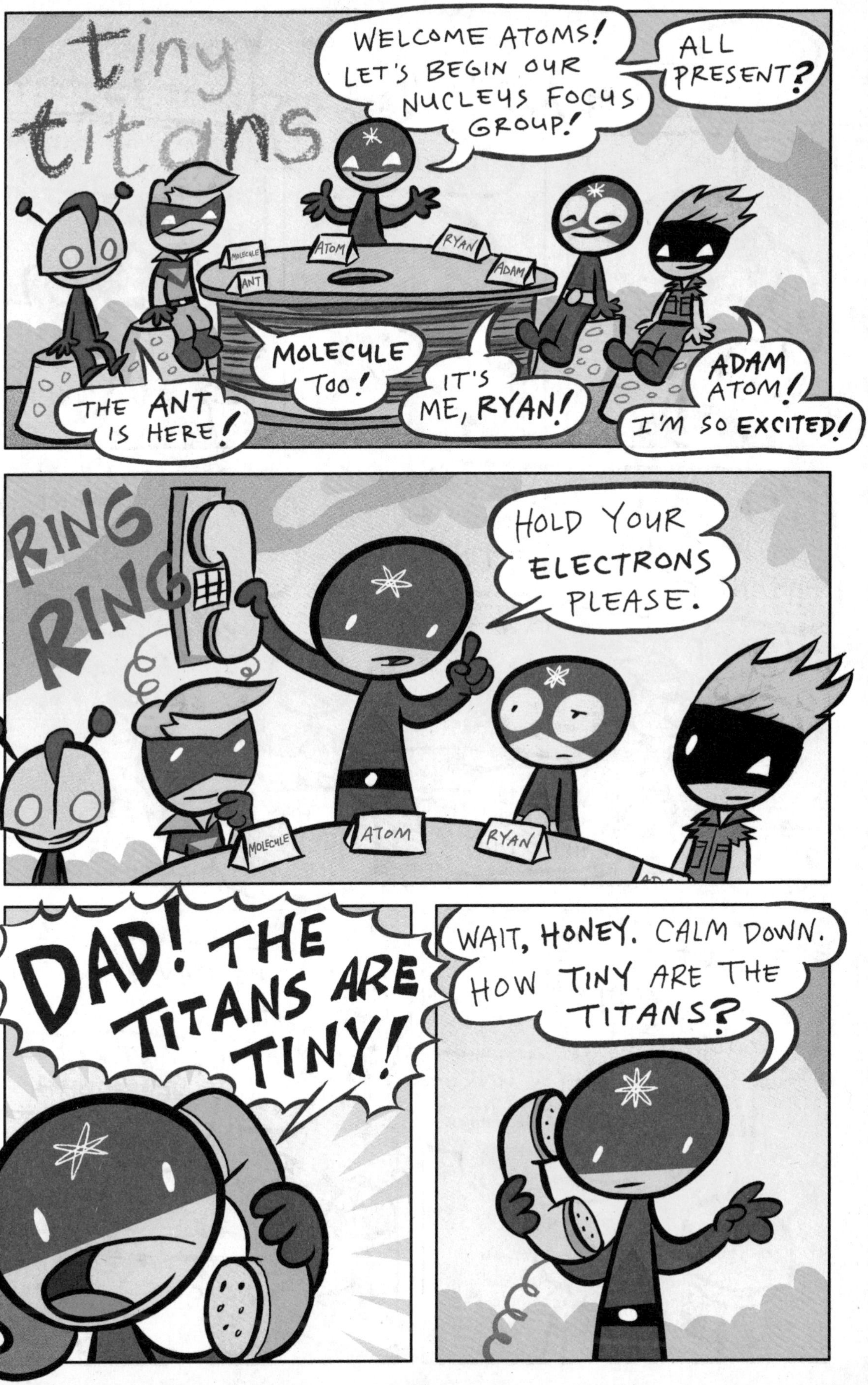
tiny titans
WELCOME ATOMS! LET'S BEGIN OUR NUCLEUS FOCUS GROUP!
ALL PRESENT?
MOLECULE
ATOM
RYAN
ANT
ADAM
THE ANT IS HERE!
MOLECULE TOO!
IT'S ME, RYAN!
ADAM ATOM! I'M SO EXCITED!
RING RING
HOLD YOUR ELECTRONS PLEASE.
MOLECULE
ATOM
RYAN
DAD! THE TITANS ARE TINY!
WAIT, HONEY. CALM DOWN. HOW TINY ARE THE TITANS?

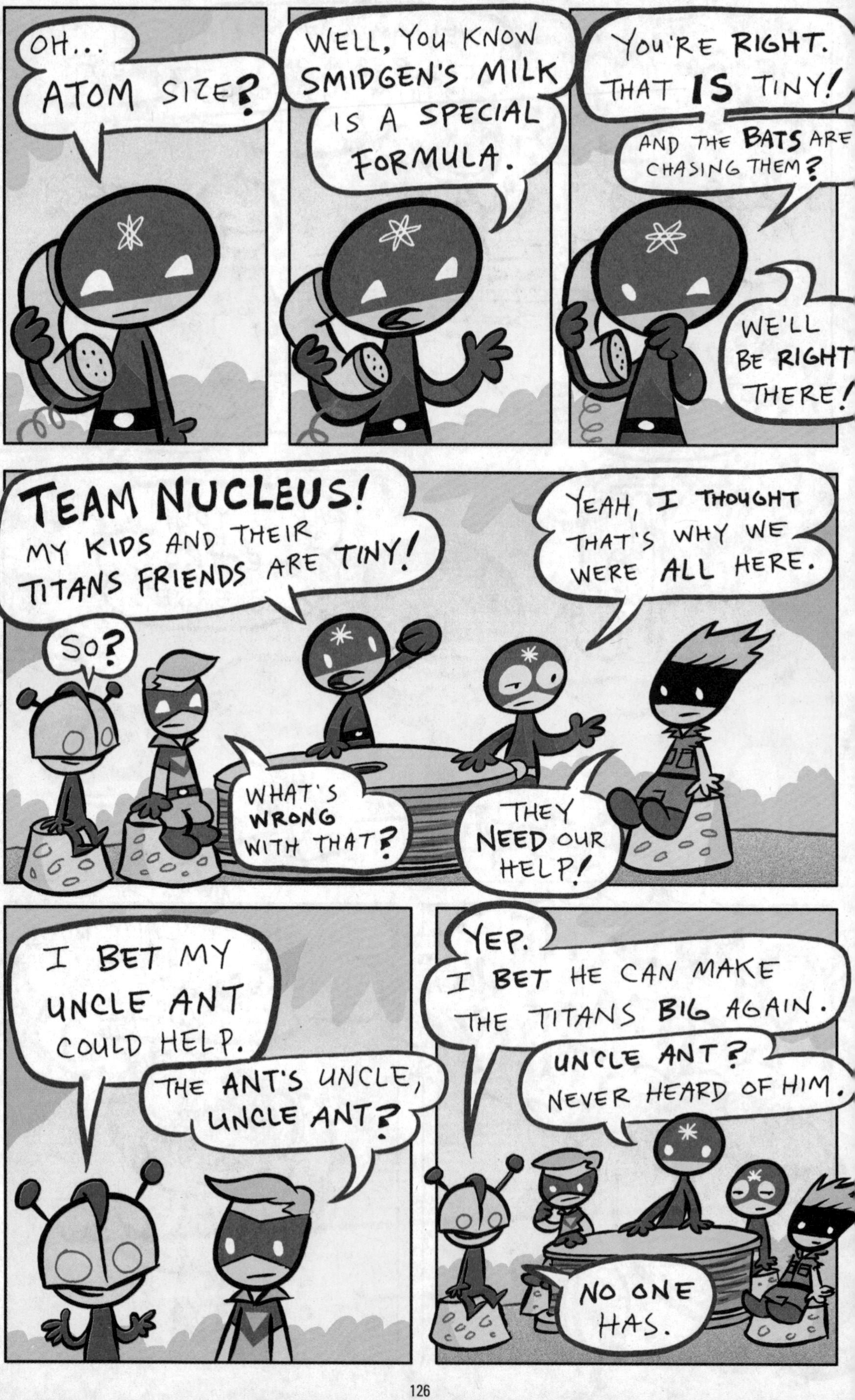
OH... ATOM SIZE?
WELL, YOU KNOW SMIDGEN'S MILK IS A SPECIAL FORMULA.
YOU'RE RIGHT. THAT IS TINY!
AND THE BATS ARE CHASING THEM?
WE'LL BE RIGHT THERE!
TEAM NUCLEUS! MY KIDS AND THEIR TITANS FRIENDS ARE TINY!
YEAH, I THOUGHT THAT'S WHY WE WERE ALL HERE.
SO?
WHAT'S WRONG WITH THAT?
THEY NEED OUR HELP!
I BET MY UNCLE ANT COULD HELP.
THE ANT'S UNCLE, UNCLE ANT?
YEP. I BET HE CAN MAKE THE TITANS BIG AGAIN.
UNCLE ANT? NEVER HEARD OF HIM.
NO ONE HAS.

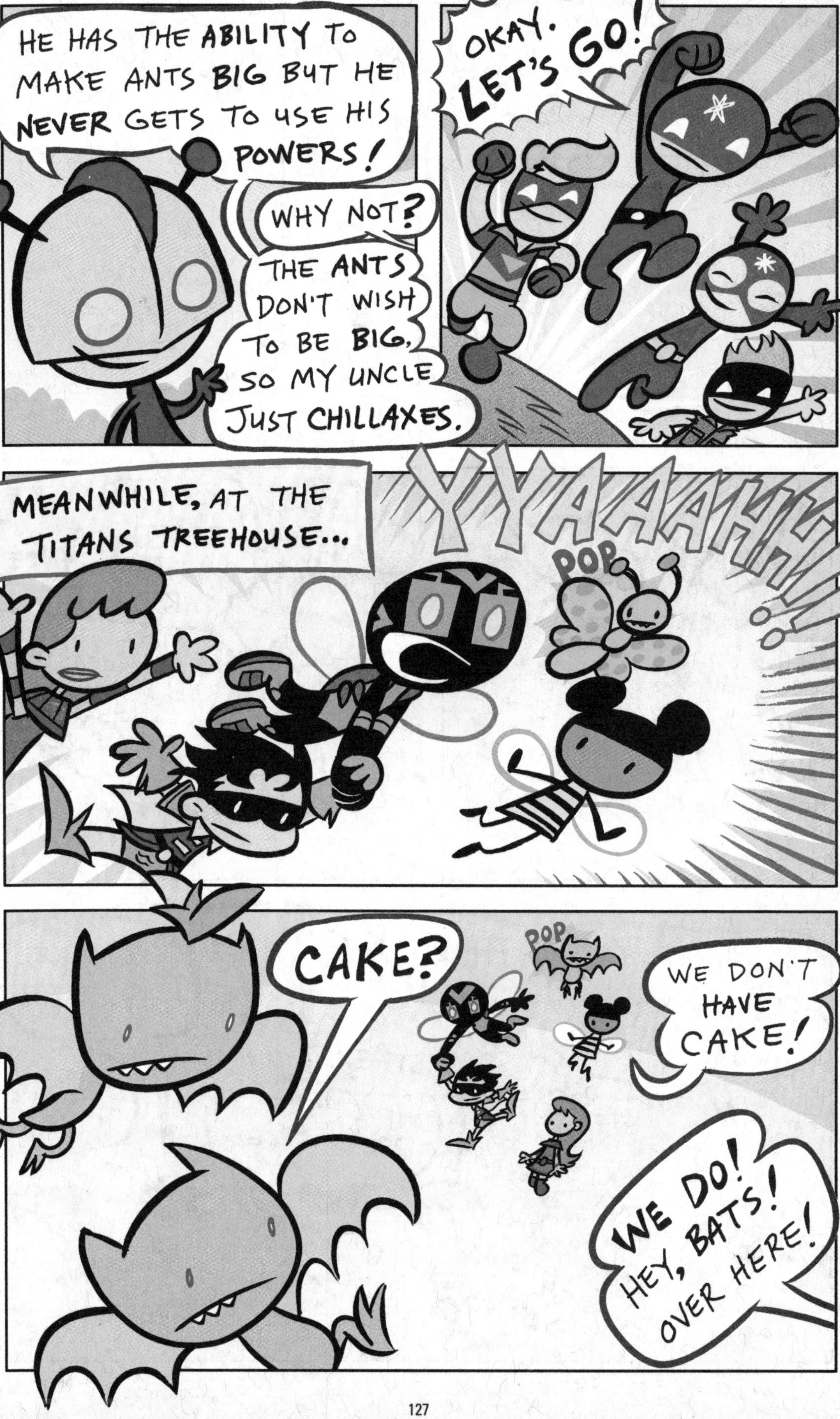
HE HAS THE ABILITY TO MAKE ANTS BIG BUT HE NEVER GETS TO USE HIS POWERS!
WHY NOT?
THE ANTS DON'T WISH TO BE BIG, SO MY UNCLE JUST CHILLAXES.
OKAY. LET'S GO!
MEANWHILE, AT THE TITANS TREEHOUSE...
YYAAAHH!!!
POP
CAKE?
POP
WE DON'T HAVE CAKE!
WE DO! HEY, BATS! OVER HERE!

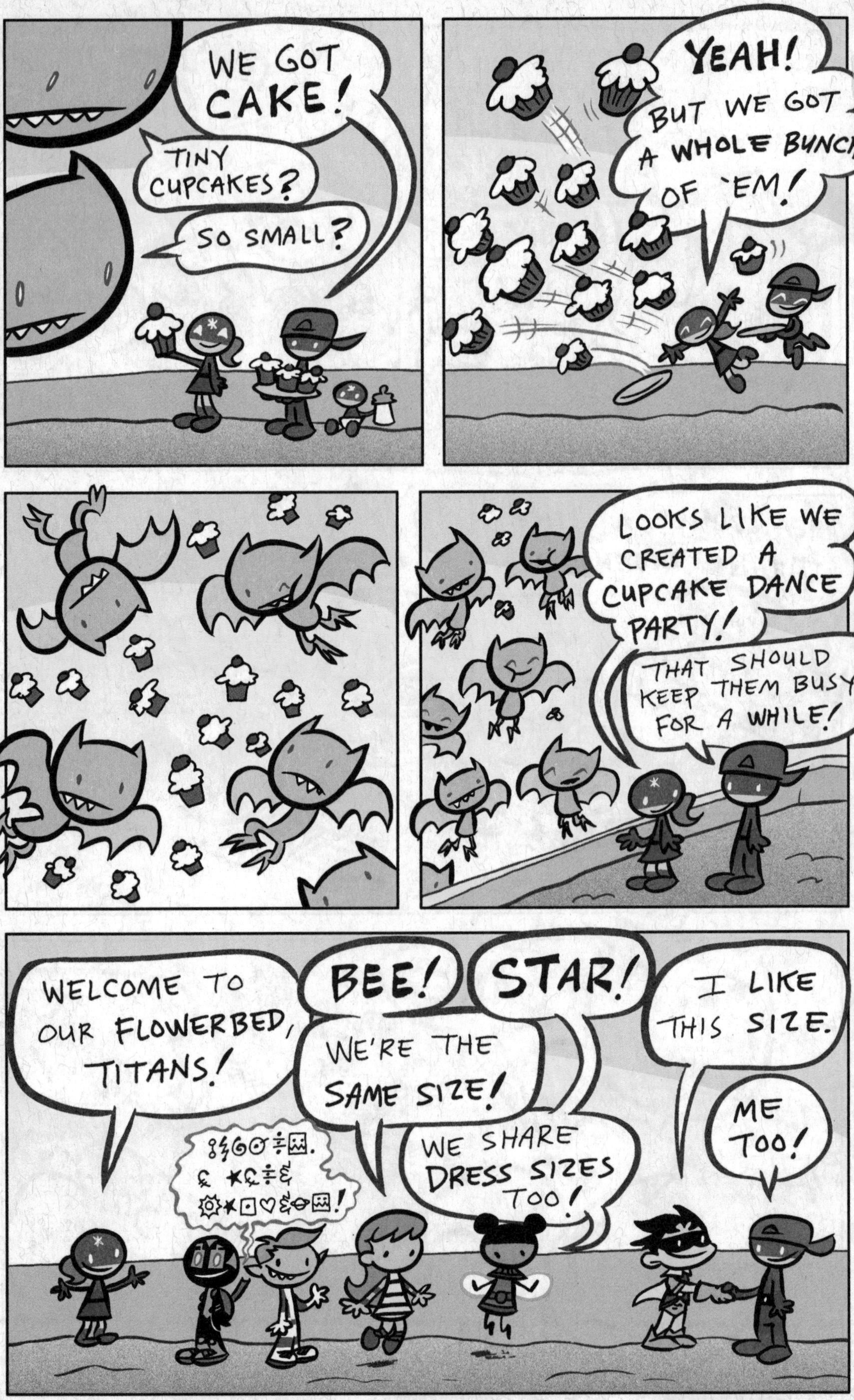
WE GOT CAKE!
TINY CUPCAKES?
SO SMALL?
YEAH!
BUT WE GOT A WHOLE BUNCH OF 'EM!
LOOKS LIKE WE CREATED A CUPCAKE DANCE PARTY!
THAT SHOULD KEEP THEM BUSY FOR A WHILE!
WELCOME TO OUR FLOWERBED, TITANS!
BEE!
STAR!
WE'RE THE SAME SIZE!
WE SHARE DRESS SIZES TOO!
I LIKE THIS SIZE.
ME TOO!

—PERFECT FIT.

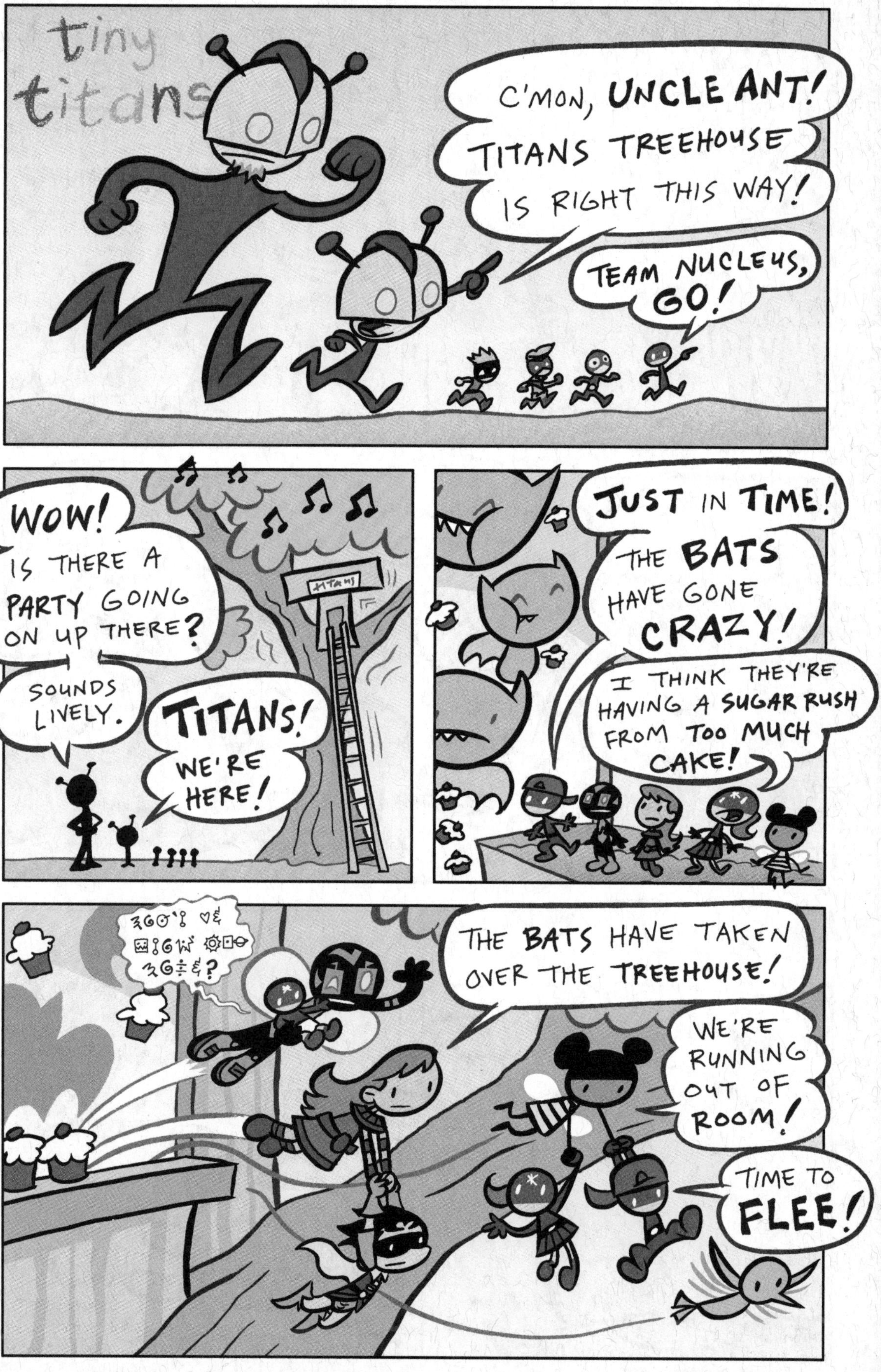
tiny titans
C'MON, UNCLE ANT! TITANS TREEHOUSE IS RIGHT THIS WAY!
TEAM NUCLEUS, GO!
WOW! IS THERE A PARTY GOING ON UP THERE?
SOUNDS LIVELY.
TITANS! WE'RE HERE!
TITANS
JUST IN TIME!
THE BATS HAVE GONE CRAZY!
I THINK THEY'RE HAVING A SUGAR RUSH FROM TOO MUCH CAKE!
THE BATS HAVE TAKEN OVER THE TREEHOUSE!
WE'RE RUNNING OUT OF ROOM!
TIME TO FLEE!

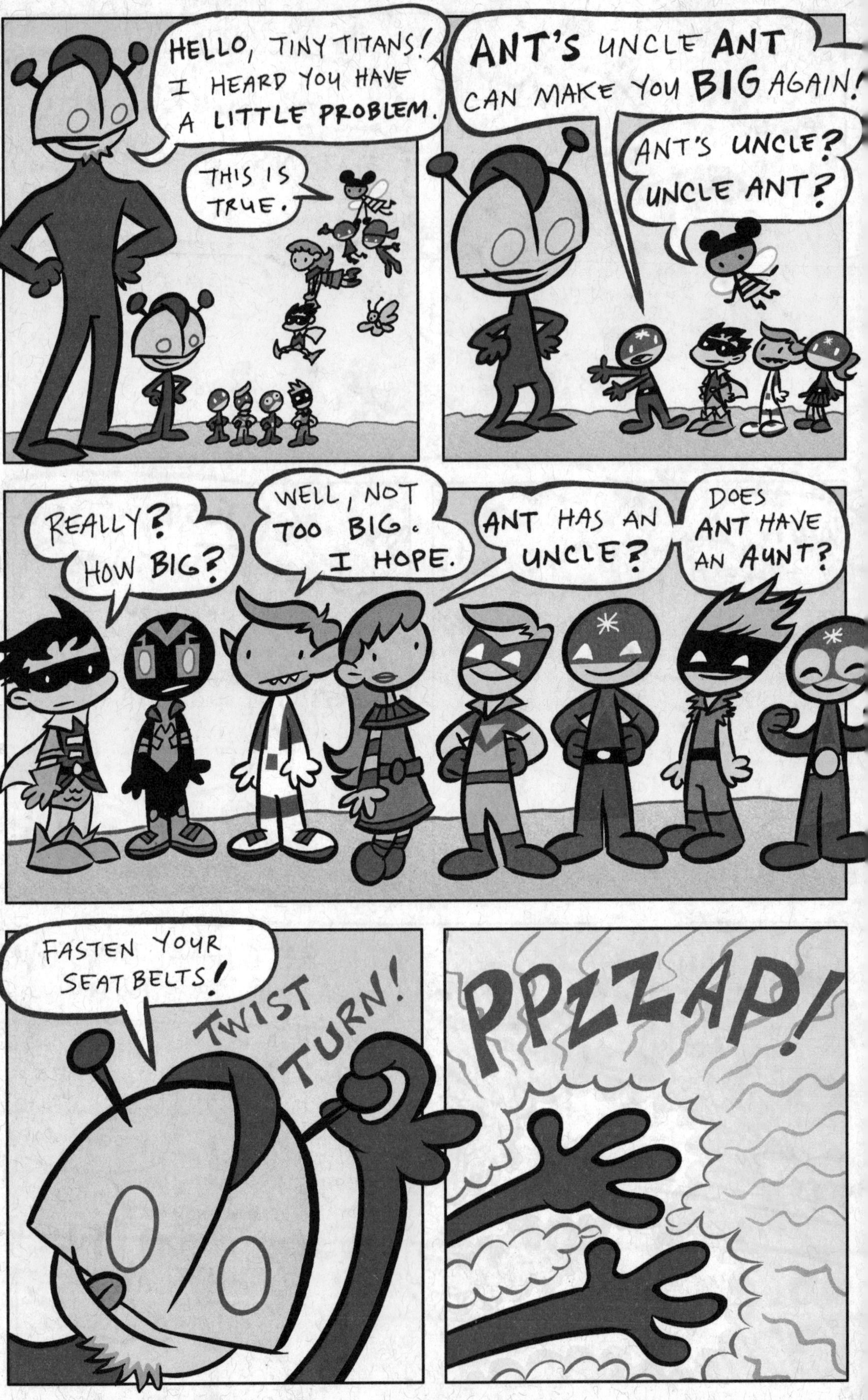

HELLO, TINY TITANS! I HEARD YOU HAVE A LITTLE PROBLEM.
THIS IS TRUE.
ANT'S UNCLE ANT CAN MAKE YOU BIG AGAIN!
ANT'S UNCLE? UNCLE ANT?
REALLY? HOW BIG?
WELL, NOT TOO BIG. I HOPE.
ANT HAS AN UNCLE?
DOES ANT HAVE AN AUNT?
FASTEN YOUR SEAT BELTS!
TWIST
TURN!
PPZZAP!

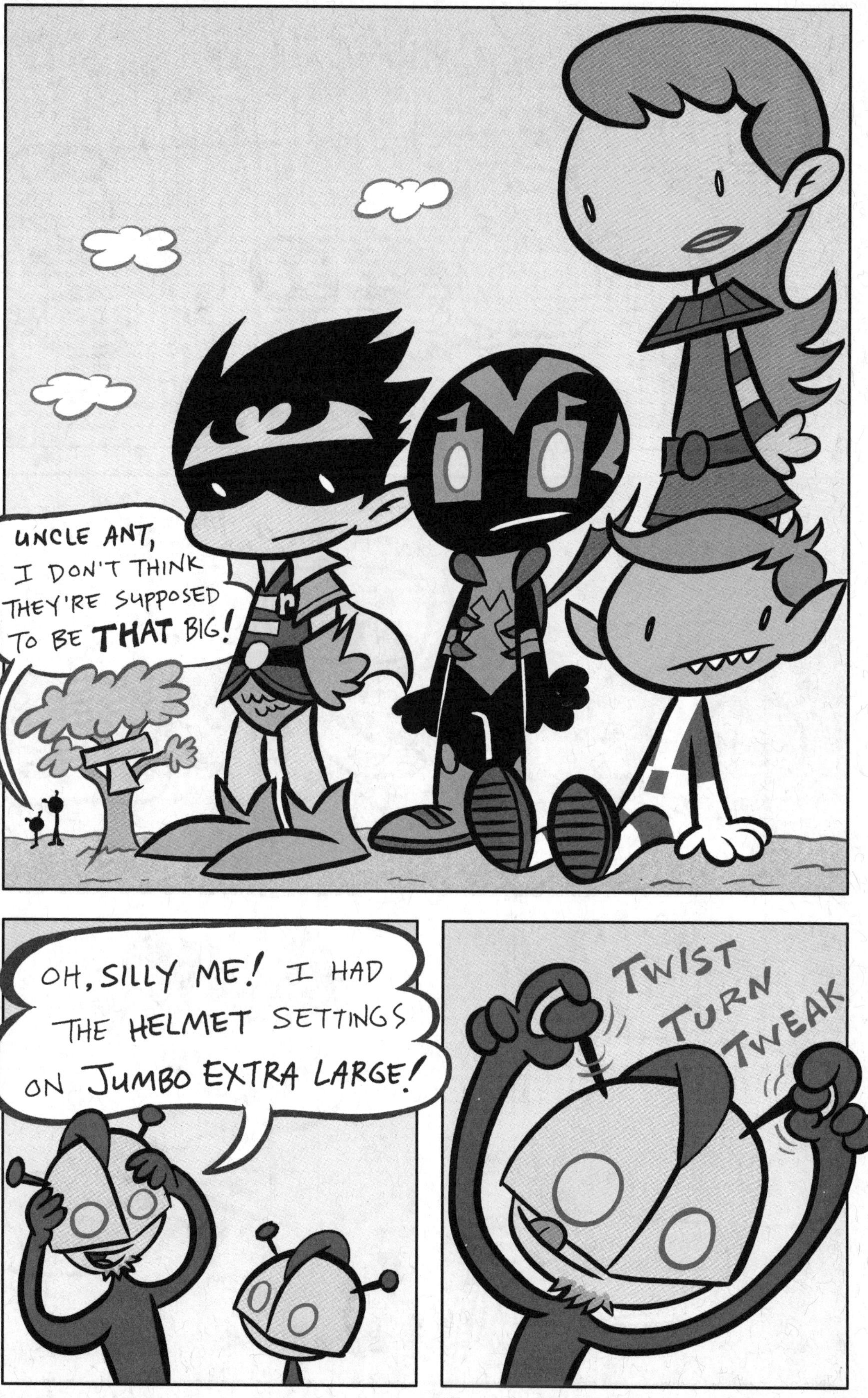
UNCLE ANT, I DON'T THINK THEY'RE SUPPOSED TO BE THAT BIG!
OH, SILLY ME! I HAD THE HELMET SETTINGS ON JUMBO EXTRA LARGE!
TWIST
TURN
TWEAK

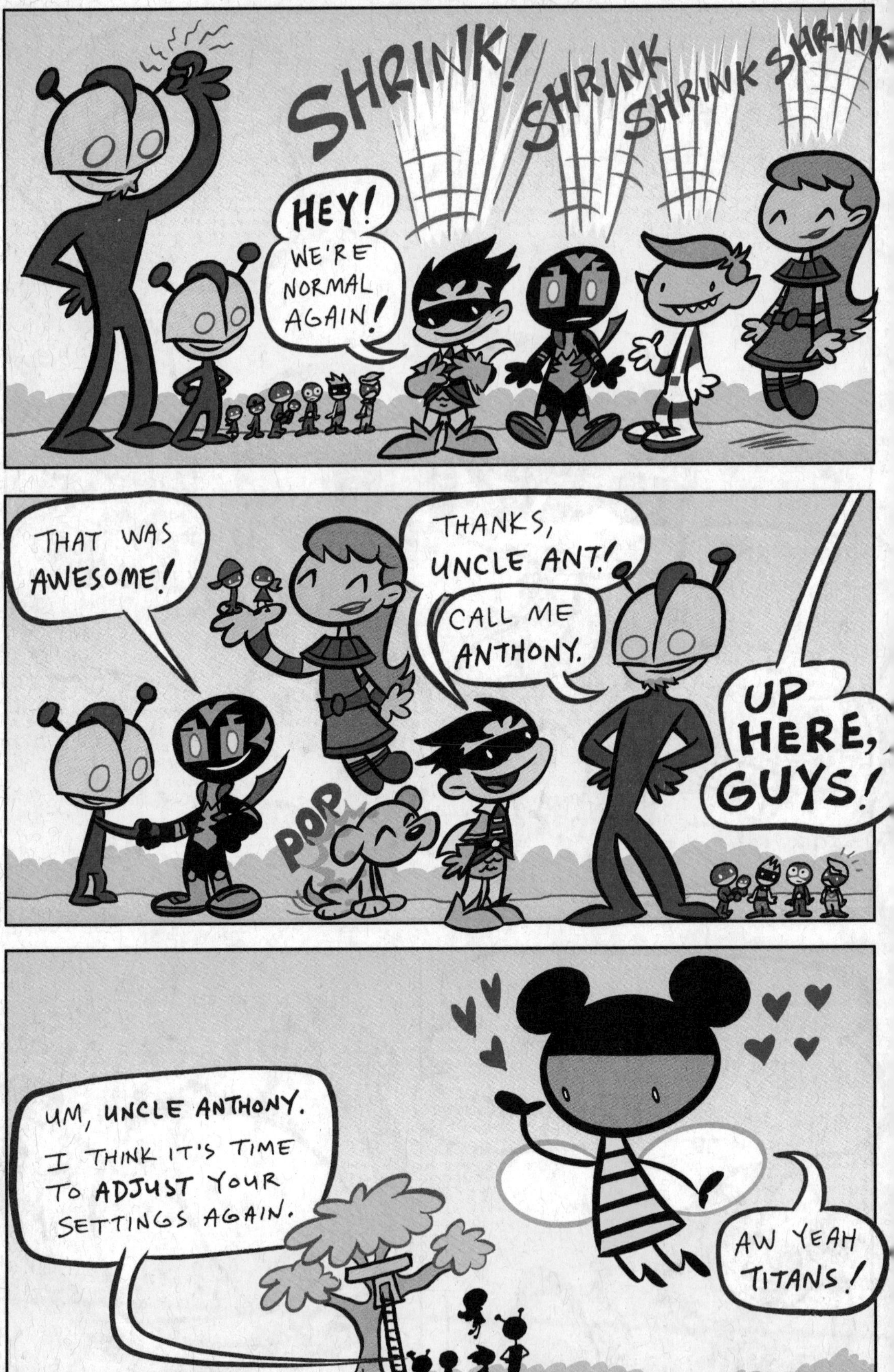
SHRINK!
SHRINK
SHRINK
SHRINK
HEY! WE'RE NORMAL AGAIN!
THAT WAS AWESOME!
THANKS, UNCLE ANT!
CALL ME ANTHONY.
POP
UP HERE, GUYS!
UM, UNCLE ANTHONY.
I THINK IT'S TIME TO ADJUST YOUR SETTINGS AGAIN.
AW YEAH TITANS!

—XXL EXTRA SMALL

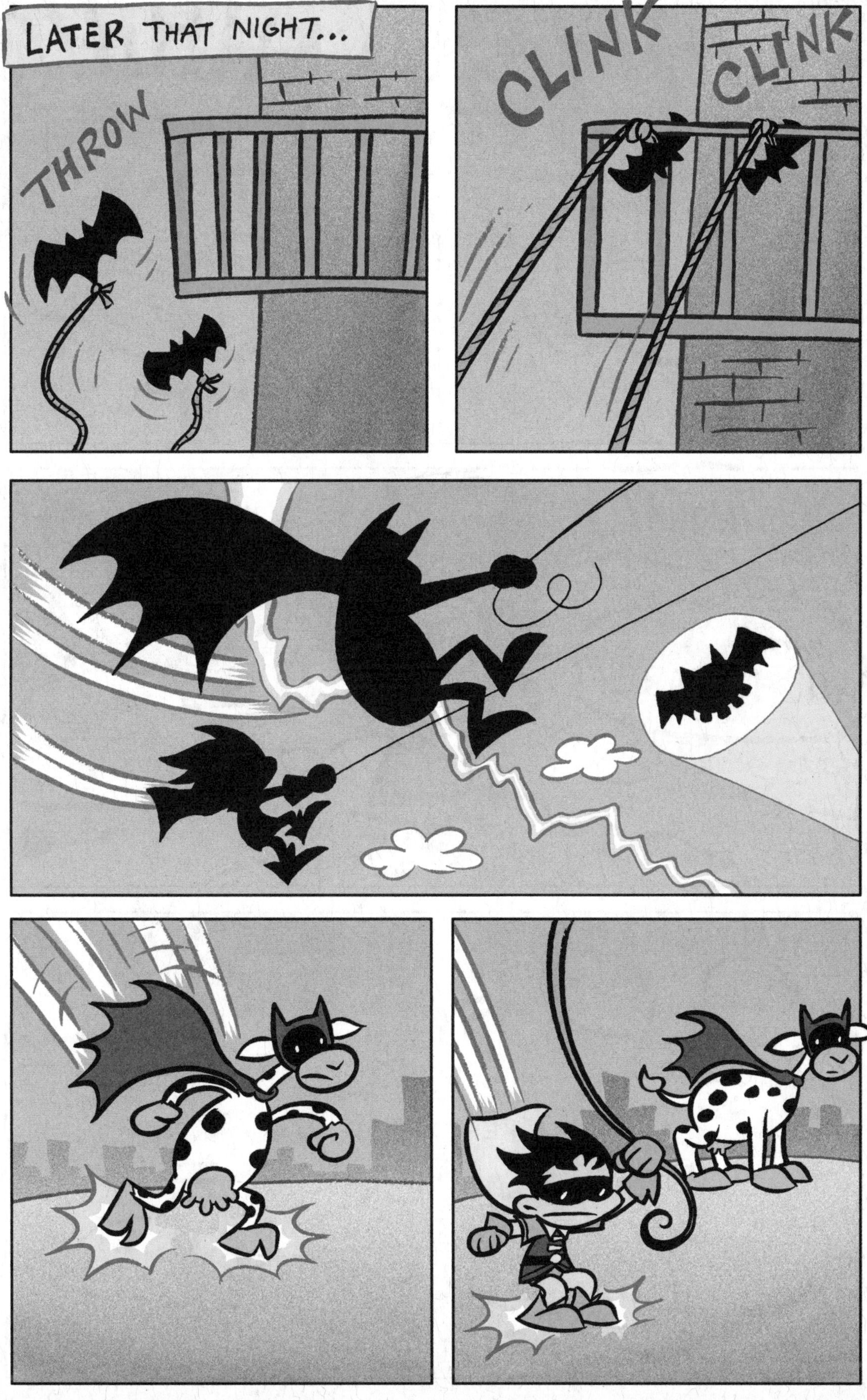
LATER THAT NIGHT...
THROW
CLINK
CLINK

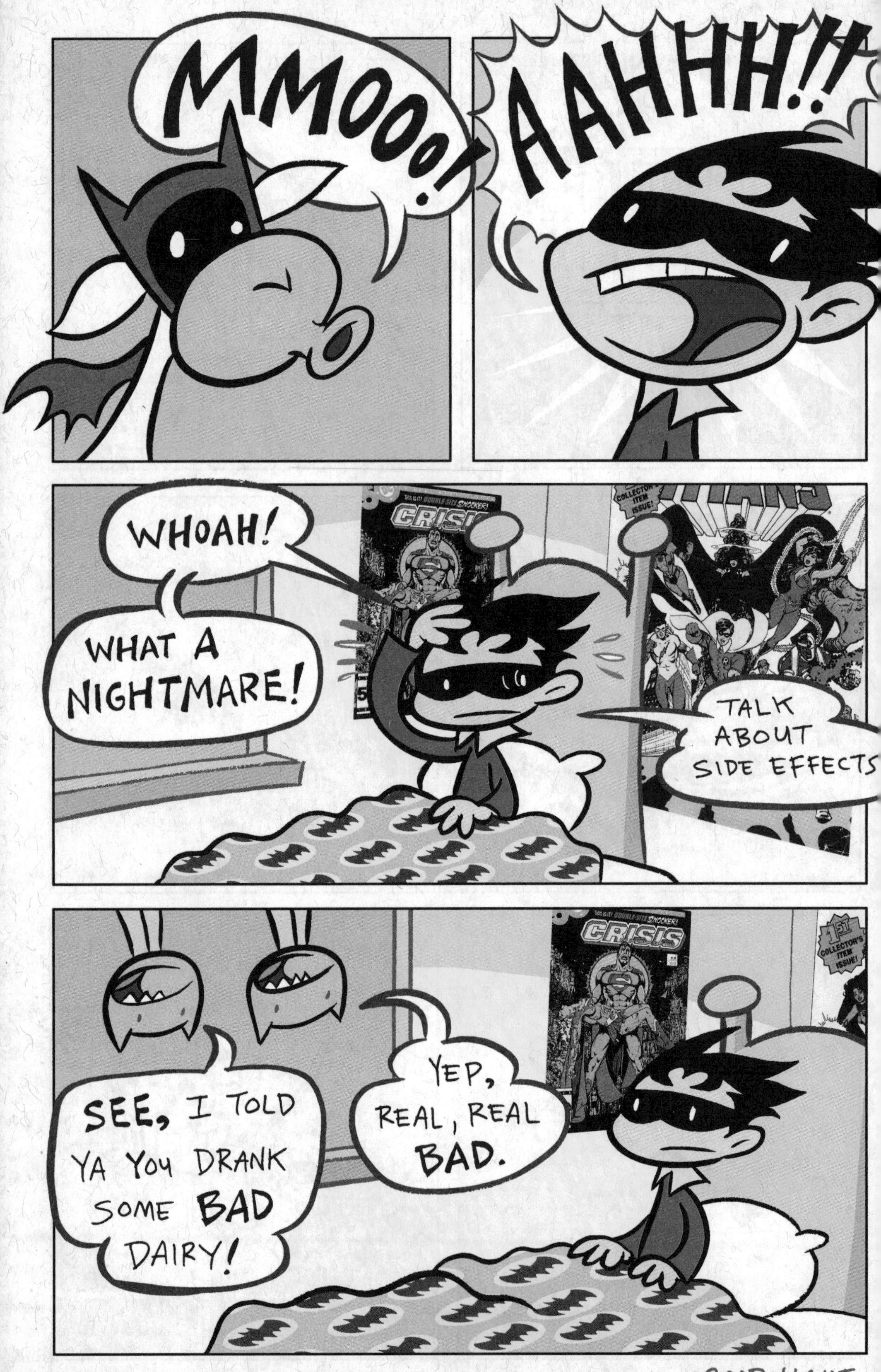
MMOOoo!
AAHHH!!!
WHOAH!
WHAT A NIGHTMARE!
CRISIS
TALK ABOUT SIDE EFFECTS
CRISIS
SEE, I TOLD YA YOU DRANK SOME BAD DAIRY!
YEP, REAL, REAL BAD.

—GOODNIGHT.

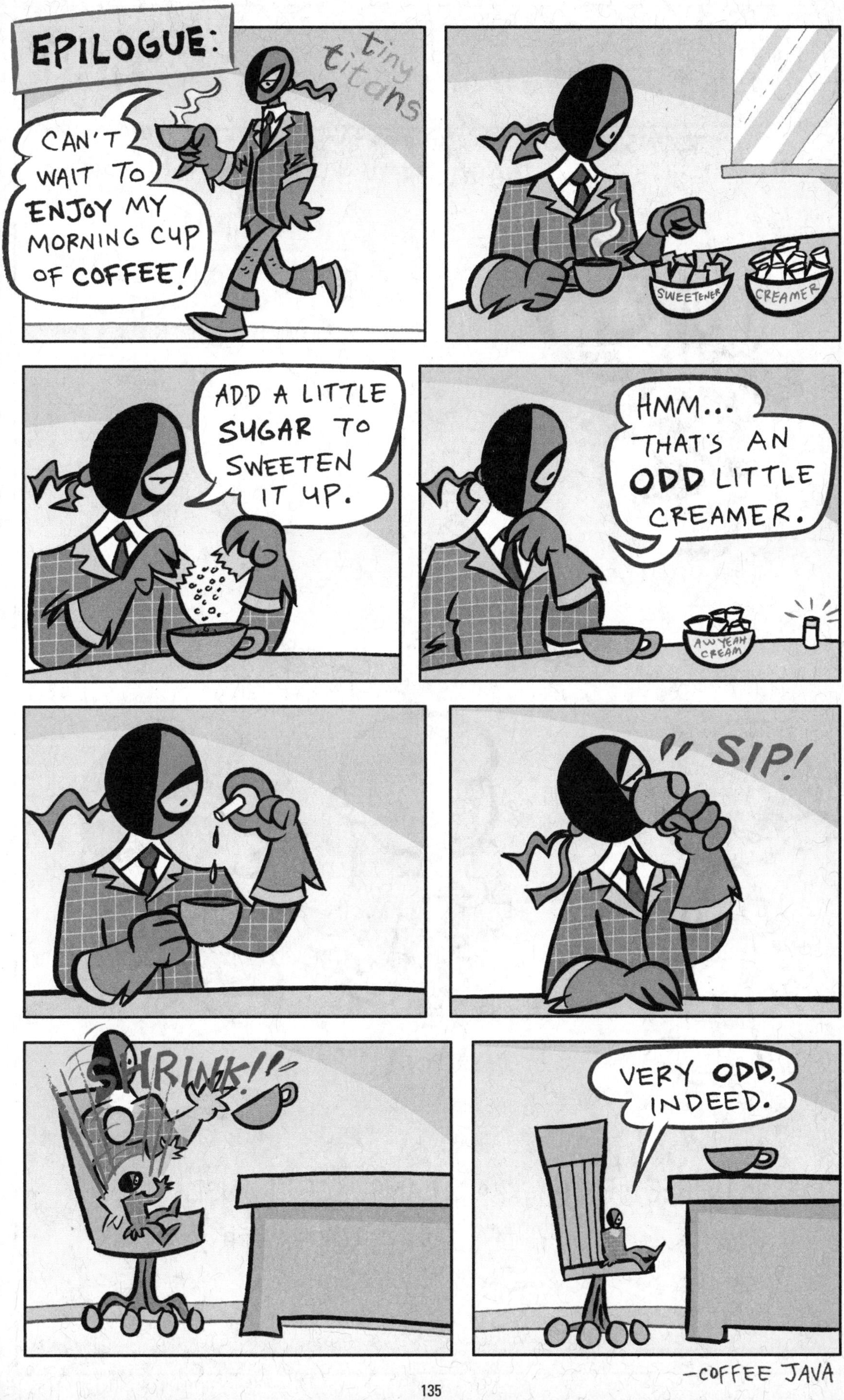
EPILOGUE:
tiny titans
CAN'T WAIT TO ENJOY MY MORNING CUP OF COFFEE!
SWEETENER
CREAMER
ADD A LITTLE SUGAR TO SWEETEN IT UP.
HMM... THAT'S AN ODD LITTLE CREAMER.
AW YEAH CREAM
SIP!
SHRINK!!
VERY ODD, INDEED.

—COFFEE JAVA

HELP THE tiny titans

TRANSLATE BLUE BEETLE'S BACKPACK
TO REVEAL WHAT TIME IT IS!

T I M E

F O R

P E T   C L U B

M E E T I N G

BONUS!
BLUE BEETLE'S BACKPACK LANGUAGE TRANSLATION!

A-🌀 B-↟ C-ʒ D-↗ E-ɛ̌ F-☼ G-⅓ H-⚡ I-ɛ̵

J-φ K-÷ L-★ M-🥛 N-☉ O-⊡ P-ϥ Q-♀ R-⊖

S-▨ T-⚲ U-♛ V-Ø W-♡ X-⚔ Y-ᨏ Z-☺

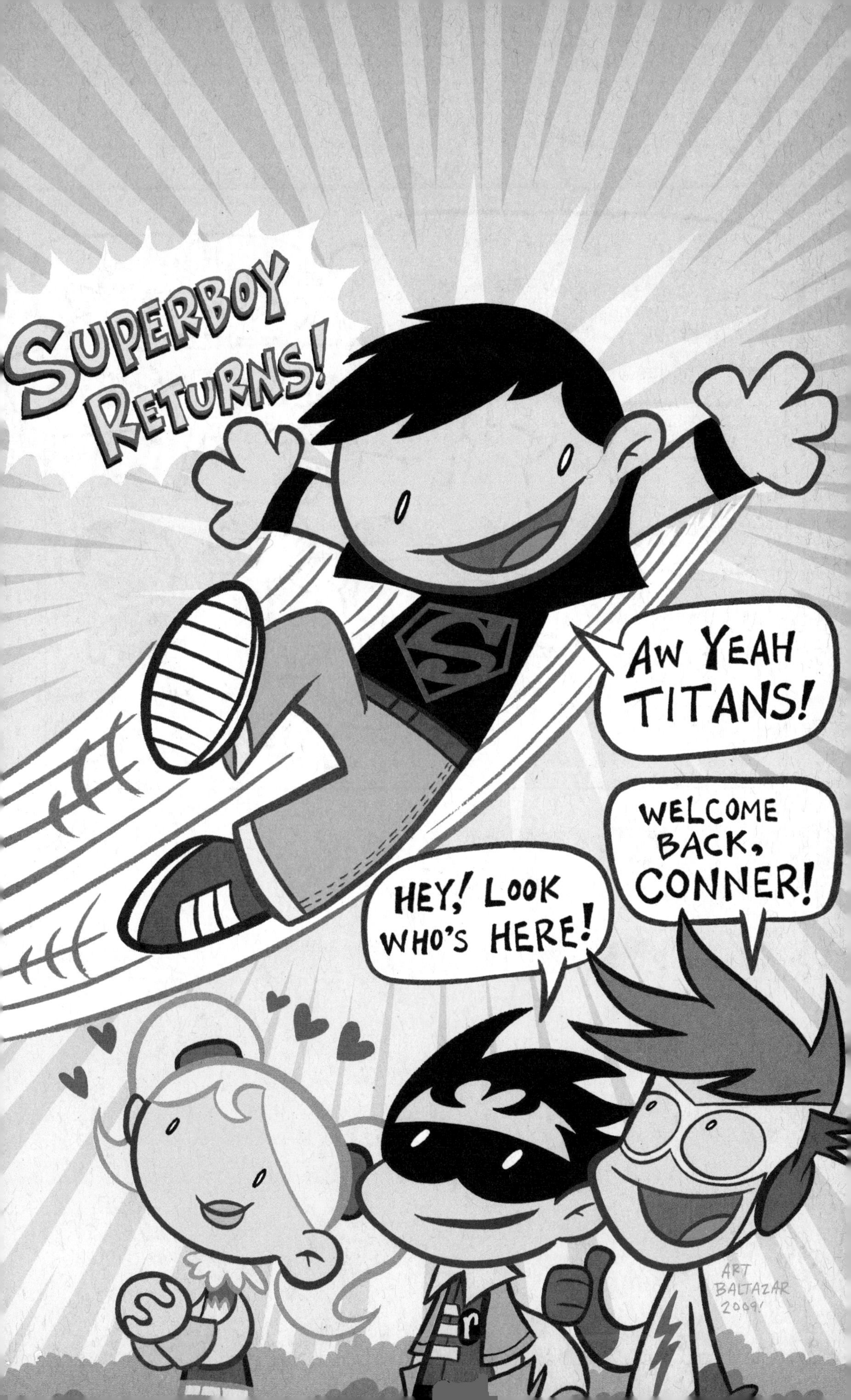
SUPERBOY RETURNS!
AW YEAH TITANS!
HEY! LOOK WHO'S HERE!
WELCOME BACK, CONNER!
ART BALTAZAR 2009!

tiny titans

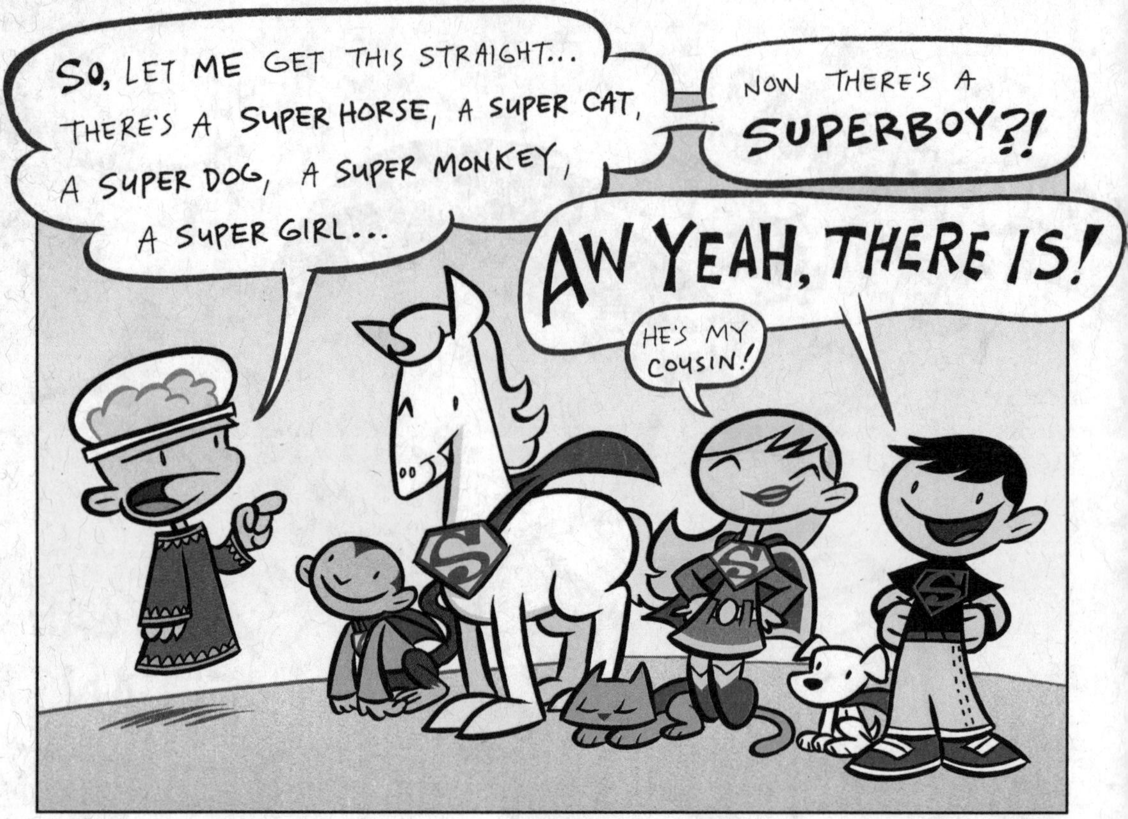
SO, LET ME GET THIS STRAIGHT... THERE'S A SUPER HORSE, A SUPER CAT, A SUPER DOG, A SUPER MONKEY, A SUPER GIRL...
NOW THERE'S A SUPERBOY?!
AW YEAH, THERE IS!
HE'S MY COUSIN!

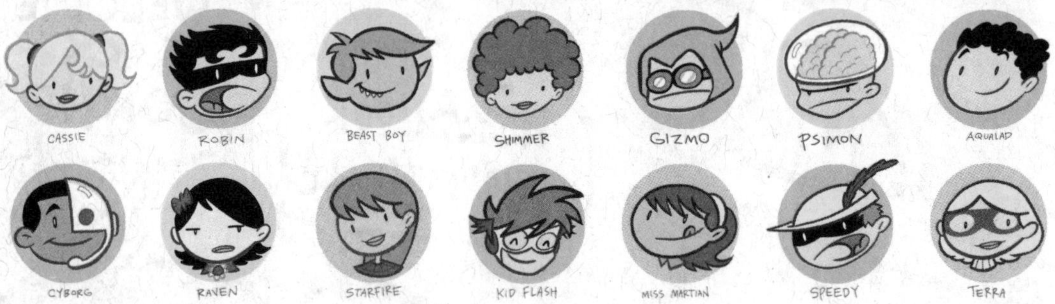
CASSIE
ROBIN
BEAST BOY
SHIMMER
GIZMO
PSIMON
AQUALAD
CYBORG
RAVEN
STARFIRE
KID FLASH
MISS MARTIAN
SPEEDY
TERRA

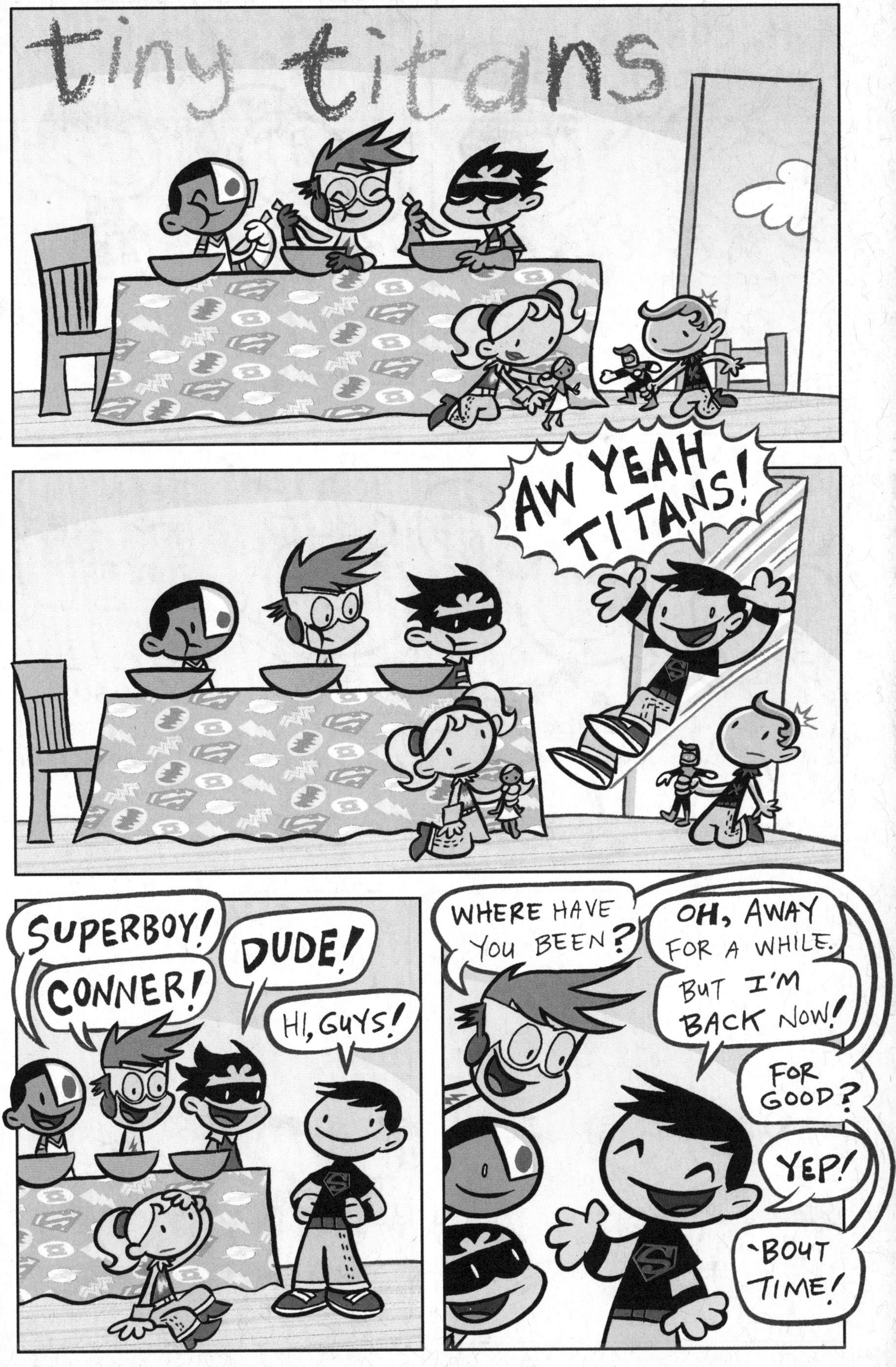
tiny titans
AW YEAH TITANS!
SUPERBOY!
CONNER!
DUDE!
HI, GUYS!
WHERE HAVE YOU BEEN?
OH, AWAY FOR A WHILE.
BUT I'M BACK NOW!
FOR GOOD?
YEP!
'BOUT TIME!

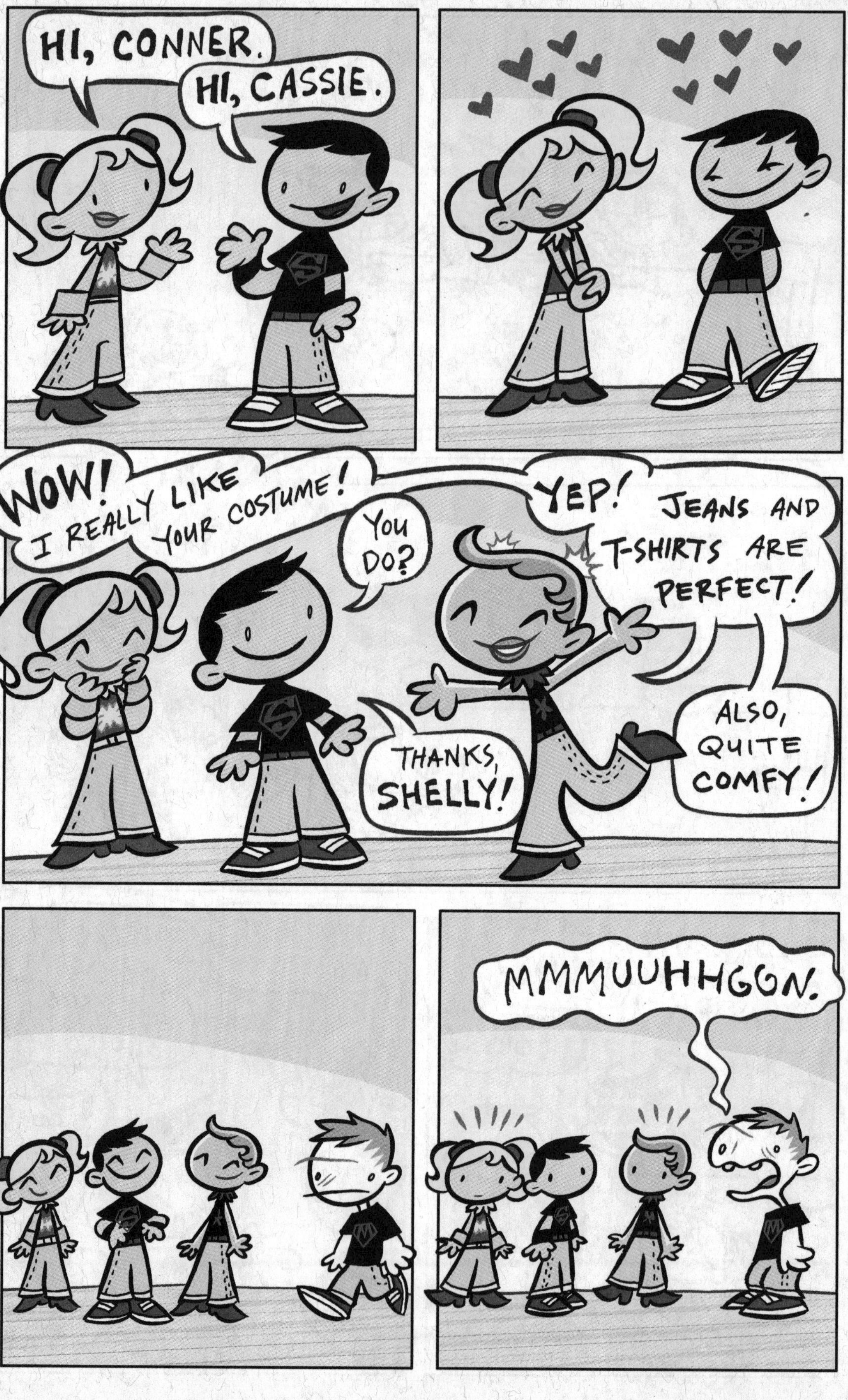
HI, CONNER.
HI, CASSIE.
WOW! I REALLY LIKE YOUR COSTUME!
YOU DO?
YEP! JEANS AND T-SHIRTS ARE PERFECT!
THANKS, SHELLY!
ALSO, QUITE COMFY!
MMMUUHHGGN.

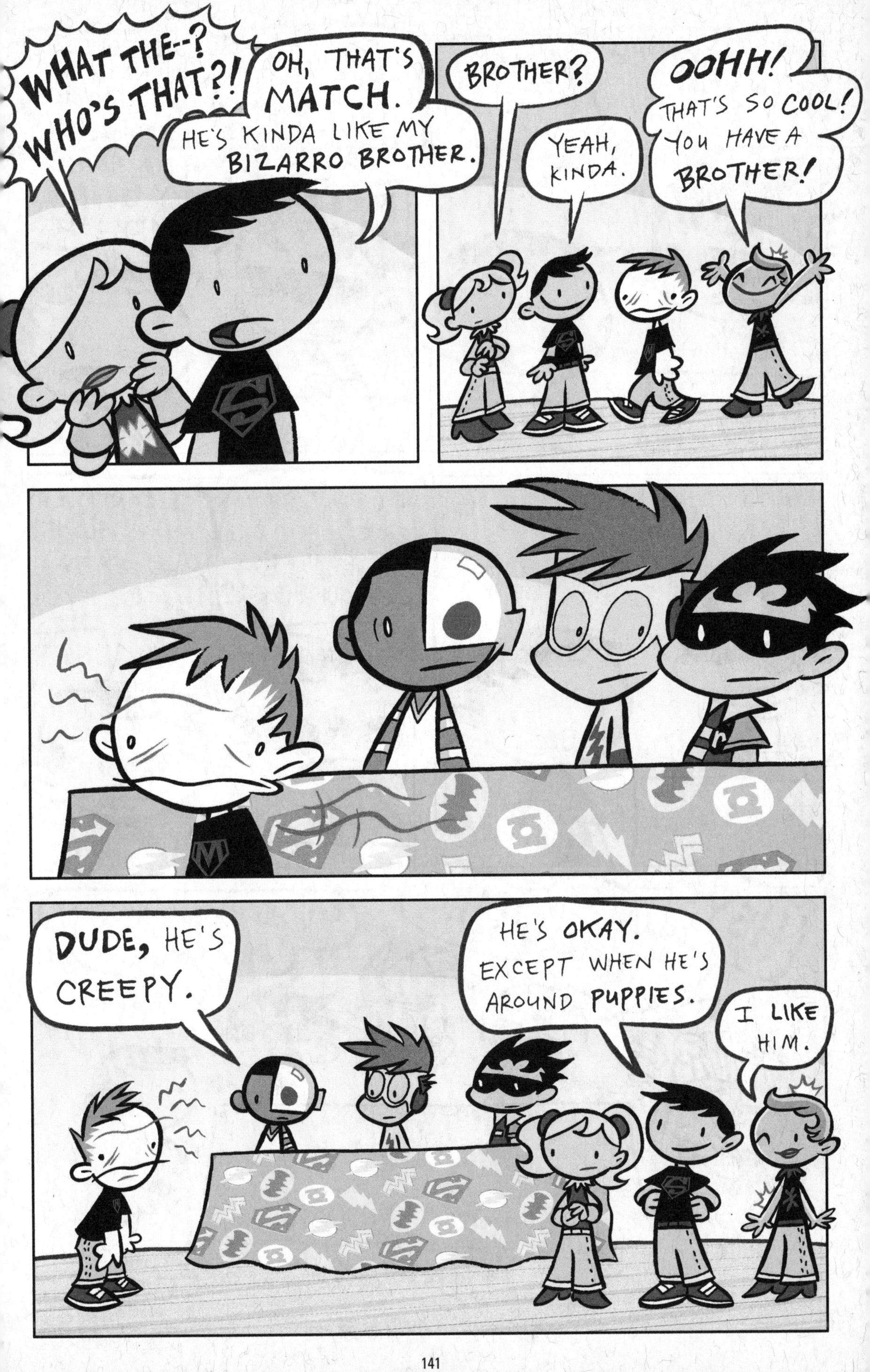
WHAT THE--? WHO'S THAT?!
OH, THAT'S MATCH.
HE'S KINDA LIKE MY BIZARRO BROTHER.
BROTHER?
YEAH, KINDA.
OOHH!
THAT'S SO COOL! YOU HAVE A BROTHER!
DUDE, HE'S CREEPY.
HE'S OKAY. EXCEPT WHEN HE'S AROUND PUPPIES.
I LIKE HIM.

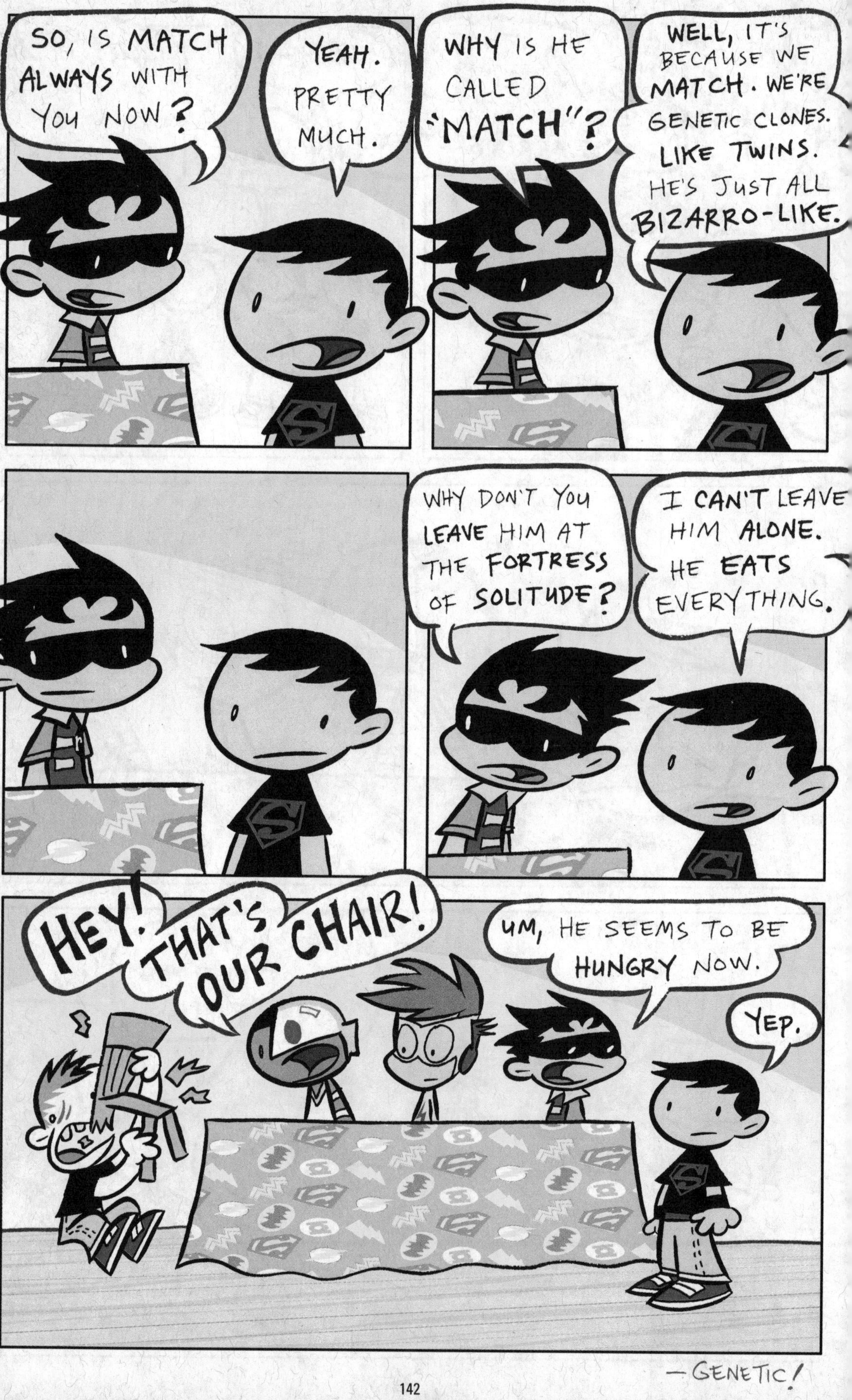
SO, IS MATCH ALWAYS WITH YOU NOW?
YEAH. PRETTY MUCH.
WHY IS HE CALLED "MATCH"?
WELL, IT'S BECAUSE WE MATCH. WE'RE GENETIC CLONES. LIKE TWINS. HE'S JUST ALL BIZARRO-LIKE.
WHY DON'T YOU LEAVE HIM AT THE FORTRESS OF SOLITUDE?
I CAN'T LEAVE HIM ALONE. HE EATS EVERYTHING.
HEY! THAT'S OUR CHAIR!
UM, HE SEEMS TO BE HUNGRY NOW.
YEP.

— GENETIC!

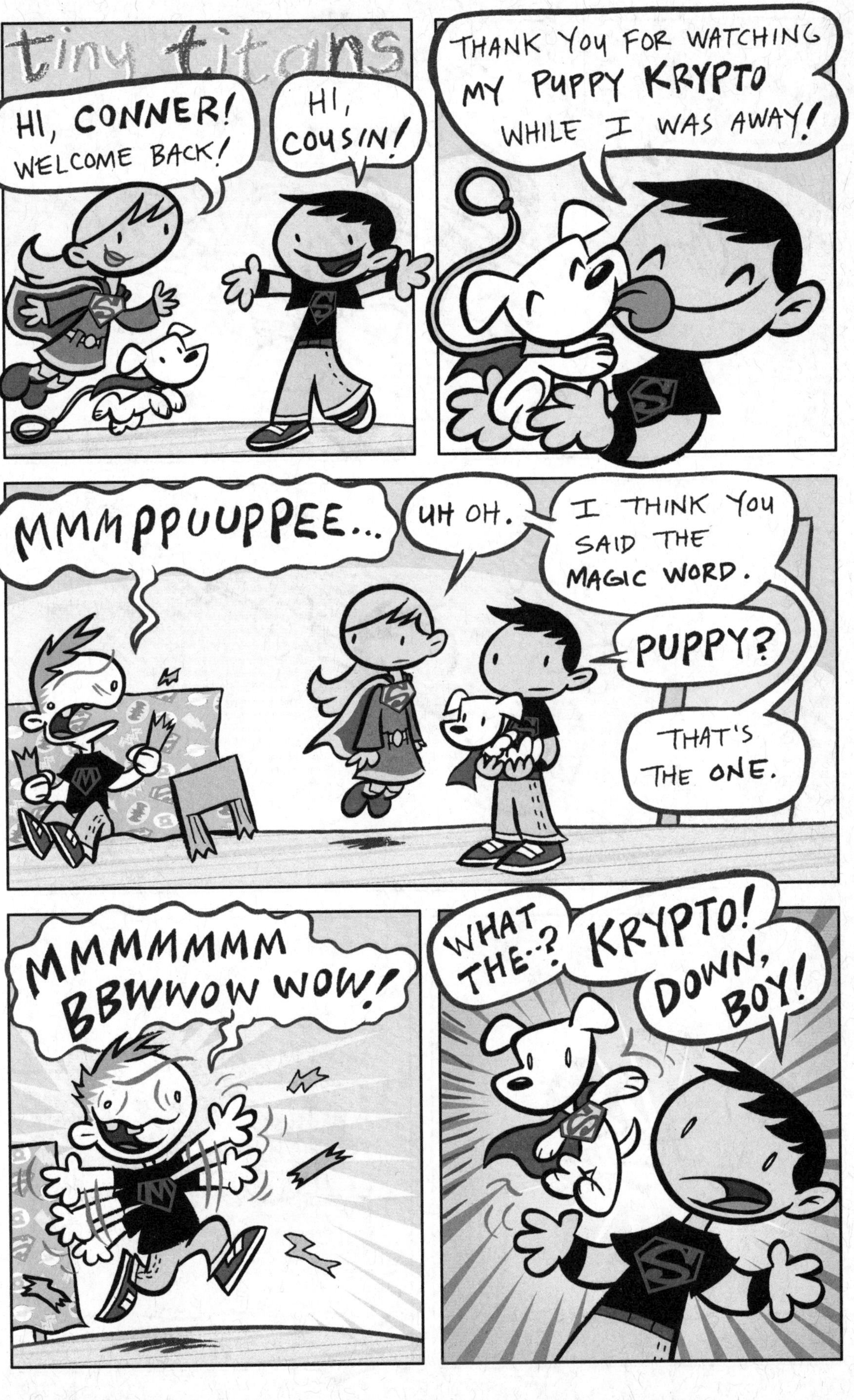
tiny titans
HI, CONNER! WELCOME BACK!
HI, COUSIN!
THANK YOU FOR WATCHING MY PUPPY KRYPTO WHILE I WAS AWAY!
MMMPPUUPPEE...
UH OH.
I THINK YOU SAID THE MAGIC WORD.
PUPPY?
THAT'S THE ONE.
MMMMMMM BBWWOW WOW!
WHAT THE--?
KRYPTO! DOWN, BOY!

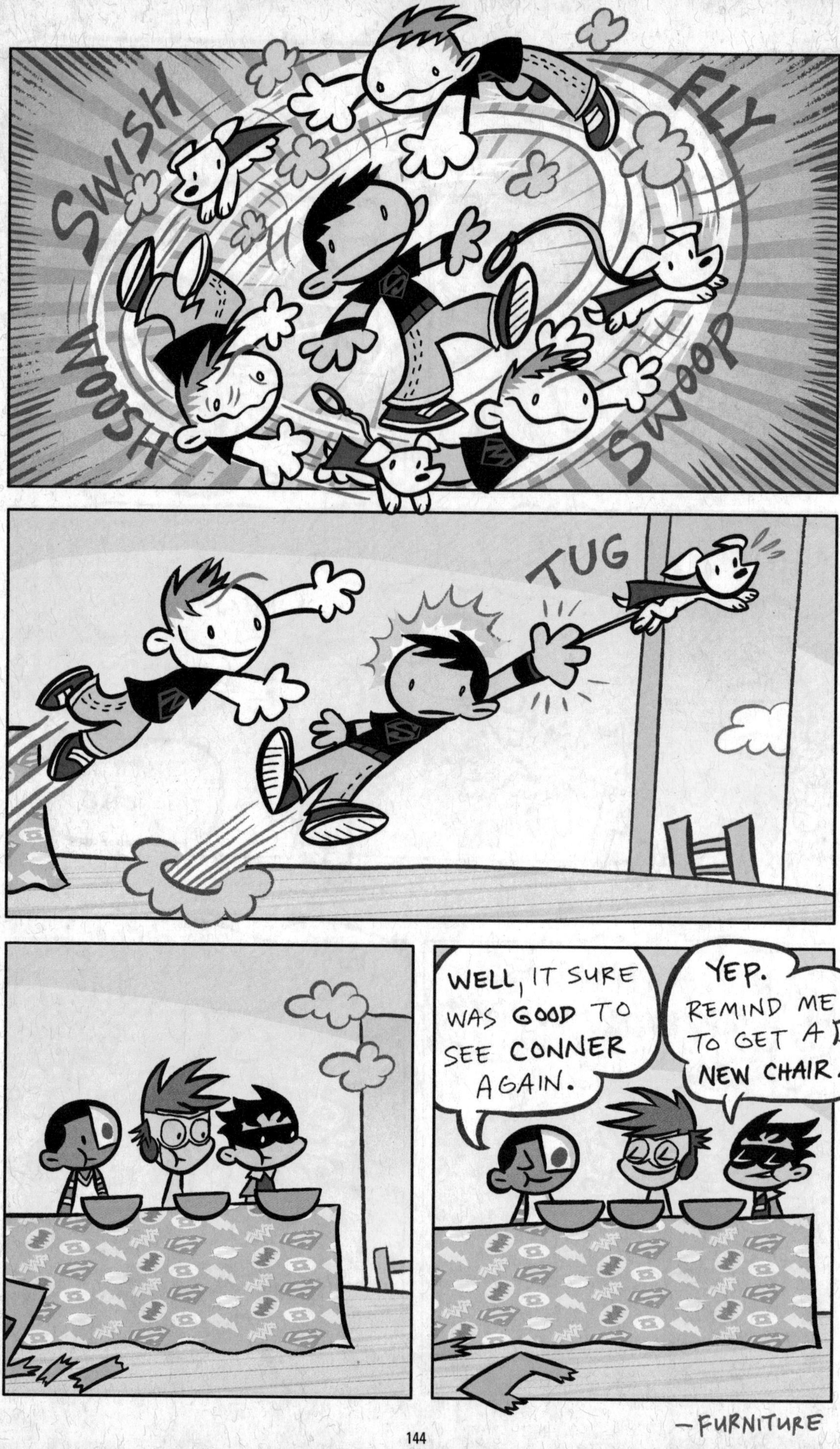
SWISH
FLY
WOOSH
SWOOP
TUG
WELL, IT SURE WAS GOOD TO SEE CONNER AGAIN.
YEP. REMIND ME TO GET A NEW CHAIR.
—FURNITURE

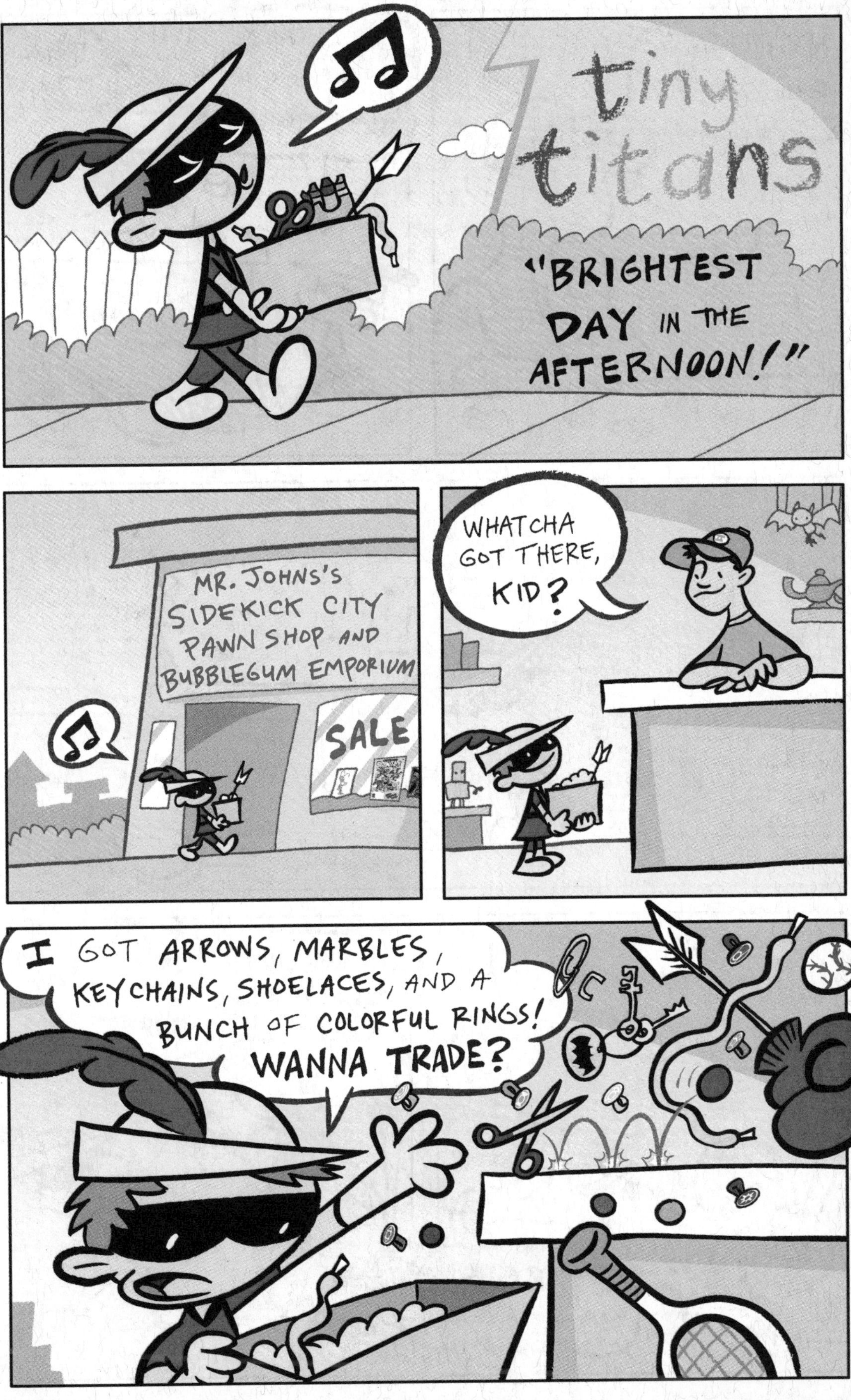
tiny titans
"BRIGHTEST DAY IN THE AFTERNOON!"
MR. JOHNS'S SIDEKICK CITY PAWN SHOP AND BUBBLEGUM EMPORIUM
SALE
WHATCHA GOT THERE, KID?
I GOT ARROWS, MARBLES, KEYCHAINS, SHOELACES, AND A BUNCH OF COLORFUL RINGS! WANNA TRADE?

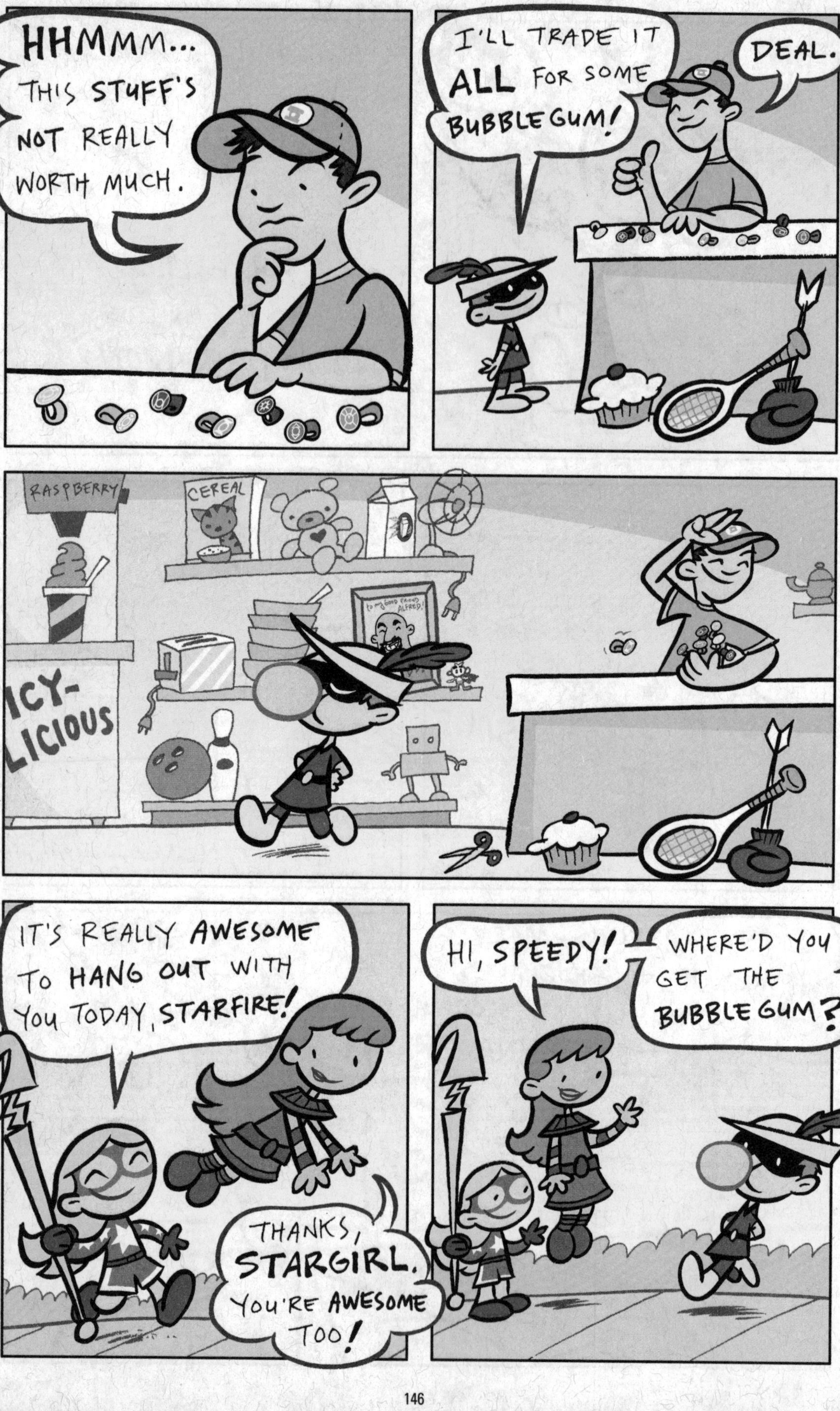
HHMMM... THIS STUFF'S NOT REALLY WORTH MUCH.
I'LL TRADE IT ALL FOR SOME BUBBLEGUM!
DEAL.
RASPBERRY
CEREAL
To my good friend ALFRED!
ICY-LICIOUS
IT'S REALLY AWESOME TO HANG OUT WITH YOU TODAY, STARFIRE!
THANKS, STARGIRL. YOU'RE AWESOME TOO!
HI, SPEEDY!
WHERE'D YOU GET THE BUBBLEGUM?

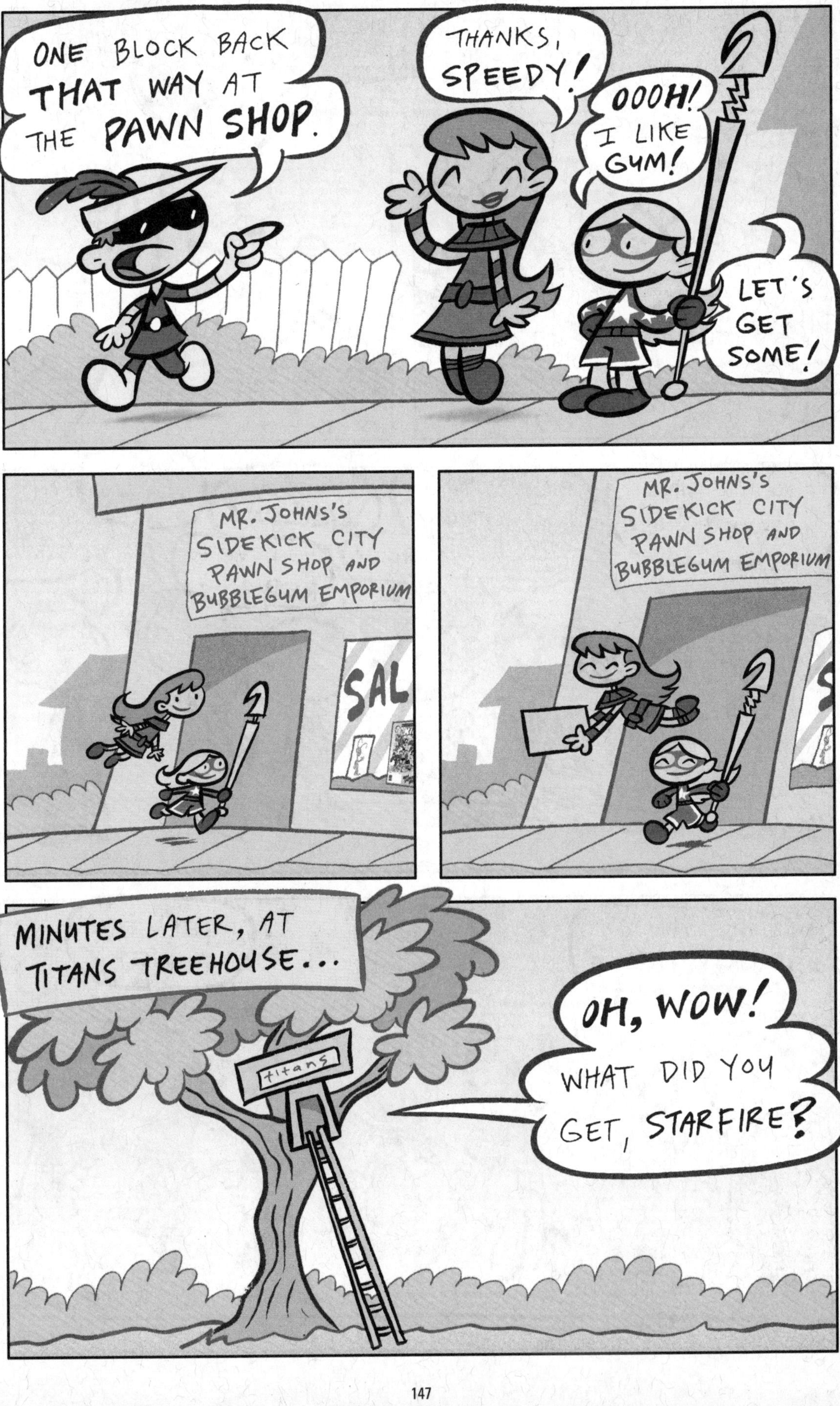
ONE BLOCK BACK THAT WAY AT THE PAWN SHOP.
THANKS, SPEEDY!
OOOH! I LIKE GUM!
LET'S GET SOME!
MR. JOHNS'S SIDEKICK CITY PAWN SHOP AND BUBBLEGUM EMPORIUM
SAL
MR. JOHNS'S SIDEKICK CITY PAWN SHOP AND BUBBLEGUM EMPORIUM
MINUTES LATER, AT TITANS TREEHOUSE...
titans
OH, WOW! WHAT DID YOU GET, STARFIRE?

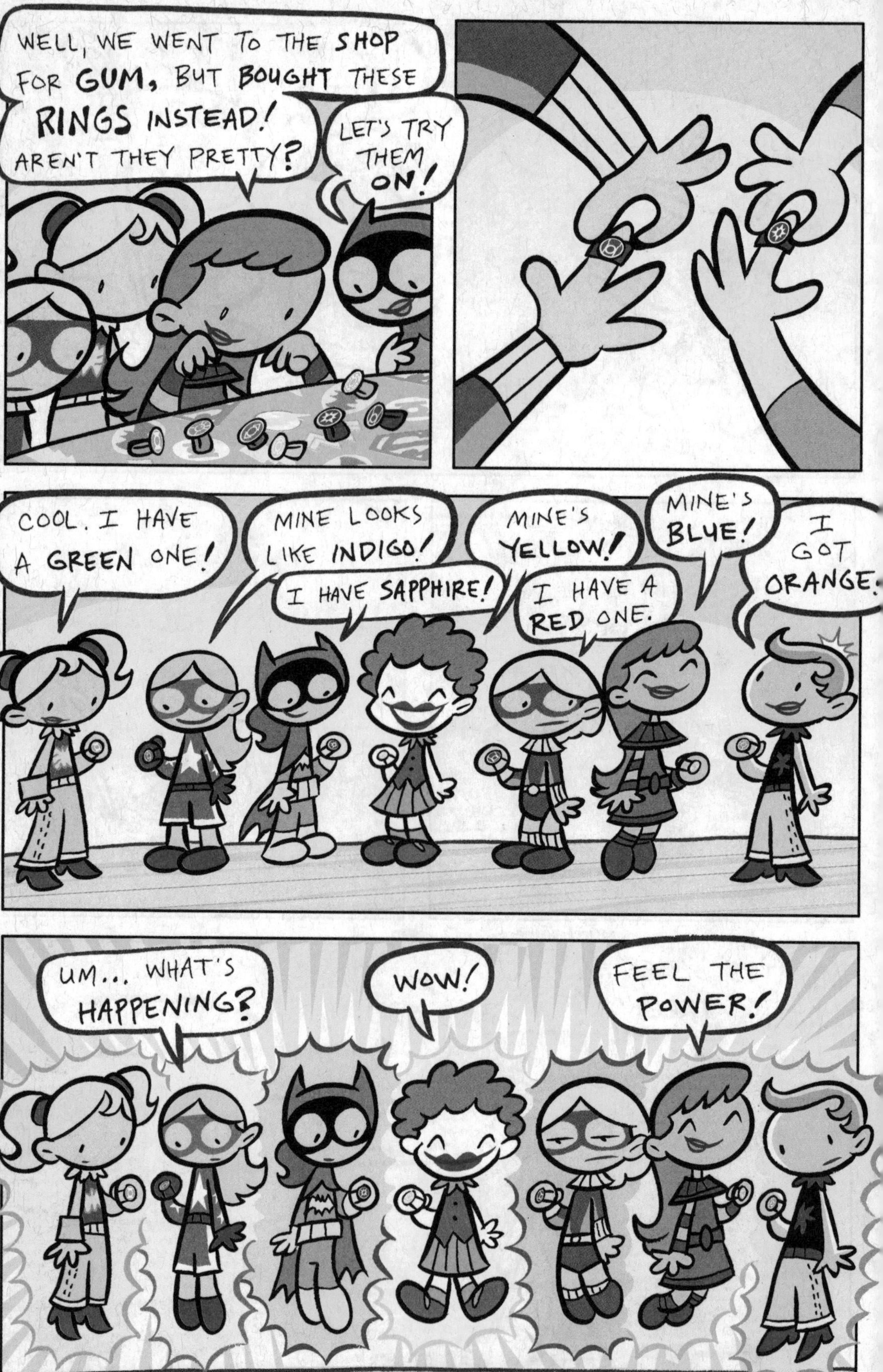
WELL, WE WENT TO THE SHOP FOR GUM, BUT BOUGHT THESE RINGS INSTEAD! AREN'T THEY PRETTY?
LET'S TRY THEM ON!
COOL. I HAVE A GREEN ONE!
MINE LOOKS LIKE INDIGO!
I HAVE SAPPHIRE!
MINE'S YELLOW!
I HAVE A RED ONE.
MINE'S BLUE!
I GOT ORANGE!
UM... WHAT'S HAPPENING?
WOW!
FEEL THE POWER!

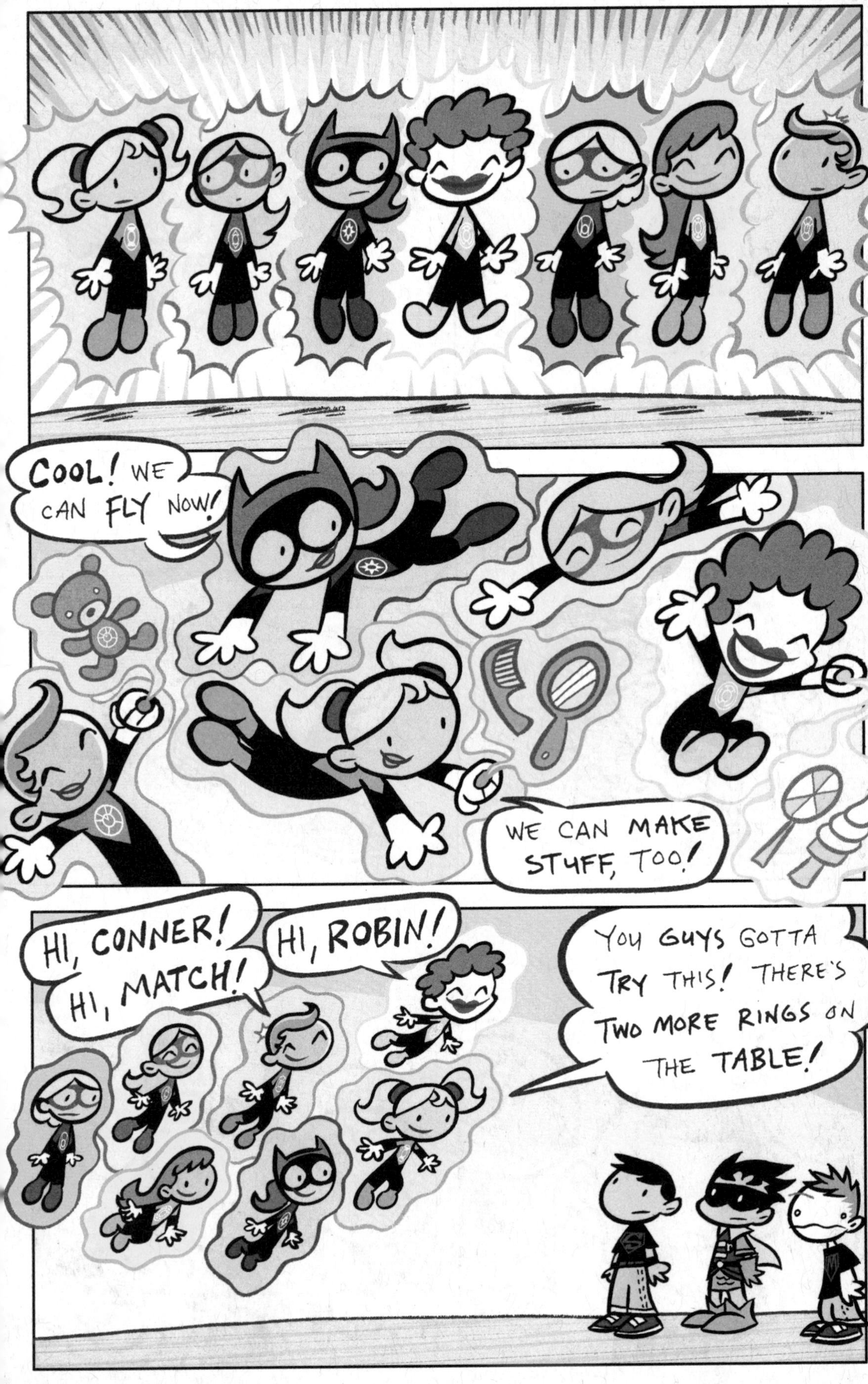

COOL! WE CAN FLY NOW!
WE CAN MAKE STUFF, TOO!
HI, CONNER! HI, MATCH!
HI, ROBIN!
YOU GUYS GOTTA TRY THIS! THERE'S TWO MORE RINGS ON THE TABLE!

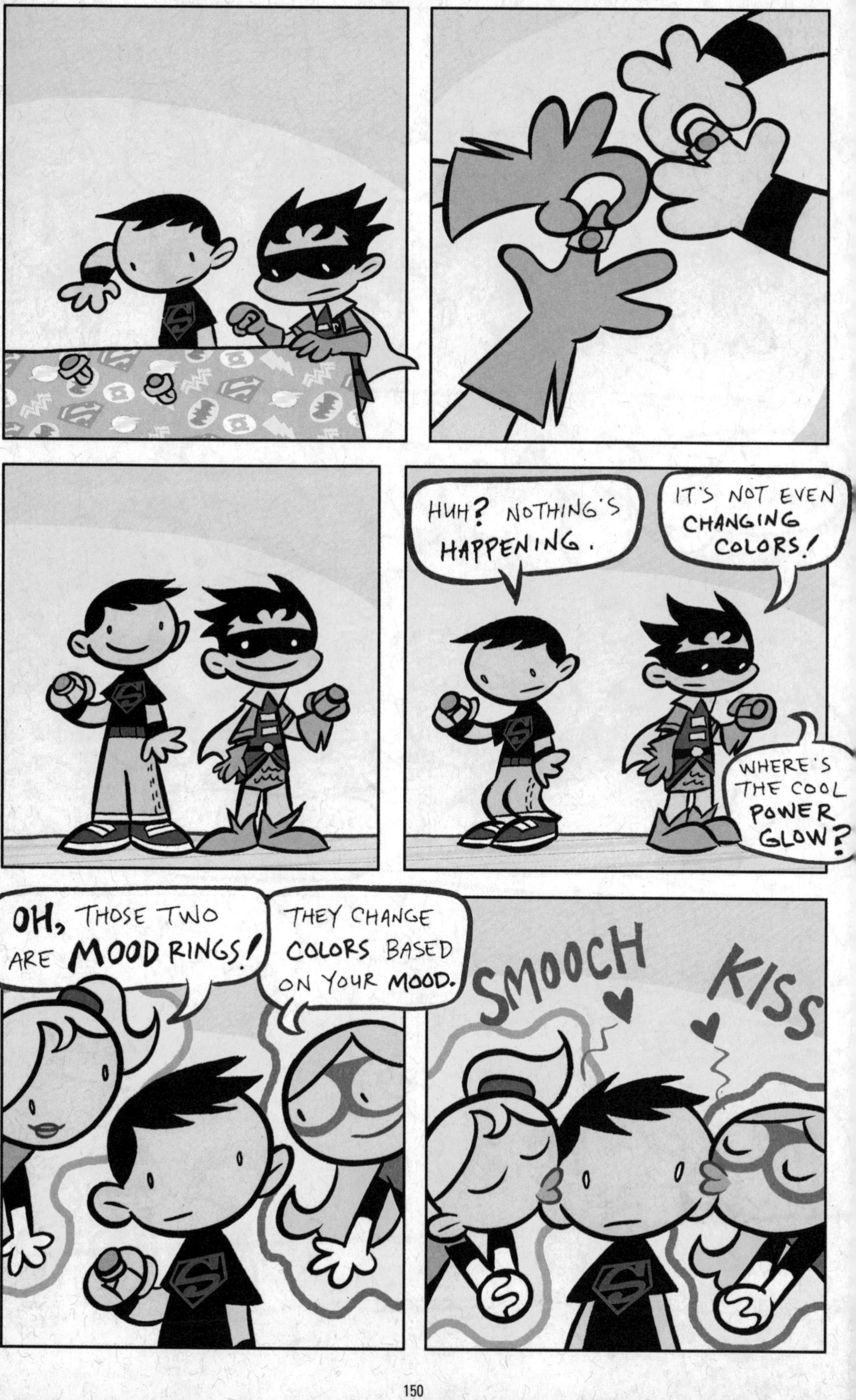
HUH? NOTHING'S HAPPENING.
IT'S NOT EVEN CHANGING COLORS!
WHERE'S THE COOL POWER GLOW?
OH, THOSE TWO ARE MOOD RINGS!
THEY CHANGE COLORS BASED ON YOUR MOOD.
SMOOCH
KISS

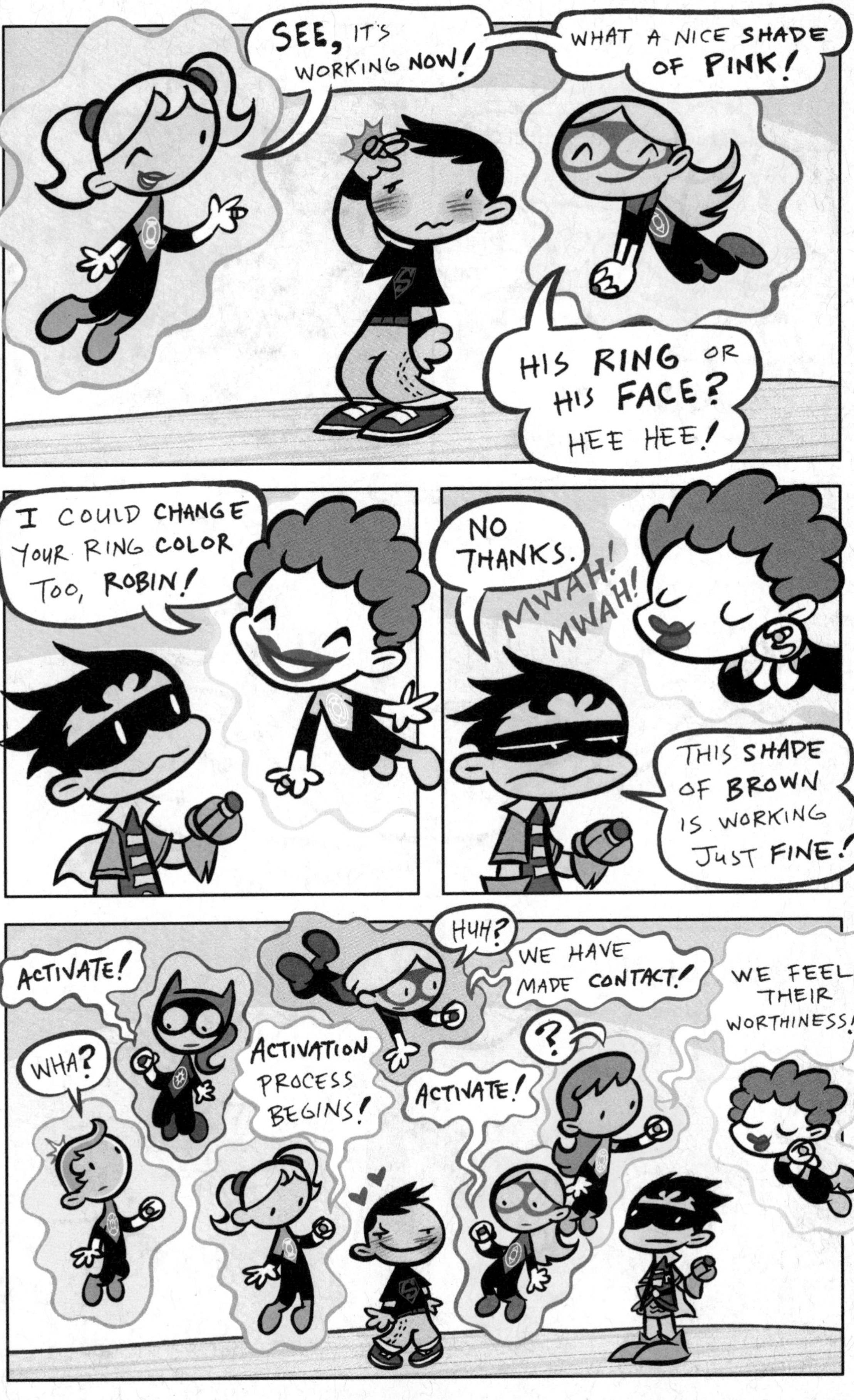
SEE, IT'S WORKING NOW!
WHAT A NICE SHADE OF PINK!
HIS RING OR HIS FACE? HEE HEE!
I COULD CHANGE YOUR RING COLOR TOO, ROBIN!
NO THANKS.
MWAH! MWAH!
THIS SHADE OF BROWN IS WORKING JUST FINE!
ACTIVATE!
HUH?
WE HAVE MADE CONTACT!
WE FEEL THEIR WORTHINESS!
WHA?
ACTIVATION PROCESS BEGINS!
?
ACTIVATE!

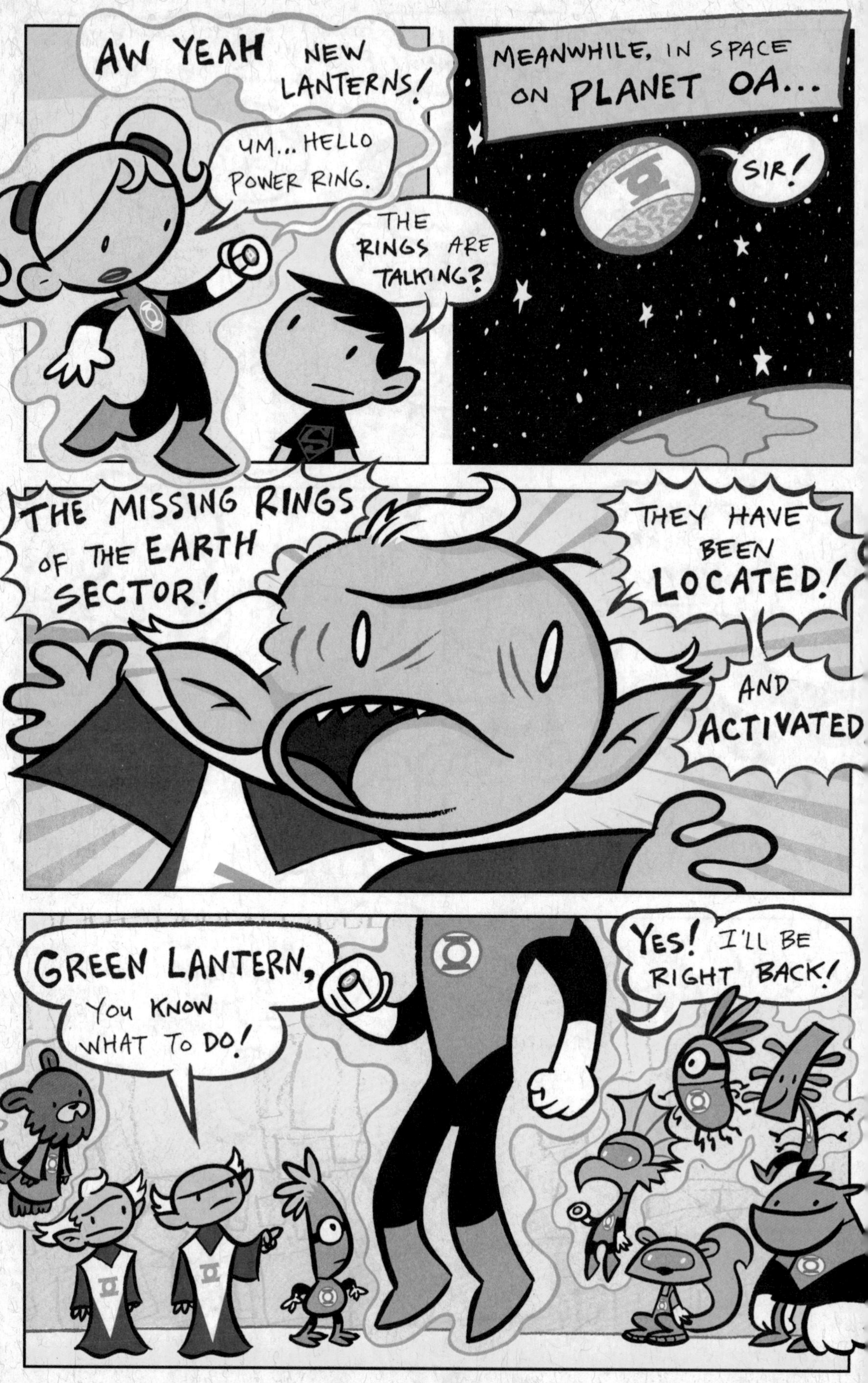
AW YEAH NEW LANTERNS!
UM... HELLO POWER RING.
THE RINGS ARE TALKING?
MEANWHILE, IN SPACE ON PLANET OA...
SIR!
THE MISSING RINGS OF THE EARTH SECTOR!
THEY HAVE BEEN LOCATED!
AND ACTIVATED
GREEN LANTERN, YOU KNOW WHAT TO DO!
YES! I'LL BE RIGHT BACK!

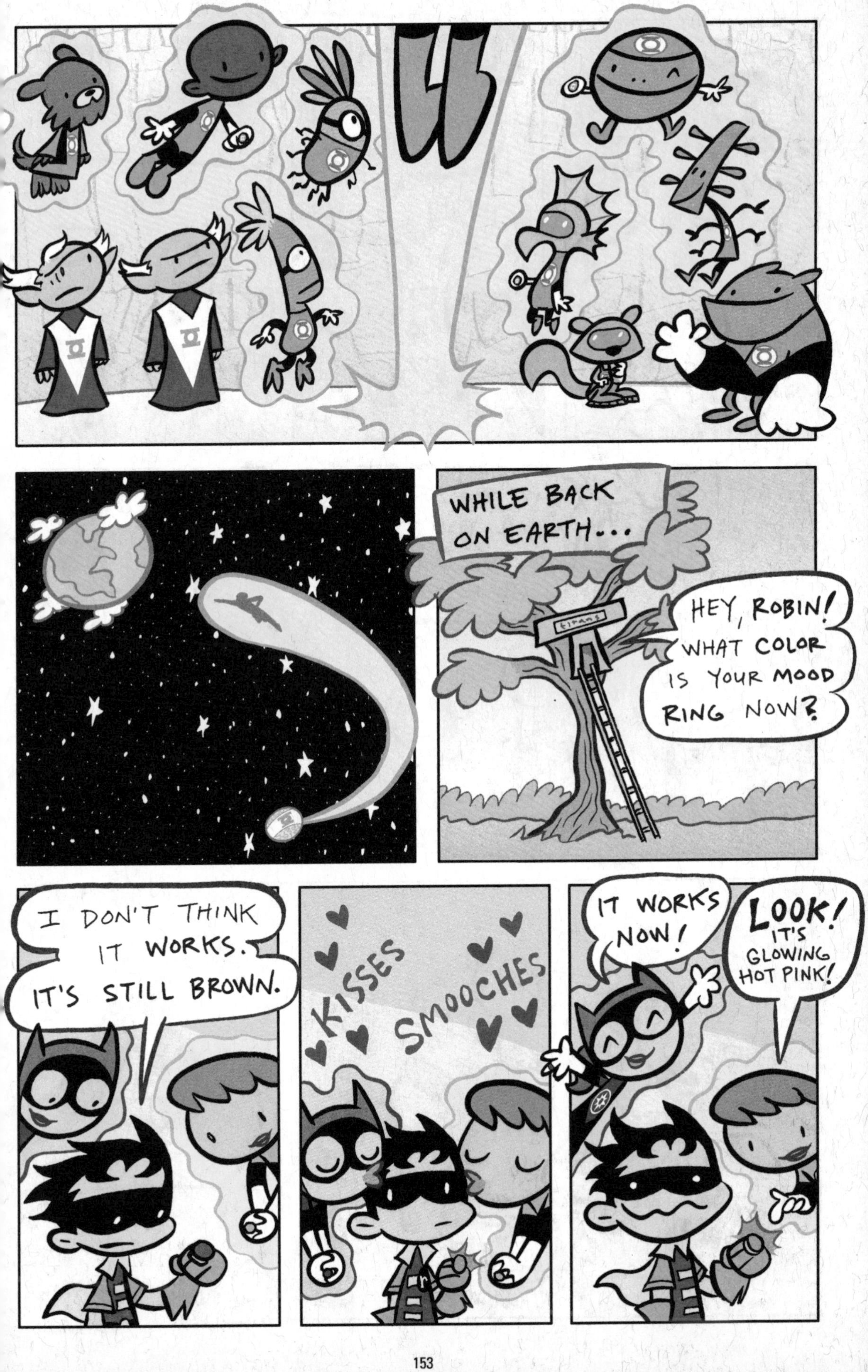

WHILE BACK ON EARTH...
HEY, ROBIN! WHAT COLOR IS YOUR MOOD RING NOW?
I DON'T THINK IT WORKS. IT'S STILL BROWN.
KISSES
SMOOCHES
IT WORKS NOW!
LOOK! IT'S GLOWING HOT PINK!

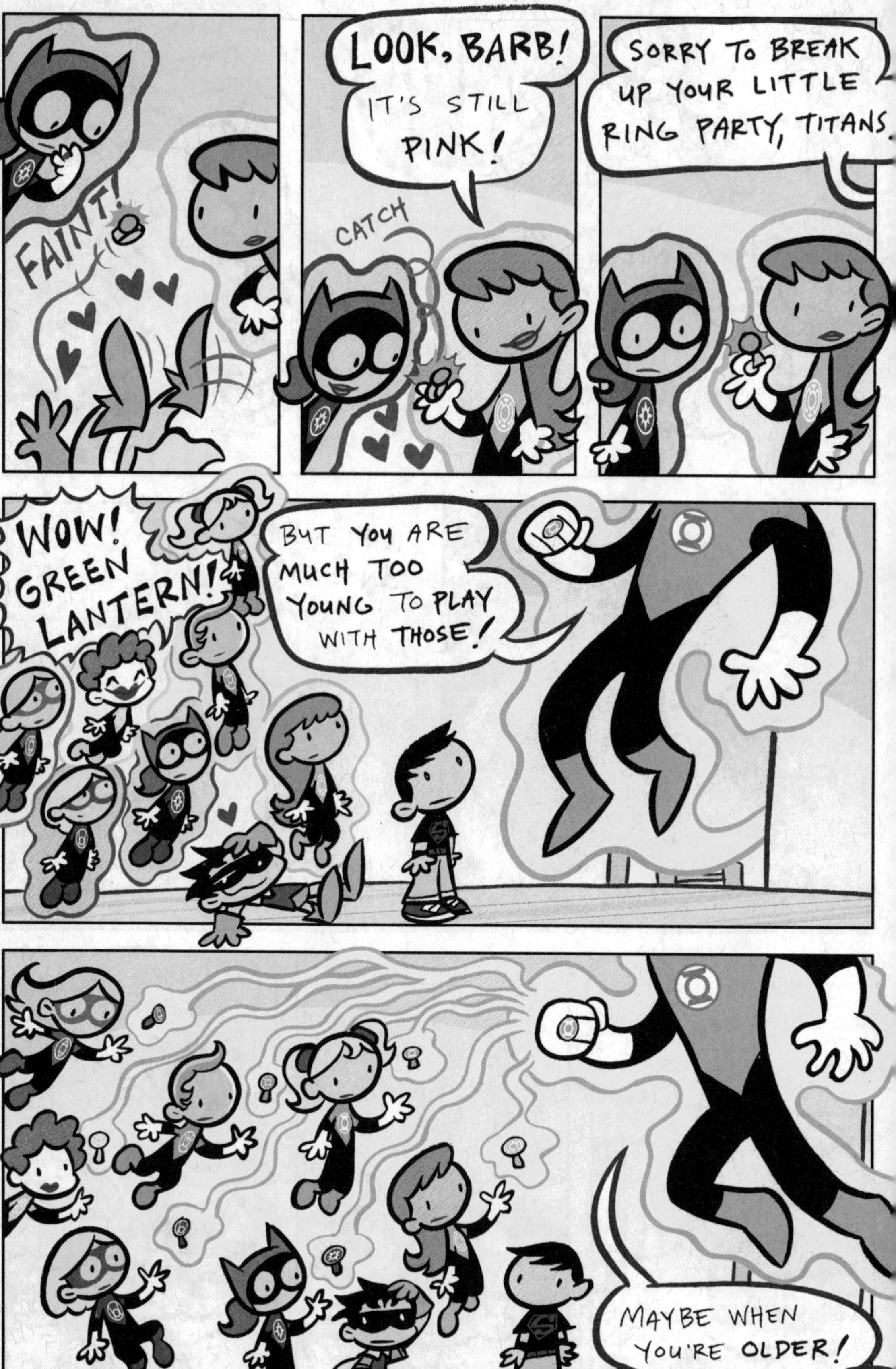
FAINT!
LOOK, BARB!
IT'S STILL PINK!
CATCH
SORRY TO BREAK UP YOUR LITTLE RING PARTY, TITANS.
WOW! GREEN LANTERN!
BUT YOU ARE MUCH TOO YOUNG TO PLAY WITH THOSE!
MAYBE WHEN YOU'RE OLDER!
UNTIL NEXT TIME...

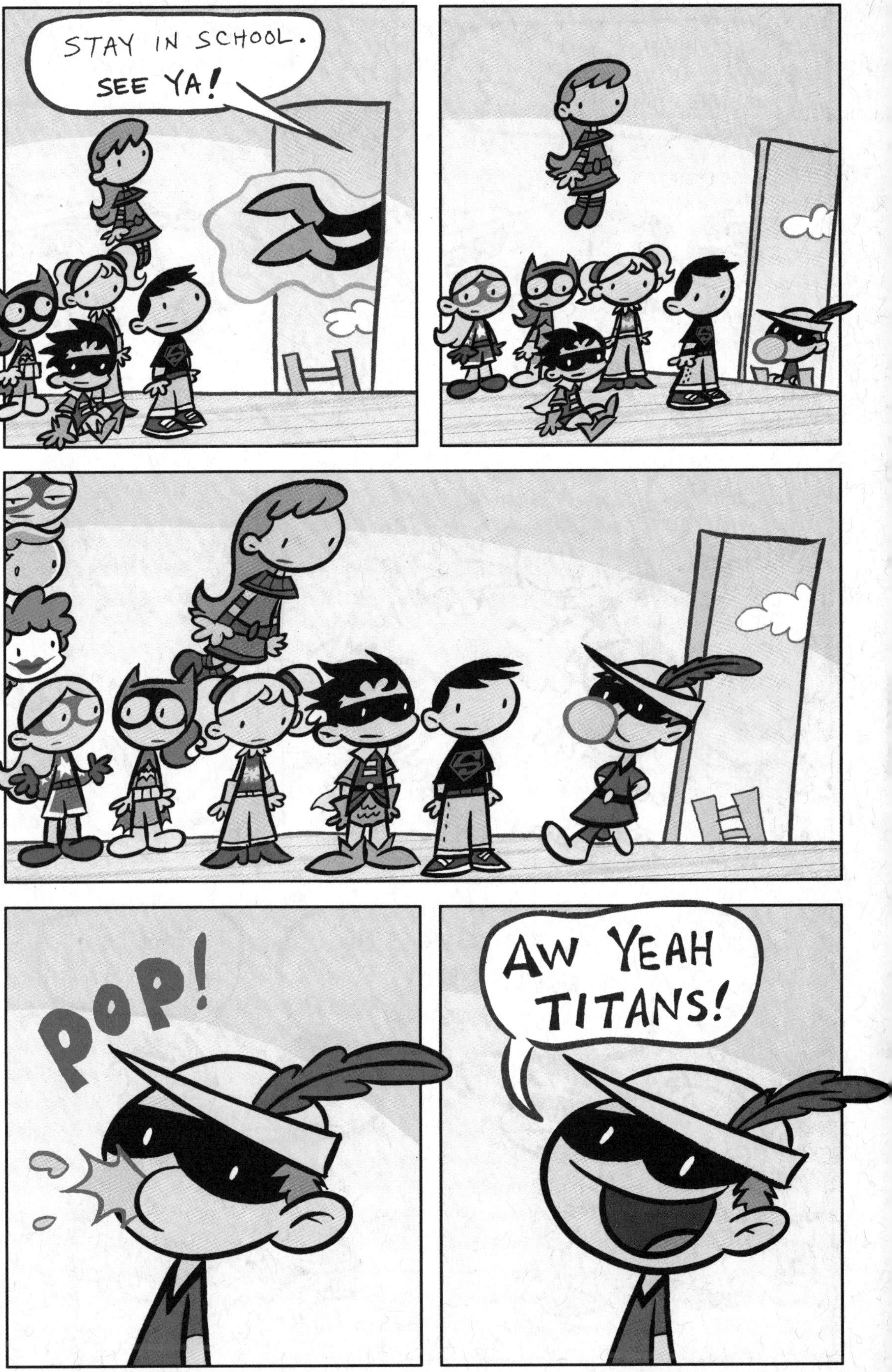
STAY IN SCHOOL. SEE YA!
POP!
AW YEAH TITANS!

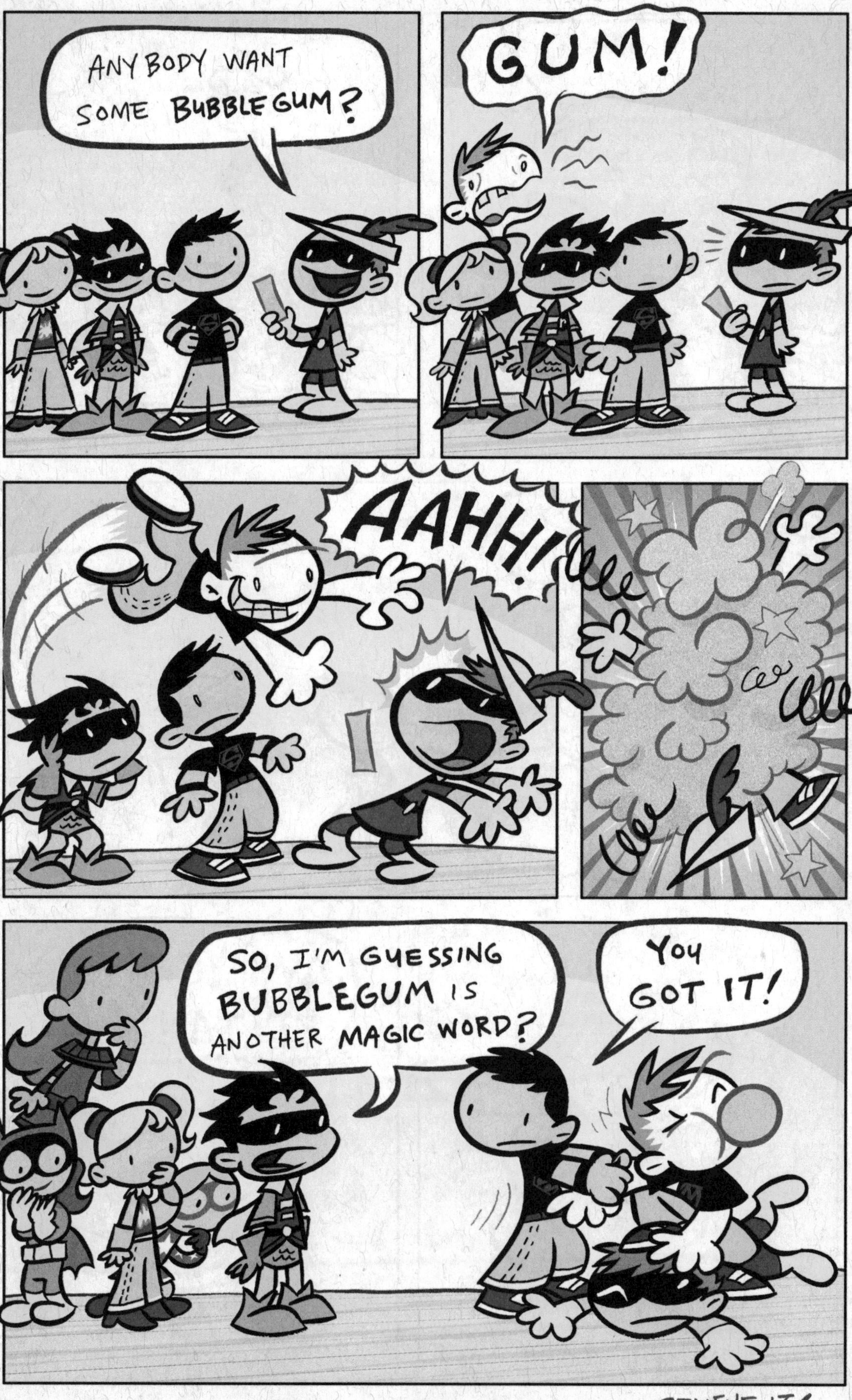
ANYBODY WANT SOME BUBBLEGUM?
GUM!
AAHH!
SO, I'M GUESSING BUBBLEGUM IS ANOTHER MAGIC WORD?
YOU GOT IT!

-BELIEVE IT!

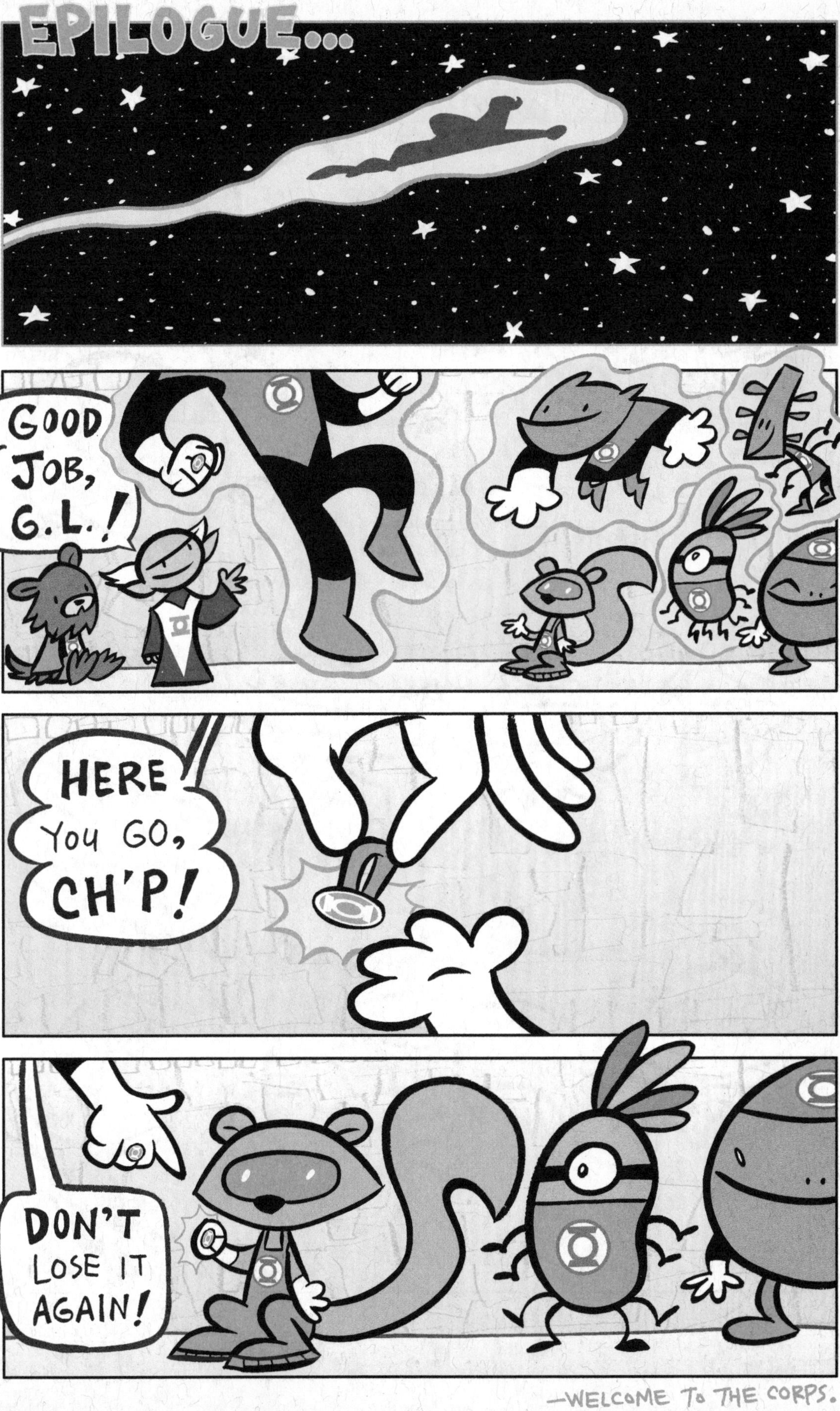
EPILOGUE...
GOOD JOB, G.L.!
HERE YOU GO, CH'P!
DON'T LOSE IT AGAIN!

—WELCOME TO THE CORPS.

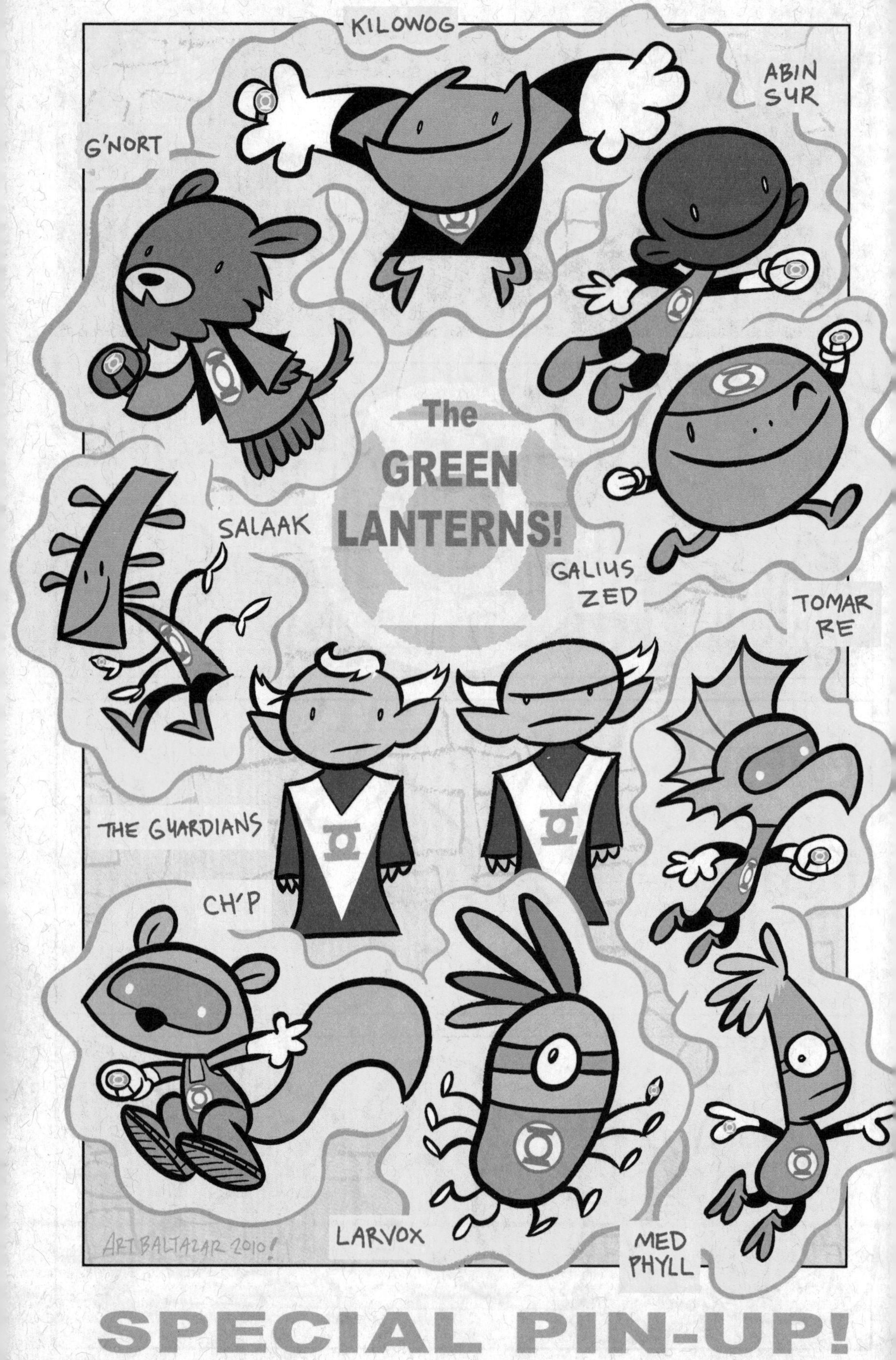

KILOWOG
ABIN SUR
G'NORT
The GREEN LANTERNS!
SALAAK
GALIUS ZED
TOMAR RE
THE GUARDIANS
CH'P
LARVOX
MED PHYLL
ART BALTAZAR 2010!

SPECIAL PIN-UP!